Second Shield

Written by
Stacy Eaton

~~~

Nitewolf Novels

Books by Stacy Eaton

My Blood Runs Blue

Blue Blood for Life

Whether I'll Live or Die

Garda ~ Welcome to the Realm

Liveon ~ No Evil

Dedication

This book is dedicated to all of those people who have inspired the characters within my stories. Thank you for being who you are.

Acknowledgements

To the two most precious people in my life, my husband and my daughter, thank you. So many times you see the back of my head, and I cannot thank you enough for your patience.

Once again, my Beta Team rocked on this story, and seemed to love every moment. Thank you to my team; Tatiana Lammers, Dodie Auglis, Jen Wolf, Pat Fordyce, Fran Nichols, Jan Galloway, Melissa Rutter, Dawn Doyle, Marie Godley, Ashleigh Danner and Scott Johnson.

As with my other projects, I have others that I wish to thank profusely for their assistance. A huge thank you goes out to Dominque Agnew for her professional editing and to Emerald Barnes for Proofreading Services. My incredible graphic artist, Natasha Brown nailed another cover for me, thank you!! And, if it wasn't for Clare Ayala, my formatting would never be correct! Thank you all so very much!

The biggest thank you goes out to my readers! Over the last few years, you have stood by me, encouraged me, and made me feel that the stories I write are worthwhile. Thank you!

Chapter 1 – MacKenzie

"Mack, please take this call! This woman is a loon."

I lifted my face from the report in front of me; my eyebrows arched as I turned to Gordon who sat on the other side of the room. "What makes you think I can talk to a bird?" I wisecracked.

"Come on, Mack, she's crazy. I can't deal with crazy today, especially not woman crazy!"

"Neither can I. Deal with it. I need to go through these reports and get these approved and off to the lieutenant." I turned back to the pages on my desk as he mumbled swear words under his breath.

"And you have your new partner coming today," Jose's deeply-accented voice reached me from the other corner of the room.

My shoulders sagged. Crap! I forgot about the new guy coming into the investigations unit today. I pulled my reading glasses off my face and dropped them on the desk before I leaned back in my chair and sighed.

"Gordon, I'll take your call, if you'll take the new guy," I proposed.

For a second I thought he was actually considering my offer, but then, a smirk spread over his wizened face as he replied, "Hell, no. It will be worth dealing with all of the crazy women in the area today just to see you deal with this rookie." He picked up the phone with a

1

grin plastered on his wrinkled face and started talking into the receiver. His voice held a note of glee that had not been there earlier. I frowned, perplexed.

I peered at Jose who was chuckling to himself. He met my eyes and cleared his throat in mock-innocence before engaging his computer again.

Something was up. We had gotten new people into the investigations unit before, and no one ever said much about it. The guys were usually seasoned officers who knew the ropes and only had to learn the ins and outs of how we did things here. Within a month's time, they were well-adjusted, unleashed, and allowed to work their own cases.

When we did bring in a new investigator, one of us was assigned to help him or her make the transition. We didn't have partners per se, as we typically worked as a group. The eight of us each had our niches, and we pooled resources as they were needed.

Jose was one of our newer guys, and he was big into white collar crime. He was also our technology guru. If it had to do with anything twenty-first century and was electronic, he was the one we went to. Cellphones, computers, software, GPSs, social media, it didn't matter, he knew them all. He was also a whiz when it came to financial crimes and knew where to get the data the fastest way possible. He even wrote the most detailed search warrants I had ever seen—and he was bilingual to boot.

Bria was our sex crimes and child investigator. She had a way with kids that I just couldn't fathom. Kids as young as three and as old as eighteen would open right up to her. Even the adult victims poured out the details when she did the interviews.

Chad was our arson investigator, among other things, but he mostly dealt with fire investigations. His job was to figure out if the fire was set on purpose or if it was accidental. You would think that he didn't have much to do, but with our large twenty-four-mile jurisdiction, he had more than his share of work.

Then, there were Mike and Will. While they didn't have any specific specialty, they dabbled in quite a bit, especially gang stuff.

Well, Will more than Mike, but they both had their hands in it. Between Gordon, Mike, Will, and me, we dealt with most of the calls that came in.

Gordon Brooks had been in the squad the longest and was a jack of all trades. He'd been investigating since I was in college, and he knew it all. Well, he thought he did, anyway.

The seventh person in our group was Lieutenant Gary Robinson, or L.T. for short. He was our supervisor, and a real prick. I should know, I was married to him a few years back, and that prick is what got him into trouble and the reason he became my ex.

I sighed as I unconsciously examined his closed door. When I had first come to the unit, working under Gary had been a nightmare, but we eventually moved on with our lives and learned to work together rather amicably.

Of course there was me, Det. Sgt. MacKenzie McAllister, or Sergeant Mack for short. The nickname fit, whether you were talking about my first name or last. I'm not sure what my parents were thinking when they named me, but after thirty-nine years, I had gotten used to it.

I'd been in the squad for almost nine years and had no ambitions to go anywhere else. I loved what I did, and what I did was my life—all of my life. Outside of work, I had little else.

I did have friends. I hung out with them and hit the movie theater and stopped for drinks often enough, but I didn't volunteer anywhere, and I didn't have kids that needed to be taxied around from one sports event to another.

Some people would be depressed by that, but not me. I loved my life. I mean, what was not to love? I worked hard solving crimes and putting people behind bars. When I went home, I curled up on my couch and read a book. I slept when I wanted, cleaned my house when I felt like it, and if I wanted peanut butter and jelly instead of a gourmet home-cooked meal, then that's what I made. I didn't have anyone to answer to and that was just fine by me.

If I did want to be with people, I had a list of contacts on my phone and could easily find a partner to fill a stool at the bar or even share my sheets for a good time, not that I'd done that in a while, but I had a list in case I wanted to, and that's what counted in my book.

Of course, there were times when I envied the guys who had families. I scanned the room and on almost every desk stood at least one framed photograph of a wife or kids. I took in my paper-strewn desk, no pictures here. Actually, that wasn't true. I did have a picture of my nieces sitting on the front porch of my sister's house tacked to my corkboard. At least I had one picture, right?

Well, I had more than one tacked to my corkboard, but wanted suspects didn't count. My desk phone rang, and I pushed the thoughts of loved ones and pictures to the back of my brain and reached for the receiver.

I was deep in conversation with Rick, a detective from another department, when I heard my name being spoken from the doorway in a deep flowing voice. It was not one I recognized, and I ignored it while I continued my conversation about a suspect we were searching for that was involved in over twenty burglaries. Whoever it was could wait.

A few minutes later, Gary's voice cracked through the squad room. "Mack!" I lifted my head from the papers in front of me in annoyance. Gary knew how much I hated being interrupted when I was on the phone. I glared at him and he returned it, "Get off the phone and get in my office."

I held up my pointer finger to tell him I'd be a minute, although the middle finger would have been more appropriate.

"Now, Mack! Get off the damned phone," he yelled. I ground my teeth, fighting to keep a blistering retort contained.

"Rick, I gotta call you back. I'm being dramatically summoned," I said sarcastically into the phone, and he laughed. I'd known Rick for a while, and he knew about the love-hate relationship I had with the L.T.

With a loud plop, I dropped the receiver back onto the phone base, hoping Rick had removed the phone from his ear before it landed, and shoved my rolling office chair back from my desk. I clicked a ball point pen with my left hand, showing my frustration non-verbally as I made my way to his office. The click of my two-inch boot heels tapped in tune with the click of the pen, and I scoured the room, trying to find a reason to delay.

Gordon, Jose, and Will were all attempting to contain themselves, but the chuckles and grins were present despite their attempts at self-control. Gordon was the only one who made eye contact, and his smile lifted. I was tempted to throw my pen at him and I didn't even know why.

"What?" I snapped as I passed in front of him.

He reached into the drawer of his desk and pulled out the small hand towel that he kept there to clean up spills. He was notorious for spilling his coffee. He tossed me the towel, "You might need this."

I caught the towel in mid-stride and gave him a curious look. What the hell was up with these guys?

"Mack!" Gary's raised voice carried out from his office, and I rolled my eyes in annoyance and clicked my pen again.

When I stepped through the threshold, I saw another person sitting in front of his desk, but I dismissed him without thought.

"What the hell, L.T.? I was talking to Rick about the burglary cases. They had another two last night." I moved to his desk to stand at the corner, the towel forgotten as it dangled from my hand.

Gary was leaning back in his chair, his hands crossed over his slim waist. He was in good shape, almost to the point of extreme. When he wasn't working, he was working out, usually with weights, sometimes with other women. I pinned his hazel eyes with a hard look and ground my teeth. Now was not the right time to remember the past.

"It can wait. Sergeant McAllister, this is your new partner, Drew Bradley." He motioned with his chin towards the other person in the room, and I glanced his way to get a cursory view, then I did a double take.

I studied his facial features: strong cheekbones, smooth straight nose, bright clear blue eyes, and a solid chin. His brown hair was trimmed short in a traditional military-style cut and the urge to run my hand over the top to see how soft it was flitted through my mind.

Holy crap! The guy was probably the hottest thing I had ever seen in person. He could have just walked off the pages of a magazine.

His neck was thick, but not as thick as Gary's, and his shoulders were wide. His light blue dress shirt fit snugly over his chest, and his striped tie accented his eyes. I looked back up to his face before my thoughts ran wild and moved lower.

The side of his mouth was tipped up in a smile. It was as if he knew that I was practically undressing him with my eyes-a freaking playboy! I closed my eyelids and shook my head slightly.

He stood up as I opened them and offered his hand to me, "Sergeant McAllister, I've heard a lot of good things about you. I look forward to working with you."

I traded the hand towel to my left hand where my pen was and reached out to take his offered hand, "It's Sergeant Mack. Nice to know one of us has the upper hand. I know nothing about you. It's Bradley, right?"

We shook hands and I found that he had a lot of strength in his palm and fingers, but I gave as good as I got. I hated men who tried to prove their strength and power with a handshake. Not that I was sure he was doing that, it could just be how he normally shook hands.

"Drew Bradley, yes," he replied as our hands parted and dropped back to our respective sides. I twisted the towel between my two palms, suddenly needing to wipe the dampness off of them.

"Pleasure to meet you, Bradley." I turned my attention back to Gary. He was biting the inside of his cheek, probably to keep from busting his gut with laughter.

"You know what to do with him, Mack." There was a leer on his lips, and I wanted to throw both the pen and the towel at him.

"Of course I do." The sarcastic comment wasn't missed by him, or the new kid—and a kid was what he was. "Can I have a word with you, L.T.? Alone?" I refrained from glancing at Bradley and stared a hole into Gary's forehead, hoping to burn right through to his stupid brain.

"Sure," the grin he had suppressed so far filled his handsome face, and I turned towards the door.

"Bradley, you see that desk over there?" I pointed to the one on the other side of mine.

"Yep, I take it that's mine?" he asked as he hesitated beside me. I tried not to stare at his solid chest. The top of my head came up to his chin, so I tilted my head back to see his face.

The bright blue irises sparkled down at me, almost taking my breath away. I swallowed. "Yes, go have a seat."

He smiled wide enough to show me bright white straight teeth and strode away. I would have been ignorant not to watch as his slacks tightened over his butt when he moved. Holy hell, he had a nice backside. I yanked my gaze away from the view to see everyone in the squad room grinning like fools.

I stepped back and slammed the door. Now, I knew why Gordon tossed the towel at me: to wipe away the drool, very funny.

Gary chortled behind me, and I spun on him. "Since when do I have to not only train someone but babysit, too?" I grilled him.

He shook his head and pulled himself up to his desk, resting his arms on the top. "You're not babysitting. Give the kid a chance, he might surprise you."

"Surprise me? I'd be surprised if he didn't need an afternoon nap. How the hell did a kid get assigned to this squad?"

He shrugged, "He tested, and from what I understand, his scores were the highest we have ever had."

"So he can read and write. At least, I won't have to teach him that." I stared at the floor, shaking my head with my hands on my hips. "How long has he been on the force?"

"A few years." He picked up a pen and wiggled it in his fingers.

"So, I not only have to teach him the ropes of the squad, but the ropes of investigation and how to be a cop in general? Great! Just freaking great! Thanks, Gary. Like I don't have enough to do already."

He laughed softly, a warm mellow sound that used to curl my toes when he did it in my ear after we made love. Now, it just irritated me.

"Hey, this isn't personal. You're good at what you do, and I

7

know if anyone can handle him, it's you." He paused for a minute. "You weren't much older than him when you joined the squad, you know."

"Yeah, but I didn't look like I was eighteen, Gary. I looked like a responsible adult, not some piece of eye candy."

He dropped his pen and laughed heartily. "Eye candy, huh?"

"He looks like he should be in an underwear ad in some fancy sex magazine," I snorted and paced back and forth in his small office.

"Come on, Mack, just because the kid has looks doesn't mean he doesn't have any brains. Give the kid a chance." He paused for a moment, and I turned to pace back the four steps that would take me to the plain beige cement wall. "Or are you concerned you won't be able to control yourself around him?"

I stopped abruptly and snapped my neck to stare at him. I stalked to his desk and put both my palms down on the smooth wood top. I leaned over as close to him as I dared.

"I'm not the one who has trouble controlling themselves around the opposite sex," I snarled at him.

He bounced in his seat slightly, and his eyes darted off to the side for just a second before he responded. "Maybe you should try it once it a while. When is the last time you had sex, Mack? It might loosen you up a little bit."

"You son of a bitch!" I yelled right before I lunged over the desktop to grab his tie. I wanted to choke him with it. He must have anticipated the move because he pushed his chair back so quickly that he was just out of my reach. The thought of vaulting over the desk came to mind, but the door behind us opened.

"Everything alright in here?" Gordon asked as he eyeballed both of us.

Anger rolled through me, and my chest heaved with the barely-controlled emotion.

"Yeah, we were just finishing up." We stared each other down as I stood up to my full five foot six inches plus the two extra from my heels. "You ever make a comment like that to me again, and I'll file a report on you, you got that?"

He didn't answer, but I knew by the tick in his jaw that I had gotten his attention.

I spun around on my heel and stomped out of the room. As I passed Gordon, I tossed the hand towel in his face and made a beeline for my desk.

The thing that pissed me off the most about what he had said was that he was probably dead on with his assumption. How long had it been since I had had sex? And why was it that as I thought about my lack of sex, I peered over at the new guy reading the operations manual at his desk?

As if he felt my scrutiny, he lifted his chin and smiled in such a way that my heart thumped against my breast bone. I dropped into my chair, closed my eyes, and took three deep breaths. This was going to be a long month of training.

Chapter 2 – Drew

I finished the half Windsor knot on my tie and shifted my neck around to make sure it wasn't too tight. This particular tie was rather reserved. Normally, I went with a bolder color, like red, but today, I needed to appear more detached.

Starting any new job was difficult, and trying to fit in with a bunch of detectives that not only knew each other well, but had worked together for a long time was enough to make my breakfast shift in my stomach. This was the one thing I hated about going undercover.

I finished straightening my tie and slipped on my silver tie bar to secure it to my shirt. With a last look, I flipped off the light switch and walked into the spare room I had turned into an office. I knew what my assignment was supposed to be, but I took a few minutes to read over my notes one last time before I picked up my suit jacket and made my way out the door.

The drive to the station was about forty-five minutes, and I used the time to replay what I had learned about the people in the squad. There were eight of them, and I would be the ninth. Most of them had been there for a few years, Jose Rivera being the newest, and he had been there almost two years. I knew he was in charge of the technology but not much else about him.

Gordon Brooks was the oldest member of the team and had been in the squad the longest. His two kids were in college now, and he worked long hours to pay the tuitions.

Will Drummond had gotten married not too long ago. I remembered seeing the wedding announcement in his file. His wife was a nurse at the local emergency room. He did major crime and also worked on the gang cases.

One of the top gang guys was Mike Weber. He'd been on the squad for about six years and knew what he was doing. His arrest record was impressive. I knew he was married and had a young child, but he kept his family pretty close and hidden, which was smart in his position.

Bria Reynolds was the youngest in the group at thirty-four. She was married to one of the street cops, and from what I was able to learn, very good at her job. Her reports were in-depth and well written, even if the subject matter was not the kind of thing you wanted to read about.

One of the other males in the group was Chad Wilcox. His certifications for fire investigation were top-notch and he had proven his ability to investigate such crimes over and over again. He was divorced about two years ago, and had a couple of kids; he shared custody with his ex-wife.

That left Det. Sgt. MacKenzie McAllister and her ex-husband and superior, Lt. Gary Robinson. They were married for just over two years with no reason listed on the divorce decree other than irreconcilable differences.

Sergeant McAllister was said to be a hard woman who went by the book. If her stats were anything to go by, she was an incredible investigator. Either that, or she was just plain lucky. She was going to be my training partner, and I wondered if she would try to break my balls like my last partner had. Although, with her reputation, I doubted she was much of a kidder.

The lieutenant had quite a bit in his past, and I was surprised that he still held his title. Obviously, he knew what he was doing and knew the right people to keep on his side, or he wouldn't still be holding his rank.

It was amazing what you could find out about people when you took the time to Google them and do some simple background work. I knew what all of them looked like, except for Mike. He didn't seem to pose for newspaper photos or have any social media accounts. If he did, I sure couldn't find them, but again with his position, that was probably a good thing.

I pulled up outside of the station, a large rectangular light brown stucco building that appeared to be somewhat new. Instead of pulling around to the back where the employees parked, I pulled into a visitor spot. I didn't know if there were any specific spots we were supposed to use, so I decided to play it safe for now.

I locked my Ford Explorer and walked up the concrete pathway to the front glass doors. Inside the entrance, I stood for a moment at the thick glass partition and waited for one of the two operators to get off the phone. One raised his chin to me in acknowledgment of my arrival.

When I told him I was reporting to duty, he buzzed me back and pointed me down the institutional-looking hallway to a door on the left side. I took a slow deep breath to calm my nervous anticipation of the new assignment and noticed the sign on the door, "Investigations Unit". I pulled the door open and stepped in to begin my case.

The large room held quite a few desks, one after another around the sides of the room. A long conference table stood in the middle, and a few doors were situated on the back and right sides. The ones at the back appeared to be interview rooms, barely furnished with no more than a table and a few chairs.

"Can I help you?" the man at the first desk asked, and I stepped up to Gordon's desk.

"I'm Drew Bradley. I'm to report to Detective Sergeant McAllister or Lieutenant Robinson." I held my hand out to shake his, and he obliged and looked me over.

"The Sarge is on the phone," he pointed with his thumb over his shoulder. "The L.T. is in that office. He's expecting you." He pointed to a door on the right side and I thanked him and headed over. I glanced briefly at Sergeant Mack's back. She appeared to be in deep conversation.

The L.T.'s office was larger than I had expected with a massive L-shaped desk that held a computer in the corner. File cabinets lined the left side, and pictures and certificates hung on the walls. His desk surface was covered with small piles of reports, one pile after another. I introduced myself, and we shook hands.

On first impression, I wanted to like and respect him, but I knew better than to judge a book by its cover. He had a firm handshake and laugh lines around his eyes and mouth as he smiled. He was a few inches shorter than my six-foot-four frame, but his shoulders were wider. His dress shirt was even tighter over his chest and biceps than mine was. Obviously, he knew his way around the gym.

I sat in the chair to the right, away from the door, assuming Sergeant McAllister would come in to join us when she was off the phone.

"I'm not sure how you found your way into this department, but I sure hope you're up to it. It's fast-paced and a lot of work."

"I think I can handle it, sir." *If only he knew how well I could handle it,* I thought to myself.

The L.T. stood and walked over to the door, yelling out to the sergeant to get off the phone. I didn't know her, but I had a feeling that wasn't going to go over so well, and boy was I right.

She all but stormed into the room, carrying a towel in her hand while I sat riveted in my seat. Did she plan on shedding blood? Was that why she had brought a towel?

The pictures I had seen of her had not done her justice. She was a beautiful woman with soft blonde hair cut short around her face. Her lips were full, and her green eyes blazed with energy as she stared down the boss. I noticed her clamp her jaw and wondered what she wanted to say.

I kept quiet, watching the dynamics of these two up close and personal. When I was introduced, she glanced my way and then started to look away. Her focus came back to me immediately, and I

13

felt like I was under some kind of formal inspection as her eyes trailed over me. I could almost feel her touching my chest. I actually smiled in response.

She flicked her eyes back up to mine, and I stood to shake her hand. "Sergeant McAllister, I've heard a lot of good things about you. I look forward to working with you." While her skin was soft, her grip was firm, so I grasped hers slightly harder.

I was tempted to ask why she was carrying a towel, but I figured I should keep my curiosity to myself, for now.

"It's Sergeant Mack. Nice to know one of us has the upper hand. I know nothing about you. It's Bradley, right?"

"Drew Bradley, yes," I answered her as I reluctantly let go of her hand.

"Nice to meet you, Bradley." She dismissed me and turned back to the L.T.

"You know what to do with him, Mack," the L.T. said to her, and I saw her clamp her jaw tightly again.

"Of course I do." Her tone of voice not only gave away that she was pissed, probably at him, but that she wasn't too happy to be dealing with me. Getting on her good side might be tough.

"Can I have a word with you, L.T.? Alone?" Once he answered, she turned toward the door, and I figured she was going to close it. But instead, she pointed out the door and spoke to me without looking my way.

"Bradley, you see that desk over there?" I moved beside her and looked in the direction she was pointing.

"Yep, I take it that's mine?" I smiled down at her, hoping to relax her a bit.

She gazed up into my face, and for a moment I was lost in her dark green eyes. "Yes, go have a seat." Her voice broke me out of my haze, and I walked in the direction that she pointed.

As I made my way to the desk, the door behind me slammed, Gordon looked up. "Uh-oh, you left them alone." He stood and glanced at the door, a look of concern written on his face. I turned back and wondered why he would be so worried.

"We don't allow them to close the door very often, and never when she's pissed. They like to push each other's buttons." He leaned back to sit on the edge of his desk and crossed his arms. "I give it less than a minute."

Jose laughed from his desk, and I made my way over to the one assigned to me, on which I found the policy manual. I sat down, flipped it open, and commenced reading the first page. Her raised voice startled me as it carried through the closed door.

Gordon jumped and made a beeline for the L.T.'s door while Jose laughed outright at his desk.

"For some reason, he feels the need to protect her," Jose said as I glanced over my shoulder at him. We both directed our attention to the now-open door, and I looked back down at the page in front of me as I heard her clipped footsteps on the hard tile floor.

I pretended to be engrossed in my reading as she returned to her desk. I peered up as she approached. I learned a long time ago that to help someone relax, all it took was a smile, so I smiled at her. Then I went back to the page in front of me as she sat down. I peeked at her, her eyes were closed and her shoulders rose and fell with a few deep breaths.

I figured it would be best if I left her alone for a few minutes, so I decided to genuinely read what I had in front of me. Five minutes later, I heard her pick up the phone and start talking to a guy named Rick. They sounded like they were discussing a stolen car, but I couldn't be sure.

I half-listened to what she was talking about, but found myself, more often than not, listening to the cadence of her voice. The inflections that she put into her words to express her thoughts intrigued me. I picked up quickly how she changed her voice from being questioning to giving commands and also how it varied pitch when she was surprised by something. She laughed a few times, and I tried to curb the urge to grin. I enjoyed the sound of her laughter, maybe a little too much.

When she set the phone down and began shifting papers around on her desk, I watched her covertly. She put on a pair of reading glasses and started scanning over some documents. A woman walked over to her desk, and I recognized her from a photo I had seen, Bria Reynolds.

"Mack, these were just faxed over for you. Did they have more burgs last night?" She handed the papers to her and Sergeant Mack flipped through them almost absently.

Mack, it seemed funny that everyone called her that, but I guess that was easier than saying one of her full names.

"Yeah, Springton had two overnight, only one where the car was stolen, but the two houses were side by side."

"How many is that now?" Bria asked and slid a flirty glance my way. "Hi, you must be the new guy. Welcome to the squad." She approached my desk and I stood, towering over her as I extended my hand to shake hers. Her grip was nowhere near as firm as Mack's, and I tried to be gentle.

Her brown hair was pulled back tightly into a bun, and she had big hazel eyes with gold flecks in them. Her round face had an olive tone to it, and when she smiled, it lit up her features. She was a pretty woman, much more relaxed than Mack was.

"Thank you. I'm Drew Bradley. I'm looking forward to working with you." I sat back down so I wasn't dwarfing her.

"I'm Bria Reynolds, it's nice to have a new face here." She peeked over her shoulder at Mack, and I saw Bria's manicured eyebrows go up and down twice.

Mack shook her head and spun around in her chair, "You're married, Bria. Remember that guy you exchanged vows with?"

Bria's laugh was high pitched, but not enough to break glass. She grinned at me before turning back to Mack's desk. "It never hurts to check out the candy aisle, even if you are on a diet."

I felt the blush creep up my cheeks as I turned my attention back to the book in front of me.

"Oh my God, he blushes! Mack, do you see that?" I peered over the book to see Mack shaking her head and laughing.

"Better toughen up, kid, or they are going to eat you alive in here," she called over her shoulder. Everyone in the room joined in on the humor which only deepened my blush.

"He's so cute," I heard Bria whisper to Mack, and I tried to pretend I wasn't listening.

"Are you ready to go back to work now," she asked Bria with a stern voice, "or do you want to keep flirting?"

She sighed dramatically, "Fine, what were we talking about?"

"You asked how many we were up to. These two make twenty-four with eighteen cars stolen." Mack spun in her chair and pulled out a document. She laid it down in front of Bria. "I haven't added the two from last night yet."

Bria studied the paper for a few moments, "Wow, still all BMWs, huh?"

"Yeah, I know."

The phone rang on Mack's desk, and she snapped it up. "Sergeant Mack," she stated firmly into the headset. She listened for a moment before her chin dropped down to her chest. I watched her pull her glasses off her face and plop them down onto her desk with what appeared to be frustration. "Where?"

I glanced around the room; everyone was watching her.

"Okay, I'm on my way." She dropped the phone into the cradle. "Make that three overnight. We just had another one in our area reported."

Jose grunted, Gordon stood up, and Bria shook her head and walked over to what I assumed was her desk.

Mack turned to me, "Let's go, kid. It's time to earn your paycheck." I stood as she grabbed a leather portfolio from the side of her desk and started for the door.

Gordon waited for her to pass by, and I followed behind her, feeling like a puppy dog. He handed me a similar portfolio and smiled, "Better start taking notes; she moves fast." He patted me on the back as I passed with a quick thank you.

Chapter 3 – MacKenzie

There was nothing like additional information on a case to calm me down and make me focus on what was really important, and Gary's bullshit was not. The piece of evidence that was left at one of Rick's scenes, however, was, a key to a BMW. Normally that would be no big deal, except the victims didn't have beamers; they had Audis. Which one of the previously stolen cars did that key fit? And could we get DNA evidence off of it?

I strode down the hall, trying to switch gears. I needed to put that information on hold and start putting myself in crime scene mode instead. I pushed hard on the panic bar to release the door to the parking lot and held it open for Gordon and the kid to follow.

The kid—I turned to glance at him. He scanned his eyes over the parking lot. His face turned in my direction, and he noticed me observing him. He released one of his heart-thumping smiles before continuing on with his perusal of the parking area. From this angle and the way his eyes methodically searched the parked cars and tree line around the back of our station, he looked older than I originally thought.

"Where we heading, Mack?" Gordon broke me out of my unprofessional thoughts as we crossed the asphalt towards a line of unmarked Ford Interceptors, typical unmarked police vehicles.

"Raven's Wood Terrace," I replied as I veered off from him towards my vehicle.

"First time they have hit that neighborhood. I was wondering when they would," he commented as he stopped beside a silver Crown Vic and put the key in the lock.

"I know," I yelled over my shoulder and moved to my brand-new white Dodge Durango. It was the only one in the fleet, and I was thrilled when I was told it was assigned to me.

The Durango was completely unmarked on the outside, and the lights were pretty well hidden inside. Most people didn't know it was a police car unless they really inspected it. The inside had everything that other patrol cars had, two radios, a computer, and special red interior lighting that was easier on the eyes at night.

The back of the SUV had my gear, an extra vest, work boots and gloves, a couple of jackets, and my crime scene gear. I was one of the certified investigators who could process a scene, and I enjoyed doing that, even if I did come out with black latent print dust all over my face from time to time.

The kid and I approached my vehicle, and he followed me around to the driver's side. I stopped at the door and pushed the unlock button on my key fob, staring at him. He reached for the door handle and pulled it open. I studied him like he had grown two heads.

"What are you doing? You're not driving. You need to get in on the other side."

"Oh, yeah." He gave me a lopsided grin that made my heart skip a beat. "I was just opening your door for you."

"Get in the car, kid." I stepped into the doorway and climbed inside the truck, grabbing the door as I climbed in and pulling it closed before he could assist. Opening the door for me, give me a break.

I started up the car as he climbed into the other side and watched from the corner of my eye as he looked around the confines of the vehicle.

"You have something against someone opening a door for you?" he questioned.

"No, but we're not on a date, Bradley. This is work. I don't need you to open my car door for me."

He observed me as I turned in my seat and looked out the back to pull out of the space.

"Would you go on a date with me?" he asked suddenly, and I stomped on the brake, jarring us both against our seatbelts, and stared at him.

"No! Are you crazy?" I was exasperated that he would even say such a thing to me. I was old, like almost forty and getting wrinkles, and he was young and hot, oh-so-freaking drop-dead gorgeous, and probably only years out of diapers.

"Why is that so crazy?" He leaned against the passenger door so he could watch me better.

I shook my head and went back to driving. "First of all, I'm too old for you; second, we work together; and, third, I'm not interested."

Lucky for him, he passed over the age issue, and lucky for me he ignored the not-interested comment. Instead, he went right to the meat of the issue. "But weren't you married to Lieutenant Robinson?"

I refused to look his way as I drove out of the lot, instead keeping my eyes on the oncoming traffic before I pulled onto the main road in front of our station.

"How did you know that?" I asked as I made the left turn and accelerated.

"I did some internet searching to see if I could find anything out about whom I would be working with. I found your divorce papers."

I peered over at him. "Stalk much?" I asked.

He laughed, the sound slithered down my spine like hot lava. It was a deep male rumble that made my nerves tingle as it worked its way vertebra by vertebra down my back.

"I wasn't stalking, I was learning." He laughed again, and I tried not to think about the sound and the feeling it created in my body.

"Did you look up everyone in the squad? Or was it just me you were trying to get dirt on?" I put my blinker on and applied the brake to make a right turn.

"I wasn't trying to get dirt. I was merely trying to find out who was who," he replied, "and if it's any consolation, the only dirt I found on you was your divorce."

"Yeah, well let's not talk about that. What else did you find out?"

"Bria got married not that long ago, and Will is a newlywed. Gordon has two kids who are track stars in college. Chad is divorced. I couldn't find much out about Mike. He's pretty good about keeping things quiet, and Robinson is a schmuck."

I laughed out loud. "Did it really say that on the internet? Because if it did, I want to see the website."

I put my blinker on again as we approached the victims' development.

"No, it didn't say that, but obviously, he must be," he retorted.

"Why is that?" I asked and glanced over at him.

He turned to meet my eyes. "Because he let you divorce him."

He looked so serious when he said those words. For a very brief moment I forgot I was driving and found myself lost in his blue eyes. He grinned at me, and I blinked and looked back at the road to make the turn.

I decided it would be better to leave that comment alone. "So, clearly you know how to look people up on the internet. Maybe there is hope for you yet." I knew my voice came out more forceful than I had intended, but I couldn't help that. I pulled a piece of paper out of my jacket pocket and looked at the address while he chuckled softly beside me.

When we pulled up in front of the house, I looked in the rearview mirror and saw Gordon park his vehicle behind me.

"Okay, I want you to watch and listen. Gordon will be getting details from the victim, and you should probably hang with him and pay attention. I have to take a look at the house and see if there is anything that should be processed." I reached for the door handle as I pulled the key out of the ignition. He reached out and grabbed my wrist gently before I could shift in the seat to get out.

I looked at his hand and then up at him. "You're not upset that I said that, are you?" he asked quietly.

Why would he even care? I shook my head and disengaged my wrist from his hand. "No, you were right; he is a schmuck." I climbed out before he could say anything else.

Gordon was already out of his car and heading towards the house. The front door opened, and a man in his late forties stood there waiting, a look of frustration written over his face.

"Mr. Timmons, I'm Detective Brooks, and this is Detective Bradley and Sergeant McAllister." We took turns shaking his hand as Gordon explained that he was going to ask him some questions while I took a look at the house.

I waited until Mr. Timmons acknowledged Gordon before I stepped forward, "Mr. Timmons, is there a room that they focused on while they were inside your house?"

"They spent some time in the dining room and in my office. They took my work laptop, but they won't be able to get anything off of it. It's protected by a thumb drive." He pulled the drive out of his pocket and showed me. "This has to be inserted before you can sign onto the computer. I keep it with me all the time."

"Alright, you can give all the details to these two detectives. I want to have a look around the house and see what I might be able to find." I made my way back to my vehicle, pulling up the hatchback. Inside the back, I pulled out some nitrile gloves and slipped them on, grabbed one of my small but strong LED flashlights to check the surfaces, and pulled my Nikon D3100 camera out of my bag, slinging the strap over my neck.

When I closed the back hatch, I walked back to the house, clicking a few pictures of the exterior as I approached. I stepped around the three men to get into the front door. Gordon knew to keep the guy outside until I was finished. The scene would have been compromised enough with him wandering around trying to see what was missing.

Inside, I stopped in my tracks. The entrance was more than just large; it could only be described as grand. The dark mahogany floors greeted me, the walls all perfectly painted in a soft warm terra cotta, with large pieces of art and family photos adorning them. The stairs were in a half circle around the room, and the chandelier looked like it should be in some fancy hotel ballroom, not a house.

How much did these people make to have a house like this? I could fit my entire house in the first floor of their two-story home. On second thought, I could fit my whole house in half of their first story.

"Hey, Mack," Gordon's voice stopped me, and I turned to him as I headed towards the back of the house.

"Yeah?"

"Entry was from the window in the powder room in the back east side of the house, forced."

"Alarm?" I asked him.

"Not armed," he replied and lifted his bushy eyebrows once.

I shook my head. "Figures," I muttered to myself and turned to move down the hall, carefully examining the floor for any prints that might be there.

I took a few photographs on my way of the general layout of the first floor. Even for someone who didn't spend much time in the kitchen, this one was to die for: tan-and-black-speckled granite countertops with dark wood cabinets, track lighting all around the room emphasized the appliances and decorations. I would bet my life that this room alone cost more than my annual salary. Wonder if they'd adopt me.

I meandered around the first floor, spotting the formal dining room, and snapped a few more pictures. The table appeared to seat at least twenty. Did I even know that many people who I would want to sit down and share a meal with? I didn't think so.

The china cabinet was huge. I wondered absently how they put it into the house, or if they built the house around it. A few of the cabinet doors were open, and I photographed them before peeking inside. There was a large void area on one of the shelves. Had something been stolen from there? I photographed it just in case. I pulled open a drawer and saw miscellaneous items scattered absently inside.

I scanned the room, taking a moment to look for anything else out of place, before I walked into the kitchen. Once I reached the cabinets, I pulled open drawers one after another. Every one of them was perfectly organized, neat and orderly.

I walked back to the dining room and took a picture of the ransacked drawer. If I were a betting woman, I'd say the suspects went through the drawer. I skimmed the items, looking for something that might have a fingerprint on it, but found nothing of value for my purposes.

I aimed my flashlight from the side across the wood drawers and cabinet, looking for any spots that were noticeable that might be oil or dirt from a hand. I didn't think I would find anything because these guys were careful and appeared to wear gloves all the time.

Criminals were getting smarter, but they still made mistakes, and it was only a matter of time before we found one of them and developed a strong lead.

I left the dining room and continued into the east side of the house, looking for the powder room. I found it on the back corner and stood in the doorway, my mouth hanging open. This powder room was bigger than my kitchen. I aimed my camera for a few more shots before making my way to the window to inspect it. Pry marks could be seen on the outside casing of the window. The screen was missing, probably lying on the ground outside.

I stood back to take a photograph of the damage to the window and then took a wider shot and stopped. I pulled the camera away from my face and bent down to examine the wall. An almost perfect footprint was on the beige painted drywall surface, the toe pointing downward. Obviously, when the subject entered, he put his foot against the wall to steady himself. I photographed it carefully. I would need some measuring tape to get accurate photographs, but I would do that later.

I heard footsteps coming my way and stayed in my crouch while I turned to the door, expecting Gordon, but not entirely surprised to see the kid standing there. He looked as awestruck as I was at the size of the bathroom.

"This room is bigger than my bedroom." He stepped into the

threshold and looked around.

"I think the wall of mirrors over there enhances it and makes it look larger than it is," I said as he stood in front of the mirrors and studied the room through the reflection. Our eyes locked, and something zinged between us like an invisible current. We both looked away.

"Did you find something?" he asked after he cleared his throat and turned in my direction.

"Actually, I did. I have a footprint on the wall. I need to take some more photographs, and then I'm going to lift it."

"How are you going to lift it?" He bent down next to me and examined the area I was photographing.

"I'll use a gel lifter. They pick up footprints pretty decently." He nodded, and I noticed how close he was when I took my eyes off the print. I stood up quickly, startling him, and he lost his balance and fell back on his butt.

A nervous laugh flitted from my lips. "You alright?" I held my hand out to help him up, and he reached for it.

"Yeah, you moved so fast. I was trying to stay out of your way." I pulled him up a little harder than I had intended and he ended up standing right in front of me. We were now just inches apart. I realized that I was staring at his chest and the boring tie he was wearing for a little too long. Then I realized that I still had ahold of his hand. I dropped it as if I had been burned and stepped around him.

I thought I heard him chuckle under his breath, but I couldn't be sure, and I didn't want to turn and look at him. "Don't touch anything; you aren't wearing gloves," I instructed as I strode out of the room, intent on getting my gear and out of his immediate area.

Chapter 4 – Drew

I wasn't even paying attention when she stopped next to the Durango. I was expecting her to go to another Crown Vic, not an SUV. That's why I ended up beside her when she unlocked the door. Opening her door seemed like a good explanation as to why I was there until she appeared offended. What woman doesn't like for a man to be a gentleman and treat a woman like a lady?

Obviously, MacKenzie McAllister didn't. I climbed into the passenger seat and looked over the vehicle. It didn't have the new car smell anymore, but it still looked brand-new inside.

I was only kidding when I asked her on a date. I wondered if I would have a bruise on my chest from slamming into the seatbelt so hard. I almost received whiplash from the quick stop, and what I said appeared to rattle her, just a tad. Maybe keeping her off balance might help my cause here.

I knew better than to talk about a woman's age. She had no idea that I knew she was only two weeks from turning forty, but that did not detract from her looks in any way. I could understand why she wouldn't want to get involved with someone at work since she worked with her ex-husband already. Talk about complicated. It was her last statement that I pondered later, I'm not interested. Was she seeing someone?

Not that it mattered or that I really cared. I hoped to get this cleared up fast and be out of here as soon as I could. I didn't need any entanglements, that was certain. I had enough to deal with at home.

The sound of her voice when she turned to me and asked me if I stalked much was so funny that I laughed, and I explained how I knew about her and Robinson and some of what I had dug up on the others. There was no way I would tell her everything, most of it I had read in my file, and that was not to be disclosed.

I watched her as she drove. She was intense and took her job very seriously, but I could see that she did have a sense of humor and I liked that. Maybe that was why I told her Robinson was an idiot for letting her divorce him. Yeah, that was the reason.

She clicked right back into cop mode, although she appeared slightly uncomfortable when we pulled up to the house, and I wondered if maybe I had overstepped my boundary with her. I barely knew her, and I needed her to not only like me, but to trust me. I was naturally a touchy person when I liked someone, so that was why I reached out for her arm. A confused looked passed over her face quickly enough that I wondered if I had really seen it. She climbed out after agreeing with me, and we went to work.

Well, Gordon and Mack worked. I stood around and pretended I was learning. Gordon was good at questioning the victim, and I piped in once or twice with a question of my own. Mack was in the house searching for evidence, and once Gordon got the victim to start listing items missing, he sent me in to make sure she didn't need any help.

I wandered around the house, my jaw hanging open at the opulence of the home. I didn't think I could ever live in a house like this. It put the one I lived in to shame. Having to clean and organize this place would be a full time job. Of course, the owners had enough money that they probably paid a cleaning company. I saw a flash down the hallway and headed in that direction.

Mack was bent down scrutinizing the wall, and I scanned the room. I examined it from the mirror image and found her watching me. It wasn't the first time she had done that. She did that in the parking lot at the station, too. What she was looking for?

"Did you find something?" I joined her near the wall. I squatted down and studied the print. It was a perfect textbook print. The labs should be able to do something with that, especially if we found something to compare it to. The least they could do was figure out the size and maybe the brand of shoe.

I was familiar with general crime scene processing, although it wasn't my niche. I saw her look my way and rush to stand up. Trying to avoid being struck by her movement, I lost my balance and fell back.

She surprised me by offering me a hand up, I stood stock still as she stared at my chest. The investigator in me wondered what she was thinking, the man in me basked in the attention.

She backed away quickly as she stood, and I tried to contain a laugh at how obvious her discomfort was at my nearness. Another way to keep her off balance, I thought.

I wandered back to the main entrance, careful to keep my hands off anything as she'd requested. I had seen what having other officers in a crime scene can do to the evidence if they weren't careful.

I stood at the edge of the office when she wheeled her large toolbox into the house and down the hallway. "What's in that?"

She stopped and started opening drawers. "My crime scene tools: powders, brushes, lifters, measuring devices, and some other things." I watched her unclip the sides and lift the top part off to reveal a deep storage compartment that had some bags and large envelopes in it. She pulled out one of the tan envelopes and pulled a large gel lifter out of a drawer, then set it aside to dig through another drawer where she pulled out a roll of tape with tick marks on it, like a measuring tape.

I followed her back to the bathroom and watched as she carefully placed the tape along the footprint in an L pattern. She took photographs of the print from a variety of angles and up close. She was about to place her camera on the floor when I reached down to take it from her. She gawked at the offered hand but gave me a genuine smile before placing the camera in my palm.

In that moment, her face looked radiant. Her features had softened, her eyes brightened, and for just a second she looked relaxed. I saved that snapshot of her smile into the memories of my mind. It was a moment I wanted to remember; I just didn't know why.

She went back to work and very carefully placed the lifter over the footprint, smoothing the back of the lifter over and over again to make sure there were no bubbles. When she pulled it off the wall, I set the camera down on the sink and picked up the protective sheet that had come with it. Between the two of us, we preserved the print as best we could.

"Good job, Sergeant Mack."

She peeked up at me with a strange look on her face.

"Thanks," she muttered when she looked away and retrieved her camera to leave the room.

We went to the office after she jotted a few things down on the back of the lifter and placed the print near her toolbox. Standing at the office door, she took overall photographs of the room while I stood behind her and inspected it over her head. Even wearing her heels, she only came to my chin. I looked down at her boots, about two inches, which meant she would come to just above my shoulder without shoes.

I dismissed the thought since it had nothing to do with what we were working on.

"Do you notice anything strange about the room?" she asked me as she stepped inside.

"It's a mess, while the rest of the house is too neat."

"Exactly," she studied the room carefully before moving to the other side of the desk and photographing from that angle. I moved outside and away from the door while she worked. "The dining room was a mess, too, but I think that was to throw us off. You can come back in," she called out, and I checked around the corner to make sure she wasn't holding the camera to her eye. She was standing over the desk pushing a few pieces of paper around.

"Why do you say that?" I asked as I stepped back into the room.

"Because in almost every burglary, they took a few things, and tossed a room or two. They never took anything too valuable, like jewelry or electronics, just the cars." She stared down at something on the floor.

"This guy owns the local BMW dealership," she stated as she bent over to pick something up from the floor.

I stepped closer and saw the victim's business card in her gloved hand. "Yeah, he told Gordon that just before I came to find you."

Her face snapped up, "Why didn't you tell me?"

I straightened at the almost ferocious look in her eye. "Um, I didn't know it was important. Besides, you didn't ask."

She huffed and looked back at the card, obviously not happy with my answer. "Well, it is important. Gordon should have sent you to tell me as soon as he learned that." She slipped the business card in the pocket of her gray sport jacket.

"Why is it important?" I watched as her jaw tightened and she scanned over the desk again, pulling open one of the drawers and moving some of the contents gently to see what was underneath.

"It's important because all of the cars that have been stolen are BMWs." She pushed the drawer closed and opened the bottom one that contained hanging file folders.

"And?" I had waited a good ten seconds for her to say more.

She clicked a photo of the drawer and gave me an annoyed look. "And, if this guy owns a dealership, they were here for a different reason than just to steal his car and burglarize his house." She stared back down at the drawer while I pondered what she said and remembered that the victim's laptop had been stolen.

She was probably right. I wondered what was on the laptop.

"Something is missing from here," she said quietly.

I looked at the drawer. It was full, not crammed, but full enough, and she was right, something looked like it was missing. One of the green hanging folders was empty, and the folders in front and behind were pushed away.

Mack looked all around the room, including under the desk and behind a file cabinet, but didn't locate any files. I didn't either, but I hadn't really been looking for one. I was watching her as I had earlier when I had listened to her voice. Now I observed her movements and tried to get a read on her facial expressions and body language.

Her jaw was clamped down, she wasn't grinding, but the muscle in the side of her cheek looked firm. She cocked her head to the right, moving her head a fraction of an inch every couple of seconds as her eyes scanned around the area. As her head came around towards me, she flicked her eyes to my face, her eyebrows arching high and her shoulders going back.

"Yes?" she said, rather indignantly.

I shook my head, "Nothing."

She bit her lip for a second while she studied me. "Then stop staring at me and help me look for the damned file."

Thankfully, she turned her head the other way because I couldn't suppress my smile. "I think you scoured the room well enough for both of us," I said lightly, she turned back to me.

"Is that so?" She leaned her head back the other way, the green of her irises darker than they appeared before. "Do you always let you partner do all the work?"

I released a short laugh, "No."

When I didn't say anything further, she shook her head as if to clear it and turned away from me. "Go ask Gordon to bring the victim in here."

I knew I shouldn't, but I felt the need to test her just a tiny bit, "Do you always tell your partner what to do?"

She paused as she walked towards the window and lifted her chin up. "If you want to work in this unit, Bradley, start getting used to taking orders from me. I'm your sergeant, you do what I ask."

"You could say please," I tried to keep my voice serious because inside I was laughing at how tense she had become. I wasn't really trying to push her buttons. I just wanted to know how hard to push before she snapped.

She turned sideways and her face came even with her shoulder. There was something in her eyes I couldn't quite place as hard as I tried. I couldn't tell if she was on the verge of laughing or taking my head off.

"And you can kiss my ass. Now go get the victim." She turned away from me.

"Before or after I kiss your—"

"Bradley! Go! Go get the damned victim, and don't you dare finish that sentence." While her voice was raised, I did catch a tiny bit of humor in her voice. When I left the room, I thought I heard her chuckle.

Gordon and Mr. Timmons were still outside. I approached them as they were discussing how Mr. Timmons's wife was either in the Bahamas or Aruba. He owned property in both, and he could never remember which one she was going to.

I'm in the wrong job, I thought. The guy has two high-end cars, a castle for a house, and he owns property in two beautiful resort areas in other countries—must be nice.

"Mr. Timmons, Sergeant McAllister would like to talk to you in your office."

They followed me back inside, and Mack met us at the door, not meeting my gaze as we approached.

"Mr. Timmons, when was the last time you were in your office?" She held the camera in one hand, the other casually slipped into her pants pocket. Gordon opened his portfolio and held his pen above the paper ready to take notes.

The victim scratched at his jaw while he thought. "I returned home from a business meeting around nine last night and came in here. I was probably in here for about forty-five minutes before I went up to bed."

"Were you in here this morning before you called us?"

He shook his head. Gordon jotted down a quick note. "No, not really. I had a late meeting this morning, so I slept in later than normal. I was coming in to get my computer and noticed it was gone and my drawers were open. I didn't touch anything and used my cellphone to call you."

"So you didn't go through any of your files?"

"No."

"Did you go through your files last night and take one out?" She peered at me briefly.

He contemplated the question, "No, I don't think so. Why?"

She glanced down at the floor. "I want you to look at your file drawer. See if you can tell if a file is missing and if there is one, if you know what the contents might be."

"Sure." He followed her into the room and around the desk. She stopped and, instead of looking down at the drawer, focused directly on his profile. What was she looking for?

His eyes tightened just the tiniest amount. If I hadn't looked at him when I did, I might have missed it. A muscle ticked in the side of his jaw, and he shoved his hands into his pants pocket.

"No, I don't think anything is missing." He glanced around his office. What was he looking for? Mack and I shared a glance.

"You're sure? Because it looks like there was a file right there where the empty hanging folder is. What could that file have been?"

He shook his head and started back towards the door. Mack watched his back as he passed me, her brow furrowed slightly in the center.

"No, I'm not missing anything. That was like that. How much longer are you all going to be? I need to get to work." He stepped around Gordon and paused to await an answer.

Gordon observed Mack very closely. I faced her again waiting for an answer.

"We are done inside. The rest we can do without you. Thank you."

As if released from custody, he bolted down the hallway, pulling his phone from his pocket as he went around the corner.

Mack grunted as she moved towards the hall. She whispered as she got closer, leaning towards Gordon slightly, "Hiding much?"

She passed by and moved to her crime scene kit, putting the pieces back together and attaching the two large pieces so she could wheel it outside. Gordon and I waited patiently for her to finish before we exited the house.

She left her kit in the driveway and went around the back of the house to take some pictures. She moved slowly towards the back window scanning the ground as she went.

"What is she looking for?" I asked Gordon.

"Probably footprints." He was a man of few words, that was for sure.

She stood beside the garden area, under the bathroom window, and snapped a few pictures.

"Gordon, can you call back to the station and have a tech come out here and cast this print? It looks similar to the one I lifted off the bathroom wall."

Gordon pulled out his cellphone. I approached Mack and came to a stop beside her, "Nice find."

"They are sending someone over," Gordon called out when he hung up.

"Okay, do you mind staying here until they get here and show them where it is?"

"Sure."

Mack and I walked back to the front of the house, and she rolled her toolkit to the Durango.

I bent to lift up her kit and put it into the back. When I finished, she was staring at me.

"Just say thank you," I said as I picked up the portfolio that I had tossed on the grass next to the curb.

"Thank you," she responded, and I grinned at her. She blinked a few times then looked behind me.

"I want a complete background on that guy," she spoke to Gordon who stood behind me. "There is something he doesn't want us to know. Can you get that started as soon as you get back, Gordon? On second thought," she flashed me a quick look, "give that to Bradley and show him how to use our program. He needs to do something other than stare at people."

Gordon laughed and she moved to the driver's door of her vehicle.

"Hey, you both told me to watch and listen; that's what I did," I threw in.

Gordon laughed louder as he leaned against his car.

Chapter 5 – MacKenzie

I started the car and tried to focus on what we had been doing, but my mind was stuck on the fact that every time I glanced at the kid, he was inspecting me. What was up with that? Was he counting the laugh lines that would soon turn into full-blown wrinkles or what?

I slid a quick glance at him as he buckled his seatbelt. He was right, we had told him to look and listen, but I didn't think staring me down every time I focused on something else was what we meant.

He should have been studying the scene. The way Mr. Timmons had examined the drawer had confirmed that something was missing, and he wasn't too happy about it. His need to get away from us only gave that theory more strength. Who had he called? It looked like I needed to work on a court order for some cellphone records. I sighed, more paperwork.

"What's wrong?" the kid asked me as I turned out of the development.

I waited until I was on the main road before I answered, "Nothing, really. Just thinking about all the paperwork that goes in on these kinds of cases and how far behind I am."

He quieted for a moment, then offered, "I'll help if I can, just tell me what you need me to do."

I laughed. "Kid, I wish you could help with the paperwork, but unless you were present at the scenes, you can't write about the processing. I have three crime scenes I need to put on paper, and it's all stored up here." I tapped the side of my temple.

"Well, I'll start working on that background check that you wanted me to do. Did you know that he owns two properties out of the country, one in Aruba and one in the Bahamas?"

"Must be nice," I snorted in an unladylike fashion. "I'll be lucky if I ever get to visit those places."

"What, you don't take vacations?"

I shrugged. "Yeah, of course I take time off, but I don't normally go anywhere," which honestly sucked because I'd love to go sit on a beach someplace and watch the sun set over the ocean while some cute little piece of eye candy gave me one drink after another that included a little paper umbrella in it. The problem was I didn't have anyone to go with.

"Why don't you go anywhere?" The kid was relentless with his questions—and getting on my nerves.

"I just don't." I flipped on my blinker to pull back into the station. "When you get inside, keep reading the manual and get with Gordon when he returns so he can get you started. I have to work on my own reports."

I started to assume that he understood the message that I didn't want to talk about it, but then again, once we parked, he opened up his sexy little mouth again.

I turned to stare at him and found myself watching his very succulent lips as they formed the words, "You really should go away sometime."

"When I go away, it will be to the funny farm." I pulled the key out of the ignition and opened my door as I heard him bust out laughing.

"You afraid to fly?" he asked as he met me at the back of my truck.

"No," I almost shouted at him, "I'm not afraid to fly, I just don't travel. My time off is spent doing other stuff." I opened my hatch and retrieved my camera bag and the envelope with the footprint.

He walked beside me as we moved towards the building. "What other stuff?"

I stopped and spun on him, "What the hell is your problem?"

A confused look passed over his face, and he shook his head, "I don't have a problem. Why?"

"Then what's up with the twenty questions about what I do on my time off? What difference does it make to you?"

He put his hands up, palms facing me. "Relax, Sarge. I was only trying to have a conversation. I didn't mean to be offensive. I was just trying to get to know you better."

I glared at him, "The only thing you need to know about me is I expect everyone to do what they are supposed to do." I turned and stalked away. "Wait for Gordon and then get to work."

So I was being a royal bitch, I was well aware of that. Why? I wasn't exactly sure. I never had a problem being friendly with the guys, and it was natural to want to get to know the people you worked with. I realized he was just trying to find a way to fit in. I opened the back door and started to climb up the flight of stairs that led to the unit, trying not to feel guilty.

Maybe it was the stress of the cases. Maybe I did need to take a break, or maybe it was because he unnerved me by watching me so damned closely. His blue eyes followed my every move, and my heart raced when I met them head on.

The conversation in Gary's office came back to mind, maybe I did need to have sex. That had to be the only reason I was lusting after the kid. I winced as I reached the door. I was not lusting after him. I was just—oh hell, I was lusting after him.

I'd only been around him half the day, yet it felt like weeks. It reminded of me of when I had been on a diet and someone had put my favorite piece of cheesecake right in front of me to taunt me. I knew I shouldn't look at it, knew I shouldn't put that tiny bite to my lips, or I would want to devour the whole thing.

Holy crap! I was referring to him as food. I was not lusting after him, and he was not one of my favorite desserts. I could keep telling myself that, but what my body was craving told me otherwise.

How could I not want it? Every time I saw his eyes on me, I felt warmth travel through parts of my body that were reserved for other things, not stuff that happened at work.

I dropped my portfolio on my desk and dropped into my seat, rubbing my hands up and down my face. I should probably slap myself. Maybe I could knock some sense into my head if I did it hard enough. Nothing like wanting to rob the cradle. Lock me up now.

I ignored Gordon and Bradley when they entered the unit, spinning so my back was to them, and picked up my phone to listen to the three messages that the LED screen on my phone said I had. Two were nothing I needed to deal with immediately, and the third one was about some evidence I'd recovered at one of the scenes. I planned to stop at the lab after lunch and see what they had for me.

I heard someone coming my way, and my back stiffened. "Hey, Mack." I released a relieved and frustrated sigh when I realized it was Gary. Could a sigh be both? Well, mine was.

I looked over my shoulder at him, not ready to forgive him for his comment this morning, no matter how true it was. I raised an eyebrow in response.

"Did you get anything at the scene?" Gary stood in front of my desk with his arms crossed.

"A footprint and the victim is hiding something, but that's about it." I swiveled my chair around to face him.

His mind was working; his eyes moved over the surface of my desk. He cleared his throat. "Why do you think he was lying?"

I observed Gary for a moment; he looked uncomfortable about something. Could he be sorry for what he'd said earlier? I doubted that.

"Because I asked him a question about something, and he lied." I continued to scrutinize Gary as he tensed.

"I doubt he was lying, he's probably just upset. You know victims, they get moody when someone takes their toys." He turned to look at Gordon and the kid while I followed his line of sight. Bradley was leaning over Gordon's desk; his pants snug over his backside as he stood studying something on the flat surface.

Damn it, there was that warm feeling again. I looked down at my hands and picked at a nail. "He was lying, Gary. I know when someone is lying."

Gary shrugged, "I doubt it. He's a good man, owns a hell of a business, he has nothing to hide." He dismissed the conversation as he walked away, and I studied his back as he left.

A long time ago, looking at his wide shoulders and tiny waist had done something for me. Now, it didn't. I eyeballed the back side of Bradley again. Now that, that did something.

"He has a really nice ass, doesn't he?" Bria whispered as she stopped beside me and leaned down.

"Yes, he does," I said without thought, then blinked and clenched my jaw as Bria snickered and went back to her desk.

I tore my eyes away from the kid and forced myself to focus on my paperwork. I still hadn't gone through the reports on my desk that needed to be approved, so I started with those. Somewhere between reports five and six, a cup of coffee showed up on my desk. I wasn't sure who put it there, but when I noticed it, I called out a quick thanks to whoever it could have been and took a sip of the still-steaming coffee.

After I finished the nine reports, I dropped them into Gary's inbox on his desk when I saw his office was empty and went back to my desk to start my own reports.

On my way, I noticed the kid was writing some notes. Huh, he's left-handed, I thought. Not that it was a big deal, but I always found people who used their left hands interesting, in an odd sort of opposite way.

He didn't look up from what he was he doing, and I sank back into my chair slightly disappointed and turned to my computer.

"Hey, Mack, before you get all engrossed in your computer, I picked up some sandwiches. They are in the break room." Jose stood at the entrance; in his hand, proof of his words, sat a thick crusty roll filled to overflowing with lunchmeat. Hot damn, I could use that right now.

I grinned at him, "Jose, you are the best." I stood up and turned to Drew, he was probably wondering if he was invited too. "Let's go, kid, time for a break. Then, if you don't need to take a nap, you can get back to what you're doing."

I heard him snort as he stood and followed us out of the room.

When we entered, the whole gang was there, well, everyone except Gary. "Where's the L.T.?" I asked.

Will shrugged, "He said he had things to do."

I pulled a chair out and reached over the table to snag a plate and half of a roast beef sandwich.

Bradley waited until I was seated and then took a paper plate and two sandwiches. "Do you do this often?" he queried.

Bria answered since my mouth was full. "We try to do it once a week. It's our time to shoot the shit and relax a bit together."

"Besides," Jose chimed in, "Mack had that if-someone-doesn't-bring-me-food-I-won't-eat look about her. She was into her work."

Everyone laughed, even me. "Sorry, who brought me the coffee, by the way?"

All eyes turned to the kid, who had just torn a large section of his sandwich off with his bright white straight teeth. Yeah, they were television-commercial perfect.

He shrugged and attempted to talk around the food in his mouth, "No big deal. You were busy, so I figured it couldn't hurt to pour you a cup when I poured my own."

Will and Gordon both spouted at the same time, "Suck-up," and everyone busted up again. The kid's face went pink, somehow becoming more attractive.

I put my sandwich down and picked up a napkin to wipe my mouth. I reached for his wrist as it lay beside his plate. I realized my mistake when a zing shot up my arm. We stared at each other as he stopped chewing. His eyes looked a whole lot older and much more mature as we contemplated one another for that brief moment.

I picked up my sandwich again. "Thanks," I tossed out before I shoved the food between my lips. Bria was watching me with a lopsided grin on her face.

"Of course, he had to come and ask how you liked your coffee before he could get it for you," Bria called out as I tried not to laugh at his reddening cheeks.

"Like we said, suck-up," Jose spoke around the food in his mouth.

During the rest of lunch, we backed off Bradley and talked about families, kids, and what everyone was doing next weekend. It turned out everyone had plans, except for the kid and me. I tried not to think about that, but my mind was hell-bent on coming up with an idea or two of what I'd like to do. Down girl, down.

With lunch finished, we all fell back into our workload. I managed to punch out my court order for the phone records with a little bit of creative help from Jose. I sent it over to the District Attorney's office for approval. I'd run by there tomorrow and get a judge to sign it for me.

When I checked my watch again, it was almost five. Gordon and Bria were already gone for the day, and Chad had come in and was sitting at his desk. The kid was typing on his computer.

I stretched my back and rolled my neck, both were stiff from sitting so long in the same position. With my hand over my mouth, I feebly attempted to stifle a yawn.

"Time to call it a night, Bradley."

He glanced up for a brief moment, barely making eye contact. "Yeah, I just want to finish typing this last bit up."

I watched his fingers move over the keyboard. He wasn't one of those hunt-and-peck types of people. He actually looked at the screen while his fingers clicked away. His fingers were long and thin, and ringless.

I turned away. Of course he didn't have a ring; he was probably barely old enough to get married. "How old are you?" I asked on the spur of the moment.

His fingers paused, and he shifted his face towards mine. He swallowed before he spoke and lifted his eyebrows. Holy crap!

"Never mind," I cut in as I spun around and straightened some papers on my desk.

"I'm twenty-eight. Why?"

I didn't turn to look at him, twenty-eight. That was twelve years younger than I was—yep, robbing the cradle. I had to get over this little fixation I seemed to have developed the moment he had entered the unit. Had that been just this morning? It had been way too long since I had gotten lost in the simple pleasures of what a man could do for me. I ground my teeth. I wasn't going to go looking for that in the twenty-eight-year-old behind me.

"Just wondering," I replied as I put the last of my papers in two neat stacks and logged off my computer. I heard him clicking his mouse, and then the wheels of his chair rolled back.

"All done. How old are you?"

I turned to him at the wrong moment. He was stretching his back. With his arms spread wide, his chest seemed to go on and on, and I wondered what those muscles looked like under the material of his dress shirt.

I mentally groaned and leaned down to pick up my small leather briefcase. "Much older than you," and that was all that mattered.

I heard the humor in his voice as he walked my way. "You're not that much older than I am, Mack."

I searched his face, noticing how strong his cheekbones were. I decided not to say anything else. I wasn't sure I could find my voice, and I turned to leave.

"Wait, I'll walk out with you," he called as I entered the hallway. I cringed, not because I didn't want him to, but because I wasn't sure how much longer I could be around him without throwing myself at him.

I slowed my steps, and he caught up halfway to the stairs. "What are you doing tonight?"

"The same thing I do every night. Go home, exercise for a little while, eat dinner, and then chill out." It was the same old routine, almost like it was my own set of general orders. "What about you?" I asked to be polite.

He grinned, "Just about the same thing, work out, eat, and see what's on television."

By this time, we had arrived at the door at the bottom of the steps that led to the parking area. He reached around me and pushed the bar on the door to release it. His body came much closer than it should but not close enough to diminish the ache I was feeling in his proximity.

I heard him clear his throat and glanced up to see him scanning the parking lot again. "Do you work out at home, or do you belong to a gym?"

I stopped and turned to him. The sun was lower in the sky, and I tried not to squint as I focused on him. Squinting would only enhance the crow's feet growing around my eyes.

"You really like to ask questions, don't you?" Unlike earlier, I wasn't angry.

He gave me his signature lopsided smile, "Sorry, I'm doing the twenty questions again, aren't I?"

"Yes, you are." I turned to continue to my car, he stayed beside me. "It's alright, I understand why you are asking. It's hard trying to fit into a new unit." I pressed the button on my key fob to unlock the doors of my Mustang.

"Nice machine." He inspected the gray body of my sports car. "I like the black racing stripes over the top."

"Thanks. This is my toy." I grinned as I pulled open the driver's door and tossed my briefcase into the passenger seat.

"It fits you." He ran his hand over the front quarter panel. I suppressed a shiver while imagining those fingers on my neck.

My voice was husky when I spoke, "Why do you say that?" He stood on the other side of the door, a barrier between us, but I felt the chemistry flowing around us like air racing inside the windows as I roared down the highway.

He moved closer, resting one of his hands on the top of the door. "Because you are a sleek machine, driven in what you do. You go fast when you need to, and you're strong. You only have to look into your face to see that, just like you only have to look at the contours of this car to know what's inside."

Okay, so being compared to a car might put some women off, but not this one. I loved my Mustangs. Over the years, I had had several of them, and I could see what he was saying. I was just finding it very strange that he could see that about me in just one day—and did I mention it turned me the hell on?

We contemplated each other, his eyes searching mine and sliding over my features, just as mine were doing to him. Could he feel this chemistry, too?

The back door to the station opened and we both turned, breaking the current between us. I sat down in my car. He gently pushed the door closed once I was inside. When I had the car started, I rolled down the window.

"I work out at home," I answered him as I put my car in gear.

"Lucky you, I have to go to the gym. Have a good night, Mack."

"You too, Drew." I drove away from him before I could invite him to come to my place to use my equipment—and by equipment, I didn't necessarily mean my weights.

Chapter 6 – Drew

After Gordon showed me how to use their background program, I played around with it for a while, but I knew I could get more information faster if I went through my own channels.

Everyone was busy with their own work, so I logged on to an email host that looked like it was a personal account and shot off a message to my buddy Rob who worked for the agency.

The cool thing about Rob was that we were best friends from high school, and he was the only reason I had taken this assignment all the way on the other side of the United States. I had lived in Los Angeles for years and hadn't seen Rob in almost that long. When the opportunity came up to do this undercover job, Rob suggested I be the one to handle it. I jumped at the chance, even though I had to juggle quite a few other things at home first.

Rob answered almost immediately, acknowledging that he received it, and tacked on a note asking when we were going out for a beer to catch up. I replied that we'd meet up this weekend.

I heard Mack get up and say something about leaving, and I glanced at the digital numbers in the corner of my screen. Wow, the day had flown by. Finishing up my email to Rob, I logged off and stood up to stretch. Mack turned my way and there was no way I could not see the look in her eye as it caressed my chest. The way she inspected me stirred lustful feelings deep inside. I escorted her down to the parking lot, and this time when I questioned her, she didn't become upset.

I gazed over her Mustang. If I had to choose a car to portray her, the Mustang would be the one. She was indeed a sleek machine, a classic, although I wasn't talking about her age. The horsepower under the hood reminded me of her determination, and the definable lines matched her ethics, smooth and straightforward, or so they seemed anyway.

She gazed at me as I spoke the words. There was a serious attraction between the two of us, but I knew she would never act on it. Hell, she thought I was only twenty-eight. It was no wonder she called me kid.

I knew the attraction wasn't right. There was no reason to get involved, other than a good roll in the hay with her. Somehow she didn't appear to me to be a one-night-stand kind of person.

We said goodbye, and I watched her drive away, wishing that I could have been with her as she revved the engine and pulled out onto the road. A woman in a fast sports car was almost as much of a turn on as a woman who could strip you naked with only her eyes. I shook my head and tried to dislodge the thought of her and me rolling naked on the sheets. Forget the workout, I thought. I was going to need a cold shower before I even started to lift.

After working out that night, I cooked some chicken and pasta and sat down at my laptop to type up some notes. I clicked open a file that had photographs of all the members of the unit. With my chin resting on the heel of my hand, I stared at her picture. I was right; it didn't do her justice. I felt a stirring inside and clicked the picture closed before opening up my word processing software to type my notes.

Thirty minutes later, I emailed my notes to my boss and finished my dinner. I climbed in bed and clicked on the small television.

With a sigh, I rested my head against the two pillows along the bare wall. I missed my own bed. The apartment they'd rented for me was decent but basic. There were no frills, but I didn't need any, although I would have enjoyed a larger television set. I dropped the remote and leaned over to pick up the only piece of personal decoration I had in my room, a picture. I ran my finger over the glass and stared at the images smiling back at me.

I didn't normally feel homesick, but tonight I did. Over the last year, due to circumstances at home, I had stopped traveling so much. I had gotten used to being at the house every night, gotten used to the rituals and the constant noise.

I set the picture down on the nightstand and fixed my pillow, turning my attention to the hockey game filling the screen and trying not to think about what I was missing at home.

Somewhere about midgame, I must have fallen asleep. I woke up to the beeping of my alarm, the television still on. I absently slid my finger over the off button on my phone and shook my head to clear it while I sat up.

Normally, I was not a morning person, but the moment my eyes actually opened, Mack's face popped into my mind, and I threw back the covers, anxious to get to work. I wondered what mood she would be in today.

After breakfast, I checked my real work email and answered a few of them. I grabbed a quick shower and dressed in black slacks and a tan shirt, ties didn't appear to be mandatory, so instead of putting one on, I'd throw one in my car, just in case.

I arrived at the station and found Mack's Mustang already parked. I felt a tingle of anticipation slide through me at seeing her again.

Yesterday, I had been given keys to the rear door, so I let myself in and climbed the stairs. I was rounding the hallway, staring at the tiles, wondering what the day would bring when I felt eyes on me— not just any eyes, somehow I knew they were hers. I looked up into her face and grinned.

"There she is," I called out as I approached. Her mouth was slightly open, and she bit her lower lip. My groin kicked slightly at the action, and I reverted to looking at her eyes again.

"Good morning, kid," she responded with a forced smile and

moved towards me, a paper coffee cup in her hand from a local convenience store.

"How are you this morning, Mack?" I stopped at the door leading to the unit, waiting for her to join me and wondering what was up, she looked tense.

"Peachy keen and you?" She passed me, and I caught a whiff of a soft fresh scent, not a perfume, more likely her shampoo.

"Oh, I'm doing well, but I think I need another cup of coffee." I followed behind her, taking in the wide shoulder width of her black sport coat.

"We can always use more coffee," she said as she approached her desk.

I logged on to my computer. "So what's on for today?" I asked as I moved over to where the coffeepot was already gurgling. I scanned the room. By the looks of things, no one else was in. I glanced at my watch and saw it was only seven-forty.

"I'm just waiting to see if there were any burglaries last night. I have to head over to the courthouse today and get that court order signed for the phone records and take care of some evidence."

I rested my elbow on the top of a file cabinet next to the coffee pot, watching her as she spoke. She never looked up but kept her attention on her desk. "What would you like me to do?" I asked and waited for her look at me. She didn't.

"Um…depending on what happens…I might put you with Gordon or Jose today since I will be running around."

She apparently didn't want me with her. I wondered why. After I poured my coffee and fixed it the way I liked, I found her watching me. I raised an eyebrow, and she turned back to her desk without a word.

"We will be having a meeting around eight-thirty when everyone gets in," she stated as she sat down.

"Is that something that normally happens?" I moved towards her desk and stopped at the edge.

She shuffled some papers around on the smooth surface, again not looking up at me. "Yeah, normally we have a short meeting every couple of days to go over what's been happening and what needs to be done."

I took a sip of my steaming coffee. "Mack?"

"Yes?" she answered, her focus still downward. I waited until she lifted her head, her eyes scanning over my face as she met my questioning gaze. "Yes?" she said again.

I cocked my head to the side, "Are you alright?"

Her eyebrows rose, "Yeah, why?" She looked away as soon as she finished speaking.

I watched her for another ten seconds as she busied herself shuffling papers again. "No reason."

At my desk, I stared at her back for a moment. Why wouldn't she look at me today?

Gordon and Jose came through the door right when I was about to ask her again. Now that they were here, I didn't think it was appropriate.One of the things in which I had lots of training was body language. I spent a lot of time watching the way people held themselves and picked up a lot of how they felt and what they were thinking just by the way their bodies moved. Obviously, something was bothering Mack, and peachy keen was not how she was really feeling.

The rest of the crew meandered into the unit, and before we knew it, the phones were ringing, and the day had jumped into full swing. Around eight-thirty, we all gathered around the conference table, notepads in hand to jot down things we needed to remember.

Instead of sitting beside Mack, I chose to sit across from her, that way I could study her better.

"Where's Gary?" she asked as she flipped her paper to an empty page.

Gordon piped up, "He said to go ahead without him. He had an errand to run."

Mack snorted, "I wonder what her name is."

There was laughter around the table, but we quickly moved on to what was happening. All thoughts of Gary were dismissed.

Mack sat back in her chair, swiveling it back and forth from time to time as someone spoke. To me, when she shifted that way, it looked like she was thinking. Her eyes tightened just slightly, and her lips were always in a tight line, not pinched together, but resting closed. I noticed she was wearing some kind of lip gloss and realized that she barely had any makeup on. She looked fresh and real.

When the meeting was over, we all had a few things to take care of, including me. I went to fill my coffee cup up, and Jose joined me.

"Did you hear anything that was said, or did you just memorize her face?"

My head snapped in his direction. Humor covered his face. "I heard what was said," I felt my cheeks heating, and Jose smirked at me.

"All I can say is good luck, man. You're gonna need it." Jose put the coffeepot back onto the burner and returned to his desk. When I turned, Mack was gone, her portfolio missing off her desk. Damn, she hadn't wasted a second getting out of here today.

Within a few minutes, I was wrapped up in my own work. Funny how I had never worked for a department like this, but immediately fell right into the workload—that was, when I wasn't watching and listening to everyone around me.

As I observed everyone, I saw nothing out of the ordinary. All of them were focused on cases, talking on the phones, sharing information, and occasionally throwing out a joke or two, most times at my expense.

I had received an email from Rob, giving me a good amount of information about Mr. Timmons and his business. I went through it, but didn't see anything that stood out. Mack might see something different since she knew the case a lot better than I did. I printed it out and put it inside a folder to give to her when she returned.

I went out with Jose for a few hours to assist him with some cases, and we stopped for a quick lunch before heading back to the station. Jose and I, both with large overflowing hoagies, sat down at a small table in the deli. "So what do you think of the unit?" he asked me as I chewed.

"The dynamics of the group are pretty cool to watch. Everyone seems to have their niche, and you all orbit around each other pretty easily. It's nice to see it work so well. I'm glad I can be a part of it. Hopefully, I will be a help and not a hindrance to you all." I shoved another bite in my mouth.

Jose watched me chew for a minute while he thought. He was analyzing me, and I realized I would have to be careful around him. "Why did you pick here? Aren't you from the west coast?"

I shrugged, "I grew up here, missed my roots."

Jose was quiet for a few minutes as he ate, "I think you'll do fine here, but you need to be careful with Mack."

I set my sandwich down and picked up my drink, "Why do you say that?"

He laughed and rolled his eyes. "Amigo, don't fool yourself. I see the way you look at her, and how she sneaks peeks back at you. You guys are like a pressure cooker, and the steam is building." He sipped from his straw for a moment and popped a chip in his mouth. "When the time comes, enjoy yourself, but don't mess with Mack's head. Keep it real."

I stared at him over the top of our lunches. Did he really just refer to Mack and me having sex?

"What?" He laughed, "You think we can't see the way you two look at each other? Talk about orbit."

I swallowed the flattened soda that was still in my mouth. "We don't even know each other, Jose."

"What does that matter? Chemistry is chemistry. You two seem to have an abundance of it. All of us can see that." He popped another chip in his mouth.

The best way to handle this was to let it slide, "Whatever, man." I went back to finish my sandwich.

"Besides, it might loosen her up some."

I stopped in mid-chew and gaped at him. He shrugged.

We returned to the office after that, and nothing else was said. The afternoon flew by as I did the reports Jose and I had taken earlier that day and learned more about the way things worked.

Gary showed up sometime while we were gone and appeared to

be in a pissy mood. He stayed in his office for the most part, and once in a while, barked out something to Gordon who sat just outside his office door. Bria entered once, and the door closed for a while. When she came out, Gary seemed to be in a better mood. I felt him watching me from his door, and I acknowledged him with a nod. He turned back to his office.

Four o'clock rolled around, and Mack still hadn't returned to the unit. Gordon called out his goodbyes, and Chad left right after him. Bria had left with Gary, and only Jose and I remained in the large room. I wrote a note on a yellow post-it and put it on the background file for Mack.

"How late you staying, Jose?" I asked as I plopped the file on Mack's desk.

"I have to finish up this project I'm working on, and then I will be out of here."

I said goodnight to him and went back to my apartment.

I was disappointed that Mack hadn't come back, but after what Jose had said, I decided it was for the better.

I had just showered and pulled up my jeans when my cell rang. I looked at the caller ID and saw it was Rob.

"Hey buddy, what's happening?" I asked as I answered it.

"How are things going? Was that information I sent any help to you?" I heard music over the line and figured he was in his car.

"Thanks for that, not sure. Mack was out of the office all day. I'll let you know that tomorrow." I buttoned the top of my jeans and was pulling a t-shirt out of my drawer when someone rapped on my apartment door. I tossed the t-shirt over my shoulder as I approached the door.

"How are things going? Find anything out yet?" he asked as I turned the knob and pulled the door open. Mack stood with her back to the door and spun to face me.

Her eyes opened wide, and her lips parted as she let her gaze slide over my bare chest. I felt the heat of her stare as if she were touching me, and I froze. How the hell did she know where I lived?

"Mack," I said as she continued to explore my chest, and I felt myself physically responding to the approval I saw in her eyes.

She flicked her eyes up to mine and straightened her shoulders. "Where the hell did you get this?" she held the folder up in her left hand.

"Rob, I gotta call you back." I hit the end button on my phone and stepped out of the way as Mack all but pushed past me.

Chapter 7 – Mack

I woke up wishing I felt more refreshed. It had been a while since I had tossed and turned because I couldn't get someone off my mind. I kept reminding myself that Drew was way too young, but my body didn't seem to care. Maybe I should just sleep with him, get it out of my system, and move on.

While the thought was nice, okay, extremely nice, that wasn't my style. I never had been one for one-night stands. Don't get me wrong, I wasn't a prude, and I'd had my share of wham-bam-thank-you-man myself, but it wasn't my normal style; however, my normal style these days seemed to be non-existent.

I'd heard people talk about the instant magnetism that they felt for a person, but I'd never been one to experience it, until now.

I stood in the communications center chatting with one of the dispatchers while I sipped my coffee, when the sound of strong, solid, confident steps reached my ears. I leaned back from where I stood to get a better angle down the hall.

Holy hell, Greek gods really did exist. I had never believed it before, but today, I saw one in the living, breathing flesh. Even the harsh flickering yellow fluorescent lights that lit the industrial-looking hallway did nothing to distract from this masterpiece. His black dress shoes reflected the light as they rapped out a cadence on the plain white floor covering. His black dress pants held the perfect crease as they slithered up his legs. With each step forward, the muscles bunched as they pushed against the polished cotton. A simple silver buckle on his dress belt winked at me, taunting me.

I locked my jaw to contain my drool. His tan dress shirt with thin black stripes, top button undone, and sleeves rolled up set off his physique to perfection, as if tailored for him.

His chin was down as he stared at the floor. Could he feel my gaze stripping him naked? Was that why he slowly lifted his chin? Immediate recognition lit his face, and something flickered in his bright blue eyes. The grin that spread over his full lips dipped ever-so-slightly on the right. Holy hell was right! This man could make an angel fall from grace with just a smile.

"There she is," his words bounced off the plain beige walls.

A shiver threatened my spine; I pulled my shoulders back and stopped it. I moved to approach him, forcing myself to act normal and not like a bitch in heat. How many heads had this man turned without his noticing?

"Good morning, kid," I joked and forced my heartbeat back to normal.

"How are you this morning, Mack?" His smile grew wider as I stopped a foot in front of him. He leaned forward slightly and tipped his head to the right, something I noticed he did when he was comfortable. His shoulders were more relaxed than the straight-backed position he used when around unfamiliar people.

I had also noticed that he normally wore a soft smile on his lips that would quickly widen, and he always looked people in the eye when he spoke.

How rare for a man to not only listen when you spoke, but actually focus on you and appear to contemplate the words you were saying. Although in our job, men were better than most at making that eye-to-eye contact. They were always looking for clues that people were giving out, watching the body language to get the full meaning of their words.

"I'm fine, thank you." Body language, I shook my head as I

walked past him to enter the unit and set about trying to clear my mind from the ogling I had just done. What I wouldn't do to let my body talk to his. Our light banter continued as he waited for his coffee, it was only when he was pouring his cup that I turned back to face him.

He looked so young, and maybe that's why I chided myself when I found my gaze running down his backside and noticing how snugly his slacks fit over it.

It's been said that women in their forties are in the prime of their lives. They know what they want and generally they go after it. Yeah, not this time, I thought to myself sadly.

When he turned around and caught me watching him, I resolved then and there to ignore him the best I could. I focused on my work, and the minute I could, I fled the unit. A day in the field would do me good.

The court order took forever. The judge was in the middle of some arraignments, and I had to wait for him to finish. I spent the time fighting the memory of Drew in the hallway. Every tap of a man's shoe down the long hallway brought back the vision from this morning.

By the time I had the court order in hand, I was tempted to run back to the station and throw him onto a desk. Instead, I went to visit Rick. We spent a few hours going over the case and had a late lunch together. When we finished, I went to visit a few other detectives that were working on similar cases.

It was almost four-thirty when I returned to the unit, and I wasn't sure if I was glad or disappointed that he was gone.

Jose was still in the office, and I filled him in on some of the info I had learned. He told me about how Drew had handled the two reports, and he appeared to watch me closely as he spoke about him.

"He's a good guy. I think he is going to fit in here." He leaned back in his seat.

I shifted away from him, not sure I wanted to hear about how good of a guy he was. "Glad to hear it," I responded as I sat down at my desk and shuffled some things around. I saw a file folder on my keyboard and picked it up, neat handwriting on a yellow sticky note telling me what was in the file and a phone number under it. Well, looks like now I had his phone number, not that I'd use it.

I flipped open the file and started reading the material inside. The more I read, the more my teeth began to grind. Where the hell did he get this?

"Jose, do me a favor and pull up Bradley's personnel file. Give me his address. I need to go see him."

"Wow, I thought it would take you longer to give in," he smirked when I turned to him.

"I have no idea what you're talking about." At least I pretended not to know what he was talking about. Anger made it even easier to pretend.

"Yeah, sure," he smugly punched a few keys on his keyboard. He called out the address, and I wrote it down on the same sticky note Drew had used.

File in hand, I tossed out a terse goodbye and headed to the door. As I drove, I wondered why I needed to do this in person. I could have easily called him and asked him, but I wanted to see his body language when he explained.

Body language, damn. I shook my head as the thought returned me to this morning and how he had sauntered down the hallway. That image was forever burned into my memory.

I found his apartment complex without any problem and took a deep breath before I climbed out of my car. With the file in hand, I entered the building and climbed the steps to the second floor. The building was newer, and the smell of dinner cooking from several different apartments assaulted me as I looked for 2-B.

At the door, I hesitated for a moment. I could wait until tomorrow to do this, I thought to myself. Damn girl, you drove all the way over here, knock on the dang door already. I rapped three times and turned my back to control my racing heart. Why was it even racing?

The door opened, and I twisted around for an eyeful. Heat flared through every part of my body as my eyes traveled down the muscular chest peppered with just the right amount of light brown hair. My earlier imaginings did not even begin to compare to the real thing. His pecs were solid and defined, and his abs, oh man, the temptation to taste each inch made me literally salivate.

When he called out my name, I snapped out of the fantasy I was having, angry with myself for allowing the thoughts to race rampant through my mind.

"Where the hell did you get this?" I glared at him and stepped into his apartment uninvited. I realized then that he was on the phone and heard him say a quick goodbye.

"What are you doing here?" he asked as he closed the door behind me.

"Where did you get this?" I turned back around, instantly my eyes were drawn back to his chest. "Put your damned shirt on."

His eyebrows shot up, and he gave me one of his lopsided grins. "You came to my house. If I don't want to put my shirt on, I don't have to. We aren't at work, so I don't think I need to take orders from you right now." He crossed his arms over his chest, expanding the definition of his biceps, and I felt the need to sink to the floor in a puddle.

I tore my eyes from him and stared at the floor. With a hard swallow, I faced him again, forcing myself to only look into his eyes, "Drew, could you please put your shirt on. I need to talk to you, and it's a little hard to talk to someone who is half dressed,"—and looks like you, I added to myself.

He tilted his head, studied me for a moment, then pulled the shirt off his shoulder and slipped it over his head. I watched every muscle movement on his chest as he did. When the soft cotton covered his skin, my body felt like it was being punished, and I fought the urge to pull the shirt back off. I cleared my throat and turned away from him to put distance between us. I knew in that moment that coming to his place had been a mistake.

I took a few seconds to glance around the room. There was nothing personal in this room. The pictures on the walls were generic, the television stand was devoid of any DVDs, although there was a player. I turned to survey the dining room, generic furniture again. This place screamed rental.

"I wanted to look around before I bought a place, so my stuff is in storage. I rented this apartment until I can get situated," he answered my unasked question, and I absently nodded at him.

"How'd you get my address?" he asked when I didn't say anything.

"Jose looked it up in your personnel file." A signature grin crossed his lips, and I wondered what that was about. I could look at that grin all night, but I was here for a purpose.

"Where did you get this information, Drew?"

He shrugged and walked around me to the small kitchen, opening up the fridge.

"You want a bottle of water? I don't have much else right now, sorry."

"No, thank you. Answer the question," I said and he arched an eyebrow. "Please," I added, trying not to sound sarcastic.

He closed the fridge, "I have a friend."

"You have a friend in the FBI, huh?"

His eyes snapped to mine, and he studied me.

"I've been around for a long time, Drew, and I know an FBI background when I see it." I tossed the file down on the kitchen counter.

He wet his lips as he peered around the kitchen. What was he hiding?

"Yes, I have a friend at the FBI. We went to high school together. He's one of the reasons I came back this way." He shrugged again, "It seemed important to you to get a full background on this guy, so I asked Rob for a favor."

It was important to me to have this information, and he had found things that I wouldn't have been able to pull up without a whole lot of digging. "Well, thank you and thank Rob for me, too."

He was surprised at my response. "You're welcome." He leaned against the counter, easing his arms apart. He had braced for an attack, and I felt sorry that I had made him feel that way.

"I guess," I took a deep breath and released it, "I owe you an apology." I looked down at the file, unable to face him.

"For what?" he asked quietly.

"I haven't made it all that easy for you. I'm tense with everything that is going on with this case, and—" I glanced up at him; he was regarding me carefully. Our eyes locked, and the air in the room crackled.

He pushed off the counter and took a few steps closer to me, almost prowling like a panther towards its prey. "And?"

My throat felt tight and my heart amped up, beating fast, I forced myself to swallow, "And obviously there seems to be something going on."

"What do you mean something going on?"

"You know what I mean," I said breathlessly as we both surveyed each other. My focus dropped to his wide, smooth firm lips that I craved.

"Mack," he said softly and bent towards me. Oh, how I wanted to feel his lips. Who the hell cared that I was twelve years older than he was? At that moment, I didn't, and he didn't seem to care either.

"What?" I said when I realized he had stopped moving closer.

"I'm going to kiss you," he said huskily, and his breath fanned out over my face. I waited a moment, but he didn't descend. What the hell was wrong with him? He said he was going to do it. What was he waiting for?

"Today?" I whispered.

He chuckled softly, the sound deep in his throat—and in the base of my spine.

His lips brushed mine gently once, and then a second time, and a vibration raced around my belly. No, wait, that wasn't him. That was my cellphone vibrating. I pulled back from him abruptly, the moment now ruined by electronic reality.

He straightened, disappointment flashed over his face, but he wiped it clear as I pulled my phone from my holder. I broke the heavy gaze he had me locked in and looked at the caller ID. It was the dispatch center.

"Mack," I answered.

"Sorry to bother you, Sarge, but we had a homicide come in." Nothing like a little murder to erase a little lust.

"Where?" I answered in a clipped tone.

"Elmhurst, looks like it might have been a burglary gone bad."

I sighed. That's why they notified me, the burglary, damn!

"Okay, I'm assuming Gordon was called out along with crime scene techs, right?" I glanced at Drew; he was back against the counter again, arms crossed, his left eyebrow quirked in question— what a freaking sexy eyebrow.

I mouthed the word homicide, and he walked out of the room down a short hallway. I took a moment to watch the motion of the tight denim.

I refocused on the phone call and asked a few more questions, obtained the correct address, and hung up just as Drew walked into the room again, dressed in tan slacks and a black button-down shirt.

I didn't have to ask him what he was doing. I knew. He was waiting for me at the door, keys in hand, and I snatched up the file I had brought with me and walked out of his apartment with him following right behind.

"Your car or mine?" he asked as we stepped into the asphalt of the parking lot.

"I'll drive," I said as I moved quickly to my Mustang.

"I was hoping you'd say that," he beamed over the roof of the car. The memory of the brief touch of his lips flashed through my mind—not a good time to think of that. We had work to do.

Drew and I climbed into the car, and he got a chance to see what the car could do as I wove in and out of traffic and headed towards the address I had been given.

"Do you normally do homicides?" Drew asked as we sped down a back road, driving faster than I should have been going.

I shook my head, "No, Gordon usually heads them up, but this one appears to have something to do with a burglary. Given the location of it, I'd say they were caught in the act of stealing someone's fancy car."

"Another high-end neighborhood?"

I saw him watching me from the corner of my eye. "Exactly." I glanced at him, "You're enjoying this aren't you?" I slowed down enough to make a sharp curve and started accelerating as soon as I hit the midpoint of the turn. The engine roared, and I felt the tires grip.

"I love this! This car handles so well. Of course, it wouldn't be half as much fun if someone else were driving."

"Yeah, why is that?" Where was he going with that comment?

He laughed. "I told you yesterday, you are an extension of this car: It's you, you're it. You handle this like a pro, and I didn't expect anything less."

I laughed along with him, "I don't think I have ever been told that I'm like a car, and most women wouldn't find that a compliment, you know."

His voice dropped slightly, "But you're not like most women."

I grinned, "No, you are absolutely right. I'm not."

Chapter 8 – Drew

The last thing I expected to see when I opened the door was Mack, especially the mixture of emotions that raced over her face when she twirled around.

Oh, there was no mistaking the fleeting anger that flashed in her bright emerald eyes before it smoldered into desire that set a flame to my blood. She might be good at hiding her feelings, but she was off balance, and in those brief seconds, I saw it clear as daylight.

"Where the hell did you get this?" She passed me and entered the living area, somehow avoiding contact with me.

"Let me call you back, Rob." I hung up the phone and twisted to face her, "What are you doing here?"

I thought it was going to be a long night when she repeated her question again, and her eyes turned a darker shade of green as she caressed my chest with a heated gaze. I could get used to that look on her face, I thought.

"Put your damned shirt on." Her voice was flustered as the words flew out, a contradiction if I ever heard one because as she said it, her eyes held vivid desire.

I liked having her off kilter, so I told her no. I saw the teeny shake of her head of surprise. She blinked her eyes as she looked at the floor, hesitated, and then asked me nicely, not looking me in the face as she did, but because she said please, I put on my shirt. My fantasy of her running her hands and mouth over my skin was doused with the cotton fabric.

I went to the fridge, biding my time, and was surprised when she asked one more time and actually added the magic word. Ding, ding, ding, now how could I refuse the spicy woman in front of me who was almost begging me for an answer and actually used the proper terminology to get it?

"I have a friend." I scrutinized her face when she made the crack about the FBI. I didn't say my friend was in the FBI. How did she know that?

She tossed the file down on the counter, and I thought for a few seconds. I ended up telling her some of the truth. I did know Rob, we did grow up together, and he was one of the reasons I was here. He did recruit me for the assignment after all.

To say I was surprised at her thank you, not only to me but to Rob, would be an understatement. I was expecting her to rant and rave about doing her own investigation and not getting other people involved. I relaxed against the counter while I analyzed her.

"I guess I owe you an apology," she practically whispered into the room.

Her passion and anger came out when she was frustrated. I loved to see her eyes blaze with indignation and surprise. She hesitated as she began to get to the crux of the matter. I felt the blaze of desire in the air, like heavy smoke, it made breathing difficult. I approached her, hoping to relieve the burning pressure in my chest.

"And?" I needed her to admit she felt something.

Her eyes caressed my face and landed on my lips, the expression almost as intense as a touch. "Mack," I hovered close. I wanted her to come to me.

"What?" she seemed confused and flustered. I felt the need to torture her just a tiny bit.

"I'm going to kiss you," I whispered.

Emotions flowed over her features, desire, confidence, and strength, but there was a slight hesitation when she whispered,

"Today?"

It brought out a soft rumble of laughter. I brought my lips to hers. I was about to deepen the kiss when she stepped out of reach and pulled out her phone.

Her pulse ticked away in her neck, and I fought the urge to yank her cellphone away and continue where we left off. She mouthed the word homicide, and like a switch, my mind changed tracks. I went to change clothes. I walked out to join her just as she hung up.

While I was disappointed we had been interrupted, knowing I was going to ride in her car was almost as good. I beamed as we climbed in and kept that grin on my face as she took off down the winding roads.

Yeah, this car was like her: smooth and sleek, and it brought back the memory of that single kiss. I imagined what might have happened if her phone had not rung. I would have tightened my hold on her, run my hands along her sleek lines, felt her chassis, and maybe gotten lucky enough to have a peek at what was under the hood. I flicked a glance over at her. She was intent on the roadway ahead. Her left hand gripped the top of the steering wheel while her right hand gripped the stick shift firmly. My groin tightened at the parallel.

I cleared my throat and shifted in my seat. "So what did you learn about the homicide?"

She glanced at me. "Not much. I prefer not to know the details of a crime before I get there. I like to see a scene and get a feel for it myself before I find out what happened. It allows me a different perspective than the cops that arrived on scene."

"What do you mean?" I watched as she down-shifted into a turn and then shifted again coming out of it.

"When the responding officers get there, they have minimal information. Usually, they only know what they were told while they were en route to the scene, what the caller is telling them. I don't know want to know that stuff until I see for myself what is there, no preconceived notions of what I'm walking into. I want to come up with my own conclusions as to what might have happened when I see the evidence."

"That makes sense." I considered that a good tactic.

"I do know that it appears that shots were fired, someone was killed, and a car was stolen, a BMW."

"You think it's related to your case?" I watched out the window as she skillfully maneuvered through another turn. God, I wanted this car. When I returned back home, I needed to get one of these.

She was quiet for a moment. "It could be, but again, I won't know the details until we arrive."

The music that was playing on her stereo muted when her phone rang. The screen above her stereo changed to display *Incoming call, Gary*. She answered by pushing a button on her steering wheel, "Go ahead."

"Where are you?" His tense voice filled the car as it came through the stereo speakers.

"I'm on my way, Gary," she ground out.

"Where the hell are you coming from?" he all but yelled, her right hand came up and pushed a volume button on her steering wheel.

"I'm coming from Valley View. I'll be there in about fifteen minutes."

"What the hell are you doing in Valley View?" he questioned her. Her jaw shifted back and forth, her teeth grinding.

"What I'm doing on my time off is none of your damned business, Gary. I'll be there in a few minutes." She hit a button with her thumb and the call disconnected, music came back through the speakers. "Prick," she muttered to herself.

"You don't like him very much, do you?" Maybe now while she was focused on something else was a good time to try and get her to talk a little bit.

"No."

Or maybe not. Okay, let's try this again. "How long were you two married?"

"Long enough." Her left hand curled tightly around the steering wheel. Her right hand flexed on the gear shift and tightened again.

"What's long enough, a few years?" I knew by the way her entire body tensed further that she definitely didn't want to talk about this. She stayed quiet for a few minutes, and just when I figured she wouldn't answer the question, she spoke softly.

"Gary and I were only married for a few months. The divorce took longer than the marriage lasted."

"Yeah, well I told you before, it's his loss."

She rolled her eyes.

"I know it's none of my business, but what happened?" Her eyes squinted for a brief moment.

She turned to nail me with a direct look. "You're right, it is none of your business." She focused back on the road. She chewed her bottom lip for a moment before the tension in her body shifted on a sigh. "Gary and I started dating when I first came on the job. He was a sergeant back then, and I guess I was enthralled with his attention. We got married, and not six months after, I found him pinning some chick up against his desk on a night shift."

My jaw dropped, "Are you serious?"

"As a heart attack." She cast a quick look at me, "Close your mouth; you're gonna drool on my leather."

"Why didn't he get fired?" I shifted in my seat so I could see her better.

"Because…I never filed a report." She glanced out the driver's window instead of looking my way.

"Why the hell not?" I retorted.

She shrugged. "I didn't want to cause waves. I was a young officer. I wasn't sure anyone would believe me."

"What did you do when you found them?"

Her maniacal laughter shocked me. "I walked right up to him, and while he was trying to get his pants back on, I punched him right in the face. I didn't really care that he was screwing some cheap piece of ass, but I was furious that he was having unprotected sex." She focused on making a turn, "God only knows how many women he slept with without protection." Her voice lowered, "After I found him, I had some serious testing done, every six months for four years

68

I went in and was tested for different STDs."

"Did you ever get any?" I asked quietly.

"Nope, and he's lucky I didn't." She slowed down and turned into a neighborhood. Flashing lights from patrol cars bounced off the darkened sky.

She pulled up behind another car and pulled the keys from her ignition while she took a deep breath. "Look, I'm not sure why I just told you all that. I shouldn't have. You work for the guy, and what happened between us was personal and has nothing to do with the job."

I rested my hand on her forearm, "Mack, it's alright. I won't say a word. You don't have to worry about that. I'm glad you told me."

She stared at my hand and then up into my face. Concern and pain rolled through her eyes.

She was about to speak when someone rapped on the driver's window, and she spun around. She muttered something before she grabbed the door handle and climbed out of the car.

"What the hell took you so long?" Gary practically yelled at her as she stepped out. I climbed out the passenger side and met his angry gaze over the roof of the car. Surprise, confusion, and then anger crossed his features as he met my stare.

Mack slammed the car door and tried to walk around Gary. He grabbed her arm and yanked her back.

"Get your damned hands off me, Gary." Her voice was low and smooth.

"What the hell are you doing with him?" He used his other hand to motion towards me. My temper was rising, and I stared at the hand still wrapped around her bicep.

Her eyes flicked to mine before she turned her attention back to him. "I told you before, what I do on my off time is none of your business."

"It is my business when it takes you over thirty minutes to get to a call." He stepped closer to her, "You sleeping with that kid?"

Her voice turned deadly when she finally spoke, "Let go of my arm."

"Answer my question," he demanded.

"How I spend my off time and whom I sleep with are none of your business. Now let go of my arm." She leaned closer to him as she spoke, "What's wrong, Gary, you jealous?"

She jerked her arm out of his hand and spun around to walk away. Gary never responded to her, but his glare at me said it all: He was.

I followed her toward the yellow crime scene tape. Gordon stood between the working area of what was roped off and the scene itself. About ten feet behind him, a complete second ring of yellow police tape encompassed the scene itself. Mack stopped outside the first line of tape.

"So what do you have, Gordon?" Her voice still held the tension from her conversation with Gary. Gordon raised an eyebrow as he looked between the two of us.

"What took you so long?" Gordon asked as he wrote something on his notepad and handed it to her. She scribbled something and handed it to me. I looked down to see it was a crime scene log. I signed next to my name to show I was now at the scene.

"I was out in Valley View." She scanned the scene. In the middle of the yard a white sheet lay over what I knew was a body.

I handed the notepad back to Gordon.

"What's in Valley View?" Gordon asked her as he took it back.

Before she could answer, I did, "Mack came out to my place to go over some information I left her."

Gordon looked between us and shrugged. "Gary's pissed," he said as he looked over my shoulder in Gary's direction.

"Who cares?" She stared at the body for a moment. "What do we know?"

"The victim just got home from work. Instead of pulling his car into the garage, he left it in the driveway. The witness said he heard gunshots. He was mowing his yard, by the time he turned the mower off, he didn't hear anything, but he saw someone running behind the houses and the victim lying on the front yard. He said the guy running was limping. The witness is a doctor so he ran over to help

70

the victim. He was dead before he reached him. My thought is the victim came home, interrupted the burglary. When he confronted the subject, shots were exchanged. There is a Ruger 9mm beside the victim. The guy's BMW has a few bullet holes in it." He pointed to where the BMW sat in the driveway. Glass sparkled along the driveway where a window had been broken. "I'm not sure if the guy was trying to steal the car or not, but since the witness saw him run away from it, I'd have to assume he was."

Mack was checking out the car, "I assume the subject got away. Do we have a description?"

"A very sketchy one. The neighbor was four doors down." He pointed down the road. "He only saw a guy in dark pants and a dark shirt, white male with brown hair."

"How did the guy get away?" I asked while Mack was scanning the street, looking at the upper middle class houses.

"The witness said he took off behind the house. He was too far away to see which way he went from there. We already sent K-9s out to track, but it ended a couple blocks away. Guy must have had a car sitting there waiting for him. There is one bit of evidence from over that way, a footprint in blood on the sidewalk. I sent techs over to photograph and swab it for DNA."

"Okay, good, so what do you want me to do?" Mack turned back to Gordon, and he looked away from her. "What?"

He looked over my shoulder again, "Gary said since you were late, you can do the neighbor interviews."

She stared at him, "You're kidding, right?"

He shook his head. "Sorry, Mack."

Mack turned around and scoured the area for Gary. When she found him in the crowd, her eyes threw daggers at his back. "Fine, I'm too tired to deal with the scene anyway." She turned away from Gordon, "Let's go, kid."

Chapter 9 – Mack

Oh, the words I was calling Gary in my mind were far worse than prick. That was for sure. What the hell was up with him? I rolled my shoulders and grabbed the notebook out of the trunk of my car.

I hadn't been assigned to neighborhood canvas since I'd been a rookie in this department. Normally, I oversaw the crime scene unit. Fine, this was fine. I could do this. I slammed the trunk of my car. After my sleepless night, I was too freaking tired to be out here working a scene anyway. Now that I was assigned to do this, and it was getting late, I would visit with whomever I could find and get out of here early. Tomorrow, I'd come back for longer interviews. I flipped my wrist and looked at the digital display of my watch, almost eight o'clock. I could be out of here by ten, good.

"Ever do any canvassing?" I questioned Drew as he walked beside me.

"Yeah, sure. Hasn't every cop done that?" He wore that easy smile, the one where his eyebrow raised over his eye. Damn, that look was so sexy. I started up a driveway.

"I'm not sure how you do it, but this is the way we do, one person asks the questions, the other takes the notes. The one writing usually only asks questions near the end to tie up any loose ends that might have been missed."

"Sounds about right. Am I asking or writing?" We stepped on the porch, the door opened before I knocked. I was about to hand him my clipboard when the man stepped out and held his hand out to Drew. The man related to him first, so he was contact on this one. I would have an opportunity to see how he did.

I pulled a pen out of my pocket and started writing as the two of them talked. This guy hadn't gotten home until after the event took place, so his knowledge was limited. His wife and kids weren't home either. We wrapped the interview up in a few minutes and moved on to the next house.

Most of the people knew nothing and spent more time asking about what had happened or putting in their own two cents. My patience was wearing thin, and I fought back a yawn as a woman started yammering on about how safe the neighborhood used to be. I had to give it to Drew, he was good at interviewing. He also had a lot more patience tonight than I did.

As we arrived at the house where the witness lived, I found myself feeling woozy. It was close to ten now, and I hadn't had anything to eat since the lunch I'd had with Rick. No sleep the night before and lack of carbs were catching up to me. I tripped on the top step of the porch. Drew grabbed my arm before I landed on my face. My cheeks burned, and my head started to buzz. I had used up all my sugar, my hypoglycemia was about to kick in, and I felt little beads of sweat start to pop out on my skin.

"You alright, Mack?"

I gave a brief jerky nod, afraid to move my head too fast, since my vision was starting to waver. I just needed to get through this last interview, and I could grab something to eat.

"Are you sure? You don't look so well."

"Yeah, I'm fine. Let's get this over with." Drew scrutinized me a moment longer before he knocked on the door. A woman answered, and as luck might have it, she said her husband had been called in for an emergency at the hospital. We told her we would catch up with him in the morning and turned to leave.

A wave of nausea crashed over me, and the beads of sweat

became gentle streams down my neck. Small black dots popped into my vision like popcorn kernels over heat. I needed to get back to my car and find a snack bar, immediately.

I must have swayed because Drew put his hand on my back. "Mack, what's wrong?"

I tried to concentrate on the feel of his hand, but the world was fading. Damn, I had waited too long. The last thing I heard was Drew calling my name as my legs crumpled under my frame.

My eyelids fluttered, and I felt a vice around my bicep squeezing. Voices mumbled around me, and I blinked open my eyes. My stomach rolled. I tried to sit up, but a firm hand on my shoulder held me down.

"Stay still, Mack," Drew's voice was filled with concern.

"What happened?" I croaked. The inside of my mouth felt like I had been sucking on sand. I surveyed his facial features to find his usual relaxed manner gone, his eyebrows low and pulled together, the small creases on his forehead more pronounced than usual.

"You passed out." Drew spoke before another voice caused me to turn my head.

"When is the last time you ate, Mack?" Gary stood by the door to the ambulance, concern and anger on his face.

"Are you diabetic?" the paramedic pulled the blood pressure cuff off my right arm.

I hated all these stupid questions. "No, hypo," I responded and tried to wet my lips with my dry tongue. "I need some water."

"Not yet. When is the last time you ate?" He lifted my hand and pricked my finger. I flinched as he squeezed the tip to bring some blood to the surface for a test.

"I think it was around eleven-thirty." I avoided Drew's worried stare.

"You know better than to do that, Mack," Gary spoke again from the door, and I glared at him. The man was on my shit list, and the last thing he needed to do was pretend he cared.

"How often does this happen?" The paramedic asked as he slipped a little strip with my blood on it into a small compact machine that would read the sugar level.

"Not very often, I didn't sleep well last night, and I didn't get a chance to eat earlier."

The machine beeped, and he looked at the numbers. "Sixty-eight, do you want me to give you sugar or do you think you can stomach something?"

I tried to sit up again. Drew's hand wrapped around my forearm and pulled me up. "Oh, hell no, no sugar push. I'll eat, I swear." I waved him away. I'd had one of those before, and they left me with a pounding headache and the shakes.

"Fine, you're lucky. I have a candy bar in my bag. Eat this, and then you need to make sure you get some real food in you very soon."

"Yeah, yeah, I know the drill." I tried to swing my feet over the side of the gurney and ran into Drew's legs. He shifted so I could put my feet on the floor of the ambulance. He still held my arm.

The wrapper of the chocolate bar crinkled as the paramedic ripped it open and handed it to me. I took a nibble and allowed the chocolate to melt over my tongue before I took a bigger bite.

"You shouldn't be driving. Is there someone who can drive you home?" the paramedic questioned as I savored the sweet milk chocolate melting on my tongue.

Drew piped in before I could find my voice, "I came with her. I'll drive her home and make sure she gets something to eat on the way."

"Bradley, take her car home for the night. I'll drive her back to her house," Gary inserted while Drew's jaw tensed.

"Drew will take me home." I glared at my ex-husband before I took another bite of the chocolate and dismissed him. He stalked off. Drew slid his hand down my arm in an intimate way. I had forgotten he still held it.

I signed off on the medical release with a signature fit for a doctor and climbed out of the ambulance behind Drew. He turned to help me.

"I'm not an invalid." I jumped down from the back avoiding his outstretched hand.

"Where are your car keys?"

I yawned, pulled them out of the pocket of my jacket, and tossed them to him as we approached my car.

Gordon met us beside the mustang, and I told him what we had learned, which was basically nothing. Drew beamed at me as he pulled open the passenger door.

"What?"

"I get to drive your car," he sing-songed.

I rolled my eyes. "Don't you dare wrap it around a tree. One ambulance in a night is enough." I slid down into the leather seat; my head falling back against the headrest as I took another bite of chocolate. I felt better, but far from recovered.

Drew climbed in and adjusted the seat and mirrors, and I watched him from the corner of my eye as he made himself comfortable in the driver's seat.

"How did I get into the ambulance?" The last time I had passed out, I had hit the dirt and awakened with a nice knot on my head. Other than feeling lightheaded, I didn't hurt.

Drew grinned as he started the car, the horsepower made the inside vibrate roughly. "I caught you when you went down and carried you to the bus." He put the car in gear and backed into a driveway.

"You carried me?" The skin of my face was burning but not from lack of sugar. This was from royal embarrassment.

He gawked at me for a moment before putting the car in gear and moving forward. "What? I don't look strong enough?"

"That's not what I meant." I turned to stare out the passenger window while he moved slowly through the crowd of cars. "Thank you."

"You're welcome." He sounded proud of himself. "So how often does that happen?"

I knew what he was asking but wanted to avoid the question. "What, letting someone drive my car? Never, you're the first one to drive this."

He grinned at me, "That's not what I was asking, but it's nice to know you trust me enough to drive it."

I snorted, "It's not like I had choice. I wasn't going to let Gary drive me home."

I thought he would laugh at that, but his features contorted into a serious expression. "Is he normally like that?"

"Like what?"

"Possessive. He didn't exactly seem thrilled that you were leaving with me." His forehead wrinkled in thought.

"Gary? He's never possessive. I'm not sure what his problem is. He seems more tense these days than he normally is. Maybe his list of young women has run out, and he's not getting any."

Again, I thought he would find humor in the comment, but he stayed serious. "He's not normally like this?" He peered over at me. A streetlight provided enough illumination for me to see his probing look.

"No," I said, unsure why he was so concerned about Gary's attitude. He quieted for a few moments.

"So how often do you have fainting spells?" he asked again when he turned his blinker on to pull into a twenty-four-hour diner.

"I'm fine. You don't need to stop," I said, although my stomach was still queasy and in need of food. I just wanted to get home and get some sleep. I stifled a yawn at the thought of my pillow.

"No, I said I'd get you to eat, and I'm going to do that. Answer the question." He pulled into a parking space, turned the car off, and looked at me pointedly.

I shrugged, "It's no big deal. I get busy and forget to eat."

"Mack, having low blood sugar isn't good, especially when you are as active and busy as you are." He studied my face for a moment, and I wondered what he was thinking. "Come on, let's go get some food. I'm starving, too."

We climbed out, and I found I wasn't lightheaded anymore. Drew put his hand on the small of my back.

"I'm fine," I feebly protested. "I promise I won't pass out again." I tried to step out of his reach, but his hand moved to my waist and curved around my hip. Now who was being possessive?

"Better to be safe than sorry," he whispered into my ear. The soft brush of his breath over my lobe brought the lightheadedness back for a different reason. I wanted to lean into him, but I refrained and moved to a table off in the corner.

Drew sat across from me and picked up the menu. I studied him for a moment over the top of mine. His left eyebrow lifted just before he looked up.

"Yes?"

"Nothing." I focused on the page in front of me.

I ordered a chicken sandwich, and he ordered an omelet. When the waitress walked away, I sat back in my seat and studied him again while I absently played with the wrapper from my straw. He was scanning the room. His eyebrow came back up as he turned to me. "Yes?"

I shrugged and took great interest in the white straw paper wrapped around my finger.

"You know, you can't keep staring at me and not tell me why." He lifted his water glass and took a sip.

"Sometimes you look a lot older than you are." I met his surprised expression head on.

This time he shrugged, "I guess I'm just more mature than most people my age." He looked away uncomfortably, and I wondered what he was holding back. I wasn't a detective for nothing.

He faced me again, and our eyes locked. The memory of our earlier kiss wove through my mind, and I wished that I could have remembered being carried in his arms. The sound of his voice whispering in my ear when we had entered the diner brought an uninvited shiver down my back. The longer we stared at one another, the more my body began to heat. His eyes seemed to be on the same wavelength as my temperature, showing signs of desire in their beautiful depths.

What if our earlier kiss hadn't been interrupted? Would we have ended up rolling around on the kitchen floor? Would he have carried me off to his bedroom or lifted me to sit on the counter? My heart was pounding in my chest as I wondered if he was dwelling on those same questions.

Loud laughter from another table broke the invisible bubble that had surrounded us. We cleared our throats at the same time and shifted in our seats.

Drew's cell rang and became another welcome diversion to the building tension. We both looked down at the phone in front of him: a picture of two children with the words, *Alex & Andy*, written under it. He shot me a quick glance as he scooped up the phone. I tried not to raise my eyebrow at his behavior. I don't think I succeeded.

"I have to take this, Mack. Will you excuse me?"

I nodded as he climbed out of the booth and started moving towards the door. Just before he pushed the chrome handle open, I heard him answer the phone.

Images of him with a wife and kids trotted through my mind, and I ground my teeth. I didn't get a good look at the screen, so I had no idea if the kids looked like him or not, but an unwanted feeling erupted when I saw the deer-in-the-headlights look he shot at me.

Our food arrived as he came back to the table. "Sorry about that."

He avoided my questioning gaze by picking up his napkin and laying it on his lap. I snatched a fry off my plate and chomped down hard. His shoulders looked tense as he cut a piece of his omelet and fed himself. He peered at me as he placed another bite in his mouth.

"Are you married?" Blunt as ever, I was.

He choked on the food he was swallowing and took a sip of his water while he shook his head, "No." I watched him as he wiped his mouth with his napkin, cleared his throat, and then pushed his plate back an inch so he could lean his arms on the table. "I'm not married, never have been."

"Then whose kids?"

"My niece and nephew. They are my sister's kids. My sister is going through a hard time." He shrugged and picked up his fork again. "The kids keep me updated."

I picked up half of my sandwich. "How old are they? They look a little young to be spying on their mother for you."

"Alexandra and Andrew are about to turn ten," he put a forkful to his lips and looked at me hard, "and they aren't spying. They are letting me know how she feels."

The tone of his voice gave off the same dark feeling that his eyes did. Obviously, he didn't want to talk about it. What was wrong with his sister that he needed the children to keep him updated? I didn't think now was the time to broach the subject, so I took a bite out of my sandwich and glanced around the room.

As much as I wanted to question him more, I let the conversation go. Somehow we managed small talk while we ate. It was safer to talk about cars and past investigations than it was to explore the looks we were giving each other, or our pasts.

I did feel better once I ate, and would have felt great, if it weren't for the fact that I traded low blood sugar for an overfull belly that wanted to fall into a dreamless sleep.

When we got back in the car, Drew started it and turned to me. "Which way to your house?"

I shook my head, "No way, I'm fine now. Just drive back to your house, and I'll drive myself home."

"No, I said I'd take you home, Mack." His voice was firm, and it made me anxious. It was one thing to let someone drive my car while I was in it, and quite another to let him take it home without me. My only other choice was to invite him to stay over. As absolutely tempting as that was, it was not happening—ever…okay, maybe someday…okay, fine, I could dream, yeah, maybe.

With an attempt to appease his male ego, I laid my hand on his arm. The warm skin and light hair tickled my palm and had me itching to rub my hands all over his body. Damn.

I cleared my throat in an attempt to remove the huskiness. "Drew, I'm fine to drive now. I know you are enjoying the car, that's the only reason I didn't take back my keys. Let's go back to your place," he lifted an eyebrow with a smirk on his face, "so I can drop you off," I added, and his smirk faded.

He contemplated me for a brief moment, "Either you don't trust me with your car, or you don't trust me with you, which is it?"

He had figured out exactly what I was trying to avoid. "I don't know what you mean," I squeaked.

He laughed and leaned to the center of the car, his mouth now only a few inches from mine. I stole a glance. My body started to tingle in low places, like my toes. I think the temperature rose in the car in that brief moment.

"You know exactly what I mean." He peeked at my lips, and I struggled not to lick them in anticipation. "I can understand you not trusting me with your car. I can even understand you not trusting me with being at your place. God knows that if I had the chance, I would devour every inch of that gorgeous body." He ran a finger down the side of my cheek, and, holy hell, I wanted to melt in my seat, "but, tonight, you need a good night's sleep."

Sleep was the furthest thing from my mind right at that moment. I was still stuck on the devour-every-inch-of-my-body comment. I nodded. He was right. I needed sleep—alone—with my eyes closed, not with a hot-blooded body over, under, and wrapped around me.

Who the hell was I kidding? I wasn't going to get a second of sleep with thoughts of his eyes, lips, and hands touching me. Shit.

I thought he would kiss me. Stupid me, I wanted him to, but instead he caressed the side of my jaw, running his thumb over my bottom lip. The urge to bite it and suck it into my mouth was strong, but I won the fight. I think it would have been worth losing that one. Who knows?

He put the car in gear, and we drove back to his house in relative silence. Jose called at one point to check on me, and I told him I was fine. Otherwise, the radio and the rev of the engine were the only sounds on the roadway. I fought to stifle a few yawns and then gave up hiding them. He knew I was tired. I dreaded the forty minutes it was going to take me to get home—so much so, I was actually considering asking if I could crash on his sofa. I knew then that I was beyond sleep deprived.

We pulled into his parking lot, and I undid my belt. He put his hand over my arm to keep me from getting out. "You could stay here."

I shook my head adamantly. Thoughts of him devouring my body shot adrenaline straight through me.

He grinned, "Not with me, as tempting as that is, I'd rather you be awake when I make love to you. You can sleep in my bed, I'll take the couch."

Oh, hell no! Was he kidding? I was already fighting fantasy images of what he could do while he tasted every inch of my body; I didn't need to lie alone in his bed with the scent of him filling my imagination.

I shook my head again and climbed out of the car before he could restrain me further. "I'm fine, Drew. Thank you for making sure I ate dinner. I appreciate that." I walked around to the driver's side as he climbed out, but stopped out of arm's reach. I kept my focus on him, refusing to look away.

He closed the door, and my back straightened. I was not staying here. I was not. He stood three inches in front of me. I tilted my head back to keep eye contact.

"I promise to behave if you stay." His blue eyes sparkled in the glow of the fluorescent parking light above us.

I swallowed, "Thank you, Drew, but I'm fine, really."

He considered me for a moment before he held up my keys. From the corner of my eye, I could see them. I never left his heated gaze as I reached up with my left hand to snag them.

Instead of releasing the keys, he snatched my hand; the keys dangling off his finger between our palms. His other hand came to my waist, and he turned me so my butt was touching the car. I leaned away so my back was against it. I didn't want to allow my chest to touch his. He somehow had maneuvered one leg between mine. The earlier tingles in my toes flew like fireworks straight to my groin at the intimate contact.

Searing heat exploded from the lower part of my stomach. He watched my face. Had I just gasped? His other foot kicked one of my legs open wider, as if I were a suspect and he was going to frisk me. The thought ratcheted up the heat. He took advantage of my surprise and stepped completely between my legs, leaning in so there was no way I wouldn't know he was as turned on as I was. Okay, that time, I was sure I gasped, or did I groan?

He laced his fingers with mine as he pushed my hands to the side. The cooler metal and glass did nothing to bring down my body temp. My heart threatened to burst through my breastbone, and I knew I would hyperventilate if I kept breathing this fast.

He pushed his hips against mine, and the hard frame of the car kept our bodies in close contact. He leaned in, our chests now touching, his lips just a mere inch from mine.

He released my hands, and I faintly heard my car keys clink on the asphalt. His hands caressed the skin of my cheeks and neck. His rough fingertips ran along my lips as I sucked in a ragged breath. I was mesmerized by the sensations he sparked inside me. When he curled one hand around my neck and pulled my face closer, I didn't even think to hold back.

The first touch was gentle, soft, and warm. The second added a tinge of passion, and the third time his lips touched mine, the world exploded, and I understood quite well how he could possibly actually devour me.

He held me firmly so I couldn't get away. Yeah, like I could want to pull away from the tantalizing touch of his mouth.

My arms encircled him; my hands spread over his wide shoulders to urge him closer. I felt every inch of his sexy frame burning my body. His left hand slipped up the side of my waist, and his thumb brushed over the edge of my breast. I wanted more. I whimpered into his mouth and pushed closer to him. Every nerve ending cried out for his touch.

Without warning, he pulled away. "You need to get home and get some sleep. That should keep you awake for the drive." He pushed off the car abruptly, and our bodies separated. I felt like I would slither to the ground without his body holding mine in place.

He bent down and picked up my keys, holding them out for me while I attempted to control my lust. I reached out for the keys wondering if there would be a round two, but he let them go as soon as I touched them.

"Good night, MacKenzie. Let me know you reached home safely." He smiled his lopsided smile and turned towards his apartment.

I stared at his back until I couldn't see him anymore. Did he really just walk away? Had he kissed me that way to keep me awake? Was he just playing with me? Are you kidding me! How was I ever going to get to sleep after that?

I groaned and plopped in my car. He was right, though, I had no problem staying awake on the ride home.

Chapter 10 – Drew

Gray shadows crept along the ceiling as another car passed outside. My left arm was tucked under my pillow as I watched the movement above me. With a heavy sigh, I rolled to my side. My eyes fell on my cellphone display sitting upright on the night table. The glowing numbers seemed to thrum with the beat of my heart. I watched the display change from 1:04 to 1:05. I was going to be beat tomorrow if I didn't at least get a few hours of sleep.

I clenched my eyes shut and tried to clear my thoughts, but the events of the night kept replaying in my mind. The memory of Mack showing up at my apartment with anger streaming from her pores and the kiss that ended way too soon brought a slight curve to my lips. Being beside her and driving her Mustang were a highlight, but was it the car or the passenger that had made the trivial event so much more enjoyable?

My small smile transformed into a worried expression as I thought about the fact that Mack didn't take as good care of herself as she should. She should never have passed out. Luckily enough, I had been there to catch her. What if she had been out on something major? I shuddered to think of her passing out amidst people who wouldn't be so kind as to help a police officer.

My shoulders tensed as I recalled our brief conversation at the diner about my family. I forced myself not to dwell on that part of our night and instead brought to mind the final moments.

I had kissed a lot of women in my life, but there was not one kiss that could compare to what had transpired between us. Never had a woman reacted so intensely to the mere touch of my lips.

The ache in my groin began to return. It had been hiding behind false images since the moment I closed my apartment door. Now, as the memory of her bent backwards against the car came to mind again, I imagined lifting her up on the hood, her legs wrapped around my waist, or bent over the quarter panel while I took her from behind. A strangled sound rasped through my throat.

Would the need that I felt for Mack diminish if I took her, or would that just stoke the fire to become a blaze that could never be extinguished? I couldn't take that chance. I had a life on the other side of the country, commitments, family that needed me.

Family—that thought alone dashed the erotic images from my mind. Alex had said that Annabelle wasn't doing so well after her treatment and wanted to know when I was coming home. Maybe taking this assignment hadn't been such a good idea.

With thoughts of home twirling in my mind, I finally fell into oblivion.

The alarm blasted me out of my sleep, and I bit back an expletive as I turned off the alarm at four-forty-five. My first thought should have been of Alex and Andy, but instead it was of a woman pushed up against a car, her body hot against mine. Obviously, I needed a cold shower.

Three hours later, I pulled into the station lot. Mack's Mustang was already backed into its usual spot. How would she act today? Would she look at me like she wanted to throw me down on a desk or would she ignore what had happened last night?

When I entered the unit, I paused. She sat at her desk wearing a light peach blouse, her blonde hair looked brighter. Her head was down as she read something on her desk, the fingers of her left hand wrapped around her coffee mug.

I moved into the room, "Good Morning, Mack."

Her head snapped up with no trace of a smile, smirk, or blush. "Morning, Drew." So we were going to ignore what happened last night. She diverted her attention back to the papers in front of her, but not before I saw the circles under her eyes. She hadn't slept any better than I had.

Jose and Gordon entered the unit as I poured my coffee.

"Hey, Mack, did you talk to that witness at the scene?" Gordon asked while he situated himself at his desk.

She shook her head, "No, I told you last night that he had an emergency at the hospital, so I was going to catch up with him this morning."

Gordon acknowledged me with a nod of his head, and we all turned to see Gary step into the room. His line of sight went right to Mack. "You feeling alright?"

"I'm fine, L.T." She went back to the papers. His eyes tightened before he approached her.

When he stopped at the edge of her desk, she didn't look up. "What are you working on?" he asked her as he scanned her messy desktop.

"I just received the phone records from the guy who owns the BMW dealership. I'm going over them." She leaned back in her seat and looked up at him.

"What? I thought I told you to leave that guy alone!"

Mack pushed herself away from him, startled by his outburst. I set my coffee cup down on my desk. "I'm working on a hunch, Gary."

He reached down and snagged the group of papers off her desk, Mack's jaw opened but no words came out. "And I told you to leave him alone! You were given a direct order to do that."

Gary spun around and stomped back to his office, almost knocking Will over as he walked into the unit. The door slammed to his office.

"Whoa, what the hell is wrong with him?" Will asked.

Mack stared at the closed door. She clamped her jaw closed and gripped the arms of her chair with white knuckles.

"Looks like he has a bug up his ass today," Jose answered Will who still stood near the door.

Mack put her palms on her desk and stood up slowly. After she took a deep breath and twisted her neck from side to side, she rolled her shoulders back and strode towards the closed door.

"Mack, give him a few minutes to calm down," Gordon suggested as she approached the closed door.

She glared at him and then slammed the door in reply as she entered Gary's office.

Jose cringed while Gordon shook his head. I surveyed the squad room and listened as best as I could for anything that was coming from the closed office door.

I sat down and turned to my computer, logging on when the system woke up. All four of us looked to the door when we heard Mack yell, "You're what?"

Nervous glances passed among us when we didn't hear anything else. I went back to my computer and was opening my email when the door flew open.

"Screw you, Gary!" Mack stomped through the doorway and slammed the door. Her face was red, and her jaw was clenched tight, just like her hands at her side.

She went to her desk and threw a few things around. With a growl, she yanked her shoulder bag off the floor from under her desk and started towards the door.

I stood up, "Mack? Where are you going?"

She kept walking. I heard the hard clipped sounds of her shoes as she entered the hallway and headed towards the back of the building.

Gordon walked into Gary's office, and Jose's phone rang. He leaned over to pick it up, and I hustled to the door to catch up with Mack.

She was already at her car when I finally caught up to her. "Mack, wait!" I yelled as I jogged across the parking lot.

She spun around. "What?" she yelled and I stopped immediately.

The anger on her face froze me on the spot. Her chest heaved as she sucked in air and released it.

I moved more slowly towards her. "Mack, what happened?"

She closed her eyes then looked at the ground. Her shoulder bag slipped down her arm, and she let it fall to the asphalt.

When she didn't look up, I lifted her chin with my knuckle, "What happened, MacKenzie?"

She laughed harshly, "I got suspended."

"You what?"

Her shoulders sagged, and she leaned down to grab her bag.

"I was suspended for working an investigation I was told not to." She turned to move the last few feet to her car.

"I don't get it. You were supposed to be working on the car theft ring. Did he tell you why he didn't want you to look at the phone records?" I stepped around her to block her progress.

She halted before she crashed into me. "Yes, I was working that case, but I have been pulled off of it." She looked away from me.

Why would Gary pull her off the case? Was there something he didn't want her to know in the phone records?

"Look, I have to get out of here. I'm sure you can work with Gordon or Jose. Gordon is going to need someone to help with interviews." She brushed past me, but I grabbed her arm before she could open her car door.

"Are you alright?"

She didn't say anything, and she wouldn't look at me, but she gave a small nod. She shrugged out of my grasp and pulled open her door, throwing her bag onto the passenger seat.

"I'll call you later," I told her as she pulled the door closed. The roar of the engine engulfed me, and she didn't waste time putting the car in gear and putting her foot on the gas pedal. I watched her until I couldn't see her car anymore.

What the hell was in those phone records that Gary didn't want her to know about? I stared at the back of the building. I didn't know, but I sure as hell was going to find out. I headed back inside the office.

Bria typed at her desk. She winked at me when she saw me, and

Jose was still talking on the phone. The headset pushed between his shoulder and ear, he glanced at me with a questioning look, and I nodded. I knew he was wondering if Mack was alright.

I glanced at the closed door to Gary's office and then at Gordon's empty desk before I eyed Mack's. There was a file box under her desk that I had seen her putting things into about the case. When I had a chance, I'd go through it and see if I could find out more on the court order for the phone records.

I was sitting at my desk when Gordon came out of Gary's office. "Drew, can you take over those interviews? You will have to do them alone because everyone else is tied up on something. Are you comfortable doing that?"

"Sure, Gordon, I can do that." I stood back up and went to Mack's desk where her portfolio was. Inside were the notes from the last night's interviews. I glanced at the box again, but decided it would be better to search through it later when no one was around. I took the portfolio with me and left the unit, glad to be getting out of the office and not having to face Gary. If I had to be near him, I might have gotten suspended myself for knocking the guy out.

Chapter 11 – Mack

Sleep was not an option. Every single time I closed my eyes, the images of our bodies pushed up against my car came back to life. Instead, I took a shower, checked my emails, and played a stupid game online.

When I felt like I would need toothpicks to hold my lids open, I finally dropped into bed. The digital numbers on the clock beside my bed read one-twenty-five.

Somehow I dropped off to sleep without thoughts of Drew drifting through my mind. When my alarm went off at five, I stumbled out of bed and started my coffee maker. Today was going to be a caffeine day if there ever was one.

I was in the office by seven-fifteen and snagged the faxes off the machine as I walked to my desk. With my shoulder bag tucked under my desk, I sat down and skimmed through the stack of paper I had in front of me. I sorted the documents according to who they were for and found, in the middle of the pile, a fax of the documents I had been awaiting from the phone company. I put that off to the side until I finished going through the rest of the papers.

When I finished sorting, I delivered them to the in-boxes where they belonged and turned on my computer. I had just finished scanning my email and turned to the phone records when I felt Drew enter the room.

I didn't need to look up. I knew he was there just by the way the air in the room changed. What was he going to say about last night?

When he said hello, I responded and went immediately back to the papers in front of me. Before he walked in the room, the text in front of me had made sense. Now, the words were just a jumble of black marks on white paper. I struggled to focus on them.

It had been hard to tear my eyes from his face. The circles under his eyes matched mine. Somehow, that didn't make me feel better.

Every sound he made registered in my mind, but I refused to look up at him. Instead, I stared at the hieroglyphics in front of me.

Gordon saved me from yet another try at reading the information in front of me. "Hey, Mack, did you talk to that witness at the scene?"

I had just answered him when Gary made his grand entrance and zoomed right in on me and asked me how I was. It drove me nuts that he even cared—and why did he? I went back to trying to decipher the information. This was going to be a long morning if I couldn't get my mind focused.

Gary stood by my desk, "What are you working on?"

I tried not to sigh and leaned back in my chair.

"I just received the phone records from the guy who owns the BMW dealership. I'm going over them," or trying to, I thought to myself.

A vein bulged on his forehead as he exploded, "What? I thought I told you to leave that guy alone!"

"I'm working on a hunch, Gary," I replied calmly.

Shock kept me from speaking when he grabbed all the documents from the phone company off my desk and made a beeline to his office.

That son of a bitch! I ground my teeth as I quietly seethed. How dare he scream at me in front of the unit about doing my job? He had no right to take my papers and walk away. I was doing what I do best, investigating.

I forced myself to calm down as I stood. I heard Gordon tell me to give Gary some time, but that was not my plan. I twisted the door knob and moved into the office with barely-concealed rage. The wall vibrated behind me as the door made contact with the frame.

"What the hell is your problem?" Although I felt like yelling, I kept my voice low.

"I told you to leave the BMW owner alone. You didn't listen."

Gary walked over to the shredder in the corner of his office and split the pile of papers he had taken from my desk into two groups. As the first set entered the grinding teeth of the machine, my anger boiled over.

"Since when do you get involved with my investigations?"

He pushed the second set into the slot and waited until it was done before turning to his desk. He never looked at me. "This is my unit, Mack, and I distinctly told you not to do something. You went behind my back and did it anyway."

I stood in front of his desk, my fists on my hips. "I did it because I guarantee it holds information that could help us with this case. Something is wrong with this picture, Gary."

He moved some papers around on his desk, still not meeting my glare. "Well, guess what? It's not a picture you need to look at anymore. You're off the case."

I reeled back like I had been slapped, "Excuse me?"

He finally met my surprised gaze. "In fact, not only are you not on the case, I am suspending you for a few days for not doing as you were told."

"You're what?" I screamed. I knew that I had yelled loud enough for probably everyone in the entire building to hear, but I didn't care.

"You are suspended for five days. When you return, you will be reassigned to another case. Your suspension begins now. Go home, Mack," he dismissed me. I stood rooted to the spot for a moment as I watched him sit down in his chair and put his hand on the mouse of his computer.

"You did not just take me off this case," my words hissed.

He clicked on something and typed for a moment. "I did and you need to leave now before I add insubordination to your file."

My jaw dropped open. I didn't have one single negative mark in my jacket, and now he wanted to cite me with not following a direct order and insubordination!

"You son of a bitch," I seethed quietly, but with enough venom that I saw him flinch. I spun on my heel and stalked out of the room. "Screw you, Gary!"

I saw only red as I grabbed my bag and left. I heard Drew call out to me, but I had to get out of the building before I did something I would really regret, namely, beating the hell out of Gary.

Drew caught up to me in the parking lot, and I spun on him and unleashed the rage I had bottled up in my chest. When I saw the startled look on his face, I realized I was almost out of control. I tried to calm down and dropped the stiff hold on my shoulders as Drew grew closer.

When my bag hit the ground, I barely noticed. The only thought on my mind was to wrap my arms around Drew and to ask him to hold me. When he lifted my chin and questioned me again, I laughed. Not because of what had happened inside, but because for a moment, I wanted him to take away the anger. I wanted him to kiss me again until it all melted away. Frustrated at myself for that thought, I informed him that Gary had suspended me.

I told him I had to leave, and he gripped my arm to hold me in place. Once again, I wanted to fall into his arms and forget all my troubles, but I knew I couldn't. I nodded that I was alright, though I was far from it, and sat down in my car.

I had to get away, away from this place, away from my fury at Gary, and away from the concerned look from Drew. He didn't have a right to be worried about what was happening with me.

I drove hard when I pulled out of the parking lot. I had no place in mind to which I wanted to go, but I knew I couldn't go home and stare at my walls. I'd drive myself crazy if I did.

I spent two hours driving north into the mountains and stopped at a diner to get some coffee and a bite to eat. I didn't need a repeat performance of yesterday.

Before entering the diner, I opened my trunk and grabbed a

duffle bag that I kept there. I entered the diner, looked for the bathroom, and made my way there without speaking to anyone. One of the ceiling lights was burned out, and the dark shadows of the small bathroom matched my mood.

I pulled out a pair of jeans and a t-shirt and traded my work shoes for a pair of sneakers. After changing clothes, I found a booth at the back of the diner and ordered breakfast.

There were twenty tables in the diner, most of them empty since it was after ten. The breakfast rush was over, and the lunch one had not begun yet. I ordered a bagel and coffee from a tired older woman and turned to stare out the hazy window towards the street.

The cars passed in a blur as I thought about what had happened this morning. What was Gary's problem? There had to be something he didn't want me to know about Timmons. Was the guy involved like I thought, or was Gary just being an ass?

My food arrived just as my cellphone pinged that I had a text message. I put my napkin on my lap and picked up my phone.

It was from Drew. *Are you alright?*

I thought about ignoring it, but if I was honest with myself, I wanted to talk to him. *Yeah, I'm fine,* I typed back.

Where are you?

I'm chilling out and, you will be happy to know, eating breakfast. I smiled as I imagined him doing the same as he read my message.

He didn't disappoint me, *Lol, good I'm glad to hear that.*

I thought about asking him what happened after I left, but decided I didn't want to know. *I'll talk to you later, be safe.*

A minute went by before he responded, *I'll call you later. Can we get together after work?*

I put my phone down and picked up my bagel, sinking my teeth into the warm bread and cream cheese as I thought about how to reply. I wanted to see him, but it probably wasn't a good idea. We needed to put the brakes on this thing between us. There was no way we could work together and have any type of relationship. Besides, he was too young.

I thought back to our dinner last night and how he had seemed older to me. It must have been a trick of the light or my tired eyes. It didn't matter anyway. There was no way we could get involved, even if it was just for a one-night quickie.

Somehow, I didn't think that one night would be enough for either of us. I finished the first half of my bagel and wiped my fingers on my napkin before I picked up my phone to answer him.

Sorry, I left town, not sure when I will be back. I'll talk to you later. I sent the message and set my phone down again.

I had just taken a bite of my bagel when my phone started to ring. I laughed because I'd had a feeling he was going to call me after I sent that message. I swallowed and thought about sending it to voicemail, but the need to hear his voice was too strong. I put the phone to my ear.

"Yes." I stared out the window, watching a family of four get out of a minivan across the street.

"Where are you?" His voice held a note of concern, and I fought a smile.

"Nowhere special. I just needed to get away for a little while."

"That's probably a good idea. How long are you going to be gone?" I heard music in the background and figured he was in his car someplace, probably off doing the interviews that we were supposed to have been doing together.

"I'm not sure." I didn't tell him I would be home later. I carried an extra change of clothes in my car, but just for emergencies. I would head home this evening after I unwound.

I heard him sigh. "Mack," he hesitated for a moment, "tell me where you are."

"Why?" I rested my chin on my palm to hold my head up.

"Because I'm worried about you, that's why." The words were said quietly, and while a little piece of me jumped up and down, excited, the rational part of my mind said to cut this crap out now.

I sat back in my seat and wadded my napkin up in my fist. "Look, Drew, I appreciate that, but I'm fine. There is no reason to worry about me. I'm sorry you got the brunt of my anger this morning. I was beyond pissed. I'm better now, and it's no big deal."

Yeah right, I tacked on to myself.

"It is a big deal, Mack, and I do worry about you," he replied.

"Why?" I asked, torn between wanting to hear he cared and afraid he would say that.

He was quiet on the other side of the line for a moment. "You know why," he finally answered.

That didn't tell me anything, well, okay maybe it did, but no, it didn't, not really—or did it tell me more than I wanted to know? I didn't know. I sighed. I was confusing myself.

I heard the heavy release of his breath whisper over the mouthpiece, "When are you coming home, Mack? I want to see you."

I shook my head, "I don't think that is a good idea, Drew." I thought for a moment, "Look, I don't think we should see each other outside of work."

"Mack, don't, don't push me away." Was there pleading in his voice? No. I must have heard that wrong.

"I'm sorry if I gave you any reason to think there was something between us." I dropped my napkin and spun my coffee cup around absently.

"Don't give me that shit, MacKenzie." The way he said my name gave me goose bumps. "You're not going to lie to me or yourself about nothing going on. You know damn well that there is."

I hung my head, "Fine, maybe there is, but it's not going any further. Drew, I'm not getting involved with you. I have too much on my plate right now, and I can't afford to deal with some crazy affair." The waitress came by my table, and I pushed my coffee mug towards her to top it off.

"I don't want an affair with you."

I wanted to ask him what he wanted, but reality was knocking on the door to my brain.

"That is all it would ever be, Drew, and that's not what I want or need in my life. I'm sorry." He started to interrupt me, but I pressed on, "Look, I will talk to you later. I need to go."

"This conversation is not over."

I closed my eyes. How I wish I could hear that every day, but I knew that was just wishful thinking. "Yes, it is, Drew, goodbye." I hung up the phone before he could say anything.

I put my phone on silent and finished my bagel. I refused to look at the screen to see why the little light was blinking. I didn't want to know that he had called or sent another message telling me that I was wrong. If I saw it right then, I might just cave, and I couldn't afford to do that.

I shoved my phone into the duffle bag beside me. I was on suspension, so there was no one I needed to be in contact with, no reason to have my phone with me.

I threw the bag in the trunk of the car and headed further up the mountain to a trail I knew that led to a waterfall. A nice walk would do me good.

Chapter 12 – Drew

I had found the doctor, and his account of what he saw was relatively short. He'd heard a popping noise over the sound of his mower after his neighbor had come home, and as the last few rounds of gunfire exchanged, his neighbor fell to the ground, and the other guy took off running behind the house.

By the time the doctor reached his neighbor, there were no signs of life. He tried to explain the medical terminology, but all I heard was he was shot center mass, right in the heart. I thanked him for his time and drove back to the neighborhood where the shooting had occurred so I could talk to the lady who had called 911. She hadn't answered her door last night.

Her account was similar: She'd heard a noise like fireworks and came outside when her neighbor yelled to call 911; she grabbed her cell to make the call. If she had looked out her back window, she might have seen the subject fleeing, but she said she was so focused on making the call, she never looked towards the rear of the house.

I climbed back into the unmarked police car I was using and glanced at my watch. It was ten-thirty. I wondered how Mack was doing. She'd been pretty upset when she pulled away, and I was curious what she did when she was angry. Did she go to work out? Head off to find a friend? Maybe go home and drink? I had no idea.

I pulled out my phone and sent her a text. I wasn't sure if she would answer me or not, and when she did, I was surprised that I felt so relieved.

I smiled when she said she was eating breakfast. I had been concerned she wouldn't if she was upset. I still sat in front of the house from my last interview. I started drumming my fingers on the steering wheel while I waited for her reply to my question about seeing her after work. When she didn't answer right away, I put the car in drive and pulled away from the curb. I was waiting to turn onto the main road when my phone finally pinged. I checked my rearview mirror and found I was alone, so I hit my pass-code on the phone and looked at the screen.

She went out of town? Where in the hell did she go? Instead of typing, I hit the icon to dial her number.

"Where are you?" I asked.

I could understand her need to change her scenery, but I irrationally wished she had confided in me. We had only known each other a few days, yet there was a connection between us that had started the moment we met. That thought kind of freaked me out.

Why did I care? I asked myself when she asked me why I wanted to know where she was. I turned into a parking lot and put the car in park. "Because I'm worried about you, that's why."

I closed my eyes and leaned my head back against the headrest while she apologized and tried to make it all go away. Thoughts of my parents flitted through my mind. They had known each other three weeks before they had married. Love at first sight, they said. Their thirty-six years of marriage had proven them right. Was that what this was? I needed to protect her and to be beside her. I cared about her after only a few days, and she had no idea that it was more than just getting her in bed. Shit, she would think I was crazy if I told her how I felt. I told myself I was crazy for thinking these things myself."Why?" she asked me softly.

"You know why." I stared unseeing out the windshield. My heavy sigh followed right behind hers. "When are you coming home, Mack? I want to see you."

"I don't think that is a good idea, Drew." She hesitated, and I was afraid to speak. "Look, I don't think we should see each other outside of work."

"Mack, don't, don't push me away." My heart thudded in my chest. Damn it!

My mouth hung open when she spoke again. "I'm sorry if I gave you any reason to think there was something between us."

You have got to be kidding me. "Don't give me that shit, MacKenzie. You're not going to lie to me or yourself about nothing going on. You know damned well that there is."

"Fine, maybe there is, but it's not going any further. Drew, I'm not getting involved with you. I have too much on my plate right now, and I can't afford to deal with some crazy affair right now."

An affair? I didn't want a one-night stand with her. "I don't want an affair with you." If that's not what I wanted, what did I want? A lifetime like my parents?

"That is all it would ever be, Drew, and that's not what I want or need in my life. I'm sorry." Before I could refute her statement, she continued, "Look, I will talk to you later. I need to go," she finished the sentence in a rush.

"This conversation is not over," I stated firmly. My fingers ached from the tension of my tight grip on the phone.

"Yes, it is, Drew, goodbye."

The phone clicked in my ear. I pulled it away to see that the conversation was indeed over, and she had hung up.

Oh, hell no! I dialed her phone, it rang four times before it went to voicemail. "Mack, this is so not over. I don't know what you think is going on, but it's more than just a one-night stand. I want more than a single night with you. What do I need to do or say to prove that to you? Please call me back."

I ended the call and stared at the phone. Since when had I become such a whiny baby? I tossed the phone into the console, put the car in gear, and headed back to the station to work on the reports for the initial interviews.

Gordon and Jose were not in the office. Gary's door was closed, and I heard muffled voices coming from inside. One sounded like a woman, and I figured it was Bria. I moved towards my desk and hesitated beside Mack's, looking down at the box and then glancing around the room.

Since no one was around, now seemed like a good time to look for the court order. When I bent down to lift the cardboard lid, I noticed that it no longer sat flush like before. Someone had been in here. I looked over my shoulder; the door was still closed on Gary's office, and no one was around. I lifted the lid.

I couldn't believe it. The box was empty. I looked to the side to read the label: *Vehicle Theft Investigation*. This was the correct box.

I scanned her desk. The piles that normally were not neat were now stacked nice and tidy in two piles on her desk. Someone had gone through her things.

I heard footsteps in the hallway and put the lid back before quickly moving to my desk. Jose, Will, and Gordon walked in as I pulled my chair out. I gave them a chin-up nod and sat down, noticing as I did that someone had gone through the few things I had on my desk, too.

I inspected my desk a little more while I waited for my computer to wake up. While Mack's desk was hardly neat, I kept mine perfectly clear; my folders neatly arranged, and, believe it or not, alphabetical in my upright holder. Someone hadn't noticed and put the *Theft from Vehicle* folder in front of the *Schedule* folder.

I scanned the labels, wondering if anything was missing, but they all appeared to be here. So far in this investigation, I had turned all the notes over to Mack. I didn't have much of a file on it at all.

I leaned back in my chair and stared at the L.T.'s closed door, biting the inside of my cheek as I wondered if I should ask where everything had gone. I needed to get a hold of the court order so I could see the affidavit and get another one. I didn't know all the ins and outs of the case or how Mack had worded the case to get the phone records.

Jose cleared his throat. I turned to him, and he made a tiny movement with his head towards Gordon. I raised my eyebrows and peered over at the older man who was writing on a legal pad.

I looked at Jose again, he raised his eyebrows and I acknowledged it by raising my own. He lifted his phone receiver and punched in a few numbers, probably checking his voicemail since the little red light on the top was blinking.

I could only assume that Gordon was taking over the case since Mack was suspended.

I opened up the reporting software just as Gordon turned to me. "You get anything this morning?" he called across the room.

"No, nothing we didn't already know. I'm typing up my reports now. I'll have them to you before I leave."

He dismissed me without another word and turned back to his legal pad.

Gordon's phone rang and he called out to Will, "Pick up line one; it's Mike."

I had yet to meet Mike. Jose had told me yesterday that he was working undercover and had infiltrated one of the local gangs.

I kept my focus on my computer but heard the tone of Will's voice change as he spoke with Mike, "That's my territory, keep your rats away from my gang."

I peered over my shoulder at him, his back was stiff and he looked pissed. "I told you to back off, Mike. Stay the hell out of this." He slammed the phone down and made a beeline for Gary's office. With a quick rap on the door, he entered and closed it behind him.

Mack hadn't said anything about gangs being involved with this case, so I mentally put it all aside. Sounded like the boys were about to have a pissing match over territory. I focused back on my reports, and true to my word, I had them finished at a few minutes before four. All the people that we had spoken with the night before, along with the two I had interviewed today, were inside the supplement now. I printed it out, read it over, and then dropped it on Gordon's disaster of a desk as I walked out of the unit.

I would have sneaked a peek at Gordon's desk, but Gary was in his office, and Bria was leaning against the door jamb outside, laughing about something he had said.

As I left, I pushed a few buttons on my phone and called Mack. She had never returned my call, and I was frustrated by the turn of events today and her not answering me.

Her voicemail came on just as my phone beeped that another call was coming in: Rob. I disconnected from Mack without leaving a message and took his call.

"What's up?" I said as I put the phone up to my ear.

"Not too much. How are things going?" He sounded much more relaxed than I felt.

I unlocked the door to my Explorer and climbed in. "It's been an interesting day." I put the key in the ignition but didn't start it. Instead, I leaned back in the seat and rested my elbow on the console between the seats.

"In the mood for a workout?" He had known me almost my whole life, and he knew when I was frustrated and needed to do something physical.

"Yeah, I could use a game." We set a time to meet at the local club, and I made my way home to change clothes. I thought of calling Mack at least a half dozen times on the ride home, but I refused to do so. She needed to make the next move. If she didn't, well then that would suck, but at least it would be easier to leave when I finished this case.

Ninety minutes later, I pulled up outside the club, grabbed my gym bag and my racket, and walked inside. Rob was waiting in the lobby for me, and I followed him to the locker room.

It had been years since we had played a good hard game of racquetball together, and the thought of slamming the little blue ball against the front wall and bouncing my body off the side walls sounded like the perfect antidote to my mood.

We hit the ball around for a few minutes, casually, to warm up. I was getting ready to serve when Rob finally broached the subject. "So what happened today?"

I made forceful contact with the small rubber ball and listened to the loud whap it made on the bright white wall in front of me. Rob returned the hit, and for a few minutes, we volleyed back and forth. I earned the point and readied myself to serve again.

"Mack was suspended today."

Rob never missed a stride, and he struck the fast-moving ball. I lost that point, and Rob moved to serve.

"Why?"

The ball came fast, and I reached it just in time to reflect it back against the wall. When the ball bounced back one too many times, he grabbed it and looked at me.

"The L.T. was pissed because she did a court order for phone records. He didn't want her investigating the guy, and when he found out she had, he suspended her and, I think, took her off the case permanently."

"Who is the guy she pulled the records on?" He bounced the ball in front of him.

"Timmons, he's the owner of one of the local BMW dealerships. My first day there, I went with her to a reported burglary at his house. She was suspicious of him, and now I am, too." He nodded, and we prepared for another round.

It was my turn to serve again and he tossed me the ball, asking, "You want me to check the guy out?"

"Give me a day or two. I am going to need you to do me another favor." Rob raised an eyebrow for me to continue. "Mack had gotten a court order for the guy's phone records. That's what set off this whole suspension thing. I'm trying to get my hands on her affidavit, so I can get you to do another one for me."

"Isn't it on her desk?" he asked when I was finished.

"Nope." I bounced the ball and geared up to serve. "While I was out doing interviews this morning, someone cleaned out her files and went through my stuff, too." I tossed the ball up, and the racket made contact with a loud whap.

We played the rest of the game without any more conversation; both of us lost in our thoughts. I wasn't sure what his were, but mine revolved around the feisty woman who wouldn't return my call and who refused to admit she wanted more.

When we finished, I wiped my face off with a small towel that I had left lying outside the door.

"So you don't think she's involved, do you?" he asked after he toweled off his own sweat.

"Who, Mack?" I shook my head. "No way, but her boss, no doubt."

"Do you think anyone else in the office is involved with it?" he asked as we made our way back to the locker room.

I thought about that for a moment. "I don't know. Bria spends a lot of time with Gary behind closed doors, but Gordon is his right-hand man. I don't think Jose is involved, he was the one who let on about who went through her files today."

He pushed the locker room door open, "Who went through them?"

"Gordon, but he could have just been doing it because he is now the lead on the case with Mack out."

"So what is Mack doing now that she's not at work?" Rob asked as he unlocked the locker.

I shook my head and sat down. "I have no clue. I called her earlier, and she said she was out of town. She wouldn't tell me where or for how long." Rob laughed, and I leaned back to look at him. "What?"

"What?" he laughed again. "You sound like you care that she's not around."

I stared at the scuffed white tiles on the floor. "I do," I said quietly.

Rob sat down beside me, "What's going on?"

I shook my head, "I have no idea, man. I just can't get her out of my mind."

"You sleeping with her?"

I jerked my head around, "No." I stood up to open the locker, "no, I'm not sleeping with her."

Rob's laughter grated on my nerves, "But you want to, that's the problem."

"Yes, no." I shrugged, "Yeah, of course I do, but that's not the problem." I pulled out his bag and handed it to him.

"So what's the problem?" He took it from me and dropped it on the ground.

I tugged mine out of the small locker and set it on the bench behind me, "You know exactly what the problem is."

"No, I don't."

"Yes, you do. I can't afford to get involved with someone. I have a life out west."

"You could transfer back here." He kicked off his sneakers and started to pull of his socks.

"I can't do that, not right now. She needs me out there and so do the kids. Besides, I don't want Alex and Andy to go through this alone."

I heard him sigh, "Then why not just take advantage of the time you have here and have an affair with Mack?"

"She deserves better." I pulled out a clean pair of jeans and a t-shirt. "Besides, I don't just want an affair with her."

"Whoa…what are you saying?" I saw him stare at me from the corner of my eye.

"I'm not saying anything. Just forget it. Besides, she thinks I'm practically jail bait at twenty-eight years old."
I pulled out my small shower kit and kicked off my shoes.

"Why don't you tell her the truth?" He yanked his shirt over his head.

"You know I can't do that; it might jeopardize the investigation." I walked to the end of the locker row and grabbed two towels, tossing one to him. He turned away and wrapped it around his waist after taking his shorts off while I did the same.

"I guess you're right." He shoved our bags back inside the locker and locked it before we went to the showers. "So what are you going to do?"

I shrugged, "Nothing, I don't really have much of a choice. Besides, she won't talk to me right now."

Rob laughed again before he walked into a stall, "Somehow, Romeo, I don't think things will stay that way."

"Yeah, well, you don't know Mack," I threw back at him.

"Speaking of which, when do I get to meet her?"

"Maybe when she gets back we can go grab a bite to eat, whenever that is," I started to step into the stall and leaned back to look at him, "and when we do, keep your hands to yourself."

Rob laughed, "No, you don't want anything from her."

That was the problem, I did, but deep inside, I knew she was right. Things would never work out for us.

Chapter 13 – Mack

I stared at the mist rising from the rocks. The sound of the water rushing soothed me—normally.

The stone under my denim-clad butt was damp, but I didn't care. I wrapped my arms around my legs, my chin rested on my left knee. The bubbling and bursting of the air bubbles in the water mirrored the explosive turmoil in my life. Why the hell had Gary been so bent out of shape because I was doing my job? Was Gary somehow involved in all of this? It wouldn't be the first time he stuck his nose someplace it didn't belong. While we were married, I had uncovered enough information to have him fired, but I'd chosen not to reveal it. He'd promised he would get out of what he was involved in and not contest the divorce if I kept quiet. That was wrong of me, but at the time, I had just wanted my freedom.

Could I sit back and allow him to be involved in something illegal now? No. He no longer had any hold over me, no evidence that he could spin around in his shifty way to implicate me—but did I want to destroy him?

Gary had to be protecting someone or himself. Which one was it? I turned that question over and over in my mind as I watched the water rush violently.

I closed my eyes and listened to the tumult of nature. Instead of calming me, the torrent reminded me of the blood rushing through my veins when Drew looked at me.

I growled and opened my eyes. Damn it! I give up! I made my way to the path to the parking lot. No matter what I did, I wouldn't be able to get away from the thoughts I had about him. Should I just sleep with him and be done with it? Who was I kidding? If I did, I would just crave him more.

When I climbed back to my car, I pulled my phone out of my duffle bag. I had three missed calls and two voicemails. Two calls were from Drew and one was from Jose. Why was Jose calling me?

I pushed the button for my voicemail and closed my eyes as I listed to Drew's voice. "Mack, this is so not over. I don't know what you think is going on, but it's more than just a one-night stand. I want more than a single night with you. What do I need to do or say to prove that to you? Please call me back."

Tears prickled behind my lids. How could the sound of a voice cause such longing? Was there such a thing as instant attraction? Could this be what finding a soul mate was about? My finger hovered over the key that would delete the message, but just as I was about to push it, my finger pushed the save button instead.

Jose's voice came on the line to remind me that they were going out for drinks after work. I glanced at the clock, I could make it back in time to meet up with them if I didn't go home and change first. I deleted his message and looked down at my jeans. I wasn't exactly dressed to go out, but who did I want to impress?

Drew.

I dropped my phone in the cup holder and started my car. Not that I knew he was going to be there or anything, but chances were someone might have mentioned that we go out on Thursday night for a few drinks.

I glanced at the clock again and picked up my phone, typing Jose a quick reply that I would be there but a little late. Could he save me a seat? He acknowledged me with a quick okay, and I pulled out on the road and headed back to town.

I made good time coming back. Rush hour was long over, and

even then, most of the cars would have been heading out to the 'burbs. I pulled up outside O'Leary's Pub and parked. After a quick scan around the parking lot, my heart dropped slightly when I didn't see Drew's SUV.

Inside, I found everyone in the back corner at our regular table. Jose, Gordon, Bria, Will, and a few others from the patrol squads were all laughing around the long rectangular table that ran lengthwise along the dark wood-paneled wall. I tried to tell myself not to be disappointed that Drew wasn't there. I mean, how many times had I told myself I didn't want to see him or get involved with him? A dozen? No, make that more like two dozen.

Jose pulled out a chair as I approached the table. "Hey, you made it!"

"Hey, guys!" I patted Tom on the shoulder as I walked by. He was one of the patrol supervisors. I noticed Bria's husband wasn't present, he was probably working.

"Hey, Mack, what the hell happened today?" Tom asked. "I heard you were suspended." A hush fell over the table, and I tried to cover my embarrassment with a laugh.

"You know Gary. Someone must have pissed in his Cheerios this morning." I sat down, and Jose handed me a tall glass filled with beer as everyone around the table joined in on the laughter. Well, everyone except Bria who was watching me closely. I grinned at her and took a sip of my beer. Thick foam stuck to my lip as I gazed over her head and practically choked on my drink.

Drew sat in the opposite corner of the room, his intense gaze focused directly on me. I put my glass down and made a hell of a mistake: I licked the foam off my top lip with my tongue.

His lids slammed shut, and I saw him visually tense. Had I done that on purpose? My cheeks began to feel warm, and I stared at my glass. Jose snickered beside me.

"What are you laughing at?" I whispered to him.

He leaned over and pushed the hair back from my ear as he came closer, "I'm not sure who you affected more, Drew or his friend." My gaze landed back on the other table, and for the first time, I noticed the man sitting beside Drew.

He lifted his chin in a greeting and gave me a wide welcoming grin. "Oh, shit," I muttered as I rolled my eyes and looked back at my glass. Jose laughed again, and my cheeks felt like they were on fire.

I hid behind my beer for a few moments, every once in a while sneaking a peek in his direction. Whenever I did, one or both of them looked in our direction, not always at me, but always at our table. Were they talking about us?

I studied Drew's friend as he threw back his head and laughed at something Drew had said. His shoulders were wider than Drew's. He had the same short hairstyle, although his hair was a lighter brown, almost dirty blond. I wasn't sure, but I would guess his eyes were either green or hazel. If he hadn't been sitting next to Drew, I would have said he was an attractive man, but compared to Drew, he was just a regular, decent-looking man.

"Why don't you go over and invite them to join us?" Jose leaned in so no one else would hear us. Most of the table was engrossed in a debate on the latest hockey game, and they weren't paying much attention to us anyway. I scanned the room and allowed my eyes to rest on their table again. Drew's friend winked at me; a smile slipped over my lips as I looked away.

What if I flirted with him? Maybe if I did, Drew would get the idea that I wasn't interested. I rolled my eyes at myself—or maybe he would just think I was a bigger bitch than I was.

"I'm going to go put more music on the juke box." I finished my beer and pushed my chair back. I forced myself not to glance toward their table and took the long way around the large rectangular wooden bar that dominated the middle of the room.

I felt him before I heard him, "I thought you were out of town." He was right behind me, almost touching me, but not quite. I was tempted to lean against him but instead leaned forward and spoke over my shoulder without looking at him. "I was."

He shifted so he was closer to me, but on my right side. "I guess you weren't that far away then."

I futilely tried to read the titles in front of me. My heart thudded in my chest, reminding me of my time at the waterfall earlier. Damn it! I would never be able to go back there without thinking about this man.

"I went for a drive up in the mountains." I pushed the number combination for what I hoped was a good song.

His hand slid to my lower back, and he leaned in closer, "Why didn't you call me?"

I shifted away from him and glanced over at the table to see if anyone was watching us. Bria turned away quickly, but Jose grinned and winked. I rolled my eyes and tried to find another song to add to my playlist.

"I didn't have a signal where I was," I lied and pushed another combination into the machine.

"But you had one when you came back."

"And your point is?" I challenged.

A smirk formed on his lips, and I forced myself to match his stare.

He waited until he had my attention again, "The point is, you didn't call me back." He paused, "Why?" His eyebrow rose. That damned eyebrow was going to be the death of me.

I shrugged, "I told you we didn't have anything else to talk about." I pushed another set of buttons and turned to go back to the table. I didn't get far. He deftly maneuvered me into the hallway that led back to the bathrooms.

Before I could find my voice, he had me sinfully pinned against the wall with his body, one hand flat beside my head, the other on my hip. "And I said we weren't finished with our conversation."

Afraid that if I touched him I would melt, I placed both my palms on the wood paneling behind me and stood up as straight as I could, putting space between us. It didn't work. Our chests had magnets inside them, and his followed mine as I tried to move away. I sucked in a shaky breath. "Drew, please."

"Please what?" He leaned closer, his lips a half inch from mine. "Please kiss you?"

I closed my eyes in response.

113

"Open your eyes, MacKenzie."

I refused to do so. I shook my head, and our noses brushed. A tingle went from that point to my lower abdomen. His hand left my waist and slipped against my neck. His thumb ran over my mouth, and I gasped. Traitors! I thought to my lips.

"Open your eyes."

I tried to swallow and forced my lids open.

"Tell me what you want," he coaxed. His thumb stroked my bottom lip and then caressed my cheek. "If you want me to walk away, tell me. If you don't talk, then I am going to assume that you want me to stay right here and keep touching you."

Oh, I wanted that. I wanted him to touch me, but I wanted him to do it while we were alone and with no clothes on. What was wrong with me? What did this guy have that could cause my hormones to take over my rational thinking?

"Tell me, Mack, what do you want?" I would blame my next move on the seduction of his voice, not on my own raging hormones.

I leaned the last fraction of an inch into him and put my lips to his. My blood rushed through my ears like the water falling over the rocks earlier today.

His hand curled around my neck, holding me tightly to him while he deepened the kiss and pressed his body against mine. He tasted like beer and bacon, the combination so perfect for him. One of my arms wrapped around his waist while my other hand ran over his short hair and down his neck.

"Oh, excuse me!"

Drew and I jumped apart guiltily at the unwelcome intrusion and turned to see Bria there with her hand on her chest and her eyebrow arched high. "Sorry! I didn't mean to interrupt. I was heading to the bathroom." She grinned at me and stepped around us, chortling as she did so.

Drew dropped his forehead to mine. I felt him fighting for control.

"Come on. I want you to meet my friend." He grabbed my hand and pulled me out of the hallway.

114

Chapter 14 – Drew

After two games of racquetball with Rob, my body felt physically refreshed, but my mind, yeah, not so much. Even voicing my thoughts to my friend didn't seem to help.

I lifted my phone out of my gym bag after I was dressed and entered my passcode. I had a text message and hoped it was from Mack. My shoulders drooped a little when I saw it was only Jose.

O'Leary's Pub 7:00 – Mack should be there.

I typed back a thanks and glanced at my watch.

"You hungry?" I asked Rob as I stood up.

"I'm always hungry. Where are we going?" He slung his duffle over his shoulder as we walked out of the locker room.

"O'Leary's Pub."

Rob's face registered surprise, and I grinned.

"Wow, we haven't been there since we were barely legal to drink. Why there?" The door to the outside opened as we reached it, and the warm evening air rushed over us.

"It looks like some of the unit is going at seven." I scanned the parking lot, always on the lookout for anything out of the ordinary. Rob was doing the same.

"Is Mack going to be there?" He stopped beside a Chevy Camaro and pushed the button on his keys to unlock it.

"From what Jose said, she is."

"Good, then we're going. I have to check out the woman who is turning you into an idiot."

I laughed at his comment, knowing just how truthful it was.

We arrived at the pub a few minutes before seven and found a table in the corner of the bar. There were a few guys that I recognized from the station at a table near the back, but I didn't know their names.

Our pints had just been set down when Gordon and Bria walked in and went directly to the table. They never even glanced around the room. I explained to Rob who they were. Jose arrived a few minutes later, but unlike the other two, he hesitated at the entrance and scanned the room, progressing slowly after looking for threats. He saw us in the corner and nodded but didn't approach.

When he reached the table he sat so he was facing us. A few other people joined them, and we ordered our burgers. When I finished my bacon burger I was beginning to think Mack wasn't coming—until I heard Rob's low whistle.

"Now there's a woman I could take home." My neck snapped to the side, and I watched her move through the crowded tables, her light-colored denim jeans snug over her backside. The dark blue t-shirt she wore floated loosely and hung down to her hips.

"Not your home," I muttered and Rob laughed.

We watched Mack join the table and sit next to Jose. She appeared to be relaxed and had everyone laughing even before she sat down, a side to Mack I didn't exactly know. I was used to the business side of her, although I had seen her laugh and crack a joke from time to time—but to see her with windblown hair, jeans, t-shirt, and sneakers, laughing while she sipped on a beer, now that was something else.

I wanted to be sitting beside her so I could hear her laughter, see the excitement of life in her face, and listen to her voice as she relaxed.

She took a long drink from her beer glass when her body and glass froze in place as our gazes locked. My heart beat in triple time as she lowered the glass and licked the foam off her lip.

"Holy…shit," I heard Rob whisper, and I squeezed my eyes shut to keep myself from becoming aroused, "and why haven't you taken that woman to bed yet?"

"Don't start." I could tell, even at a distance, that Mack's cheeks were red from embarrassment, and she kept her attention on her glass until Jose whispered something in her ear, and her wide eyes flashed to Rob.

The waitress brought us another round of beer and cleared off our plates. We sat and rehashed the old days while we kept an eye on the table. Every few minutes, Mack would scan the room and land on us. I saw her stop once and smile at Rob. A small little bolt of anger wound through my veins, and I wanted to give Rob a right hook when he returned the smile.

I understood the emotion for what it was and kept myself from bruising not only his face but my hand. Was I jealous? I couldn't be jealous unless I cared about her. I must have sighed out loud because Rob turned to me, "What's up?"

I shrugged, "I have no clue what to do. I don't know her very well, and the only things she knows about me are lies. But what I do know about her, I'm crazy about." I took a chug of my beer and set the glass back down with a heavy thud. "She's a strong woman, confident, but she's reserved. Everyone likes her, and damn, when she kisses me—" I shook my head.

"Does it blow your mind?" Rob stared at me expectantly.

"Yeah, it blows my mind, and I can't think straight. Whenever I'm around her, all I can think about is her safety and wanting to slam her up against the wall or bend her over her desk. Shit, I was even fantasizing about doing it on the hood of her car." I shook my head in exasperation, "When I'm not around her, I think about her constantly and worry about her. I've never dealt with this before, not even with Annabelle."

"I hear you, buddy. I had that with Julie, or at least I thought I had. I guess she didn't feel the same way since she slept with Drummond."

"Sorry about that, man. I wish I could have been there for you." I watched Mack talking to her coworkers. She appeared to be more relaxed and laughed often.

"Yeah, I wish you had been here, too. There were quite a few times I needed a partner to help let out some frustration on the court."

"Next time, I promise next time I'll be there." I followed Mack with my eyes as she stood up and moved to the other side of the bar.

"Let's hope there isn't a next time." He laughed. "So why don't you go over there and slam that little lady up against the wall?"

I dragged my eyes off her backside and turned to Rob, "You think I should go for it?"

"Dude, with the look in your eye, it's obvious you are already half in love with the woman. If you feel that way, don't let her go. Life is too short." He slapped me on the back as I stood up and moved towards her.

My hands shook ever so slightly as I approached her. The urge to scoop her up and walk out was coursing through my veins, but I fought it. "I thought you were out of town." I said loudly enough that she would hear it over the music but so that no one else would.

She smelled like fresh air and beer. The combination made my head spin. I tried to get her to look at me, but she kept avoiding eye contact with me. Even when I touched her she wouldn't turn my way, so I challenged her—and bingo!—I got what I wanted.

I nearly pushed her up against the juke box machine when she stared at my mouth. I struggled to get the words out, "The point is, you didn't call me back. Why?"

Once my body was holding her up against the wall in the hallway, I told her we weren't finished. Mixed emotions whirled in her eyes. "Drew, please."

"Please what?" I wanted her to ask for it, to tell me that I wasn't the only one who wanted this. "Please kiss you?" She hid from my scrutiny behind her lids. "Open your eyes, MacKenzie." I caressed the side of her face, her mouth parted as my thumb ran over her bottom lip, so tempting. "Open your eyes."

Her entire face glowed with passion. "Tell me what you want." I swallowed before I told her if she wanted me to walk away to just say it. I wasn't sure I could do it, but if that was what she really wanted, then I would try.

She stared at me for a few moments, waging an internal battle. "Tell me, Mack, what do you want?"

Please say me, I prayed internally.

My prayers were answered as she fell into me and wrapped herself around my body. The touch of our lips ignited a hunger that had been slowly burning. I felt the flames licking up my back as I crushed her to me.

I briefly remembered that we were in a public place and needed to put the brakes on when Bria ran into us. Somehow, I didn't think it was a coincidence. I had watched Bria sneak looks at Mack all night. She moved past us, and I tried to rein in the heady feelings that Mack elicited. I rested my forehead on hers until our breathing calmed.

"Come on. I want you to meet my friend." I grabbed her hand and pulled her out of the hallway, and I didn't care who saw me holding her hand. We were going to get past this we-work-together bullshit.

As we wound through the tables, I cast a glance over to her friends. Jose looked too satisfied. For a moment, I wondered if he might be involved. Maybe he wanted me to keep Mack out of the way. I pushed the thought to the side for future contemplation.

When we reached the table, Rob had a classic cat-that-ate-the-canary look on his face. "MacKenzie McAllister, this is my longtime friend, Rob McNeary."

"It's nice to meet you, Rob." She shook hands with him, and I felt that strange emotion again when Rob smiled into her eyes.

"A pleasure to meet you, too. Drew was just telling me about you." Mack peeked over at me. "It's the first time we have been able to hang out since he started in your unit."

She laughed, "Oh, I'm sure that has been some interesting conversation."

"Actually," he studied her face for a moment, "he didn't do you justice."

The thought of that right hook was sounding really good again. I let go of Mack's hand and slipped my arm around her waist. She leaned into me. I leered at Rob whom I could tell was holding back laughter.

Jose saved the moment by approaching us, "Hey, Drew, why don't you guys come join us at our table." I introduced Jose and Rob to each other, and we followed him to the back of the room. Jose had pulled another two chairs up to the table, and I sat on Mack's left side while Rob took a seat across from her. Names were exchanged from the guys around the table, and we quickly fell into the conversation.

Mack yawned beside me, and I took in the dark circles under her eyes. I glanced at my watch and saw it was eleven-thirty. My arm rested along the back of her seat, and I wondered if Mack would respond to it the first time she leaned back and felt it against her shoulders.

She had checked over her shoulder, seen it belonged to me, and rubbed up against my arm the slightest bit. I ran a finger along the back of her arm and saw her shiver. That was how it had been the last hour. Little teases, subtle looks that weren't so subtle.

I knew, and I was sure Mack was aware also, that everyone at the table could feel the crackling sexual tension between us. Rob must have seen Mack yawn, too, and he glanced at his watch and pushed his chair back.

"Nice meeting you all, I have to call it a night. You ready, Drew?"

Mack leaned on her elbows on the table and reached for my arm. I had been spinning my empty glass for the last thirty minutes. She looked at my watch and blinked, "Wow, it's eleven-thirty." She let my arm drop back to the table and scooted back in her seat. "It's no wonder I feel so tired."

"Come on, Mack, we'll walk you out to your car." I pulled her chair out, and we said our goodbyes to everyone else before leaving.

When we walked out the front door, I felt something flutter in my lower stomach. Was I actually nervous about saying goodnight? Geez, this woman had turned me into a wimp!

"'Night, Mack, it was good to meet you. I'm sure we'll see each other again." Rob bent down and kissed her on her cheek. She had a soft smile on her lips, and if it had grown bigger, I would have finally gotten a chance to use that right hook, but it didn't, and Rob walked away to give us privacy.

I threaded my fingers with hers and stood in front of her. "You finally going to accept there is something between us?"

She bit her lip while she thought about her answer. "Yeah, for now we can see what happens."

"Okay," I let go of her left hand and brushed her cheek with the backs of my fingers, "it's about time."

She chuckled, "Um, we have only known each other, what, a few days?"

I grinned, "Long enough." We met in the middle and shared a sweet goodnight kiss. "Get some sleep, Mack. I'll talk to you tomorrow."

"You too, Drew." She gave me another light kiss and turned to open her car door.

"Yeah, tonight, I might just be able to sleep."

She laughed and threw me a smile over her shoulder. "If your last night was anything like mine, then I know how tired you are right now."

"Oh, I have no doubt you know how I feel." I winked at her, "'Night, Mack."

I closed her door and watched while she started her car and drove out of the lot. I felt like a teenaged boy who was about to get lucky. Rob pulled up in his Camaro, and I climbed in.

I slugged him in the arm before I put my seatbelt on.

"What the hell was that for?" he yelled, rubbing his arm.

"You ever kiss her again, and I'll deck you," I growled at him.

Rob's laughter filled the interior of the car as we headed back to the gym to get my car.

Chapter 15 – Mack

How did he always manage to slide right under my skin and crawl right up close to my heart and make it beat the way it did? Did anyone else find it strange that some sexy-assed kid who was twenty-eight could be interested in someone my age?

I drove home wearing a stupid grin. Maybe I just needed to forget about the age difference and just enjoy a wild time with a hottie for a while. How long had it been since I'd had any kind of relationship?

I climbed out of the car and leaned against the cool metal door. The stars were bright, and the moon glowed almost full in the clear sky. It was almost midnight, the street behind me deserted. A dog barked off in the distance, but otherwise, silence reigned—well, until my cellphone pinged quietly in my pocket.

I pulled it out, entered my pass code, and beamed when I saw a message from Drew. *You home yet?*

Why did I feel like bouncing on the tips of my toes and dancing under the moonlight? It had to be the few beers I had consumed. At almost forty years old, I shouldn't get giddy over a text from a man. Well, I shouldn't, but I certainly did.

Yes, just got home. Standing in the driveway staring up at the stars. You home?

Lol. Ironically that was just what I was doing. Looking up at the stars and wondering what you were doing.

Well…now you know, I typed back.

Are you thinking about me? I could just imagine his eyebrow raised high on his forehead with his lopsided smile adorning his lips as he typed his message.

Nope, I replied, giggling as I did. I hit the send and then stood up straight. I had just giggled—like a teenager. Oh man, I needed counseling.

Yes, you are, he replied quickly, as if he had already expected my answer.

Lol. I'm going to bed. Goodnight Drew. I smiled as I sent the message.

You had to say that. Now I won't be able to sleep.

I laughed as I walked to the trunk of my car and took out my duffle bag. *Yes, you will. Just think about all that work you need to do tomorrow since I won't be there,* I typed the message good-naturedly, but as I sent it, a melancholy feeling washed over me, knowing I wasn't going to be there to work the case. Damn, Gary!

True. I read his reply as I unlocked my door and heard another beep, *You have a good night, I'll talk to you tomorrow, Mack.*

'Night, Drew. I stepped into my house and flipped on the front hall light. Instinct stopped me in the foyer. Something felt wrong, and the hairs on my neck rose as I slid my phone into my pocket. I heard it beep quietly in my back pocket, but I ignored it.

As I scanned the hallway and front room, I squatted and set my bag on the floor. I unzipped it as quietly as I could and stuck my hand inside to pull out my firearm. My eyes never left the area in front of me as I slipped it from the paddle holster and grasped it tightly in front of me. I flipped off the foyer light again and allowed my eyes to adjust to the darkness of the house.

I listened as hard as I could. There were no sounds, but that didn't mean someone wasn't waiting for me just out of earshot. I was glad I wore sneakers and was able to step quietly over the hardwood floors to the living room entrance. I scanned the room, my gun stretch out in front of me as I examined the dark space.

The only place to hide would be around the back side of the beige suede sofa that faced me, so I skimmed the far wall and made a wide arch around the couch—nothing.

I exited the room, stopping at the foyer to listen carefully again, but no sounds filtered to my ears. I crept slowly down the hallway to the kitchen, pulled my gun close to my chest as I reached the corner, and then sprang around the edge to extend it. I surveyed the area, nothing. I checked the short hallway off to the left that led to a powder room, and then checked the family room off in the back corner.

The first floor was empty, and nothing seemed disturbed. I returned to the main hallway, and my eyes stopped on the rear slider. I had long drapes that hung from a silver rod down to the floor. The right edge fluttered from bottom to top. I moved closer and pulled the drape back to find the sliding door open about a half inch.

Shit! Someone had been in the house, or someone was still in the house. I pushed the door closed with the back of my hand so I wouldn't leave any prints on the nickel-plated handle and turned to survey the room again. My television was still in place, so were my blue ray player and stereo. There wasn't anything else of interest down here to steal.

It was time to check upstairs. I continued quietly, once again trying to listen as hard as I could to the sounds in the house. The toilet gurgled upstairs and reminded me I had a small leak I needed to repair, later.

As I approached the stairs, I held my gun in front of me and pointed it up. I leaned my back against the railing to keep steady and slowly climbed the stairs, making sure my foot was planted firmly before adding my weight. I didn't need to slip down the stairs and break my leg.

Now that I had found my door open, the adrenaline that had been slowly climbing spiked. My blood pumped hard, and I had to focus to hear over the sound of it pulsing through my ears.

When I reached the top, I stopped. I closed my eyes and took a long slow breath to calm myself. I took the last step and spun around the corner. The hallway was dark. All four doors were as I had left them this morning, open. I approached the first one, and peeked in quickly. It was the bathroom, and the glass shower door showed me it was empty inside.

I took another two steps and peered around the corner into the guest bedroom. Nothing looked disturbed, and I stepped in and checked the other side of the bed. I even went down on one knee and peeked under the beige bed skirt, nothing.

I checked the closet as quietly as I could before I left the room. The master bedroom was next, and as soon as I entered, I knew someone had been in here. My pillows were flipped over, and the drawer to the nightstand was partially open. I glanced at my dresser and looked at my jewelry box. It didn't appear to be open. I checked the room, the closet, and the attached bathroom, but there was nobody present.

There was only one more room to check, my office. I stepped back into the hallway and walked to the end and the door of my office. The room was darker than the others, which wasn't surprising. The blinds had been open in my bedroom, letting in light from the street lamps. Normally, I kept the blinds in my office closed so I could see my computer better and not get distracted by daydreaming out the window.

I had no choice but to flip on the lights as I entered, I blinked furiously at the brightness and scanned the room.

"Son of a bitch!" I let my gun fall to my side. I wasn't a neat person when it came to my desk, but compared to what it looked like now, I could have had an award for a neat desk before. Papers were strewn everywhere over the wood surface and onto the floor. My trash can was overturned on my desk and the contents spread all over. I walked to the back side of my desk and leaned over my chair to tap the mouse with my knuckle. My screen came to life, and three screens were open: my personal email, a document folder, and my Dropbox program. I studied the screen. What were they looking for? I studied the files. What was missing?

Well, that was easy to figure out. Why did I get suspended today?

The damned court order! Had Gary broken into my house and taken the file off my computer? If it wasn't Gary, who could it have been?

Should I call this in? I glanced around the room. No, I couldn't call this in, but I could document it. I slipped my gun into the back of my jeans waistband and grabbed my cellphone out of my pocket. I snapped a few pictures and thought for a few seconds.

While I hadn't known Drew long, there was something about him that I trusted. Plus, while I was suspended, he was my eyes and ears inside the squad room. The fact that he was new meant he was unbiased and would absorb more of his surroundings.

I sent a picture via text to Drew. *Save this.*

A moment later he wrote back, *Why am I saving a picture of your messy desk?*

Funny, that is not my mess. Someone broke into my house and tossed it.

I didn't need to look at the screen to know who was calling. I just put it to my ear after pushing the button, "Yes."

"What do you mean someone broke into your house?" he asked tensely.

"What part of that don't you understand?" I tersely replied.

"Did you check the rest of your house? Are you alone?"

"Of course, I checked the house. There is no one here. They left the back slider door open when they took off."

"Anything taken?"

"Nothing worth anything, not really." I shook my head and sank down into my leather desk chair.

"What do you mean not really? What's missing, Mack?"

"I mean it doesn't look like they took any property, but they messed around with my computer and removed some files."

"Were these case files, MacKenzie?"

"Yes," I replied as I tried to take inventory of what else was in the Dropbox file.

"Was your court order in there?" His voice had picked up an added measure of tension.

"Yeah, that was the first thing I noticed missing. Why?" I swiveled back and forth in my seat for a moment as I waited for him to reply.

I heard him sigh, "Someone took all your case files from the office today. Mack, there has to be something in those phone records that someone doesn't want you to see."

So, all my case files were taken. I should have expected that since I was tossed off the case.

"Do you think the Gary broke into your house?" he asked quietly.

"I don't know. It could have been, but if he is involved in this, then he's not working alone. He could have had someone else do it."

"True." We both were lost in our thoughts for a moment. "Mack, where is the original court order?"

"It was in my case file box." I picked up the trash can and started to deposit the garbage back inside from the top of my desk.

I heard him mutter, "Damn." He blew out a heavy breath that made a deep low sound over the phone. "Are you alright? Do you want me to come over and stay there with you tonight?"

My mouth opened for a moment. I don't think so! "I'm fine, Drew. I just wanted someone else to have a copy of the picture of my desk. I'm going to send you a few more, just in case."

"Just in case what? Just in case something happens to you? I don't like the sound of that. Maybe you should come over and stay here." His words were rushed as he spoke, and I wanted to laugh, but I didn't.

"Come on, rookie hero, I'm a big girl, I can take care of myself. I'll be fine. I just thought it would be a good idea if I sent the pics to someone else so they had them."

"You sure you don't want me to come over there."

I laughed, "Nice try, Casanova, but not going to happen." I heard him laugh.

"Fine, what are you going to do?" he asked as I finished pushing the trash into my can and set it down.

"I'm going to take a shower and then go to bed. I'll figure this out tomorrow."

"Okay, promise me if anything else happens tonight, you'll call me."

I laughed again, "Go to bed, Drew, I'll be fine. I'll talk to you tomorrow."

We got off the phone a few moments later, and I sat staring at my computer. The only files that were touched were the ones that dealt with the car thefts. All the dates and times had adjusted to the moment they had been accessed, and it looked like I had missed the bad guy by about fifteen minutes.

He had probably heard my car pull up and had taken off out the back while I was staring at the stars. Maybe it was better than me coming into my home and finding someone inside it. No, that wasn't better. I would have preferred to put two into the chest of the person who had invaded my privacy and stolen my work.

I made my way to my bedroom, grabbed a t-shirt and shorts to sleep in. With my gun set on the edge of the tub, I climbed in for a quick shower, wondering who had been saved by the stars: me or the bad guy.

Chapter 16 – Drew

Like I was going to get any sleep worrying about her, yeah right. I plopped down on the couch and dialed Rob.

"I don't want to hear you whine," his voice was husky from sleep.

"I'm not calling to whine. I needed to let you know something. Mack returned home tonight and found someone broke into her house. They went through her computer and took off some files."

"I assume these files have to do with what she was suspended for today, right?" Rob sounded more awake now.

"Yeah. The first thing she noticed missing was the court order." I leaned back on the couch and scratched the top of my head.

"Is her computer still intact?" he asked as I rubbed my eye with the heel of my hand.

"I assume so. She didn't say they destroyed it, just that they took off some files, so I assume it is running."

"Give me her number." I heard him moving around.

"Why?"

"Why the hell do you think? I'm going to ask her to go out on a date, idiot!"

"Screw you, Rob." I almost wondered if he was serious.

"I'm going to call her tomorrow and see if I can check out her computer. Maybe I can get her to give it to me, and I can recover the file if they didn't wipe it."

"I could get Jose to do that. I'm pretty sure he knows how."

Rob hesitated just long enough that I knew what he was going to say even before he said it. "But, do you trust him?"

I contemplated that for a moment and remembered my early concern about him. Was he using me to keep Mack busy? Or was he really interested in seeing us hit it off? I knew he hadn't broken into her house; he was at the bar the whole time. He could be involved in all of this and have gotten someone else to do it for him while he knew we were all at the bar.

"Fine, I'll give you her number." We hung up a few minutes later and I climbed in bed, wishing my mind to quiet so I could get at least four hours of sleep before I would have to get up and deal with another day.

The alarm went off at five-thirty, I slammed my hand onto my phone and slid the button over to silence it. I had probably fallen asleep at around two-thirty: three hours of sleep. I groaned as I pushed myself up to sit on the edge of the bed.

I picked up my phone and scanned through my emails. I had one from home. I set my phone on my thigh and rubbed my eyes. I wasn't ready to read that one yet. I tried to clear the blur out of my eyesight by blinking. I stood and dropped my phone onto the bed and went to find clothes for work.

Inside the shower, I tried not to dwell on the fact that I had an email ticking in my inbox from Annabelle. Was she just giving me a heads-up on the kids, or was something wrong? She didn't normally email me when I was away—not that I was away much. I was usually close to home these days.

I finished my shower, wrapped a towel around my waist, and plopped back down on the edge of the mattress to see what she had to say. My finger hovered over the email on my screen, and I finally opened it.

Andrew – I hope you are doing well and your case is progressing. The kids miss you. Can you please try to contact them today? Do you have any idea when you will be coming home? Not that I am rushing you, I am doing well these days, but the kids do tend to wear me out and with them missing you so much, it's hard to keep them preoccupied all the time. I hope to hear from you soon, Love Annabelle.

I sighed and dropped the phone back onto the disarray of the bed before hanging my head in my hands. What the hell was I doing getting involved with Mack? Did I think that I could just pretend that I didn't have a life on the other side of the country? What an ass I was to even think such a thing when there were Alex and Andy to worry about.

I grunted to myself, slapped my palms down on my knees, and stood up to get dressed. I needed to get this case finished. With the way things were going, and now apparently Gary starting to show his hand a bit, I didn't think it would be that much longer before I could break it and turn it over to Rob.

I needed to get away from here, get away from Mack before I hurt her—shit, before I was hurt in the process, too. I already felt more for her than I should.

Finally dressed and off to work, I stopped at the local convenience store to grab a large coffee and a muffin. I needed some carb energy this morning, and a protein bar wasn't going to be enough.

As I drove into the station, I wondered how Mack was doing. Did she get any sleep last night? Had she found anything else missing? Was she alright?

My heart skipped a beat as I asked myself that last question. She had to be alright. No one would try to hurt her over this, would they? It wasn't that big of a deal, right? I slammed my fist against the steering wheel after I parked and huffed out a heavy breath of air. I didn't have a good feeling about this case.

I pulled up my text messaging on my phone and sent her a quick message asking her to let me know she was alright when she woke up. I put my phone into my pocket, grabbed my coffee and muffin, and walked into the station.

As I entered the unit, I noticed it was darker than usual. I glanced at my watch and saw it was only seven-ten. I was much earlier than normal. I put my coffee and bag down on my desk and turned to survey the room. A box was sitting under Gordon's desk. Did I have time to check it before someone came in? I scanned the corners of the room. I had never thought to check for cameras before. Now as I checked, I didn't see any in the main room.

It was now or never. I walked with purpose to his desk and squatted down beside the box and lifted the lid. It was empty. Shit! I glanced at the other boxes under his desk, but they were all about other cases. Flustered, I stood up and ran my hand over the back of my neck as I examined his desk: nothing.

I turned to look at the L.T.'s door. It was closed and most likely locked. I heard footsteps in the hallway and spun around to go back to my desk, flipping on my desk light as I arrived there. Gordon walked in just as I pulled my chair out to sit down.

"You're early, kid," he called as he flipped on the main fluorescent lights, and a buzz filled the air.

"Yeah, I couldn't sleep." I pulled the blueberry muffin out of the bag and laid it on top to pull the paper liner off it.

Gordon laughed, "What, she didn't wear you out enough to give you a good night's sleep?" He kept his back to me as he spoke, which was a good thing because my stare would have given away my anger.

I didn't even know how to respond to that. I was glad that the phone on his desk rang and that he picked it up and sat down.

My phone vibrated in my pocket, and I pulled it out to find a message form Mack, *Awake and alive. Have a good day at work. I'll talk to you later, I'm heading down to work out.*

I read the words three times and smiled to myself. How could reading that little bit make me feel better than anything else today, especially my earlier email? I fought back the frustration and remembered I never responded to Anna.

I'll touch base with you around lunch. Have a good workout. I sent the message and then opened my email to respond to Annabelle.

Anna – glad to hear you are doing well. Tell the kids I will call them tonight. Not sure how much longer, couple of weeks, maybe. I'll advise when I can, Drew.

I sent the email before I realized that I signed it Drew and not Andrew. Oops, guess I was getting used to Mack calling me Drew. Oh, well, Annabelle probably wouldn't even notice.

Jose walked into the unit as I took a bite of my muffin. He glanced at Gordon who was still on the phone and then gave me a nod as he approached my desk. He stopped in front of me and glanced over his shoulder.

"Meet me at the diner at lunch. I have something for you." He walked away as quickly as he approached and went to his desk just as Gary walked in.

Our eyes met, and he paused in front of his door, his keys in his hand as we scrutinized each other. I forced myself not to pulverize the last half of my muffin as we continued to eyeball one another. What had Mack seen in that man? How much was he involved in this whole scheme?

Gordon dropped the handset of his phone, and Gary broke off our staring contest and glanced at Gordon's desk. He ignored me when he turned back to his door and unlocked it. After he stepped inside, he closed it with a swift click, and I glanced over my shoulder at Jose who raised his eyebrows and then shook his head.

What did Jose know? Would I find that out at lunch when I met him at the diner?

Bria sauntered in a few minutes later, smiled sweetly and winked as she stopped by my desk, "Did you have a good night, Drew?"

I knew she was referring to my time with Mack, but I played it off a different way. "It was fun hanging out with everyone. Been a while since I kicked back like that and enjoyed a few drinks and a game."

"That's not what I meant, and you know it." She looked over her shoulder at Jose, who had his attention on his computer screen and a puzzled look on his face.

I waited for her to continue as I had no intention of giving her anything else.

She leaned down on my desk, "I'm glad you and Mack are hitting it off. She needs someone to help her get over Gary." Her voice was low, and I knew no one else could hear her speaking.

"Gary?" I asked as if I had no idea about that part of her life.

She looked surprised, "Yes, Gary. They were married. He divorced her a few years ago. She is still trying to get him back, has been ever since he filed the papers."

Okay, that was a lie. I knew Mack had filed. She was listed as the plaintiff on the divorce proceedings. Why was Bria lying, or didn't she know the truth that Mack was the one to divorce Gary?

"I didn't know that." I leaned back in my chair in fake surprise. I snuck a peek at Jose who obviously was tuned into our conversation and trying to not act like it.

Bria leaned a little closer, "Yeah, but he told me she's crazy, so just be careful, okay? I'd hate to see such a sweet guy get hurt."

She straightened up and I nodded. What the hell had just happened here? I thought Bria and Mack were friends. Maybe I should warn Mack not to turn her back on Bria. Was she involved in this situation with Gary? Was she involved with Gary? No, she was married, right? Shit, when had that stopped anyone?

Gordon broke me out of my stupor as Bria walked over to her desk. "Hey, kid, can you help me do a few interviews? I'd like a second set of ears on some of these."

"Yeah, sure." I swiped the crumbs from my muffin into the wastebasket, picked up my notebook and coffee cup, and joined Gordon who stood at the threshold waiting for me.

I was sort of surprised that I was working on the case since Mack was pulled off, but I'd take any part of the case that I could get. I turned to view Jose just before I walked out and he mouthed the word, one, before I nodded once and followed Gordon out the door.

Chapter 17 – Mack

I set my phone beside me and crossed my arms over my chest. I wasn't on my way to work out, I was still lying in bed, thinking. I had just fibbed to Drew so he wouldn't worry about me.

I spent most of last night listening to the settling of the house with my eyes wide open. Who had come into my house and why was that court order so damned important? I had to find a way to get my hands on that again so I could request another copy of it from the phone company. Maybe if I tried to call them and told them my fax machine was broken they would resend it.

I flipped back my covers and climbed out of bed. I knew that wasn't going to work. Without the court order to back up my request, they wouldn't so much as talk to me.

I stood in the doorway of my office and stared at my desk with my arms crossed tightly over my chest. I hated feeling like a victim.

I went down to make coffee and sat at the kitchen table, my foot tucked under my leg as I inhaled the aroma of the fresh brew and listened to the water drip into the carafe.

I could only guess now that Gary really was involved. Had he gone that rogue that he was running a chop shop? Were they collecting these cars, cutting them up, and selling them for parts? Or were they shipping the cars out whole to someplace else? What was in it for him?

My cellphone lay on the table and buzzed with a number I didn't recognize. I let it go to voicemail, not really caring who it could be.

I heard the vibration of the voicemail registering on my phone at about the same time that the coffeemaker gurgled that it was done brewing. I grabbed a mug out of my cabinet and noticed for the first time that my kitchen window wasn't locked or closed correctly. I set the mug down and leaned over my sink to get a better look.

This was how they gained access. They jimmied the lock open from the outside. The screen was missing and the window wasn't completely closed. It was about time I put in an alarm, damn it!

I searched the glass trying to ascertain if there were any fingerprints on it or the frame. I didn't see any on the inside of the glass, but without powder, I couldn't be sure. I stepped back and looked at the counter closely and then the floor. No footprints were obvious, but my counters were granite and dust prints wouldn't show up very well. My cream-colored ceramic tiles looked clean. The weather had been dry, so no mud prints on the floor. Why couldn't it have been raining last night instead of a clear sky?

I poured my coffee and went back to the table. The light blinked on my screen, and I swiped it to listen to the message. I was surprised and intrigued to hear Drew's friend calling me. I listened to the message and dialed his number back.

"Rob," he answered on the second ring.

"Hi, Rob, it's Mack. I just got your message."

"Morning, sweetheart!" he called lightly into the phone, and I smiled at his unexpected endearment. I had liked Rob right from the start last night, and seeing him and Drew chatting and joking had helped lighten the mood around the table.

"How did you get my number?" I asked him.

He laughed, "I had to beg your boyfriend to give it up."

The laughter left my voice, "He's not my boyfriend, Rob."

He laughed loudly into the phone, and I pulled it away from my ear until he quieted down, "Oh, really, who you trying to convince?"

I cleared my voice, "Um…is there something that I can do for you?"

"No, actually there is something that I want to do for you. Can you meet me for lunch?" His voice sobered as he asked.

I tilted my head, "Something you can do for me?"

"Yeah, and I'd rather speak to you in person."

"What's this about?" What could Rob want to help me with?

"Mack, trust me, come out and meet me for lunch. I'll fill you in on some of Drew's little habits."

Somehow I didn't think this was about Drew, but I took the bait anyway. "I don't think I want to know his dirty little habits."

He chuckled briefly, "I didn't say they were dirty, unless they have to do with breaking and entering."

Did Drew tell him about someone breaking into my house? He must have, why else would he throw that particular detail out there.

"Okay, maybe I do need to know about his little secrets. Where do you want me to meet you?"

"Antonio's on Third Avenue? One-thirty work for you?""Sure, I'll see you then."

He said goodbye and we hung up. I stared at my phone for a few moments wondering if I should text something to Drew, but decided not to.

I sipped my coffee and wondered what Rob knew about the case we were working on and what Drew might have told him about my house being broken into. This phone call had to have something to do with that.

I spent the next few hours going through my house, carefully looking for anything out of place or missing. I'd even checked the weather to make sure we weren't expecting rain. I wanted to get a hold of latent powder to dust my window and frame when I could. Luckily, there was no bad weather in the forecast, so a day wouldn't make a difference. Maybe I could get Bria to bring me a small dust kit.

Thinking about Bria made me dwell on last night. She had seemed especially interested in my relationship with Drew. Why? As I thought more about her, I realized that she had also been spending a lot of time with Gary, behind closed doors. Was she involved with this? Damn, why did I just get a shiver up my spine?

I took my time getting dressed around noon. The restaurant wasn't that far away and would only take me about twenty minutes to drive to. I was in the parking lot at one-twenty.

I scanned the lot but didn't see any cars that I recognized, but then again, how could I? I had no idea what Rob drove on or off duty. I climbed out of the car and headed into the restaurant.

After getting a table in the back corner, I looked over the menu for a few moments before the little bell over the door chimed, and Rob walked in. I set the menu down as he took a moment to study the room taking everyone in and making me feel like I had missed something.

He examined one man off to the side for a few moments before he crossed the room. I turned to check out the man as Rob grew closer. He was an older man dressed in old jeans and a flannel shirt. He stared out the window and appeared to be lost in thought. I dismissed him as Rob leaned down and kissed me on the cheek.

"Your thoughts?" he whispered before he stood up with a quizzical look on his face, and I must have appeared confused since he bucked his head in the direction of the old guy.

Was he asking me if I thought something of the guy? I shook my head. He turned to throw a cursory look over his shoulder at the man who sat pensively staring out the window.

He slipped into the bench seat across from me. "Ever eaten here before?"

"Yeah. Actually, I used to come here a lot when I worked the street. They treat patrol guys pretty good."

He smiled and picked up the menu.

He considered the menu for a moment as I studied him. His eyes were a hazel with a lot of yellow striations in them. I bet in the bright sunlight they might look more gold. He had a square jaw that was closely-shaved and eyebrows that were full, but not bushy.

He glanced up and grinned, "You're checking me out."

"I was not." I put the menu in front of my face, hiding the blush because that was exactly what I had been doing. Although it was not for the reason he thought I was doing it. I was trying to gauge his age. Drew and he had been friends for a long time. How had they met? How long had they known each other?

"Yes, you were, but I promise I won't tell Drew. In fact, if things don't work out with you two, you need to keep me in mind." I lowered the menu and met his direct gaze.

"How are you two friends?" I asked him and quirked my head to the side to study him. He was an attractive man, but even without Drew sitting beside him, he couldn't hold a flame to him. His shoulder shook with silent laughter as he turned his attention back to the menu.

After the waitress left us, he glanced over his shoulder again, and the man met his gaze. They watched each other for a moment and then the man stood up, dropped cash on the table, and walked out without a backwards glance.

"Why the interest in him?" I said when he turned his attention back to me.

"I wasn't sure if someone was watching you. I was parked across the street, watching the lot when you pulled in to see if anyone was following you."

I eyed him warily, "Why?"

He pulled a pen from his suit jacket pocket and wrote on a paper napkin, "Is your phone on?"

I leaned back slightly and nodded.

He glanced around the room again and wrote quickly, "Turn it off."

I inspected the serious features on his face, and took my phone out, powering it off and setting it down on the table. He slipped the napkin into his pocket.

He studied me for a moment, "Let's just say, I know that you have stumbled onto something. I don't know if your phone is bugged; that's why I had you turn it off. If it doesn't have power, it can't transmit."

"Why do you think my phone might be bugged?"

He waited to answer until the waitress had dropped off our soft drinks. After pulling the paper off his straw, he took a sip and met my wary stare.

"Drew told me about your house being broken into and what was taken. He told me about the case you are working on, and how he is concerned about what is going on, especially with you."

I shrugged and scanned the room, "So, it's just a case." I sure as hell didn't know if I could trust him. Yeah, he might be a fed, but I didn't know anything about him.

"It's more than just your average case, and you know it," he paused and focused on me. "Look, Drew is concerned about this. He's worried about you."

I pushed back from the table and sighed. "He has no reason to be worried. He doesn't even have the right to be worried," my voice came out flustered.

"What else were you missing off your computer besides your court order?" He dismissed my comment easily.

"He told you about the court order?" What the hell was Drew doing? This was my case, and now he was talking to federal agents about it. What if guys in my unit were involved? What was going to happen if the feds got messed up in this?

"Yes, he told me about the court order and about you getting kicked off the case because you applied for it and received the results."

"What else did he tell you?" I asked quietly as I watched him intently.

He contemplated me for a moment, "That he likes you."

I threw my head back and guffawed at the ceiling. "Like that has anything to do with this." I set my hand on the table and started tapping my nails.

Rob watched my fingers tap a cadence over the Formica tabletop, but didn't say anything for a long moment. "Well, it might not have anything to do with what is going on, but he does like you."

I shook my head, "I'm not here to talk to you about Drew." I stopped tapping my nails. "What is it that you think you can help me with?"

He leaned back and straightened his shoulders, "I want access to your computer. I might be able to get the document back if it was only deleted and not swiped clean."

I watched him closely, "Why?"

He stared me down, and I almost one hundred percent believed his answer. That was until at the last moment when he flicked his eyes to the side as he spoke, "I'm just trying to help you out."

What was he trying to help out? What stake did he have in this case? "Are you involved in this case?"

"No," he said the word slowly, and I had to believe him.

"Then why?"

He took a long deep breath and released it, "Because it's important to Drew, and I'd do anything to help him out."

Chapter 18 – Drew

Gordon kept me busy until almost one, and I rushed out of the station and took off to the diner to meet up with Jose. I arrived ten minutes late, but Jose was sitting in the corner booth patiently waiting for me.

He waved the waitress over, and she set a menu in front me. "Sorry I'm late. Gordon had me making a few phone calls."

"No problem. I'm not surprised. He's keeping an eye you."

I rested my elbows on the table and tried to look like I was reading the menu. "I'm sure he was told to keep his eye on the new kid."

"I know you're not who you say you are," he said quietly. I tensed but didn't look up right away. He didn't continue until I met his eyes. "If I'm right, then you are working for someone else to figure out what is going on in the unit."

"Why would you say that?" I tried to keep my hands from fisting. I had been made, but how?

He shrugged and appeared to relax a little bit. "It's my job to figure these things out." He picked up his coffee cup and took a sip. "I did some research on you."

"And?"

"And your paperwork is nice and tidy, but I don't believe it." He eyed me carefully.

I figured this was either going to be trouble or this was going to be helpful. I had to figure out which one. "Your point is?"

He grinned, "I want to help you."

I leaned back against the cracked vinyl, "How do you think you can help?"

The waitress interrupted us, and we both ordered a burger and fries before she bustled away to put in our ticket.

"I can probably get those phone records for you. I know Mack probably has the file saved on her computer at home. I've seen her save everything to her Dropbox program. If I can get a copy, I can get it sent back over and get another copy of the records."

"Why are you willing to do that?" I put my hands in my lap and wiped the dampness off my palms on my slacks.

He glanced around the diner. "Because big shit is happening in the unit, and I don't want to go down with it."

"Do you know what's going on or who is involved?" The waitress put my coffee cup down on the table, I nodded thanks to her.

"I can only assume that Gary is involved. I think Bria and Gordon might be, too, but I'm not certain of that yet. I've seen a few emails go back and forth between Gary and Bria, but they don't make sense—and maybe Will."

"You hacked into their email?" I asked, surprised.

"Among other things." He leaned forward and rested his elbows on the table. "I need to get to her Dropbox program, but I don't know her password for her computer. Can you get it from her?"

"You can hack into things, but you can't get her password?" I looked at him funny.

"Dude, she uses the most obscure passwords I have ever seen," he laughed.

I sighed, "Well, that might all be well and good, but that's not going to work."

"Why not?"

Okay, so I either had to trust him or not. What was it going to be? I studied him for a moment, and it was obvious he knew I was doing so.

"I'm on your side," he said as he waited for me to respond.

"Someone broke into her house last night and wiped those documents off her computer."

"Mierda," he muttered in Spanish and looked down at the scarred white Formica. "When?"

I shrugged, "Not sure. She found it last night when she got home. She was gone all day, so who knows."

Our burgers arrived, and we made small talk as we dug into our food.

Jose swallowed and wiped his mouth with his napkin. "Does Mack know who you are?"

I stopped chewing and met his direct gaze. "No," I said around a mouthful of food.

"Are you going to tell her?" he asked as he picked up a fry and held it in front of his mouth.

"Are you?" I threw back at him when I managed to swallow my half-chewed mouthful.

He contemplated that for a moment, "No, but I think you might want to tell her." He popped the fry in his mouth, chomped down a few times, and then continued, "She's going to be pissed if you don't."

I could just image how pissed she was going to be when this all came out. I took another bite of my burger.

"So what are you going to do now?" Jose asked. "With how Gary threw a fit about that court order, you know there has to be some incriminating evidence in it."

"Actually, I have someone working on that right now."

"Well, if there is anything that I can help with, just let me know. I'll do what I can to protect myself and Mack. I know she's not involved in whatever is going on."

"Thanks, Jose, I appreciate that, more than you know." We finished eating our lunch over idle chat about the people in the unit and if there were any others that could have been involved, but from what Jose had been able to find out, no one else appeared to be in the mix.

We finished up and headed back to the station. Gordon was in Gary's office, and Bria didn't appear to be around. I sat down and sent Mack a text.

Hey, how was your workout? I waited a few minutes, but didn't get a response. Was she away from her phone, or was there something wrong? Why did I have this gut feeling that something bad was going to happen to her?

My burger rolled in my stomach, and I wondered if there were any antacids lying around someplace. Damn, I was too young to get heartburn already.

I tried to focus on the reports from the interviews earlier this morning, but my thoughts kept drifting back to the fact that Mack hadn't returned my call yet.

At three-thirty, I was almost at my wits' end and looking for an excuse to get out of the office and head over to her house, but someone sent a call over to me that needed to be dealt with concerning a potential sexual assault. With Bria out of the office, I was the only one around to take the initial information. By the time I finished with the call, it was almost four-thirty and still no response from Mack.

I tossed my phone into my pocket and hustled out of the unit, intent on getting to her house. Just as I reached my car, my phone rang. I snagged it out of my pocket and released the pent-up air that had been in my lungs.

"Hey, did you get lost in the basement?" I asked, trying to calm my nerves.

She laughed. "No. I've been busy doing other things. Sorry I didn't see your message until a little while ago. I turned my phone off and forgot to turn it back on."

I climbed into my vehicle. "You have plans tonight?"

"No, not really," she said softly.

"Not really? What is that supposed to mean?" I put my elbow up on the door handle to hold the phone closer to my ear.

She laughed again; the sound went right to my heart, and I closed my eyes to savor the moment. "No, I was just gonna sit down and maybe watch a movie."

I smiled at the simple words she said. "Why don't I take you out to a movie?"

"Why?" she asked, and her voice sounded breathy over the phone line.

"Because I want to spend some time with you, Mack." "Alright," she finally replied a few moments later.

I couldn't keep the smile off my face. "Let me go home and change, and then I'll come over and pick you up."

"Why don't you tell me where to meet you and that way you don't have to come all the way over here? You still have to work tomorrow, right?"

"Tomorrow is Saturday, Mack, unless something comes in tonight, I'm off."

She hesitated, "I still think it would be better if I met you someplace."

I laughed, "You don't trust me."

The laughter that crossed the line from her sounded more nervous than humorous. "Why do you say that?"

"Because you obviously do not want me to come to your house. Afraid I'll try to take advantage of you?" I grinned because I knew I was right, and I heard her sputter on the phone.

"No, I know you've had a long week. I'm just trying to help you out a bit."

"Stop trying to help me out," I paused, "but if it would make you feel better, then fine, I'll meet you." While I started my car and got on the road, she pulled up the movie schedule online, and we picked a time and place.

When I hung up the phone, I felt more relaxed and excited than I had in a long time. Well, that was until my phone rang and I looked down to see Alex and Andy's picture on my screen. Damn it, I had forgotten to call the kids.

I answered the phone and spent the next twenty minutes

catching up with what was going on back west.

When I finally arrived at the movie theater, I found Mack standing by the front door. She pulled two tickets out of her back pocket as I approached her.

"I bought the tickets. I figured you could spring for the popcorn." I moved up close and personal on her. I had been waiting all day to look into her eyes again and to taste those lips.

I ran my hand around her neck and pulled her to me for a soft kiss. Her surprise was apparent as she stiffened in my hold for just a brief moment before returning the kiss.

"Give me another one of those, and I'll even buy you a box of candy," I said to her.

"Oh, a kiss for candy, huh? I think I can handle that." She stepped up on her toes and pressed her lips to mine. Fireworks went off in my head.

When the kiss ended, I glanced around and noticed some teens watching us. They were smirking and talking under their breaths. I turned away and wrapped my arm around her waist as we entered the theater.

As the previews started, I tried not to dwell on the conversation that I had had on my way home. Alex said Annabelle wasn't as well as she had implied in her message, but Alex could have been stretching the truth. Nine-year-olds tended to do that from time to time. Both Alex and Andy had asked several times when I was coming home.

I turned to look at Mack's profile. How could I go back home to what was there when I had found her? What the hell was I going to do? She turned a searching look at me, and I winked at her.

"You're hogging the popcorn, give me that," I joked. I pulled the bucket closer and pushed the conversation out of my mind so I could enjoy the precious time I did have with her.

Chapter 19 – Mack

There was nothing like a good comedy and a sexy man sitting beside you to help you unwind and forget about the bad things in life. As the movie progressed, the sexual tension increased between us. Every time our hands met in the popcorn bucket, I felt a tingle run up my arm. His leg would brush mine from time to time at the start of the movie. By the time it was over, they were joined from mid-thigh to knee.

Memories of my teenage years and making out in the dark theater were foremost in my mind until the credits started to roll.

He took the bucket from me, dropped his empty soda cup inside it, and grasped my hand as I stood up. I followed him out of the theater. We stepped outside and both of us scanned the parking lot.

"You want to take a walk? It's a nice night." I bent my neck back to look up at the sky above, the stars were sparkling and the moon was bright.

"Yes, it is," he agreed.

We wandered away from the parking lot towards a shopping strip mall that was still open. His thumb rubbed over my knuckles as we walked, and I tried not to overthink my feelings for him.

"So what did you do today?" His words were innocent, but I knew there was more to them.

"I had lunch with Rob," I responded and saw his profile stiffen from the corner of my eye.

"Yeah?"

I squeezed his hand and laughed. "Yeah. Why? You jealous?" I teased him and it brought him to a stop. He pulled me closer, taking my other hand in his, and stepped back so we were against the building and not standing in the middle of the sidewalk.

"What if I am?" He eyed me cautiously.

I threaded my fingers more tightly in his hands, "There is no reason to be jealous of him." I considered him for a moment before I spoke again, "Obviously, you trust him, and I think we need someone on the outside we can trust."

He nodded but didn't respond.

"Although," I turned and looked down the sidewalk for a moment, "I'm not sure I want the FBI involved in this." I felt his hands stiffen in mine, and I turned back to face him.

"Why not?" His facial expressions were guarded, and I tried to analyze them.

I shrugged, "I don't know. I know something is going on, but I have no idea how bad it is or who is involved. The thought of them taking over this case and maybe finding things out about the unit kind of freaks me out."

He burst out a quick laugh, "Freaks you out, huh?"

"Yeah, I've known these guys for a long time. They're like family. I don't want to think about some of them going bad."

He regarded me for a moment, "Sometimes good guys go bad. What about Gary?"

I tensed. I knew deep inside that Gary was involved. How much could I trust Drew and tell him? In my heart, I wanted to trust Drew completely, but how well did I know him? Trust wasn't easy, not after what Gary had done to me.

"I know Gary is involved," I spoke softly and tried to step back out of his reach, but he held my hands tight.

"That bothers you, doesn't it?"

"Of course it bothers me. I was married to the man for a little while. When we were divorced, I knew he was involved in things; I just thought they revolved around women and not cars."

"I know he cheated on you."

"With about a dozen women." I tried to move away again, but Drew once again held my hands tight for a moment before pulling me to him. His back rested against the beige stucco of the building.

"I'm sorry, Mack. I know you don't want to talk about that, but if you ever do, I'm here."

I rested my cheek on his chest as he wrapped his arms around my back. The thumping of his heart was comforting. Yeah, but for how long will you be here, I wondered.

I muttered a thanks and held onto him for a few more moments. A car horn blared, and we both turned to look in the direction. Drew asked, "Hey, do they have an ice cream parlor around here? I could use some mint chocolate chip."

I raised my eyebrows and looked at him, "Mint chocolate chip, huh?"

"Either that or a peanut butter chocolate concoction."

I pulled out of his embrace and took his hand. "Ah, now there is a flavor! Yeah, there is one around the other side of the strip mall." We wandered off towards the ice cream parlor and spent the rest of our evening casually talking about life in general and staying off the topics of work and the unit.

I was up early Saturday morning and put in a quick workout on my treadmill in my basement. Rob was stopping by in an hour to take a look at my computer, and I had just enough time to get in a run and to dress before he arrived.

When the doorbell rang, I was surprised to find Drew standing on the front porch with Rob. Drew took advantage of my shock and pulled me into his arms to kiss me hello. Rob muttered something under his breath behind him.

"Why are you here?" I asked when they were safely inside the foyer.

"You think I'd allow Rob to be alone in your house with you?" He quirked his eyebrow and gave me one of his smoldering grins.

"Come on, you still don't trust me?" Rob slapped him on the back.

Drew stared at him seriously, "Hell, no. Not after what you did when we were growing up."

"Hey, that was one time. Okay, two," Rob declared and held his hands out in front of him.

"Doesn't matter, that was enough."

I watched the conversation and concluded that at some point, there must have been a confrontation about another woman or two between them. I'd have to ask Drew about that later.

"You guys want coffee?" I turned to head down to the kitchen. "I just put a new pot on."

They tagged behind, and I poured them both a mug before we sat down at the kitchen table. Rob set a black duffle back on the seat beside him.

He unzipped the bag and pulled out a small black plastic box. My eyes lit up, a latent kit.

He slid it over the table, "I figured you could check out your window while I take care of your computer. I'm not a crime scene guy, just another computer geek."

I grinned up at him. "Thanks."

"What window?" Drew asked.

"I noticed yesterday morning that the person who broke in entered through the kitchen window. I wanted to dust it for prints, but I didn't have access to a kit." I put my chin out towards Rob to indicate his help.

"You didn't notice anything else missing, did you?" Drew asked as he took a sip of his coffee.

"No, although someone did try to gain access to my lock box. I'm surprised they didn't just take it with them."

"What is in your lock box?" Rob asked as he dug around in his duffle bag.

I glanced guardedly between the two of them. "Just some records I needed to keep safe." There was no way I was going to explain that it contained evidence against Gary, not the kind of evidence that had anything to do with what was going on now. This was my own personal evidence to use should I need to in the future.

They both studied me for a moment, and I tried to stay as calm as I could.

We finished our coffee, and I showed Rob where my office was and left him to do his thing. Drew stayed downstairs and was inspecting the window in the kitchen when I returned.

I picked up the latent kit and walked to the sink. "What's in the lock box?" he asked without looking at me.

I was startled by his question and stared at him. "Just papers."

"Is there anything in there that could be used against Gary?" He scrutinized me as I stood with my mouth partially open.

I shook my head. "No. Just my important papers, birth certificate, social security number, divorce decree, things like that." I popped open the box and turned to open a kitchen drawer where I kept some nitrile gloves for cleaning. I pulled a pair on before I picked up the dusting brush and powder. Drew appeared to have accepted my answer, for now, and stepped back to watch me work, his arms crossed over his chest as he leaned back against the counter.

I made quick work on the inside of the window and found a partial print on the window frame. I lifted it using one of the hinge lifters. Drew glanced down over my shoulder, and I pressed the two sides together and studied it. "It could be mine."

"Or it could be someone else's," he said, and I looked over my shoulder at him. "You're going to do the outside too, right?"

"Yeah, but I'm going to need your help. Ever dusted anything before? I'm not tall enough to do the whole window."

"Yeah, I know how to dust for prints."

I pulled open my kitchen drawer and took out another pair of gloves for him. He slipped them on while I packed up the small kit and headed for my sliding door.

I watched him as he dusted the outside window; the muscles under his t-shirt moved fluidly as he reached over his head, and a craving to run my hands over them overwhelmed me. I spun around and examined my yard to clear the yearning.

It didn't work.

"Do you have a flashlight?" he asked as he studied something on the window ledge.

"Yeah," I went back inside and grabbed a small LED flashlight from my kitchen drawer. When I came back out, I handed it to him, and he shined it sideways over the area he had dusted. Even I could see the detail from where I stood two feet behind him.

"Bingo," he whispered. "These probably aren't yours, now are they?"

I shook my head andheld my breath as he attempted to lift the print. I knew how easily it was to destroy such tangible evidence. When he sealed the hinge lifter, I released the air from my lungs.

"I'll give these to Rob and see if he can find a match."

I turned around, and he pulled his gloves off after handing me the lifter. "Are you sure we should give this to him. I could just put it through our lab."

"What if someone in the lab is involved? Besides, you're on suspension. Won't they question that?"

I stared at the ground, "Yeah, I guess you're right."

We went back inside and poured another cup of coffee and sat down to wait for Rob who joined us a few minutes later.

"I mirror-imaged your drive, both of them." He set the duffle bag he had with him down on the table next to him. "Did you get anything off the window?"

I pushed the hinge lifters over the table to him, "One inside and one outside."

"Rob, can you run them and see what you come up with?" Drew asked as Rob inspected the hinge lifters.

"Good lifts. Yeah, I can do that." He slipped the lifters into an envelope and put them in his bag with the latent kit he had allowed me to borrow. "I should be able to get some results by week's end."

Chapter 20 – Drew

As much as I didn't want to leave Mack, I had already promised Rob that we would hit the gym for another round of racquetball. I told Mack I would call her later that day.

When Rob and I returned to the club, he parked and turned in his seat.

"What are you going to do about her?" he asked me out of the blue.

"What are you talking about?" I knew what he was talking about. I was just trying to come up with an answer.

He knew me too well and laughed, "You couldn't keep your eyes off her, and I could feel the electricity between you two while I was sitting at the table. You were making my hair stand on end. How are you going to go back west?"

I looked out the passenger window, "I have no choice, man. I have to go back."

"Why don't you transfer back here? You know they would take you back in a heartbeat. We need some new blood around here."

"I can't. Annabelle and the kids need me."

"Why not move them back here?" he asked after a moment.

"I can't do that. Her treatment is set up there. I can't put her or the kids through that and move them back here. Not now."

"What if she doesn't make it?" His voice was soft, but it thrust a tight feeling through my chest that burned.

I swallowed the tightness in my throat, "If she doesn't make it, then maybe I will transfer back."

He didn't say anything else, and a moment later we climbed out of the car and headed into the gym to work off some steam.

We had finished three games and were heading back to the locker room when I finally asked about Mack's computer, "Do you think you found the documents?"

He shrugged as he pushed the door open, "As long as they didn't wipe it, I'm pretty sure I can pull it out."

I followed him in and set my racket down to untie my shoes. "If you pull it off, can you get it ready to put in front of a judge again, this time under either your name or mine?" He turned, a question in his eyes. "I don't want her getting into any more trouble," I explained.

He unlocked the locker, "Actually, I think it would be better if it was coming from one of us, you more so. I think that with all that happened, the rest is going to move quicker. I'll go into the office tomorrow and try to abstract it. If I can, I could have it ready for you by Monday morning to get signed. Think you can get away long enough to meet up with a judge?"

"I'm sure I can find a way." Maybe Jose could give me an excuse to be out of the office.

"You intend on seeing Mack later today?" Rob asked as he tossed his sweaty t-shirt into his gym bag.

"I was hoping to, but I don't know what she has planned. Why?"

He shrugged, "You know, I told her if things didn't work out for you two, she should give me a chance." He raised his eyebrows at me as he stalked off to get a couple of towels for the rack.

"You did not." I stared at his retreating shoulders, trying to hold back the flashbacks his words had caused.

He grinned over his shoulder, "Oh, yes I did."

I stood up, "Why the hell would you do that?"

He tossed a towel at me, and I swiped it midair. "Hey, you're planning on going back west. You have a life out there, you said so yourself, one that needs your attention. Why should I sit back and let someone like her be alone?"

"Why are you always interested in the women I like?" I wasn't sure if he was joking or not, and I watched him carefully.

"Let's not bring Julie up in this conversation, or Annabelle either." He cut a quick look at me before he grabbed his shower bag and headed to the stalls.

"You brought it up. You stole Julie right from under my nose," I spoke to his back as I followed.

He turned to answer over his shoulder, "Yeah, and she cheated on you with me, married me and then cheated on me with another guy. No winner there. Be glad I took her off your hands."

"What about Annabelle?" I said as I walked into the stall next to him and pulled my towel from my hips. "You tried to steal her away from me, too."

I heard him laugh, "And for that, I'm glad I let you win. Too much baggage there, man."

Baggage…having cancer wasn't baggage. The kids weren't baggage either. Although what I wouldn't give to pack up all the hypothetical luggage I could and get away from it all. I hung my head. No, that's not what I wanted to do.

I wanted Annabelle to get better. I wanted the kids to be raised with a mother. Mack's face flashed in front of my eyes, and I wondered what she would think if she knew the truth.

We left the gym, and Rob dropped me off at home. I sent Mack a text message, but she didn't answer. I had to run a few errands so I gathered up my cleaning and made out a short grocery list. Maybe she would answer me, and we could grab a bite to eat, or maybe I should stop pestering her and leave her alone. What did I have to offer her? Absolutely nothing.

By dinner time, I had not heard from her and started to get worried. I dialed her number, but it went straight to voicemail. My apprehension grew as I listened to her message. Instead of leaving one, I hung up.

I jumped in my car, not sure what I would say when I arrived at her place, but knowing I needed to check up on her.

My hands gripped the steering wheel firmly as I made the turns leading to her house. When I pulled up on her street, I noticed right away that her car was gone and her house was dark. Where was she?

I pulled over and picked up my phone, dialing her number again, voicemail. Damn it. Should I sit here and wait for her to get home? She would probably be pissed if she found me sitting in front of her place, but I had to know that she was alright. I still had the feeling that she was in danger, and I didn't know why.

For two hours, I waited. It was after ten now, and no signs of her. My bladder was full, and I was tired. I turned the car back on with a snap of the wrist. In the time I had sat there, I had tried her cellphone at least seven times. It always went straight to voicemail. My tension ratcheted up, but what was I supposed to do? Nothing, mind my own business. Go home and get some sleep.

My palm struck the steering wheel, "Shit!" I put the car in gear and headed back to my stark apartment all the while thinking about how cozy Mack's place was. Her family room had been large and comfortable with a big plush couch and two lounging chairs. I had almost hoped she would come home so I could pull her down on one and kiss her senseless.

Obviously, that wasn't happening tonight. When I returned home, I called her one more time. "Mack, It's Drew. I've been trying to reach you. Can you please call me and let me know you are alright? I'm worried about you."

I hung up the phone. What would she think about my message? She had to know I cared about her. Would it bother her that I was I worried? I was beginning to feel like all I ever did was worry: worry about Annabelle, the kids, the case, and now I was worrying about a woman with whom I shouldn't even be involved.

By Sunday night, I still hadn't heard from Mack, and I was past worry and getting close to panic. I did talk to Rob, and he had been able to extract the court order. The file hadn't been wiped clean. He had the court order prepared and would get a judge ready to sign it for me on Monday.

"Have you spoken to her?" I asked Rob when we finished talking about the court order.

"No. She hasn't called?" His concern matched mine.

"No, I left her a few messages, but I haven't heard anything from her." I released a pent up breath as I leaned back on my couch.

"Don't worry about it, maybe she went back up into mountains. She said where she was there was no signal."

"Yeah, but for two days?" I shook my head at the empty room. "I just wish I knew she was alright."

"She was put on suspension, forced vacation. Maybe she decided to go away for a little while." I heard what sounded like a soda can opening over the phone, it was more likely a beer though.

"If that's the case, why didn't she tell me?"

"You're whining again, stop it," he barked into the phone, I rolled my eyes.

"Whatever. Look if you hear from her, tell her to call me." He grunted into the phone when I finished, I heard him slurp from his drink.

"If she calls me before she calls you, all bets are off, brother." I could hear the smile in his voice, and I clenched the phone harder in my hand.

"Stay away from her, Rob. I'm not kidding."

"Yeah, whatever man, go get some sleep." He disconnected the call, and I sat there staring at my cell. Was he really interested in her? When I went back west, would he stay in touch with her, maybe take her out on a date?

That thought bothered me so much I almost threw my phone at the wall. Where the hell was she?

Chapter 21 – Mack

After Rob and Drew left, I wandered around my house for a little while. I was restless, and the perfect opportunity to do something about that came in the form of a telephone call from my little sister, Cindy.

I packed a bag with clothes for a few days and jumped in the car to take the five-hour drive to her house. As I got on the road, I turned off my phone and slipped it into my console. I needed to step back and think about everything that was happening.

I rarely turned my phone off. Normally, I was always on call, but while on suspension, part of me just needed to disconnect from everything.

I spent the ride trying not to dwell on the happenings of the unit or how deeply involved Gary could be. When I wasn't mulling all that over, I fought the hungry thoughts that Drew brought to mind.

By the time I arrived at my sister's, I was more flustered than when I had left home. My two nieces, Suzie and Linda, ran out to meet me, and I squatted down to wrap my arms around them. Cindy stood on the white wraparound porch smiling, and I watched the glow in her eyes at the sight of her two children.

We were totally different in that aspect. She had always wanted to settle down and have a family. She only had two children who were six and eight, but since her childhood, having four had been her dream. Her husband, Jeff, worked for a large corporation, and the money was good. He provided well for her, and as he stepped out of the house onto the porch and put his arm behind her back, I could see the love in his eyes for his family.

Envy punched me deep in the gut. It was the first time I had ever noticed such a feeling when it came to my sister. Cindy called to the girls, and they each tugged one of my hands and dragged me to the front porch.

Cindy met me on the bottom step and wrapped her arms tightly around me, "I missed you, Macky." I laughed at her pet name for me and fought to hold back the tears that threatened to explode from my eyes the moment she pulled me to her.

When she leaned back, she kept her hands on my forearms and looked me straight in the eye, "You alright?"

I bit my lip to try to bring my emotions under control and started to nod, but she tilted her head to the side and looked at me harder. I gave her a quick shake and felt the tears pooling in the back of my eyes.

She threw her arms around me again, and I heard Jeff say something to the kids about going inside to get me a drink.

"What's going on?" she asked as she released me. I wiped at a stray tear that had fallen and sucked in a rapid breath.

"How much time do you have?" I asked as I tried to smile.

"How long are you staying? Because I have that amount of time." She rubbed my arm and pulled me up the stairs, "Come on, let's get you something to drink. I have to get the kids ready for soccer practice, and Jeff can take them while we sit and talk."

Jeff bundled the kids into his car, a BMW SUV of all things, and drove out of the driveway. All the while, I was aware that Cindy waited patiently for me to speak.

"So is this about a guy? Or work?" she asked when I finally turned my attention from the empty driveway.

We were seated on her back porch in deep floral-cushioned wicker chairs. I put my foot on the stool in front of me. "Both."

She raised an eyebrow, "Okay, so which one do we start with?"

I ran my thumb along the condensation of my lemonade glass, "They are kind of intertwined."

"Oh, damn, Mack, you aren't involved with another guy on the job, are you?"

My halfhearted shrug was all I needed to give her to make her shake her head.

She went completely still, "Please, tell me it's not Gary."

A burst of laughter flew from my throat, "Oh, hell no!"

She scrutinized me, and I peered over at her for a moment before turning to look at her neatly-manicured back yard. A vegetable garden grew in the back corner. A large wooden playset beckoned on the opposite side next to a sandbox.

My sister was so domesticated, set into her happy life, and what did I have? I had an ex-husband who was into more trouble than I could probably imagine, a house with nobody to share it with, a job that devoured my life, and off-the-chart fantasies about a kid who was twelve years younger than I was. Where the hell did I go wrong?

"I was working on a case, and it looks like some of the guys in my unit are involved."

"Seriously?" she asked quietly.

"I think Gary is dirtier than I originally thought." I studied her face as I said the words, her eyes tightened. She was the only person on this earth that knew what I had on him. She was also the only one who had seen the proof, and actually had a copy of that locked up safe for me, just in case.

"What is he involved in now, another sex ring?" The words she spoke caused the memory to sting.

"No, more like a stolen car ring," I hesitated, "at least, that's all I think it is."

"But it could be more?" She took a sip of her lemonade, and I nodded slowly. "So what does this other guy have to do with it?" Drew's face flashed into my mind, and I smiled unconsciously. Cindy giggled, and I tried to hide the smile. "Oh, do tell! The look that just came over your face was priceless."

I threw my head back and laughed, "Priceless? What the heck does that even mean?"

She grinned at me, "It's been a long time since I saw a sparkle in your eye when you thought about a man. How serious is it?"

I put my feet back on the ground and leaned forward to rest my elbows on my knees, swirling the ice in my glass. "It's not anything serious."

"Why do I think you aren't telling me the truth?"

I sighed; she knew me so freaking well. "Sometimes I wonder how we aren't twins with the way you know me." I lifted my glass and finished off the refreshing liquid in two more swallows. The glass made a loud click as I set it down on the side table.

"Yes, I know, spill. What's his name?"

I ran my hands over my face and leaned back in the cushion again. "His name is Drew, and I swear Cindy, if you saw him, you'd be awestruck like I am when he is around. He has this way of quirking his eyebrow up and giving you a lazy smile that could melt you to the ground."

"And?" she added when I stopped to relive the feeling of his smile.

"And he takes my breath away." I leaned my head back against the cushion and allowed my eyes to drift with the fluffy white clouds in the sky.

"Why do I get the feeling that you are fighting this? What's wrong with him?"

I groaned, "What's wrong with him? He's perfect! He's smart and sexy and so damned nice—but he's almost twelve years younger than I am."

Her eyes popped and mouth dropped open, "Wow, never thought of you as a cougar."

I laughed, "I'm not a cougar. Trust me. The age thing is driving me nuts, but—" I stopped and went back to staring at the sky.

"But what?" she said a few moments later.

"I don't know him that well. Like I said, he's new to the unit, like he's only been there a week. He said he's twenty-eight, but sometimes when I look at him, he seems so much older. I almost feel like I'm missing something."

"You've only known him a week? With the way you are talking, I thought you might have known him for months." She took a sip of her drink.

"I know it's crazy. I feel like I've known him a lot longer," I spoke softly.

"You do know that there is such a thing as soul mates, right?" Her left leg was pumping up and down from where it was crossed over her right.

I snorted, "I don't believe in soul mates. Do you?" I studied her as she nodded her head emphatically.

"Of course I do. Jeff's mine. I knew he was the one I needed to spend the rest of my life with in just a few weeks. Maybe you two connected quicker."

I thought about what she said but didn't want to dwell on it, "Yeah, but he's twenty-eight years old."

She was quiet for a few minutes. "Does age really mean that much? Nowadays, it doesn't seem strange for that kind of age difference."

I laughed, "I know that, but he's young enough that he needs to have a family, kids. I can't give him that."

"Wow, this is serious enough that you have thought that far?" She sounded surprised.

"No," I shook my head, "it's not serious, not really. I mean nothing has happened between us, but the thought has crossed my mind."

"If it's not serious, then why has it crossed your mind?" she asked tentatively.

I met her questioning gaze, "Because part of me wants to settle down, wishes I had started a family, but it's too late for that."

"No, it's not," she laughed. "Macky, women still have kids in their forties."

"Cin, I don't want to be sixty-five years old when I can take my kids out for their first legal drink." We both laughed.

"Have you spoken to him about this?"

I almost gave myself whiplash when she spoke those words. "Oh, hell no! He'd think I was crazy," I sputtered out.

"Why? Maybe he doesn't even want kids." She raised an eyebrow which only reminded me of the quirky way he did it. It looked a lot sexier on him.

"I doubt that. He has this niece and nephew that he talks about once in a while. He seems really close to them. I can't imagine him not wanting his own." The thought depressed me, but what was I supposed to do?

"You'll never know unless you ask him."

"I'm not going to ask him. I haven't even slept with him yet. I'm sure not going to ask him about his future plans with a wife and children." I laughed uneasily.

"But you plan to sleep with him?"

A rumble left my throat and closed my eyes, "I don't know about planning, but trust me, I've thought about it. Man, have I thought about it, and the thoughts make me feel like a dirty old woman."

Her laughter filled the air. "Then sleep with him. He's an adult; you're more than an adult."

"Gee, thanks!" I sputtered as she laughed harder.

"I'm just saying, enjoy it. Don't take it so seriously. You're in the prime of your life, take advantage of it!"

"Maybe," I said quietly.

"I'm glad you came up. How long are you planning on staying?" she changed the topic of conversation and I was glad she did, but when I remembered why I was here, I felt the frustration settle down over me.

"Well, I'm not sure. I was suspended the other day, and I have a few days off, so at least until Monday, I guess."

The shocked look on her face passed quickly. "Okay, what the heck did you do to get suspended? Wait, let me refill our glasses." She stood up and checked her watch, "Better yet, it's almost four; let's have a glass of wine."

I followed her into the house, and we spent the rest of the afternoon and evening catching up on what else was going on at work and what her family was doing.

As I sat at the dinner table, sadness wrapped around my heart as I watched the children giggle and talk over one another about their day. I had missed my chance for a young family, but could I manage to still have a happy family someday?

It wasn't until almost noon on Monday when I even thought about checking my cellphone. That was a first, but it just went to show you how much I had needed some down time. Sunday had passed in a blur of activity. With a big breakfast, two soccer games, and then a picnic with friends, the day flew by.

It felt good to unwind and not worry about work or what was going on back home, but after almost two days of being tuned out, I needed to check in and see if Drew had contacted me.

I was surprised when I found ten messages in my voicemail. Six were from Drew, two from Rob, one from Jose, and even one from Bria. Everyone was wondering where the hell I was, and Drew sounded exasperated in his last message.

I'm alive and well. I typed to him after listening to his last message.

I had barely looked through my other text messages, many of which were from Drew, when my phone rang.

"Where the hell have you been?" he practically shouted in my ear, and I pulled the phone away.

"I came upstate to visit my sister," I said calmly.

"Jesus, Mack, I've been worried sick about you." He released a flustered breath.

"I'm fine, stop worrying about me." Even though I was happy that he was worried, I didn't think he had a reason to be.

"I can't stop worrying about you." He quieted, "When are you coming home?"

I considered that for a moment. Hearing his voice and remembering the conversations I'd had with Cindy, I had the intense urge to jump in the car right at that moment and get back to him, but I wasn't going to do that.

"Probably tomorrow." I leaned against the outside of my car.

"Okay." He paused for a moment, "Are you having a good time? I didn't know you had a sister."

"I am, and I do. My two nieces are cute, and we've been having a good time." I smiled as I watched Suzie chase after a ball that her sister Linda had kicked.

"How old are they—your nieces?" he asked, and I could tell he had calmed down.

"Suzie is six, and Linda is almost eight." The ball rolled my way, and I kicked it back to them.

"Do you like kids?" His question reminded me of the other part of my conversation with my sister, and my stomach fluttered.

"Sure, I like kids, when they belong to someone else," I laughed, trying to remove the nervous feeling from my stomach.

"When they belong to someone else," he repeated, "What, you don't want kids of your own?" He sounded so serious, almost too serious. How had this conversation turned in this direction?

"I'm a little too old to be having kids," I threw back to him playfully.

"I don't think so," he said quietly.

"Look, Drew, this is not a conversation to have over the phone." I kicked at a clump of grass in front of me.

"You're right. Call me when you get back tomorrow. We can finish it then." He sounded like he was about to hang up.

"Wait! I don't think we should be having this conversation then either."

"There are some things we need to discuss, MacKenzie, and I want to do that as soon as we can."

His words put me on alert, and I instinctively looked around the area, "What things?"

"About us, about me, about where this is going." His voice was husky, and it made me shiver.

"Drew—" I started to refute what he said, but he stopped me.

"Don't, Mack. When you get home tomorrow, call me. I want to see you, and don't you dare turn your damned phone back off. I want you to stay in touch with me and let me know you are alright."

"What are you, my father?" I busted out with a laugh.

His own laughter filled my ear and traveled straight to my heart. "No, thank god, but I want to know you are alright. Is that too much to ask?"

I shook my head, not that he could see that, but I did. "Fine, I'll leave my phone on and let you know when I get back. Did Rob have any luck?" I asked just as he started to say goodbye.

"He did. I'll explain it tomorrow night. Enjoy your visit, thanks for letting me know you're okay." He paused again, and I waited to see if he was going to say anything else. "I miss you, Mack."

I smiled as I absorbed those words, "I miss you too, Drew." I pushed the end button before he could say anything else or before I could try to take back the words.

Maybe my sister was right, and I needed to just go with it for a while. Who really knew what the future held?

Chapter 22 – Drew

Sleep was overrated, and right now, I was jealous of anyone who had obtained more than three hours. I, of course, had not—not in one stretch of time anyway. The longer I went without hearing from her, the more of a mess I was.

Even Rob's taunting couldn't pull me out of the funk I was falling into, wondering where the hell she had disappeared to and if she was alright.

I was awake before the alarm sounded on Monday, dressed and ready to walk out the door an hour before I needed to. I'd checked my cellphone so many times throughout the night that I was starting to wonder if it was still working. How many times had I shut it off to make sure it was reset? Four? Five times?

I knew I wasn't the only one concerned when I received a text late from Jose asking if I had heard from her. She hadn't even touched base with him.

The really bad thing was I knew next to nothing about her. What if she had just decided to take a quick vacation and went to visit friends or family?

I didn't like not knowing. I left for work forty-five minutes early and drove past her house. The steering wheel vibrated after I hit it with the bottom of my fist when I saw her driveway still empty.

Cops had good instincts, and right now, mine were firing in all kinds of directions. I knew something was going to happen. I just didn't know what or when.

I arrived at the station a few minutes early. Jose was already at his desk, he nodded as I approached his.

"Anything?" I asked as I slowed down.

He glanced at Gary's door and shook his head. I cast a peek over my shoulder and saw the door open and his light on. He was in early. When I turned back to Jose, he shrugged his response to my unanswered question.

I put my paper coffee cup on my desk and pulled out my chair. Gary stepped out of his office, "Hey, Bradley, where's Mack?"

I forced indifference into my features and shrugged, "I don't know."

He was staring hard enough at me that I could actually feel it. I made eye contact with him and sat down. "What do you mean, you don't know? I thought you two were together."

"Sorry, sir, but I don't know what you mean." I knew exactly what he was fishing for, and I wasn't falling for it.

He cocked his head and strutted towards my desk, scrutinizing me carefully as he approached. His dress shirt tightened over his biceps as he flexed them. Was that supposed to impress me or intimidate me?

"I heard you two were seeing each other. That's not true?" He stopped at the corner of my desk, his hands hanging at his sides, his fists partially closed.

"I'm not sure what you heard, L.T., but Mack is my Sarge. That's all." I picked up a pen and flicked the button. He continued to study me.

"Yeah, right," he sputtered and spun away. "If you hear from her, tell her to call me." He threw the words over his shoulder as he reentered his office and slammed his door.

I turned to Jose, who was shaking his head. I tossed the pen onto the desk. I had to find Mack.

I rolled my chair towards his desk, "Any idea where to start looking for her?"

He spoke softly, "No, I wish I did. She hasn't tried to contact you at all?"

I shook my head, "Nothing. Does she have family anywhere? Close friends she might have gone to visit?"

"I know she has a sister that she visits sometimes, but she's never said anything about visiting friends."

"Where does her sister live?" I leaned closer to his desk.

"I don't know, but I'll see if I can find out." We heard footsteps coming down the hallway; I turned my chair back to my desk and scooted under it as Bria walked in.

"Morning, boys!" she called out happily as she sauntered around the conference table to her desk.

"Good morning, Bria," I replied as she whizzed by and winked at me. Why did that annoy me?

"Hey, Drew, where's Mack hiding?" My eyes glossed over Jose as I turned to her.

I shrugged, "Don't know. Wasn't my turn to watch her." I spun back to my desk when she gave me a dark look.

"I kind of figured things were different now. What, you two have a lovers' spat already?" She sounded catty.

"Sorry, no arguments." I shook my mouse and woke up my computer.

She hummed to her herself for a moment before she cruised back by my desk and walked into Gary's office without knocking.

When the door closed, I heard Jose ask softly, "Why does everyone want to know where she is?"

"I don't know. I was wondering the same thing." Jose's phone rang then, and before we knew it, things were business as usual in the unit.

I still glanced at my phone every few minutes to see if I had a text from her, but so far, only Rob had contacted me with a quick note that the court order was ready. Now, I had to find a way to get out of the office.

I had my chance at lunch. Gary said he was going to a meeting, and Bria was going out to do an interview with the sexual assault I had taken last Friday. Gordon was lost in his paperwork, and Jose and I said we were going out to lunch.

My phone vibrated as I climbed into my car, and I dropped my head back against the headrest for a moment when I saw her message. Relief gave way to frustration as I dialed her number.

"Where the hell have you been?" So Jose was right; she had gone to her sister's upstate. At least she was safe.

The conversation of children was a touchy subject, and I knew that as soon as we had time, we needed to talk, and seriously. There was a lot I needed to explain to her.

I grinned like a kid when she told me she missed me, and I shot a message off to Jose that I had heard from her and that she was fine. Like me, he was relieved.

Rob had things set up, and the court order was signed quickly. Rob was going to send it from his office and would let me know when the results arrived. I went back to the station feeling better than I had in two days.

The afternoon went by in a blur, and I dragged myself home. The lack of sleep from the past few days had caught up to me. When I arrived home, I sent Mack a quick message, and I was happy to see she had left her phone on and responded back for a short conversation.

I was passed out by nine o'clock and didn't wake up until my alarm went off at five the next morning.

I had a spring in my step when I entered the unit. I knew Mack was coming back today, and I couldn't wait to see her. I thought about the conversation that we needed to have, and it almost put a damper on my spirits, but I didn't let it.

I would make her understand what I was dealing with, and I would find out how she felt about me and if there was any chance for us.

Gordon walked up to my desk while I was typing a report. "You remember that footprint that Mack lifted at that burglary?"

"Yeah," I nodded as he dropped two pictures in front of me.

"It's the same tread as the bloody footprint we found at the homicide."

I studied the two pictures, "It sure looks like it."

"Now we just need to find the feet that go inside the boots."

He picked up the pictures and walked back to his desk.

That was some good evidence. If we could find that person, we would have a major lead. I knew they had put a rush on the DNA sample, so maybe that would lead us to the guy. I went back to my report.

A little after three, I received a message from Mack saying she was home. I had packed casual clothes in my car that morning, so I wouldn't have to go home and change.

I was staring at my watch, waiting for it to get closer to four, when Gary stepped out of his office and called out, "We just got a double homicide. Gordon, Drew, Jose, I need you guys to head out. It sounds pretty bad."

I stared at him. Are you kidding me? I wanted to scream.

Gordon jumped up and started grabbing things off his desk. Jose sighed, and I joined him. When we got out to the parking lot, I climbed in beside Jose and sent Mack a message.

Not sure I'm gonna make it tonight. We were just dispatched to a double homicide.

Oh, dang! Okay, let me know.

I replied that I would and slipped my phone into the holder.

On our way to the scene, we listened to the radio and the units on scene. The shooter appeared to be on the loose, and it was possible it was related to drugs. Of course, drugs, guns, jealousy, and money—that was what homicide boiled down to most often.

Rob called me just as we were pulling up. "Hey, what's up?" I said by way of answering.

"You on your way to Mack's place?"

"No, I have to go out on a double homicide." I climbed out of the car. "We just arrived on scene. Did you need something?"

"No, go take care of business. I'll catch up with you tomorrow." We hung up and for the next six hours, I was elbow-deep in investigating a crime I had no interest in investigating.

It was almost eleven when Jose dropped me off back at the station to get my car. I sent Mack a message, wondering if she would still be awake, but doubted it. When I didn't get a reply right away, I backed out of my space and headed to my apartment. I would get some sleep and pop over to see her in the morning before work.

I was just pulling down the street to my apartment when my phone rang, and I looked down to see Jose's name on the screen. "What did we forget?" I asked, feeling bone-tired after working the scene and dealing with hysterical relatives for hours.

"Where are you?" Jose's voice was abrupt.

"I'm just about home. What's wrong?" My fingers clamped around the phone as he began to speak.

"Get to Mercy General. Mack was shot tonight."

His words echoed through my head before they finally registered, and I breathed out a soft, "What?"

"I don't know the details. All I know is that she was shot. She's alive, but that's all I know."

I thanked him and did a U-turn in the middle of the road to head to the hospital. As I slowed down for a turn, I spun through my contacts to Rob's name and dialed him. It went to voicemail after four rings.

Shit!

Chapter 23 – Mack

I had a good time at my sister's, but I was glad to be on my way home. I missed the peace and quiet of my solitary life—okay, not really, but it sounded good. What I missed was Drew—more than I wanted to acknowledge.

I let him know when I arrived home and looked forward to seeing him that night. We did have things to discuss, and I finally admitted to myself that I wanted to talk about them.

When he sent me the message to say he was going to be tied up, I tried not to be disappointed, but I was. I flopped down on the couch, knowing that there was no way I would see him tonight.

My cellphone rang a few minutes later, and I smiled when I saw Rob's name. "Hello, there," I said as I answered.

"I hear you were blown off tonight." We both laughed.

"Yeah, the story of my life." I leaned back on the couch with my arm resting behind my head.

"Well, what if I take you out to dinner and keep you company for a little while. I could give you some good dirt on Drew." I could imagine the smirk on his face.

"You know what? I think I'll take you up on that offer. I wasn't expecting to be sitting around all night alone. I need to get out for a little while. Besides, it would be good to quiz you on your buddy."

His hearty laugh filled the line. "Okay, fine, use me to get to him, that's alright. Where do you want to meet?"

We decided on a place outside of town, and I went to get dressed. Wearing casual gray slacks and a light purple button-down, I climbed into my car and headed to the restaurant to meet up with Rob.

I arrived a little before seven and found him waiting in the bar for me. We had decided on a steakhouse, and it was busy for a Tuesday night, but that only added to the atmosphere in a good way.

We sat in a back booth and snacked on peanuts right out of the shells. I tossed one at Rob, and he caught it in his mouth. The second one bounced off his tooth and landed in his beer. We both burst out laughing. After we had ordered, Rob stopped talking and looked at me hard, "You really like him, don't you?"

I fought the urge to glance away and instead lifted my chin and said, "Yes."

"He's a good man, a lucky man." He grinned, and I shook my head and lobbed a peanut shell over the table at him.

"He's more like a kid," I said as I leaned up to the table.

"You know, there is a lot you don't know about him."

"And I suppose you are going to fill me in on that?" I questioned him hopefully.

He lifted his beer glass, "Sorry, that stuff has to come from him, but what I can tell you is what a sucker he was in high school."

"You knew him in high school?" I took a sip of my beer.

"Oh, yeah. Well, actually he was good friends with my little brother, Mark, all through school. They used to try and tag along with me everywhere I went."

For the next two hours, we kicked backed, stuffed ourselves, and laughed over the antics of Drew, Mark, and Rob as they grew up.

It was almost nine-thirty when Rob finally paid the bill, and we were getting ready to leave. "Hey, I have something for you."

He pulled out a stack of papers from the inside of the suit jacket pocket.

"What's this?" I asked as he slid them to me over the table.

"The court order results you were looking for." He crossed his arms on the table and leaned on his elbows as he watched me.

"You got them?" I flipped the papers around in my hands, my fingers began to tremble. "Have you looked at them?" I tried to pull my focus from the folded copy, but barely lifted my gaze for a second.

"I did and I found a few things, but I think you are probably going to find more. You know this case a lot better than I do."

"Thanks, Rob." I set the papers down on the table. I knew I should look at them, but I wasn't ready to. "I really appreciate this."

"No problem. Take them home, look over them, and if you need something else, let me know." He picked up his jacket and moved to slide out of the booth. "You ready?"

"Yeah, I'm ready." I stuffed the pages into my purse and slipped out of my seat. Rob kept his hand on my lower back as we exited the restaurant and walked to my car. When we reached it, he stood in front of me, "You're a good man, Rob. Thank you."

He tipped his head back and laughed, "For what?"

"For everything, for being Drew's friend, for being mine, for helping with this whole mess." I stepped closer and stood on tiptoes so I could put my arm around him to hug him.

It was only as he wrapped his arm around me that I heard the tires squeal and felt the piercing pressure in my back as the shot rang out.

I staggered forward against Rob and fell to the ground with his arms still wrapped around my waist. The pain in my body didn't register as fast as the look on his face did. Blood bubbled up to his lips as he rasped out his last breath.

"Rob!" I pushed off his shoulder to get up off of his chest, noticing the blood staining his light blue shirt. I gasped as pain roared through my shoulder, and I realized that I had been shot, too. I heard tires squealing towards the street, but I couldn't take my eyes off of Rob's face as a drop of blood slipped down from the side of his mouth.

"Rob!" I shouted again and heard screaming in the distance. The voice was muffled, and I yanked my cellphone out of my purse and dialed nine-one-one.

A man came to my aid and asked me if I was alright, I couldn't answer him. The pain in my back radiated through my body, and I couldn't look away from Rob.

How was I going to explain this to Drew? Oh God, Drew! I scanned around me but couldn't find my cellphone. I had made the call, but someone had taken the phone from me when I started to babble, and I didn't know where it was anymore.

Police cars showed up one after another. Medics whisked me away on a stretcher as my eyes started to grow heavy. I remembered the oxygen mask going on my face and the bright lights inside the back of the bus, and then I passed out.

When I woke up, I was lying in a hospital bed, and a nurse was taking my vitals. "Detective, how are you feeling?"

"Like I've been shot." I tried to move, but the pain burned through my shoulder and stopped me from trying again. "How bad is it?"

"It could have been much worse. It went through your shoulder. They already cleaned it and stitched you up."

She patted my arm and stepped around the bed to push a few buttons on a monitor.

"What about Rob?" I already knew the answer, but I needed to hear it.

She glanced down at the sheet for a moment, "I'm sorry. I was told he died at the scene."

I clenched my eyelids shut. Rob was dead, and I could almost guarantee it was my fault, and it was all about those damned court orders. I turned my head, "Where is my purse?"

"I think it is in that bag over there." She pointed to the large white plastic bag that was stamped *My Belongings*.

"You have some people waiting for you. Do you feel up to a visitor?" she asked as she moved around to the other side and poured me a glass of water. I gulped down a few sips from the straw and sat back, "How long am I going to be here?"

"Actually, once you feel well enough, they are going to release you. There was no major damage done, just tissue. With some rest and rehab, it will get better pretty quickly."

Thank god, I thought. I wasn't sure I would be able to handle being in the hospital overnight.

She headed towards the door, "I'll let your friends know you are awake."

Before I could ask who was out there, the door closed behind her. I found the bed controls and put myself more upright, shifting slightly to my right to avoid putting pressure on my left shoulder.

My eyes were closed, and the image of Rob lying under me on the asphalt assaulted my senses. I could hear the tires, the shot being fired, and feel the projectile entering my body. My mind swayed as I pitched forward while his body fell back, and I landed on top of him. The last burst of air as it blew from his lungs into my face and the bright crimson of the blood dripping down the side of his mouth.

I stifled a sob and gripped the sheet as if it were a lifeline.

I heard the door squeak, and my eyes popped open. Bria stood at the door, and her body language said more than her words did. "You're alive." She seemed surprised, or was that disappointment I saw in her eyes.

"Yeah, lucky me," I stuttered as my emotions surged at the thought that I was the lucky one and Rob was not.

"How are you feeling?" She moved to the edge of the bed and sat down.

"I've been better, but I guess I could be worse." I leaned my head back against the pillow. "Is Drew here?"

"No, I don't know if he knows yet. What were you doing out with his friend? I thought you were seeing Drew?" She watched me more carefully than I cared for.

"We were both stood up tonight. We decided to commiserate together, no big deal." Except he was dead, and Drew didn't know yet.

The nurse popped back into the room, "You feel up to leaving?"

I forced myself to sit up straighter. Even though the pain

threatened to make me pass out, I had to get away from here. I didn't trust Bria, and I needed to get to Drew.

"I'll help her get dressed," Bria smiled sweetly over her shoulder at the nurse before she left to get my paperwork ready.

"I'm sure I can do it by myself." I turned to put my feet on the floor and felt my body sway. Bria gripped my right arm and laughed.

"If I don't help you, you might pass out. Here let me get your clothes." She stood up and grabbed my belongings bag.

"Can you hand me my purse?" I asked as soon as her hand went inside.

She looked surprised when I asked, but pulled it out and set it beside me on the bed. Her eyes latched on to it for a second too long, and I knew she had an interest in what was possibly inside.

As much as I hated to admit it, I did need the help getting dressed, and the fact that I was furious that she had played me as a friend and was now on the wrong side, kept me upright and focused.

The focus started to fade the moment the door whooshed open and I heard Bria speak, "Give us a minute, Drew." Oh, thank God he was here. I wanted to rush into his arms, I wanted to beg him to tell me it hadn't happened, but I knew I couldn't.

Bria helped me put on the scrub top from the hospital. The paramedics had cut off my own blouse in the ambulance. When I finally gathered up the nerve to face him, I didn't expect to see so much pain in his eyes. There was fear there, too, fear for me, and it made me want to fall into his arms and weep.

He held my face with such utter care and wiped a stray tear from my cheek.

"I'm sorry," I whispered.

Chapter 24 – Drew

The adrenaline shot was like explosive lava in my veins. What the hell had she been doing? She told me she'd be home.

Did she lie to me? Was she doing something behind my back and didn't want to tell me? That was the only thing I could come up with in how she could have been shot. Damn it!

I whipped into the parking lot of the hospital, pulling into a spot as close to the emergency room door as I could, and threw my SUV in park before it was even completely stopped. The transmission rocked the vehicle back and forth at the drastic change.

I jumped out the door and slammed it behind me as I took off towards the entrance. Over my shoulder, I heard the tell-tale beeps of the locking mechanisms clicking, and I pushed my keys into my pocket.

The automatic sliding doors opened as I approached, and a blast of medicinal air burst over me. Gordon and Will stood in the corner of the waiting room, both with coffee cups in their hands. I made a beeline towards them.

"Where is she?" I asked as I grew close enough to ask without having to raise my voice too much.

"In back, she's doing alright. You okay? You look upset." Will said as he turned to study me.

"I'm fine," I tossed back and redirected my footsteps to the doors that led to the treatment area. I stopped at the window and looked at the lady behind the desk. She stared at me, and I pointed at the door. She shook her head.

"I need to get back to see Sergeant McAllister," I said as I approached her.

"I'm sorry, sir, are you family?" she asked as politely as she could, although it was obvious she was aggravated with me.

"No, I'm not family, but I need to see her."

"I'm sorry, but only family can go back." She turned to dismiss me, and I hated what I was about to do, but I had to see Mack. I glanced over my shoulder to make sure Gordon and Will couldn't see. They were still in the corner and paying no attention to me.

I slipped my hand into my pocket and pulled out a wallet. I stepped closer to her desk and lowered my voice, "Excuse me, ma'am, but I'm with the FBI, and I need to see her now. Please open the door." I flipped open my credential wallet and held it out close enough so that she could see the details.

She looked at the wallet, and then up at me. "Oh, I'm sorry. I thought you were just another one of the officers that was concerned about her. I'm sorry, sir, for everything." She had an empathetic look in her eyes that I did not understand, but right then I didn't care. I just needed to get back to Mack.

Like most emergency rooms, chaos reigned. People moved quickly, phones rang, machines beeped, and nurses and doctors bent over charts and tests. I studied the board that listed the patients and found her last name next to the number three. I started towards her room, only pausing when an orderly needed to pass by in the opposite direction with a stretcher.

The orderly had a somber look on his face, and I glanced at what he was pushing, a black body bag. A shiver raced down my spine as the image of Mack lying inside it crossed my mind. I shook the image away and moved once the stretcher was out of the way.

I found room three and didn't even think to knock before I burst in.

Mack was standing up trying to get her shirt on. Bria was helping her slip it over the bandage on her left shoulder. I cringed as I saw how big the bandage was and how painstakingly slowly she moved.

Bria's eye flashed up to mine at the interruption. "Give us a minute, Drew," she said as she pulled a light blue scrub top over Mack's head and helped her to get her arms inside the sleeves.

Mack had not turned or made any sound since I entered. I waited patiently for Bria to finish so Mack would be covered. Then I waited again while Bria adjusted a sling on Mack's arm.

Finally, Mack began to turn, and I stepped forward so that I stood right in front of her. I took in her pale face and the dark circles and noticed the red rimming her eyes and how, when she met my gaze, they filled with tears that she tried to blink back. She was always trying to be so damned tough.

I slipped my hands onto the sides of her face, pulling it up so her hair fell back away from it, and I stared at her. "MacKenzie," my voice came out husky. I wanted to kiss her, wanted to pull her into my arms and not let her go. She was alive, and suddenly, I realized how much I cared about her and how much I didn't want to lose her. I stared into her face and a tear ran from the corner of one. I wiped it away with my thumb.

"I'm sorry," she whispered as another tear rolled down her cheek.

"I thought you stayed home tonight. I can't believe you went out and did something that could have killed you. What were you thinking going out without me?"

I saw a moment of confusion roll over her face and then it cleared. "I wasn't working. You said you were tied up. My going out had nothing to do with work."

I stood straighter and studied her more closely. She wasn't showing any signs of lying to me. "Then what the hell happened?"

She inhaled deeply, but made no move to distance herself from me. I wouldn't have let her anyway.

"You were working tonight. Both Rob and I knew that, so we decided to go out to dinner together."

"Rob?" I loosened my grip on her face. "You had dinner with Rob tonight?"

"Yes," she said softly.

That single word felt like a slap. I knew they had hit it off. I even knew that Rob was interested in asking her out, but he hadn't told me he did.

I took a step back, dropping my hands to my side, "So where is he now? Why isn't he here with you?" Anger at Rob for asking her out surged through me and then doubled as I realized he had left her alone after she had been shot.

Tears filled her eyes again, and she stepped closer to me. A strange feeling crept over me; one that I didn't like.

"Rob and I went out to dinner. After we were done, he walked me to my car and someone drove by and fired several rounds at us." She looked down for a minute and then took my hand. "I was standing in front of him like I am with you, and the bullet that struck me, went through my shoulder and into his chest." Her tears ran down her cheeks unchecked, and I silently watched them, not comprehending.

She swallowed tightly and squeezed her eyes shut, causing creases to cover her forehead. I felt her hand shake, I squeezed it to encourage her to finish.

"The bullet struck his heart, Drew." She opened her eyes and looked at me. "He died instantly."

"What?" Did she just say that Rob was dead?

"I'm so sorry, Drew, there was nothing anyone could do." I dropped her hand and was thankful that her hospital bed stood behind me because I sank down onto the side, my legs suddenly weak.

"Rob's dead?"

She nodded slowly, wiping the tears off her chin before they could drip down.

My best friend was dead? How did that happen? Was it just a random act of violence?

Images of Rob and me hanging out as we grew up, of us in

college and at the FBI Academy flipped through my mind. No way. We had been in more scrapes and shootouts before; there was no way some random bullet would take him out. I stood up so quickly, Mack had to step back and wobbled on unsteady feet. I absently wondered what kind of pain medicine she was on.

"I need to see him." I started towards the door and glanced around and noticed for the first time that Bria was gone. She had left us alone to talk. I wondered when she had slipped out and what she knew about this.

"Wait. Let me go with you." She grabbed my arm and pulled me to a stop. I turned to face her.

"You don't need to do that."

She stood in front of me, her internal strength shining in her eyes, and slipped her hand onto the side of my cheek, "I want to. I want to be there for you."

I pressed my cheek into her hand for a moment, pulling on the warmth of her palm before nodding once and turning to open the door.

"I just have to get my discharge papers and then we can go down to the morgue." That final word made my stomach heave, and I swallowed the bile that attempted to rise.

I waited while she grabbed her purse off the bed and went to the counter. I stood behind her with my hand on her back as she wobbled again. She leaned into me, and I slipped my hand around her hip to pull her tighter. It felt good. It felt right to have her in my arm.

The nurse put the papers down in front of her and held them as Mack attempted to sign them one-handed.

With her copies in hand, she faced me, "You ready?"

We moved to the elevators before I could change my mind. I kept my arm around her waist, not only for my own strength, but because her body shook. We entered the elevator when it arrived, and she pushed the down button. Obviously, she knew where the morgue was. When the doors slid open after our descent, we both hesitated before we stepped forward in unison.

What was going through her mind? Had she really liked Rob?

Something close to jealousy reared its ugly head, but I pushed it aside. I couldn't be jealous of a dead person.

We walked quietly except for the staccato taps of our shoes on the hard tile floor. Noises from the basement of the hospital surrounded us, hissing and grinding came from behind closed doors. A fluorescent light flickered once ahead of us, almost like being in a horror movie. What was going to come out to get us?

Oh, wait, Mack had been shot, and Rob was dead. This was my own personal horror movie.

Mack wound us through a maze of hallways, and we finally stopped in front of a door marked with a large biohazard plaque. She knocked on the door and waited. About thirty seconds later, the door opened, and the orderly I had seen upstairs stood there looking at us.

With a sick feeling, I realized that the body he had been moving down here was probably Rob's. Damn it, and here I had been thankful that it wasn't MacKenzie inside that bag. My knees began to shake.

"This is a very close friend of Rob McNeary. He would like to see the body and do a positive identification on it for the family." Mack's professional voice was in place, and I was thankful because I wasn't sure I could have spoken just then.

"Yeah, sure, Sergeant McAllister. Come on in." He pulled the door wide so we could enter the office and reception area. Mack moved into the room ahead of me. Another door stood off to the left, and I could see harsh light coming from it. "They were just getting ready to do the autopsy. I'll let you see him before we start."

"Thank you," Mack said and reached for my hand, lacing her fingers with mine. "Are you alright? You don't have to do this," she said quietly.

"I'm alright, and I'd rather do it than have his family do it." I groaned at the reminder. "Does his family know? Oh, God." I dropped my head back and stared at the yellowed ceiling tiles. "I bet they don't. I'm going to have to go tell them."

"I'm sorry, I have no idea," she replied as the orderly stepped back into the room.

"He's all ready for you."

"Thank you," Mack said and looked at me again. "Are you sure?"

I nodded because a lump had formed in my throat. She pulled me gently towards the door, my feet on autopilot as they followed her, and we stepped into a cold, light green room. I had been in morgues before, and this one was no different: bright lights, stainless steel fixtures, large sinks, and lots of cabinets for tools. In the center of the room, a metal table stood alone, the body shrouded in a white sheet. My own body shook as I stepped closer. Someone in medical scrubs, I assumed the medical examiner, stepped forward.

"Sergeant McAllister, it's good to see you are alright. I'm not sure I could have been the one to do this if it had been you here." The older man directed his words to Mack, and I agreed with him. I don't think I could have done this for her.

"Thanks, Dr. Nickels. It was just a through and through. I'll heal, and it won't be until you are well retired that I'll be lying here." Her voice was genuine as she spoke, but I didn't look at her face. My attention was on the sheet in front of me.

"This is Drew Bradley. He is a childhood friend of Rob. He wants to make the identification so the family doesn't have to." She squeezed my hand.

"Kind thing for you to do. No matter how long I do this, I hate to see parents come in and ID their children, no matter how old they are." He reached for the edges of the sheet and pulled it down to reveal Rob's face and shoulders.

I slammed my eyes closed and swallowed the tight ball that lodged in my throat. With a deep breath that filled my lungs with antiseptic and the smell of death, I opened them again and forced myself to look down into the face of my best friend.

"That's Special Agent Robert McNeary of the FBI," I stated with a thick gravelly voice.

"Thank you. I will treat him well, and he will have a hero's funeral, I'm sure. Please tell the family that I will be able to release his body tomorrow morning."

I nodded and heard Mack say something to the guy, but I had tuned out. My brain was buzzing with memories and feelings, and I left the room alone.

Mack found me a few minutes later in the hallway. My head tilted back against the wall, my eyes closed, and my hands jammed deep in the pocket of my slacks.

She stood in front of me, and I spoke to the ceiling. "I need to go tell his parents. They need to hear this from me and not from some stranger at the Bureau."

"Do you want me to go with you?" she asked as she touched my arm. I pulled my head off the wall as if it weighed a hundred pounds. I pushed off the wall with my back and stepped close enough to pull her into my arms. Very carefully, I held her to my chest, cautious not to hit her left arm or shoulder. I ducked my face in her shoulder as she wrapped her good arm around my neck and held me tightly.

Breathing in the scent of her hair and skin, mixed with the antiseptic smell of the hospital, I finally lost it. The not so manly tears filled my eyes and spilled out. My body began to shake as the loss of my friend struck home. Mack pulled me tighter to her, her hand brushing softly over my neck and shoulders.

"Let it out, Drew," she whispered. "Let it out."

And I did. I held her there in the empty hallway with the fluorescent light above our heads blinking every now and then, and I cried like a child. Somewhere along the way, I had pulled her tighter to me, and I realized that I must be putting pressure on her shoulder, yet she had not said a word.

I composed myself and pulled back. She wiped a stray tear from under my eye and kissed me gently on my cheek. I turned my head towards her, her mouth so close to mine, and I moved the last distance to claim her lips.

It wasn't a passionate kiss, or a demanding one. It was a soft gentle kiss of which she took control.

She pulled back a moment later, smiling softly and taking my hand in hers. "Come on, let's get out of here."

We returned to the elevator, and she faced me, "Do you want

me to go with you?"

A bell dinged, and the elevator doors opened, and we stepped in. "You've been through a lot tonight, I should get you home." The doors slid closed.

"I didn't ask you to take me home. I asked you if you wanted me to go with you. That is a question that requires a yes or no response." She stood tall and stared me down.

"I don't want to let you out of my sight."

I thought I saw her lips twitch, but she didn't allow the smile to grow. Instead, she leaned back against the stainless steel wall and replied, "Then, it looks like I'm going with you."

I examined her from head to toe, "But not before I get you out of those clothes."

Her eyebrow arched up, "Um, you think now is the right time to have sex?"

I actually laughed for a moment. "While that idea has quite a lot of promise, that's not what I meant. I think it might be better if you changed out of the scrub top."

The elevator jolted to a stop, and the door opened. I noticed her cheeks were slightly pink. "Wow, did I just make you blush?" I stared at her cheeks intently as she walked past me. "I did!" I laughed out loud again.

"Yeah, whatever," she retorted and headed towards the waiting room.

Just as we entered the waiting room, my cellphone buzzed, I glanced down at it. "Excuse me, Mack, I have to take this call." I pointed over to where Gordon, Will, and Bria were waiting and watched her walk away as I lifted the phone to my ear.

"Yes," I answered.

"Andy, did you hear what happened tonight?" my supervisor, Todd asked me.

"Yes, I just identified him at the morgue." I turned my back on the group and moved towards the windows.

"I'm sorry about that, Andrew. I know you guys were close." He hesitated for a moment, "We haven't given notification yet, thought you might want to do it."

"Thank you, sir, I was just going to ask that. It would be better coming from me." I looked down at my feet, clenching my jaw, dreading the moment I would have to face his parents.

"I think it would be, yes. Do you want someone to come with you?" he asked, and I heard voices talking in the background at the other end of the line. I knew the office would be in an uproar right now. The loss of one of your guys was a hard thing to handle, no matter what time of day it was.

"No, sir, I can do it myself. Do we have any idea what happened?"

"Not at this time, but we will find out. How is the woman who was with him? She was a cop, wasn't she?"

I turned and looked over to where Mack stood, talking quietly with her co-workers. "It was Sergeant McAllister, and she is going to be fine. It went through her shoulder."

"Are you with her now?" he asked me.

"I'm at the hospital. She's talking to her coworkers," I responded.

"Alright, keep us updated on your case. If you need to take a few days off, we understand that."

"Thanks, Todd, I'll let you know how things go." I pulled the phone away from my ear after he said goodbye, slipped it into the holder on my belt, and walked to the group.

"You ready to go, Mack?" I asked as I moved closer.

Everyone turned to face me.

"Yeah, I'm ready." She started to move towards me when we heard her name being yelled from the door. I was not too happy about who was coming our way.

Chapter 25 - Mack

We all turned to see Gary rushing over. His normally-handsome face filled with anxiety. "Mack, are you alright?" He grabbed me by the shoulders. Pain lanced through me so fast I thought I might pass out. Gary let me go just as quickly as he grabbed me, but the damage was done. My body shook, and Drew put his arm around me to steady me.

Gary didn't miss the movement and practically sneered at Drew. "I'm sorry. I didn't mean to hurt you."

He tossed a look around the group. "Does someone want to tell me what the hell happened?" He put his hands on his hips and glared at us. I couldn't comprehend why he was so angry.

"I was having dinner, and I was shot in the shoulder. The bullet went through my shoulder and into the guy I was with. It killed him."

His face, usually so healthy-looking, paled, and the hardness in his jaw seemed to grow more rock solid. He scanned the area. "I'm sorry that happened to you." His feet became interesting as he avoided eye contact and shuffled for a moment. "Who was the guy you were with? I didn't know you were dating anyone," as he said the last words, he glanced at Drew.

"I wasn't out on a date, I was out with a friend, and like I have told you too many damned times before, that part of my life is none of your business." I was furious, and the anger was coming out in my words, "What should be your business is helping to find out who took a shot at me and who killed a federal agent."

"What?" he sputtered as his eyes grew in size. There was more white visible than color now. Good, he was shocked. How tempting it was to ask him right at that moment what he knew about what was happening, but I didn't.

"Robert McNeary, the guy she was having dinner with was a special agent with the FBI," Drew supplied.

"Oh, shit," he wiped a hand down over his face before regarding me with tired eyes.

"Mack, I'm so sorry." He started to reach out to me again, and I stiffened. Drew pulled me more tightly to his side.

"Don't feel sorry for me. Find the bastard that killed Drew's best friend." I looked up at Drew, "I'm ready to go."

"L.T.," Drew said as he stepped around Gary, guiding me as we left the emergency room arm in arm.

"That son of a bitch," I seethed as soon as the cool air outside his us.

"Are you alright? He grabbed you pretty hard. You don't have to go with me, Mack. I could drop you off at home."

I shook my head, "No, I'm going with you. I don't want you to be alone when you tell Rob's parents, and to be honest, I really don't want to be alone right now."

"You're not alone, Mack." He kissed the side of my head.As he drove, I tried to ignore the little jolts of pain that darted into my shoulder when he hit bumps. I must have moaned once because he apologized.

My house was dark when we pulled into the driveway, and I unlocked the door. I flipped on the entrance lights as we moved into the foyer, and I started heading towards the stairs, but halted when I began to ascend. "This is going to sound very strange, but I think I need your help to get undressed."

"I think I can do that."

"But it's only my shirt I need help with. The rest is staying on.

Got that?" I gave him a pointed look.

He let out an exaggerated sigh, "Fine, if that's all I can do, fine." He winked as he approached me. A butterfly took flight in my stomach as if set free by the movement of his eyelashes.

It's just him helping me with my shirt, nothing else, I told myself.

When I got to the top of the stairs, I turned right and went down the short hallway to my room. I flicked on the main light before moving to turn on the small table light on the nightstand. Bright lights are less romantic, right? I asked myself. Pain was so not romantic, that I knew for sure.

I walked to the closet and found another shirt to wear. I ended up pulling a button-down blouse from a hanger and walked back into my bedroom.

Drew was waiting at the threshold of the room, leaning against the door jamb, his arms crossed lightly over his chest as he inspected the room. His focus came back to me as I stopped at the side of the bed.

He stood watching me. I returned the look for a moment. My whole body was aware of him there, and if my shoulder didn't hurt so damned bad, I would have been at war with myself over what I wanted to do to the sexy man in my bedroom.

After the conversation with Rob earlier, I wanted to get to know Drew better. Thoughts of my early conversation with Rob reminded me of what we still had to do and doused the smoldering flame inside of me.

"I need help getting the sling off. It hurts to shift my arm right now, so I'll hold my arm still while you take it off."

He nodded and went to move the sling. I tried not to cringe or show the pain I felt, but I knew he saw it.

"I'm sorry, Mack, I'm being as careful as I can."

"I know. It's alright, just finish it," I said through clenched teeth.

When he removed the sling, he moved to lift the shirt. His fingertips grazed the sensitive skin on my sides and I sucked in air. He helped me to get my right arm out, and then we slowly slid the shirt off my left arm. No matter how much I hurt, standing in front of a man that I wanted awakened desire. We shared a long look, and I saw my feelings reflected in his eyes.

When the shirt was off, he looked straight at my breasts. "You need to change your bra, but I'm not sure I can help you without touching you."

"I'm sorry. This is really uncomfortable for both of us, isn't it?" I tried to keep the shake out of my voice and stepped around him to go to my dresser to find a bra that would be easy to slip into. I glanced in the mirror and realized why he suggested a new bra. The light blue material on the left side was now completely red from my blood.

My mind flashed to the scene on the sidewalk: Rob's face going from handsome and alive to surprised, pain-filled, and then peacefully dead. I shuddered at the memory and watched as Drew approached. His mirror image moved directly behind me; his eyes held mine in the reflective glass.

His hands moved to the back of my bra and unfastened the hooks. His eyes never left mine.

"It's only uncomfortable because we both want more than just this, and we can't have it right now," he said. He pulled the back of the bra open, the front went slack. My breasts weren't huge, but they filled out my C-cups nicely. Without the support of the bra, they shifted slightly lower. Thanks, Old Age.

His eyes followed the movement, and his hands slipped the strap off the right side, fully exposing my breast. He inspected it for a moment before carefully lifting the strap off the left shoulder and pulling it past the bandages. When it was off, he dropped it on the floor. His hands rested on my waist. His eyes soaked in my reflection.

He was right, I did want more. With his eyes on my body, I wanted to feel his hands moving over it, too. He shifted his hands to slide up my sides enough so that his fingertips lay just under the swell of my breasts. I sucked in another quick breath.

His face moved closer, never breaking the gaze we shared, and he placed a kiss on my right shoulder just where it met my neck. I gasped at the feeling. His left hand moved and held the weight of my breast in it, his thumb rubbing over the nipple slowly. My knees weakened, and I slouched back against him. I could feel the hardness of his erection pushed tightly against his pants as I leaned back. He kissed my neck again and released my breast. I ached to be touched again. My entire body wanted to be touched by this man.

"Someday soon, we'll finish this. When you aren't in pain and you can enjoy it, we will start where we left off," he whispered. I put my hands on the top of my dresser to help my balance and winced at the pain that ran up my arm from straightening it.

He opened a drawer and sifted through it, pulling different bras out and holding them up. I was shocked when he found the oldest and most boring bra and pulled it out.

"This one looks like it will be as comfortable as it can be." He held it out, and I laughed.

"I can't believe this is happening." I shook my head and felt his other hand leave my side. I opened my eyes to find him trying to figure out how the bra was supposed to go, and I used my right hand to lay it down on the dresser and straighten it out. I was able to get the right side on but had to wait while he shifted the left strap up.

Once it was on, I told him to hook it, and then I adjusted myself the best I could. He picked up the new blouse I had chosen and helped me to get into it.

I left it untucked because I couldn't imagine asking him to put his hand down my pants. Nope, couldn't do it. Oh, how I wanted his hands down my pants, but not right now, not when I couldn't enjoy doing the same to him.

He stepped away from me once I was dressed, his eyes trying to shutter the passion he was feeling.

"I guess we better go do this," I said and he nodded. I flipped the main light off, forgetting about the smaller one next to my bed.

We had just climbed back in his car when I glanced at the house. "I forgot to turn the lights off," I said as I looked back at my small two-story house.

Drew was backing out of the driveway and stopped halfway out.

"Do you want me to go back in and turn them off?"

"No, that's alright. I think I would rather not have the house dark when I return." I gave him a small smile.

"Why don't you sit back and close your eyes? We have a little bit of a drive." He squeezed my hand, and I laced my fingers with his and pulled his hand in my lap. I laid my head back against the headrest and fell asleep. Drew's hand squeezed mine, and I opened my eyes to see a neighborhood I didn't recognize.

"Sorry to wake you, but we are almost there."

I pulled my hand away to wipe my eyes.

"It's okay. I guess I needed a nap." I tried to stifle a yawn but didn't do so well and ended up using my hand to cover it.

"What kind of pain medication did they give you?" he asked as he slowed to make a turn.

"No idea. I didn't take it. They gave me a few pills and I put them in my pocket. I don't like pain meds, they make me feel funny." I looked out the window, it was almost one in the morning and all of the houses were dark.

"You haven't taken anything?" he asked, surprise in his voice.

"Nope," I said to the window.

"When we get done here, you are going to take some so you can get some sleep. You need it."

I shrugged and winced because I had no intention of taking any pain medication stronger then Tylenol. He could think what he wanted.

We had pulled up to a small ranch home. A light was on in the living room. The flicker of a television set could be seen through the front window.

"Aw, crap, they're up." Drew put the car in park and put his head back against the headrest.

I saw someone peek out the window. "They know we're here," I remarked.

I heard his loud exhale as he took the key out of the ignition. Very carefully, he helped me out and took my hand as we moved to the front door.

The door opened before we stepped on the porch, and a man with a sad expression on his face watched us approach. He looked like an older version of Rob.

"I was hoping it wasn't him, but we had a feeling," he said as we grew closer.

Drew and I stopped on the porch. His hand was shaking in mine.

"Drake, I'm so sorry."

Tears came to the older man's eyes, and he motioned for us to enter the house.

I followed Drew inside and waited as Drake closed the door quietly and skirted around us to the living room. A woman sat in a chair, a picture frame in her hand.

"Please, Andrew, tell me it wasn't Robbie," she said as her voice cracked.

"I'm sorry, Rose, I can't. Robbie was shot and killed tonight."

The woman stood and walked to Drew. I stepped out of the way to give them space. She cradled him in her arms, and the two of them cried. I looked at the carpet, feeling out of place. Drake joined the emotional scene as he put his arms around them both. All three of them stood crying for a man that they had obviously loved very much.

Drake pulled back, but kept his arm wrapped around his wife. "Does Mark know?"

Drew shook his head, "I don't know, but I doubt it." He glanced over his shoulder at me, "I'm sorry, I forgot to introduce MacKenzie."

"This is Sgt. MacKenzie McAllister. She was with Rob tonight when they were both shot." I expected there to be anger in their eyes that I had lived and their son had died, but there wasn't.

Rose and Drake both examined me and focused on the sling. Rose came forward and pulled me into a tender hug, "My dear, I am so very sorry. Thank goodness you weren't killed, too."

I hugged the woman gently then pulled back. "I'm so very sorry for your loss. Rob was a wonderful man."

"He was, wasn't he?" she said and wiped tears from her face. "Were you dating him long?"

"Oh no, we weren't dating. We were friends and went out to dinner. Actually, we spent the whole night talking about Drew." I pointed to Drew with a shrug of my head.

"Drew?" A confused look passed over her features, "Oh, you mean Andy. Oh, okay, well, I'm glad Rob wasn't alone when he died. I always worried about that."

I was amazed at how easily they were taking the news. Rose moved back to the chair and sank into it. It probably hadn't really hit them yet.

"We better go call Mark," Drake said to Drew as he came to my side and put his hand on my shoulder. "No, we don't wish it was you and not him. We learned long ago that this could happen. I was a cop for thirty years. It's part of the job."

I forced back the tears that threatened and nodded while I bit my lip.

"Do you mind staying here with Rose while I go with Drake to call Rob's brother?" Drew asked me.

"Not at all," I replied and moved to sit on the couch as they left the room.

"So you were shot, too? Can you tell me what happened?" Rose asked as she picked up the picture again.

"Rob and I had just finished dinner, and he walked me to my car. We were talking in the parking lot and someone fired off some shots. One went through my shoulder and struck Rob," I finished quietly.

She kept her focus on the photograph. "Did he suffer?" her voice shook as she asked.

I forced myself to say the words, "No, ma'am. He died instantly."

She nodded at the picture. "Good, at least he didn't suffer."

We were quiet for a moment.

"Is that a picture of him?" I asked.

"Yes, it's a picture of when they graduated from the academy."

She handed the frame to me, and I grasped it with my right hand and turned it so I could examine it.

I wasn't surprised to see the four men in the picture. I recognized Rob and his father right away, and there was no way I could miss Drew. I assumed the other person was Rob's brother, Mark. What surprised me was that Rob and Drew were both holding identical badges in their hands, and they weren't normal police badges.

"What academy was this?" I asked, suddenly very confused.

"The FBI Academy, of course." Yes, of course. "We were so proud of both Andy and Rob when they graduated. You know Rob waited two years for Andy to finish school before he would apply to the FBI because he wanted to go through it with him."

Andy…Drew…Academy…FBI…the words spun in my mind. He had lied to me. What the hell was an FBI agent doing pretending to be a police officer?

Wait a second, she had just said he had waited two years for Drew to graduate, but Drew was eight years younger than Rob, right?

"Rose, how old is Andy?" It sounded strange to say that name and be talking about Drew.

She appeared surprised by my question. "He's thirty-four, the same age as Mark." I handed the picture frame back to her, trying to contain my anger. This was not the place to unleash it.

Just then Drew, or Andy, or whatever his name was, came rushing back into the room. "Mack, we gotta get back to your house."

There was so much alarm on his face that, as I stood up, I completely forget about the fact that he had lied to me. "What's wrong, Drew?"

"Jose and Gordon have been trying to get ahold of you. Where's your cellphone?" He stepped closer.

"I have no idea. I haven't seen it since I called nine-one-one at the scene." I glanced at Drake as he took a position next to Drew. "What's going on?"

"MacKenzie, your house is on fire. From what it sounds like,"

Drew took a deep breath and released it, "it's pretty much totally destroyed."

Chapter 26 - Drew

I had never been so thankful for a woman to fall asleep than I was when Mack dozed off in the car. I needed a few minutes to not only get my hormones in order, but to get my mind focused on what was coming next.

Being in her bedroom and seeing her half naked and vulnerable had practically undone me. If it wouldn't have caused her pain, I would have made love to her right then. I had never wanted a woman as much as I wanted her.

I turned to the right and studied her while she slept. The red light gave me a few moments to take my eyes off the road so that I could appreciate what was beside me. How peaceful she was in her slumber, I thought. Her blonde hair was haphazardly messy around her face, but that only added to her beauty. I could have pulled my hand away from hers, but I enjoyed the feel of her slack fingers in mine. Every once in a while, I ran my thumb over the back of her soft skin, and it reminded me of our moment in the bedroom.

I finally had to push all those thoughts away and instead, brought up the image of Rob lying on the cold steel table. I wasn't sure how Drake and Rose were going to take the news. No parent should hear that their son or daughter had died before them; it wasn't natural. The thought of losing one of my own children made me weak in the knees.

I woke her up when we were close to the house. I wanted to give her enough time to get her wits about her before we arrived.

My stomach churned as I stopped in front of the small ranch house. I knew they were watching the television, had probably seen a news blurb about an agent shot. Most likely, they had attempted to call Rob and hadn't reached him. In other words, they already knew.

A few years ago, an agent had been killed in the area we were working, and Rob's phone had started ringing the minute the information hit the news. He joked about how he had to check in with the parents and his brother so they would know he was alright. No matter what we were doing, or where we were, he always answered his phone for his family.

There was little doubt in my mind that they knew.

As we approached the door, I was thankful for Mack's hand in mind. When I saw the look on Drake's face, I wanted to turn and run. I didn't want to face this—face them—with the truth.

Drake's eyes filled with tears, and I fought back the sob that wanted to tear from my chest. When Rose asked if it was Rob, I couldn't say anything more than the truth, as much as it hurt us all. For a few minutes, I forgot that MacKenzie was there as we consoled each other in the loss of such a great man.

Mack spoke about being with Rob, and guilt filled her words. I was glad that Drake tried to comfort her, even though he was the one that truly needed the comfort.

Drake and I left the women alone to go into the kitchen and call Mark. Telling him over the phone was going to be difficult, but he lived a few hours away. It was the only way to do it before word hit the street, and his name was leaked to the press.

I held the cordless phone to my ear and listened to the ring. It only rang once before Mark picked up. "Is it him?" he demanded.

"Mark, it's Andy," I said quietly.

I heard a loud thump through the earpiece. "Damn it! It was him!"

I hung my head, "I'm sorry, Mark. Yes, it was Rob." Drake put his hand on my shoulder.

"What the hell happened? What case were you working on?" he asked, his words filled with anger and pain. He would need someone to blame. Unlike his parents, he would probably try to blame Mack for what had happened.

"Rob was out to dinner with a friend. They were standing outside and someone drove by and shot them. I don't know if it is related to anything we were working on, or if it was a random act." I turned to see Drake sink onto a nearby stool.

My pocket began to vibrate and I pulled it out to see who was calling. It was Gordon, I sent it to voicemail.

"Was anyone else hurt?" he asked, and I heard a horn through the phone.

"Are you driving?" I changed the subject, afraid to bring up Mack being alive.

"Yeah, I'm on my way home. I had a feeling. I'll be there in about an hour if the stupid cars stay out of my way. Why is there so much traffic at this time of night?" He mumbled something under his breath. "How are my parents doing?"

"Taking it about as well as they can." My phone started buzzing again, Jose's name showed up on my screen this time. Something must be up. "Here, talk to your dad, I have to take another phone call."

I handed the phone to Drake, as I answered my cellphone. "What's up, Jose?"

"Please tell me Mack is with you!" he yelled into the phone, and I jerked it away from my ear. There was a lot of background noise and it sounded like a fire truck horn blowing close to him.

"Yeah, she's with me. We're in Hillsdale; we just told Rob's parents. Why, what's going on?"

I thought I heard him say, "Thank you, God," but I wasn't sure with all the noise around him.

"Look, Mack's house was just torched. Well, we think it was torched. She wasn't answering her phone, and we all thought she might have been in the house."

"What the hell are you talking about? We were just there an hour ago." I spun in a circle, confusion and concern spiked my adrenaline again.

"We aren't certain. The fire marshals haven't gotten into the house yet, but a neighbor said they saw someone throw a few Molotov cocktails in through the windows, and the house just went up in flames. It exploded, man! We think someone cut the gas line in the house before they threw the bottles."

"Please, tell me you're joking."

"Sorry, I wish I could. None of us knew if she was in the house. Her car was out front. Can you bring Mack back here?" I heard someone talking in the background, and it sounded like Jose put his hand over the mouthpiece for a moment because the sound became muffled.

"Give us a few minutes, and we'll start heading back." We talked for another few seconds and I ended the call.

Drake had hung up the phone and was observing me curiously, "What's wrong now?"

"Mack's house was just blown up." I ran my hand over my short hair and laced my fingers at the back of my neck. "Like she hasn't been through enough today."

"Could it be related to the shooting?" he asked quietly.

The thought crossed my mind as he said the words, and it put a sharp pain right through my heart. Because suddenly, I realized that the shooting might not have been random, but an attack directly on her, and Rob had died because of it.

I shook my head, "I don't know, Drake, but you can bet I'm going to find out." I put my hands down on the counter and stared at them, lost in thought. "I hate to leave you all alone, but since Mark is going to be here soon, I need to get Mack back and see what's going on."

"It's alright, Andy, we understand. You need to take care of this, and her. Is she an agent, too?" He spun the cordless phone on the counter aimlessly as he spoke.

"No, she's a local cop. I've been undercover working on

something. She doesn't know I'm an agent; she thinks my name is Drew Bradley."

He studied me for a long moment. "I think you need to tell her the truth—unless she is the one you are investigating."

I shook my head, "No, I don't think she's involved, but people in her unit are, and obviously things have just become a little bit more intense."

I turned and moved toward the living room. "Mack, we gotta get back to your house," I said as I entered and saw the confusion roll over her face as she stood.

"What's wrong, Drew?"

"Jose and Gordon have been trying to get ahold of you. Where's your cellphone?" I walked to stand in front of her.

"I have no idea. I haven't seen it since I called nine-one-one at the scene. What's going on?" She looked between me and Drake as he stood next to me.

"MacKenzie, your house is on fire, from what it sounds like," I hesitated, "it's pretty much totally destroyed."

"What?" Her brow furrowed, and she took a small step back. "What the hell are you talking about?"

I reached out and took her right arm, "Look, we have to get back. I'll explain on the way." I started to pull her towards the door but stopped abruptly and turned to Rose.

"I'm so sorry, Rose. I wish I could stay until Mark gets here, but I need to get MacKenzie back."

"No, that's alright, you go. We understand." Rose moved to Mack and put her arms around her. Mack barely registered the gesture as she looked at me in shock.

"I'm so sorry, honey, take care of yourself. Andy, take care of this young lady." She gave me a quick hug, and I hustled Mack out the door after telling Rob's mom I would be in touch very soon.

Once Mack was back in the car, I turned around and started the car moving towards her house.

"What happened?" Her voice was so low I barely heard it over the sound of the engine.

"Jose said it looked like it was torched. A witness saw someone throw something into the windows."

"I have fire alarms; it can't be that bad," she tried to sound hopeful.

"I'm not so sure about that. He said something about the gas line being cut."

"What?" she yelled from the passenger seat. "Oh, my God! Someone is trying to kill me, aren't they? And Rob was caught in the middle of it."

I turned to her; her shoulders slumped while her right hand covered her eyes.

"Mack, don't jump to conclusions. We will figure out what's going on." Just then my phone rang, and I shifted in my seat to pull it out. Drake was calling, why?

"Yeah, Drake, is something wrong?" I asked and peeked at Mack who hadn't removed her hand from her face.

"Two things: One, she knows you're an agent. Rose said something about it. Sorry, she didn't know."

I clamped my eyes shut for a fraction of a second. Damn it. I could only imagine what was going on in her mind right now. "No, that's alright, she didn't know. Tell her not to worry."

"Okay, I think with what is going on that she needs to know anyway, so maybe it was good she said something. The other thing is," he paused for a moment, "I don't think you should be taking her back there."

"Why is that?" I asked and peered over to see Mack staring out the passenger window.

"Someone tried to shoot her today, and missed. For some reason, they torched her house, probably hoping she was home recovering. I was in this business for a long time, Andy. I have a bad feeling about this. I think you should take her to a safe house."

I considered his words, and it made sense. He continued before I could respond.

"If someone is attempting to get to her, obviously they are going to have to go through you, and I don't think we could stand to lose you, too." His voice dropped, filled with emotion.

"I agree with you, Drake. It all kind of fits now. It's a smart idea. I'll call the bureau and get a place. Thanks."

He acknowledged me, and we ended the call. I pulled into a parking lot and put the car into park.

Mack turned to me. "What now?" she asked quietly, her voice devoid of any emotion.

I searched her profile and saw stark pain, physical and emotional, written all over it. I reached for her hand, but she tried to pull away. I grabbed onto it and pulled it closer, shifting in my seat so I could see her better.

"Mack, I did not lie to you on purpose."

She turned away and stared out the front window. "I don't know what you're talking about," she evaded.

"You know exactly what I'm talking about. You know I'm a federal agent. I'm sorry I couldn't tell you. I have been working undercover."

"Who were you investigating? Me?" Her emotions burst free, and anger was the first one to rear its head.

"I was investigating the unit as a whole, but I know you're not involved." I lifted my hand to push some hair behind her ear, and she flinched at my touch.

"Mack, look at me please." I understood her anger, but I needed to break through that and get to her. "Please," I begged her.

She closed her eyes tightly for a few seconds before she opened them and met my gaze. The circles under her eyes were deeper than they had been just an hour ago.

"You have to understand, I was doing my job." The expression in her eyes softened ever so slightly, and she turned her attention to her lap.

"I know," she replied softly.

"I'm not taking you back to your house."

"What? Why?" She reared back from me, trying to pull her hand free.

"Mack, I think the shooting earlier was aimed at you. Someone just burned your house down, thinking you were in it. I can't take you back. I'm afraid someone is going to realize you aren't dead and is going to try again."

If I could have taken the pain from her, I would have. Tears filled her eyes and slowly rolled down her cheeks.

"I have to keep you safe, MacKenzie," I whispered to her and brushed a few tears away from her soft skin.

"Why would someone want to kill me, Drew?"

I shook my head, "I don't know, baby, but I swear I'm gonna find out." I paused. "You understand why I can't take you back to your house, right?"

She peered out the passenger window for a long time, "Yeah, I get it, but where are we going to go?"

"I'm going to call into work, get us into a safe place. Then we will figure out what to do next."

She nodded and closed her eyes, leaning her head back on the seat. She looked broken, so extremely vulnerable, totally the opposite of her normal self. I brushed her cheek again with the back of my hand and picked up my phone.

After explaining my thoughts to my supervisor, Todd, he told me to check into a hotel for the night in a rural town about two hours north of where Mack lived and put it under my real name. They shouldn't be able to connect me with Mack, although they might pick up on my car.

He told me to make a trip to the airport and get a rental for now. It might throw someone off if they see the car parked at the airport, thinking we caught a flight. It would buy us some time.

I explained everything to Mack when I hung up the phone, and she accepted it with a silent nod as I started moving the car again.

She was either lost in her thoughts or asleep again, I wasn't sure, but she didn't move much during the drive. I parked the car in the lot at the airport and left her there while I went to get a rental. I would be a lot less recognizable than if I were with a woman who looked like she was in shock and had her arm in a sling.

Once I returned, she climbed into the new SUV that I'd rented and I grabbed two bags out of the back of my vehicle. Within a few moments, we were headed off to the hotel where my supervisor had booked us a room.

"I'm sorry." Her voice was so soft that I almost missed what she said.

"You have nothing to be sorry for." I considered what she said for a moment and realized that she was blaming herself for Rob's death. "It wasn't your fault, MacKenzie."

"If what you are thinking is correct, that bullet was meant for me, not Rob. How can I not blame myself?" Grief was palpable in her tired voice.

The more I had considered everything on the drive, the more I knew I was correct, but how was I going to get her to believe that his death was not her fault? I wasn't. It was something she was going to have to deal with on her own.

"Mack, I understand how you feel, but you aren't to blame. You're having survivor guilt, and that's normal." I reached for her hand, and she yanked it out of my reach.

"Normal? You call this normal?" she yelled from the passenger seat. "This is so very not normal!"

I didn't know how to respond, so I stayed quiet and so did she.

We pulled up to the hotel a few minutes later, and I grabbed the two bags from the back, helping Mack get out of the truck, and we headed inside.

The bright fluorescent lights on our tired eyes made us both blink furiously for a moment. I pulled out my wallet and withdrew my real driver's license. I slipped it across the counter along with a credit card. As the clerk slid it back, Mack reached for my license and picked it up.

She studied it for a moment, huffed out a breath, shook her head, and handed it back to me.

After they gave us our room cards, we headed over to the elevator and ascended to the fifth floor where our room was located.

"Sorry, we're sharing a room." I hadn't thought about telling her beforehand.

She shrugged and winced, "I figured, and right now, I don't care. I just want to lie down."

I slid the card through the key slot and pushed open the door so Mack could enter.

She practically stumbled through the doorway and walked right to the bathroom and closed the door. A few minutes later, I heard the toilet flush and the water turn on. I thought maybe she had needed time alone, and forgot that it would take her longer because of her arm. Dumb me, I should have asked if she wanted help.

The door opened, and she walked right to the bed. She kicked her shoes off and started to climb on the mattress.

"Wait," I called out, and she rolled her eyes at me.

"What?" She looked so damned tired, and the tight lines in her face told me how much pain she was in.

"I have a t-shirt you can sleep in, and I want you to take the pain medicine you have in your pocket."

"Fine on the t-shirt, no on the meds." She practically crawled off the bed, barely able to hold herself up.

Chapter 27 - Mack

"Yes, Mack. You need to get a good night's sleep." His voice was stern, and normally, I would fight being told what to do, but my mind and body were crashing. I didn't have the energy to do it.

"Fine," I muttered and stood up as he approached. He carefully helped me take the sling off and undid my shirt. Unlike earlier, there was no passion in his eyes nor urges in my head. I just wanted to get changed and go to bed. When he slipped my bra off, I barely noticed.

He put the t-shirt he had pulled out of one of the bags over my head and it filled my nose with his scent, calming me. After my shirt was changed, he slipped the sling back on me, and lifted the end of the t-shirt to help me get my pants off. They dropped to the floor, and I stepped out of them.

He pulled the covers down for me, and I felt like a small child being put to bed. On a normal day, I would have never allowed this, but at this moment, I was thankful someone was here to help guide me.

"I'll be right back. I want to get you some water." He picked up my pants and fished around in my pockets until he found the small package of medicine from the emergency room. I leaned back against the pillow, trying to find a comfortable position with my shoulder.

I heard the tap go on in the bathroom and then the sound of his feet moving towards me. I sat up and took the pills from his one hand, popping them in my mouth before taking a drink of the water. I handed him the glass and sank into the fluffy pillow.

I closed my eyes, wanting to shut everything out. I was hoping that when I opened them again, this would have all been a bad dream.

"Get some sleep, MacKenzie." He kissed my forehead, and I would have answered him, but I was already fading into the dark recesses of my mind where people didn't get shot and houses didn't get blown up.

Sometime during the night, Drew climbed into the other bed. I opened my eyes as the light tried to filter in around the heavy maroon curtains. The room was your standard boring hotel room: two queen beds, a dresser, television, desk, and small table with two chairs. I glanced at the clock on the table between our beds, 12:40 p.m.

I noticed his laptop sitting open on the desk. How long did he stay up after I fell asleep? What did he work on while I was passed out cold? Probably trying to figure out who killed his friend and why.

Grief filled me as I remembered the handsome friendly guy with whom I had enjoyed a nice dinner just last night. Was it less than twenty-four hours since my entire life had been turned upside down, and for what? What had I stumbled across that would make people want me dead? There must be something in the case I was working on, but what the hell was it?

I contemplated everything I knew about the investigation and allowed my eyes to trail over Drew, or Andy, or more correctly, Special Agent Andrew Bradley Cooper. I should have been angry with him for lying to me, but I understood what being undercover was about, so how could I really use that against him? I couldn't. Besides, he was helping me.

His face was relaxed. The furrows in his brow that normally were there while he was thinking were gone now as he rested. He looked young while he slept, but now I knew he wasn't as young as I had believed. I was thankful for that, because having lustful feelings for a man twelve years younger had played too many mind games for me. In truth, he was only six years younger than me. I could handle that.

211

Handle what? What exactly was there to handle? Nothing. He was working a case, and I was probably the easiest person to get close to. Did he want more, or was that all a ploy? I studied him, suddenly afraid that it was nothing but an investigation to him.

His cellphone rang softly, and I reached for it, trying to stop it from waking him. He shifted in his bed, but didn't open his eyes. I answered it on the second ring.

"Hello?" I said quietly into the phone.

There was a long hesitation on the other end, "I'm looking for Andy? Is this Sergeant McAllister?"

"Who is this?" They knew who I was so I had every right to ask who they were.

"This is Todd. I'm Agent Cooper's supervisor." The name on the phone matched what he said, so I relaxed.

"Yes, this is Mack. I'm sorry, Drew is sleeping. I'm not sure what time he went to bed."

"That's fine." He hesitated again, and I heard his chair creak through the phone. "We had some people from the ATF go out to your house last night. I'm sorry for what you are going through, Sergeant McAllister."

"Please call me Mack, and thank you. Did they find anything at the house?" I sat up in bed as quietly as I could, shifting so my voice traveled towards the wall behind me and away from Drew.

"Your guys weren't too happy when the ATF showed up, but they allowed us to take over since we believe Agent McNeary's death is related to this incident." I could just imagine Gary blowing a gasket when he was told the feds were taking over one of his investigations. "I am assuming I can be frank with you?" he asked.

"Yes, sir, please do."

"Someone threw three bottles of flaming liquid through your window. Before they did that, someone cut the gas line outside of the house. After they tossed the bottles inside, the last bottle they threw was against the side of the house where the gas line was. It exploded, taking most of that side of the house out. If you had been home and in your bedroom, it would have killed you immediately."

I swallowed and tried to speak but couldn't. I heard rustling behind me, but shock held me motionless.

"The neighbor told investigators they thought you were home. They said they saw someone put your car in the driveway, and there were a few lights on in the house."

"Drew and I had gone back there to change my clothes before going to see Rob's parents. I left lights on, but my car wasn't there when we left. Someone must have dropped it off for me after we left." I heard more rustling behind me. I felt the bed dip and turned to see Drew observing me.

"That's probably what happened. They assumed you were home. I'm glad you weren't. We are going to move you to a safer location. Another agent will come in and take over for Agent Cooper, and they can go over the case with you and see if they can find anything that links what he was working on with what has been happening."

"I need to go back to work," I said and stared at Drew.

"Mack, you know something or you are close to finding something. You're injured, and someone is trying to kill you. It's best if you let us handle this. Agent Cooper is capable of going back in and finishing this." His voice reminded me of a parent talking to an errant child, and it pissed me off. But deep inside, I knew he was right.

"Agent Cooper just woke up. I'll let you speak with him now."

I handed the phone to Drew and tried to throw back the cover to get out of bed. He stood up so I could get out from under the blanket and pressed the phone to his ear.

I slipped into the bathroom, trying to control my anger at being told I was basically being locked up for my own protection. I looked in the mirror and muttered an expletive. I looked like hell twice-warmed over. My hair was everywhere and in knots, my eyes bloodshot, my face pale, and the circles under my eyes made me look like Ricky the raccoon.

I found two toothbrushes on the counter, one still in plastic wrap. I tore open the plastic with my teeth. Putting the paste on one-handed was tricky, but I managed and felt a little bit better after I brushed away the morning fuzz.

When I walked back out, Andrew was sitting against the headboard of the bed in which I had slept. I stared at him as he walked to the bathroom. He was only wearing gray boxer briefs. My eyes followed the movement of his backside as it moved away from me.

Memories of the scene in my bedroom came to mind, and I plopped back down on the bed. There was a hungry feeling in my stomach that had nothing to do with food.

Drew came out of the bathroom a few moments later and climbed on the bed behind me. His hand rested on my back, and he began rubbing small circles over it. He tugged at the end of the t-shirt that I was sitting on and pulled it out from under me so he could slip his hand under the material. The warmth of his fingers sent a thrill through my body, and I closed my eyes with a sigh.

"Feel good?" his voice was still husky from sleep and didn't do anything but increase my hunger pains.

I mumbled something that was an answer but wasn't. I stretched my back like a cat and ended up wincing when I inadvertently stretched my shoulder. I grabbed it with my right hand.

"How's it feeling?" he asked as he sat up behind me. His hand now back on the outside of the shirt.

"Hurts like hell."

"Did you sleep alright?" He moved closer to me while he rubbed the back of my neck.

"I slept like the dead." His hand stilled on my neck. "I'm sorry, I shouldn't have said that." I turned to try and look at him, but all I received was an eyeful of sexy muscular legs. My hand itched to reach out and touch them.

He started rubbing my back again. "It's alright. I know what you meant."

My hand rested beside me on the mattress, and as if it had a mind of its own, it crept closer to his legs. Just a touch, my hand thought, just to see if the hair that looked so touchable, was. I made contact near his knee and felt his leg tense under my fingers. I hesitated, but then realized I didn't have to anymore. He wasn't really one of the guys in my unit. He worked for a different organization, so that rule I had for not dating guys I worked with didn't apply.

I also knew he wasn't twenty-eight years old, and six years wasn't that much of a difference with consenting adults. I rubbed my hand gently down his leg, enjoying the feel of his skin beneath the soft hair.

His circles grew a bit smaller, and he applied more pressure. It felt good, almost too good, and I was about to say something when he stopped and moved to sit up against the headboard. He looked at me and patted the bed beside him.

I didn't think about what I was doing. My only thought was how I could get as close to him as I could without hurting my shoulder. I cuddled into his side; my right shoulder tucked under his arm. If felt good to be this close, but my right hand wasn't able to move much, and I wanted to touch him. I had the urge to rip the damned sling off my arm, but I knew I would probably tear something in my arm if I did.

He held me for a few minutes, placing a kiss or two on my head. He reached down and pulled my knee it up so it lay over him, putting pressure on the full erection that strained to escape his boxers. With a finger under my chin, he lifted it so my lips were just a few millimeters away from his.

We considered each other, and I realized that we both wanted the same thing, at least at that moment we did.

"I don't know what I would have done if you had been killed Mack," he whispered.

There were no words to answer him. I closed the space between us and placed my lips on his. The kiss began gently but grew in urgency in mere seconds. I needed to taste him, needed to feel him. I wanted to feel passion and life and forget about death and destruction. I shifted and winced. Drew pulled back from the kiss.

"You have no idea how much I want you right now, MacKenzie." He pushed the hair back from my face and ran his hand down over my throat. I watched his face as his eyes followed his hand down over the t-shirt I wore. He cupped my breast through the material and squeezed gently. I pushed up into his hand.

"Yes, I do know because I want you, too."

His gaze flicked back up to mine, and I watched his blue eyes smolder with passion before his lips returned to mine.

He rolled me to my back, careful to keep the pressure off my shoulder, which allowed my hand to free itself and wrap around his back. I felt his tight muscles under my hand and yearned for more. His lips left mine and traveled to my neck, teasing, licking, kissing his way down.

He stopped when he reached the edge of the t-shirt and lifted his head. "I have an idea."

I laughed, "Yeah, I have some too, but they don't include talking." I was rewarded with one of his heart-thumping smiles and a raised eyebrow.

"We have to get out of here soon. I'm taking you to a safe house, so let's take care of two things at once and take this to the shower."

"I know I should be asking you where this safe house is, but right now, all I want to know is how hot you like your water," I said with a seductive smile.

"Doesn't matter what the temperature is, we will make it hot enough, no matter what." He moved off the bed and pulled me up by my good arm.

Before he moved further, he placed his hands on my face and kissed me so deeply that I felt lightheaded—or maybe that was from getting up so fast. No, it was his kiss, and I knew it.

He led me by the hand into the bathroom, turning the water on to warm up before helping me get the sling off. After placing it on the counter, he slowly lifted the t-shirt off of me. I held my left arm close to my stomach as he pulled me into another kiss.

His hands moved to my hips and slid under the waistband of my panties, slowly removing them. I tried to reciprocate, but it was hard pulling his boxers down with one hand with his erection getting in the way.

"Take those off," I muttered against his lips.

He smiled before he removed his own underwear. The feel of his soft hot flesh against my stomach warmed my body all over. He was right, no matter what the temperature was, we would heat it up.

He stepped away to test the water, then pulled the curtain back so I could enter. He followed right behind me and closed the curtain. I had my back to him, and he pulled my hips to his, grinding against me slowly. I let my head fall back against his shoulder. The warm water fell on my head and ran down my face and chest. His hands came up to hold my breasts, and I could imagine him watching the water slide over my skin and around his hands.

I turned my head to take his lips in mine, and he continued to touch me. My right hand went down to his leg, and I palmed the strong muscle there as his hand slid lower into the soft curls between my legs. I caught my breath as he touched me and tried to stop the shaking of need that coursed through me.

He turned me around and wrapped his arms around me tightly before he moved them down to my backside and palmed it roughly.

He lifted me then, and I wrapped my good arm around his neck while I pulled him closer to me with my legs. It didn't take much movement for him to find where he wanted to be, and he slid into me deeply the first time, his head falling back.

"Oh damn, wait." He closed his eyes and strained to control himself. When he opened his eyes again, he stared deeply into mine. "I have to put you down for a moment." He pulled out of me and slid my legs to the ground. "Stay right here."

I wondered what the hell had gotten into him to start and then stop. Please tell me he wasn't teasing me!

He stepped out of the shower, and I heard the bathroom door open. I stood under the water and allowed it to flow over me. When he returned, I heard a rustling and then the curtain zipped open. I took the moment to examine him from head to toe. The sight of his naked body alone caused my hormones to go crazy.

"I forgot protection," he said softly as he stepped back into the shower and pulled me back into his arms. "Where were we?"

I grinned at him, at least he was thinking, because the thought of him having to wear a condom had never crossed my mind. I should have been more responsible, perhaps, but the shock of the shooting, the need to feel alive after being around death, and my intense desire for Drew, drove all accountability out of my head.

He lifted me back up, and I gingerly moved my left arm so it was around his back. The warm water from the shower ran over the bandages and helped to relax my muscles. I pulled him tighter, trying not to shiver as the cold plastic from the wall behind me hit new patches of my hot skin.

He pulled me in for another kiss, sliding back to where he had been before he stopped, and started moving inside of me, going as deep as he could. I shifted my hips to accommodate him further, and we moved together like we had been doing this for years. We both hit the pinnacle at the same time, and even the pain in my shoulder did not affect the pleasure of my release mixed with his.

He leaned heavily on me, using the wall behind me as support until he gained control of his breathing and then very gently allowed me to slide down his body and back to my own legs.

He smiled and leaned his wet forehead onto mine. "You amaze me, Mack."

"The feeling is mutual," I replied and placed a small kiss on his lips.

"Are you alright? I didn't hurt you, did I?" His brow creased in a way I had gotten used to when he was questioning someone.

I wiped my hand over his forehead, "No, just the opposite." I pulled his head down to mine, kissing him again, and savored the minty taste of his toothpaste.

"We need to get your bandages off and take a look at this." He held me back from him, "Turn around. Let me work on the back side first."

With the warm water running down over the bandage, the tape was easy to pull off, but still, he did so with care. We both examined it, the wound was angry and red, the stitches dark against my pale skin. He took a bar of soap and very gently cleansed it, and then he helped me to wash my hair and body.

It had been a long time since I had taken a shower with someone, and while his help was needed, his company made it the best shower I had ever taken.

Once we were done, he helped me towel dry my hair and pulled out a clean t-shirt for me to wear.

"There is a Target around the corner, I saw it last night. I'll run down there and find some comfortable clothes for you." He handed me the small pad of paper that had the hotel's name printed on it. "Write down your sizes, shoes, too. I don't think you are going to need dress shoes for a little while."

I stared at the pad, and then my arm, "How about I tell you my sizes and you write them down."

"Oh yeah, right." He leaned over the desk and took dictation.

He left me resting on the bed, and I smirked at the ceiling. We were good together, not just as partners fighting crime, but as friends and lovers, too. I didn't want to get ahead of myself and wonder where our relationship would go, but I couldn't help but do just that for a few moments.

When he returned, I woke with a jerk at the sound of the heavy metal door clanging shut behind him. I sat up and rubbed my eyes as he dropped five large bags on the other bed.

"How long were you gone?" I glanced at the clock. It was almost four.

"I'm sorry I was gone so long. I had to check in with work and find out what was going on, and then I was a bit sidetracked shopping for you." He pointed at the bags, as if to say, See?

I chuckled, "That sure looks like a lot more than just an outfit to be comfortable in."

His face lost its humor. "I realized that you really didn't have anything. With what happened to your house, I figured you would need a few more things."

I looked at the bed and realized that what I had to my name was in those five bags, and I hadn't even paid for them. I had lost everything. I swung my legs over the side of the mattress, the jovial mood I had been in now long gone.

Chapter 28 – Drew

I searched her face and knew exactly what was going on inside that mind of hers, but I had no clue how to make it better for her. I sat on the bed, my arm wrapped around her.

She leaned into my side, resting her head on my shoulder. "There was nothing left, was there?"

"No, because of the gas leak, they had a hard time putting the fire out. It burned to the ground. I'm sorry, Mack."

She didn't speak for a few moments. Finally, she lifted her head, inhaled deeply, and released her breath. "Okay, so let's see how well you shop for a woman."

I gave her a gentle squeeze before I stood up and dumped out the bags. I had gotten her a variety of things: socks, underwear, jeans, some lounge pants, and t-shirts. I had also picked her up a lightweight jacket and two pairs of shoes: sneakers and flip flops. I had even thrown in two sports bras.She chose a package of underwear and tore it open, pulled a pair out and dropped them on the floor at her feet. I bent down and helped her pull them up. Our eyes met as I slipped them to her knees, and I stopped when I saw the expression in them.

The stark sadness that showed on her face pierced my heart, and I wanted to take that away from her, if only for a minute. I let go of the panties and allowed them to fall back to the floor as my hands skimmed up her thighs to the edge of the t-shirt she wore.

Her breath fanned over my face, my heart beat faster the closer I moved. She lifted her hand and put it behind my head, pulling my lips to hers. Kissing her was a slice of heaven. My entire body tingled, my heart thumped wildly, and my mind came up with all kinds of images that it wanted to make come true.

I ran my hands under her shirt, allowing one to slide around her back and pull her closer, while the other moved to cup her bare breast. I had made love to her only a few hours before, but at that moment, my body needed her like it needed air to breathe.

I was between her knees, and I considered yanking the shirt off of her until I remembered her shoulder. I pulled back and slowly lifted it, tossing it aside. "You are so incredibly beautiful," I said to her. I examined every inch that I could with my eyes and vowed to myself that I would touch and taste every other part of her before I was done.

I moved to kiss the column of her neck and ran my hands over her thighs; my thumbs rubbing the insides of them. I felt her tremble and knew it was not because she was chilled.

"You have too many clothes on," she said to me as she tried to pull my shirt over my head with one hand. I helped her out, but instead of taking more off, I moved back to her body, branding her chest with my lips and tongue. My hands slid closer to her hips, and then returned to her sensitive skin between her thighs, teasing her.

"Lie back," I whispered, and my lips trailed down her stomach. I spread her thighs wider. The hair tickled my nose, and I inhaled her scent, drinking her in as I tasted her. She whimpered, and the sound sent all the blood straight to my groin.

I touched and tasted her until I brought her to her breaking point. I watched her as she clenched the bedspread with her one good hand, her stomach muscles bunching as her orgasm rocked her, and then I kissed my way back up, stopping when I reached her breast.

She lifted her head. "Get your damned pants off, now!" she demanded, and I wasn't going to fight her. I leaned back and took my jeans off before moving right back to where I had been between her thighs. I teased her with the tip, and she arched her hips.

She put her hand out to me, and I kissed her fingers, pulling one into my mouth and sucking on it for a moment before pulling her up to me. She sat up and looked at me with passion-glazed eyes. "Your turn."

Before I knew what she was doing, she shoved me back, and I lost my balance and almost fell on my butt, but caught myself with my hand. She raised an eyebrow, and I moved slowly to sit on the other bed, never taking my focus off her.

She was like a tiger hunting her prey as she moved to her knees on the floor in front of me. My heart was thudding, and my erection jumped at every move she made. When she took me in hand, I growled, not sure I could handle her doing this. I needed her too much.

She used her right hand, and grasped me tightly, sliding up and down a few times before she put her lips to the head and licked. There was no way I could allow her to do this right now. I wouldn't make it two seconds. I put my hand down to stop her, and she looked up into my face.

"I won't last if you do that. I want you too badly, MacKenzie." My voice was so husky, I barely recognized it.

"Fine, lie back on the bed." She stood up, and I gazed at her, wondering what she had in store for me. "Where are your condoms?"

"In my wallet, in my jeans." I leaned up on an elbow, but she put her hand out to stop me.

"I got it." She picked up my jeans, dropped them on the bed, and dug through my pocket. When she found my wallet, she tossed it to me. I made quick work of pulling one out and putting it on.

She watched my every move before she climbed over me, straddling my hips, and I stood at attention, waiting for permission to enter. It didn't take long before she slid down, encasing me completely.

She grinned down when I opened my eyes, and I put my hands to her breasts as she moved up and down, back and forth on top of me. I knew I wouldn't have lasted with her mouth on me, but this was almost as bad, or good, no, better, and I knew I wasn't going to make it more than a few moments. I put my hands on her hips and helped to guide her, faster, deeper until we were both panting.

Our release was simultaneous, and I sat up to hold her so she wouldn't put pressure on her shoulder lying on my chest while we calmed down.

I wished that we could stay here longer, but we were already supposed to be on the road. Another agent would meet up with us at the safe house, and tomorrow morning, I would head back into the station to resume the investigation.

We finally pulled apart, and I put clean bandages on her shoulder before I helped her get dressed. We put all her stuff back in the shopping bags, and then I took two trips to put everything in the car before she came out. By the time we were on the road, I realized it was dinner time, and neither of us had eaten all day. We didn't need a repeat performance of her low blood sugar.

"What can I get you to eat? Whatever it is, it has to be something you can handle in the car because we are already running late."

She laughed, "It was worth it."

I joined her good mood, "That it was." We decided on a fast food restaurant and hit the drive thru before venturing onto the highway. While we ate, she chatted lightly about everything but what was really happening with us and with the case.

I wouldn't allow my mind to dwell on what would happen when this case concluded. My choices were limited, and I wasn't ready to talk about that yet.

When she finally spoke again, I had to bring myself back to the inside of the car and away from the city it was in on the other side of the country.

"So what happens now?" she asked.

I tightened my hand on the steering wheel and wondered if she was talking about the case or about us. "With what?" I glanced over at her.

"With me, with the case, with anything," she answered.

I paused before I replied, "Well, I'm going to get you settled, and then I have to get back to work."

She sighed, "I hate that I can't go back and help you. This was my case."

"I know, Little Miss Control Freak, but you need to stay hidden and safe." I winked at her to lessen the blow of my words.

She dropped her head back to the headrest. "Yeah, yeah, yeah, it still sucks."

She reached over and turned up the volume on the radio, letting me know she didn't want to talk anymore.

An hour later, we pulled up to a small house in the mountains, set back off of a long drive. Around the house, cameras were perched inconspicuously among the trees, so that the agents in the house knew if anyone was coming towards them.

Another vehicle was already there, and I knew it would be Chris, the agent who would stay with her while I went back to finish the job. Mack clambered out of the truck on her own and looked around.

"Nothing like being hidden in the woods," she said more to herself than to me.

I fought back a smile. "It's a nice place. You should be comfortable here and it won't be for too long, I promise."

She scrutinized me. "Don't make promises you can't keep." She turned away and walked towards the house. The front door opened and Chris held it for Mack.

I grabbed the shopping bags and headed to the cabin. Mack was already inside chatting with Chris when I entered. I set the bags down inside the door.

Chris held out his hand, "I'm sorry about Rob, man. He was an awesome guy."

I shook his extended hand, "Thanks, Chris. He was." I surveyed the inside of the house. It was a log cabin, and the interior went with the design. Heavy wooden furniture and thick rugs covered the area.

"Is everything good to go?" I asked as I moved over to the window and pulled back the heavy drapes.

"Yep, she's going to be safe here. This house is like a tank, and with motion alarms, we will know when the squirrels come our way. I've stayed out here before. It's a great set up."

I nodded and turned to Mack. She had gone to the couch and sank down. She looked tired.

"Did you get those other things I asked you for?" I turned to Chris.

"The pain meds? Yeah, I have them and enough groceries to last us a solid week."

Mack piped in, "A week?"

"You never know, Mack. We are hoping to have this taken care of within the week, but it could take a couple."

She grumbled under her breath and picked up a throw pillow from the couch. She hugged it to herself while she put her head back against the hunter green cushion.

A week or two and then this would be cleared up, and I would be sent back, and she would go where? What did she have here? No home? Maybe no job when this was over. Could I talk her into coming with me? I considered this as I watched her stare at the ceiling.

She stood up slowly, "Which room is mine? I think I want to try and get some sleep."

I turned to Chris, "We grabbed a bite to eat on our way up here. Which room did you take?"

"I'm in the one there," he pointed to the right side of the building. "Mack can have the big one over there." He pointed to the opposite corner.

I picked up her bags and carried them to the room while she followed. She moved to sit on the bed and began to take her sling off. I walked over to help her, but she stopped me.

"I gotta learn to do this myself. You're leaving tomorrow, remember, and I'm not going to ask Chris to dress and undress me."

I smiled down at her attempt at humor, "Glad to know you aren't going to share that with him."

She took the sling off, and even managed to get her t-shirt off. I watched her from the corner of my eye, wanting to see how she would handle getting her bra off. I was surprised at how easily she did it by slipping the straps off her shoulders and then twisting the hooks to the front to undo them. Thank god I didn't have to wear those things, I thought to myself as I placed her clothes into the dresser.

I emptied my pockets and placed everything on the nightstand while she managed to get a nightshirt on. When she was done, I pointed to a door on the side of the room where the bathroom was and handed her a small bag with toiletries in it. She closed the door, and I heard the water running in the sink.

I went in search of a glass of water and the pain medicine that Chris had picked up for me.

"Is she all settled?" Chris asked as I entered the kitchen area. He was working on his laptop, and it appeared that he was going through some emails. "I put a pillow and blankets out on the couch for you."

I ignored the last comment, "Sorry you were roped into this. I know how much it sucks to be stuck in a house babysitting someone." I started opening cabinets looking for glasses.

"No worries. I needed a break. I just finished doing a three-month undercover gig. I'm looking forward to a week or so of sitting back and catching up on my sleep and television."

I found a glass and filled it with water, setting it on the table opposite him. I pulled the chair out and sat down, rubbing my face with both hands.

"Been a rough twenty-four hours, huh?" Chris remarked.

"No shit, and by the way, I won't need the couch." I put my forearms on the table and wrapped my hands around the glass. Both his eyebrows rose in question. I shrugged.

"What are you going to do when this is done? Take her back to Los Angeles and set her up in an apartment?" He pushed the lid of his laptop down to give me his undivided attention.

"I have no clue. I doubt she would go if I asked her. Right now, she doesn't even know I live there. She just found out early this morning that I'm an agent and not some young rookie cop."

"Tough spot, man, I'd hate to be you." He leaned back in his chair and crossed his arms. "How do you feel about her?"

"I'm crazy about her, but I have no idea if it would work or not."

"I guess you need to use this time to figure that out, huh?"

"I guess so." I replied as I stood. "I better go give her these. I'll be back after she falls asleep and tell you what's going on with the case."

He acknowledged me and turned back to his email.

The room was dark when I entered. "Mack, you awake?" I asked quietly, and received no reply from her.

I moved around to the side of the bed, using the light from the cracked bathroom door to allow me to see. She was snuggled down in the bed, her hair falling over her face, and I put the glass of water down gently and pushed the hair off her cheek. She didn't move. I stared at her face in the darkness, an emotion I had never truly felt rolled through my chest and almost brought me to my knees.

She must have been more tired than I thought. I put the pills on the table next to her before I walked out, closing the door with a soft click.

"That was fast," Chris said when I entered the kitchen again.

"Yeah, she's already out like a light. All of this has drained her physically and emotionally." I sat down again. "I can't imagine going through what she has and still holding it together."

"She must be a strong woman," he replied.

"The strongest one I have ever met."

Chapter 29 - Mack

When I returned to the bedroom from the bathroom, I was alone. Drew's phone was vibrating on the bedside table, and I picked it up. The screen said Andy & Alex, his niece and nephew. I answered the phone, meaning to take it to him.

"Hello," I said in a much more friendly voice than I felt.

There was a pause. "Hi, who is this?" a young girl's voice asked.

"This is Mack," I answered and sat down on the side of the bed.

"Mack? You sound like a girl, who calls a girl Mack?" She sounded confused, and I laughed.

"My real name is MacKenzie, my friends call me Mack because it's easier."

"Oh, okay, that makes sense. Are you working with my dad?" Her dad? I glanced at the phone.

"Um, you mean Andrew?" I questioned, hoping the answer was no, and that she had dialed the wrong number.

"Yeah, are you working with him?" Her voice was so innocent. She did not deserve the wrath of anger that was creeping up my chest. He had kids! Did he have a wife, too?

"Yes, I'm working with him," I answered as smoothly as I could while trying not to allow the steam to blow a gasket.

"Oh, is that why you answered his phone?" I heard a noise in the background that sounded like a woman talking, not a child, a woman.

"He stepped out for a minute and forgot his phone. I knew he would want to know you called, so I answered it for him. He has told me a lot about you," not as much as he should have, I wanted to tack on, "so I thought I would say hello." How I was keeping my voice level and friendly was beyond me, maybe I should have been an actress.

"Oh, okay," she replied, and I heard the woman talking again in the background. I cringed.

"Is there something you wanted me to tell him when he comes back?" I asked, needing to find a way to get off the phone before he came in the room.

"I wanted to know when he was coming home. Mom asked me to ask him next time we talked." Mom wanted to know. I bet Mom wanted to know! That son of a bitch!

"Tell me something, Alex, where is home?" I needed to know this one last thing before I hung up.

She giggled into the phone, "Los Angeles."

"I am sure he will be home to Los Angeles before you know it." I heard the woman asking her who she was talking to, and she attempted to cover up the phone, but she missed the speaker.

"I'm talking to MacKenzie; she works with Daddy."

"Alex, you need to hang up the phone. Your daddy said never to talk to anyone who answers his phone. Hang up the phone now." She sounded angry, and I could just imagine how angry she was. It was something we shared at that moment, aw hell, something else we shared!

"I have to go. Will you tell Daddy I called?" Alexandra said into the phone, and I heard her mother yell at her to hang up.

"You can bet I will, Alexandra. You better get off the phone before your mom gets any more upset."

"Yeah, I know." She hung up the phone. I held it to my ear even though the line was dead.

I slowly pulled the phone from my ear and set it down on the side table again. With absolutely no energy, I crawled over the bed to the opposite side and pulled the covers back, sliding between them. I clenched my eyes closed and willed myself to sleep. How many other lies had he told me?

A moment later, I heard the door open. He called my name, but I pretended to be asleep. My senses were fine-tuned right that moment, and I heard every step he made as he moved closer.

I needed time to process this, and tomorrow, he would be gone for a few days. I could do it then. I heard a glass being set on the nightstand and fought to hold still when he touched me. Every ounce of me wanted to lash out at him, but I wouldn't.

I heard something else drop on the table and then he turned and walked out of the room. When the door closed and I heard his footsteps on the other side moving away, I opened my lids and looked at the pain pills. They blurred in front of me as my eyes filled with tears that slipped down onto the pillow.

I don't know how long I cried, but I assumed I cried myself to sleep. When I next opened my eyes, the room was completely dark, and his hand rested on my hip. I wanted to push it off, wake him up, and ask him what the hell he was doing, but instead, I gently removed his hand and slipped out of bed.

Pain radiated down my arm, and I bit my lip to control the discomfort. At some time during my slumber, I had rolled over onto my bad shoulder. I glanced at the pain pills before I went into the bathroom to empty my bladder.

When I came back out, I scooped up the pills and swallowed them dry. They left a chalky aftertaste in my mouth, but I didn't care. I climbed back into bed as carefully as I could and studied his sleeping face.

Why did he have to lie to me? I had fought our attraction, and once I had given up fighting, I had let down my wall and fallen for him. I had to believe my sister was right, and soul mates did exist. It was the only way I could explain how I had come to care so much about him in just over a week.

I rolled over and closed my eyes, not wanting to even think. A few minutes later, I fell back asleep.

When I woke, the room was bright. I turned my head to find the other side of the bed empty. I looked at my watch and saw it was almost eight-thirty. Was he still here or had he left already?

Part of me wanted him to be here so I could question him. I almost laughed; it would have been more of an interrogation than a questioning. My other reasonable side hoped he was gone, so that I could deal with what I had learned and get used to him not being here.

I heard movement on the other side of the door and could smell bacon cooking. My stomach growled, and I climbed out of bed. I could use some food and hopefully some coffee.

I threw on sweatpants and socks, trying not to think about how he had purchased them for me. No wonder he knew how to shop for a woman so well; he had a wife and kids! I stumbled into the kitchen in a haze of anger. Chris was at the stove, flipping the bacon, and I saw that the coffee pot was still half full.

"Hey, there. How did you sleep?" he asked as he glanced over his shoulder.

"I slept better than I expected to." I figured I would have tossed and turned all night thinking about Drew, but I had fallen into a deep, dreamless sleep.

"If you want coffee, the mugs are in that cabinet over there." He pointed with his spatula. "Make yourself at home here; use whatever you need." He went back to his cooking, and I opened the fridge to look for cream. There was a large bottle of French vanilla. I pulled it out, thankful for small favors.

I had finished pouring my coffee when Chris spoke again, "Cooper said to tell you he was sorry he missed saying goodbye. He said he would call you later today."

I had to think for a minute when he said Cooper, but the fog in my brain cleared, and I remembered that Drew's real last name was Cooper, not Bradley. "Fine." I carried the mug back to the table. "Tell me something, Chris, is Chris really your name or is that an alias?"

He gave out a hearty laugh, "My birth certificate says

Christopher Carley, and my death certificate someday will read the exact same thing. Is that good enough?"

I smiled, "Yeah, that's good enough."

Chris and I chatted while he finished cooking breakfast. He was an intelligent and humorous man, and I decided having his company for the next few days, or longer, wouldn't be so bad. It did not take long for the anger to dissipate, and I relaxed and enjoyed the conversation until he mentioned Drew again.

"Cooper gave me strict instructions that you needed to take a shower when you woke up and then have me clean your wound." He paused while I stared at him. "He also told me you haven't been taking antibiotics, so you need to start taking those, too. I picked some up when I bought your pain medication."

"Well, aren't you a goodie-two-shoes. You always do everything you're told?" I asked.

He belted out a hearty laugh, "No, but in this case, Coop's right. You need to take care of the wound. Why don't you go take a shower, and I'll clean up. Then I'll take a look at your shoulder." He went to the counter and turned back, "Here are your antibiotics."

I took the vial and read the dosage before taking the childproof cap off and tipping a pill into my palm. I swallowed it with the last of my coffee.

"Yes, sir," I replied and stood to salute him with my right hand. He laughed and shook his head, picking up our plates while I headed back to the bedroom.

It was a challenge to take a shower alone, and more than once, I wished that Drew was there with me. Each time, I forced myself to let go of the feelings, and told myself that it was better to end it now. I was not going to be sorry I had slept with him, but I sure as hell wasn't going to do it again.

When the shower was over, I put on a pair of sweatpants, and it only reminded me again of Drew. I wrapped a towel around my chest and went out into the kitchen. The table looked like a mini-triage area with the antiseptics and bandages.

"What were you, a doctor, in your previous life?" I stared at the array of medical supplies.

"I was a paramedic before I joined the agency. I keep my certifications up. You never know when you might need it."

I had to give him credit, not once did he look below my neck. I knew that was a hard thing to do when a woman was standing there half dressed. "Let's get this over with," I huffed as I sat down in one of the chairs.

"Do me a favor, and climb up on the table, being right under the light will make it easier to see." He stepped to the table.

"Yes, sir, doctor, sir." We shared a laugh as I tried to climb onto the table. Chris finally scooped me up and set me down.

"My knight in shining armor," I joked when he let me go.

He went right to work, pulling on nitrile gloves and looking at the entrance wound on my back. "Pretty clean, although it is very red in this one area. Glad I have the antibiotics."

I winced as he poked at it. "That's tender right there."

"I bet. That is where the infection is trying to take hold. I'm going to have to push on it, make sure there is no infection inside."

I grabbed the edge of the table, preparing myself for the pain.

"I'm going to wrap my arms around you for a moment; that way I can get at it better." He slipped his arms around my shoulders, and I stared at his wide chest. Normally, I would have paid attention to it, even checked it out, because it was a nice chest, but Drew had ruined it for any other man.

"Okay, this might hurt a bit," he warned right before he pushed on it.

The pain was so intense I thought I might pass out for a second. When it started to subside, I realized that I had my forehead up against his chest. I wanted to move it, but I was still trying to catch my breath.

He rubbed the back of my neck, "That was the worst of it. I know it hurt. Relax for a minute, and I'll put some ointment on it."

I grunted in response and took a few deep steady breaths. When I felt I could lift my head without passing out, I did and was rewarded with a smile that in no way made my heart thump like someone else's did.

Damn it!

Chris finished cleaning up my back before he looked at the front. I could see that while it was red, it didn't look infected. Thank God for small miracles. He put medicine on and then bandaged me up with large but very gentle hands. When he finished, he pulled off the gloves and lifted me off the table, placing me on my feet.

He walked over to the counter and picked up a pill bottle. He turned to me, "Take these, I know you are hurting, and it will only get worse for a while."

"I hate taking pills," I grumbled at him.

"It's not like you have anywhere else to go, right? Take it, you'll feel better." He dropped the pills into my outstretched hand, and I filled up a water glass and swallowed them.

"Go lie down on the couch. Let me clean this up and then we can watch a movie or something."

I went back to my bedroom and pulled on a t-shirt without a bra. If he was gentleman enough not to look at my towel-clad body, I doubted it would bother him that I wasn't wearing an over-the-shoulder-boulder-holder. I made my way back to the living room and collapsed onto the couch, closing my eyes, wishing that blocking out the light could block out the pain. A few minutes later, I fell fast asleep.

Chapter 30 – Drew

"So tell me what this case is all about and what you need me to do, besides keep her safe?" Chris asked me as he pulled two beers out of the fridge.

I took the offered beer and twisted off the top. "Do you know anything?"

He shook his head. "Not really. Todd told me that it had to do with a stolen car ring and that you and Rob were involved, but that's basically it."

The mention of Rob made the beer I was swallowing lodge in my throat. It took a moment for the muscles to relax enough to allow the liquid to go down.

"I can't believe Rob is dead."

Chris didn't say anything for a moment as we both thought about what had transpired. "He was a great guy. He's going to be missed, and that's for sure," he finally offered.

I pulled at the paper label on my bottle, "Yeah, he was." I sucked in a deep breath and leaned back in the chair. "They called me out here to go undercover because they wanted someone who appeared young. They figured if a rookie cop breached the unit, the others wouldn't pay too much attention to him."

"Did that work?" he asked right before he took a swig of his drink.

"It did. I'm in and act the part of the newbie. I don't think anyone thought much of it at first, but one of the guys figured out who I was."

His right eyebrow came up in question. "Hopefully, it wasn't someone on the wrong side."

"I don't think so. Jose told me that he knew something was going on, but he wasn't sure how to handle it."

"Do you trust him?"

"Yeah, I do. My gut tells me he's okay."

"Okay, so what does he have to offer?"

I took a drink before I answered him. "Like me, Jose thinks Bria and Gary are involved. He's not sure about Gordon or anyone else." I paused to think for a moment. "Gordon is like the father of the group. He's older, has a couple of kids in college. I'm not sure if he's involved, or if he is just doing what he is told. Now Bria, on the other hand, I have no doubts about. She is too interested in what is going on with Mack, and she's definitely involved with Gary."

"How deep do you think they are into it? Do you think they are masterminding the operations or just pawns in it?"

"That, I don't know. My first day there, we went to investigate a burglary at a BMW owner's house, and Mack picked up on the fact that something was missing in the office. When she questioned the guy about it, he lied. It was obvious that he was lying. The moment he was away from us he made a phone call. Mack filed for a court order on his phone records, and Gary flipped his lid when he found out she had gotten them." I took a sip before I continued, "That's how Rob became involved. Someone broke into Mack's house and deleted files from her computer. Rob extracted the deleted files and obtained another court order for the phone records. I don't know if he ever received the results." I paused to think. "Hey, I need you to do me a favor and see if Mack will tell you if Rob said anything to her at dinner about the court order or anything else to do with the case." The thought that maybe he said something to her made my head spin because I hadn't thought to ask earlier.

Chris nodded, "Yeah, I can do that. Anything else you want me to ask her about?"

I contemplated asking him to find out what she thought of me, but decided that was pretty immature. When the time came, we would talk about it face to face. "No, that's it." I chugged down the last of my beer. "Now, I need to figure out if they are actually chopping the cars, or if they're just shipping them out. Plus, I need to figure out the involvement of Gary and Bria and see if anyone else in the unit is involved."

"Be careful, Coop. It's obvious they don't value human life. They killed McNeary and tried to kill Mack. Don't be the next victim." He finished his beer and set it down with a final thump on the table.

Chris didn't know that one of the victims was dead, too, but he was correct, they didn't value life. I would be careful, and I would figure this out.

I climbed into the bed about thirty minutes later. Mack was breathing deeply, and I lay on my side and watched her. Her back was to me, and her shoulder slowly rose and fell with each breath she took.

I needed to solve this so that Mack could go on with her life. She had lost a lot, and I was determined to help her at least get started rebuilding it. How much I wished that I could stay here and be part of her new life.

My thoughts turned to what was waiting for me on the other side of the country. Was Annabelle going to make it? Would the cancer rob her of her life? The prognosis wasn't good. Her oncologist told her that her chances were dwindling, but we all held out hope that she would somehow beat the brain cancer that had started eating away at her mind.

She had good days and bad days, and I tried to help the best that I could by keeping the kids out of her hair when she was going through bad times. When she had first been diagnosed, we had decided that we would not hide anything from the kids, no matter what. Yes, they were young, but we were not going to lie to them. Annabelle had two live-in nurses that helped her around the clock along with other medical personnel that came in as needed.

If Annabelle lived, could I leave her and come back here to be with Mack? Could I leave my children? But if she died, wouldn't it be easier to bring the kids here to start a new life?

Guilt washed over me as I imagined Anna dead and me starting a new life here with Mack. Not that the life I led was all that great out west. I was only there because of the kids and to help Annabelle. I turned away from Mack and closed my eyes.

The alarm went off at three A.M., and I silenced it quickly. My sleep had been interrupted with frustrating dreams throughout the night. The haze of images drifted out of my mind as I became more conscious, but I knew what the meaning was.

I needed to let Mack go. I had no right to bring her into my life and subject her to what was going on in it. I had to deal with what was happening in California, and later, if there was a chance, then I would come back and ask her if we could start again.

I climbed out of bed and tiptoed to the bathroom to pull my clothes on from the night before. I would head back to my apartment where I could shower and get ready for work after I changed cars again.

I thought about leaving a note but decided against it. Chris was awake when I walked into the kitchen. He knew I had planned to leave early and had put on coffee for my drive. I thanked him again for helping me and for watching over Mack.

My first stop was the airport where I traded in the rental car for my Explorer. When I got back to my apartment, I wasn't surprised to find the place ransacked. Nothing was missing because there wasn't anything to take. My laptop had been with me. It was the only thing that could tie me to the FBI.

I drove into the station with a mix of steadfast resolve and nervousness. Everyone would know that I had been with Mack and that I knew where she was.

I arrived just before eight and entered the unit to find it already buzzing with activity. Gordon was behind his desk on the phone. Jose searched my face the moment he saw me, and I nodded to him.

I wasn't sure if I nodded to say hello or she's fine, but his shoulders seemed to relax just a tad.

Will was actually sitting at his desk typing on his computer and turned when he heard the sound of my footsteps. "Hey, how's Mack?"

Was he asking because he cared or because he was part of this? I didn't know much about Will; he usually worked nights and was out of the office.

"She's fine. She's resting," I replied and casually glanced at Jose who met my gaze for a fraction of a second.

"Good to hear that. Where is she?" He turned in his seat so he was facing me and not just looking over his shoulder.

Chad walked in and slapped me on the back, "Mack doing alright? Freaked me the hell out when I showed up at the scene and thought she was inside. That was one hell of an explosion, man."

"So I've heard. You have pictures, Chad? I haven't seen it yet." I was aware that I had ignored Will's last question, but I pretended I had gotten distracted.

"Sure, I have the ones I took. The ATF boys won't give me a copy of theirs yet, but at least I was able to work with them at the scene. I know what evidence they have." He walked over to his desk and sat down to pull up the pictures. I stood over his shoulder and watched as the first one showed up on the monitor.

Flames were still shooting out of the ceiling of the house and most of the windows. The picture showed that the one side of the house had major damage but not how much.

Chad moved on to the next photograph, and my stomach twisted. The side of the house had been blown away. I could just make out the corner of the dresser in her bedroom. The bed that would have been across from it was gone. Mack would have died if I hadn't taken her to see Drake and Rose. Chad ran through more photos, and I leaned on his desk with my palms, trying to keep the shaking out of my limbs. The more I saw, the sicker I felt. Before he could get through all of them, I stood up.

Luckily, Gary walked out of his office at that moment. His eyes scanned the office and hesitated on Bria's desk before coming to me. "Bradley, can I talk to you for a minute?"

We regarded each other over the expanse of the office, and I wondered why his voice sounded so defeated. There were dark circles under his eyes, and the shoulders that were normally held high were rounded forward.

I nodded and started towards him. He dropped his head to look at the floor and spun around slowly to enter his office. When I entered he asked me to close the door, I did and then took a seat.

"L.T.," I said as I sat and laced my fingers over my stomach while my elbows rested on the wooden chair arms.

He leaned to the side in his chair and studied me while he rested his chin on his fist. Unlike the past when he had studied me, I didn't get the feeling that he was trying to intimidate me. From the way he was searching my face, I had the feeling he was trying to ask for something, and I had a good idea what that would be.

The air in the room grew heavier the longer we sat there in mutual contemplation. When he lifted his head and wiped his face with his hand, I knew he was finally going to speak.

"How is she?" His voice held emotion, and I was trying to decipher what emotion it was supposed to be. Was he really concerned about her or pissed that she wasn't dead?

"She's alright." I leaned back in my seat and put my legs out in front of me, crossing my right leg over my left at the ankle, an attempt on my part to appear relaxed and in control of the situation.

He rolled his chair closer to his desk and put both of his elbows on it, resting his face in his hands. Was he trying to pretend to be concerned?

He wiped his face again. "You're not going to tell me where she is, are you?" He stared me in the eye, but I already had the answer shining there. No way in hell.

"Sorry, L.T., but the only thing I can tell you is that she is safe." He leaned back in his chair to stare at a point over my head.

"Is there some way I could talk to her?" he asked without looking at me.

I shook my head, and he finally made eye contact, "Sorry, but you can't. If you have a message you want me to get to her, I can do that, but I can't let you call her or tell you where she is. She doesn't want to speak to anyone right now."

His eyes tightened ever so slightly, and I realized that I had just thrown down the gauntlet, and a large red bull's eye had been drawn on my forehead. Bring it on, I thought to myself.

He considered my suggestion for a moment before shifting in his seat. The fact that he was under a lot of pressure was very evident, as he couldn't sit still. "Look, tell her I'm sorry about everything, and I mean everything. Things aren't as they seem."

I raised my eyebrow at him, and he stopped talking.

"Look, Bradley, you have no idea what is going on here, but Mack really pissed some people off. I can't control that." His voice rose an octave as he spoke. "I wish I could, and I'm glad she's safe, but tell her to stay the hell out of it and don't put her little nose into this any further."

Now was my chance to see if he would talk to me, "Who did she piss off?"

He stared at me, and I knew there was little chance that he would confide in me; but the way he was searching me made me think he was actually considering it.

He shook himself from the urge and thumped his right thumb on the arm of his chair a few times, a nervous gesture. "If I'm right, Mack cares about you."

"What has that have to do with anything?"

"I'm not going to endanger your life by telling you anything else. You need to stay out of this, too."

"You do realize that the feds are involved in this now. How long are you going to be able to hide what is going on? One of your officers was shot, an agent was killed, and then immediately after, Mack's house gets blown to smithereens. You think they aren't going to start digging?" I paused for a moment and let that sink in. "If you know something about this, Gary, you need to speak up."

Gary sat still for a moment before he wiped his face again.

"Bradley, stay out of it." He rolled his chair closer to the desk and shook his mouse. "Tell Mack I'm glad she is alright. I never wanted anything to happen to her."

He said the words, but they sounded hollow. He didn't say anything else and kept his eyes trained on his computer screen as he clicked away. Apparently, the conversation was over.

I stood up just as the door opened, Bria had questions written all over her face as she looked between Gary and me.

"Bria," I tipped my head to her and walked out of the office. I felt her drilling a hole into my back with her eyes, but I didn't turn to her or bother to look in her direction as I sat at my desk. I heard the door close with a thud as I logged on to my computer.

Gary's concern bothered me, but I wasn't sure if it bothered the professional agent in me or the man in me who cared about Mack. I glanced at my watch, eight forty-five. I wondered if Mack was awake yet.

Chapter 31 – Mack

I hated pain medication. It made me feel like a freak, unable to be in control of my thoughts, feelings, or movements. Plus, it gave me the weirdest freaking dreams! I awoke from a very disturbing one where I was wandering around in the woods and the trees were talking to me. I'm not sure if I was more concerned that the trees were speaking to me or that they were telling me to run.

I shifted on the couch, my right shoulder sore from lying on it. I heard a shuffling sound behind me and tensed.

"Nice nap?" Chris asked as he leaned over the back of the couch and looked down at me. Thank God it was only him and not a talking tree.

I chuckled at that thought and sat up, rubbing my eyes with the tips of my fingers to clear the blur out of them. My head felt woozy, but my left shoulder wasn't throbbing like it had been when I lay down.

"How long was I out?" I cleared my throat when I heard how husky it was. Chris dropped down into a chair across from me.

"About two hours." He crossed his ankle over his knee, and I examined his orange and black socks.

He followed my line of vision, "What? I'm a Flyers fan."

I laughed. "I can't believe I slept for two hours when I had only been up for an hour before that." I leaned back on the couch and curled my feet under me.

"Pain can do that." His lips lifted in a soft smile.

"Yeah, I guess I'm one of those people." I yawned and didn't bother to try and hide it.

Chris laughed, "Can I get you something?"

"I could use something to drink, but you sit, I can get it." I started to get up, and he beat me to it.

"Nope, I've been sitting around waiting for you to get up. What would you like, juice, water, or a soda?"

I wanted a beer, but I didn't think he would let me have one while on pain medicine. Now that could have been fun. I wondered what else would have talked to me, the couch maybe? Or the deer head on the wall? "Soda will do for now."

"Coke or ginger ale?"

"My stomach is kind of upset, I'll go with the ginger ale over ice if we have it."

As he walked toward the kitchen, I changed my mind, "Wait, make that a coke over ice, please. I could use the caffeine to wake myself up."

"One coke over ice coming up," he repeated as he entered the kitchen.

I closed my eyes and listened to the clinking of the ice cubes falling into the glass. My mind was still full of fuzzy remnants of my dreams thanks to the narcotics.

He handed me the glass, and I sat up to take it from him. He settled himself in the chair again. The coke was sweet and cold. I didn't realize how thirsty I was until I started drinking. I finished half the glass in one turn and wiped my wet upper lip with my hand.

"Thirsty much?" Chris laughed as he asked, and I replied back with a small burp which only made him laugh harder.

I apologized as I looked around the room. If I were on vacation, this would be a nice place to kick back and relax, maybe spend some quality time with someone. I clenched my jaw, knowing that someone wouldn't be Drew. I pushed him to the back of my mind again.

"So now what?" I asked as I tried to close the door on the memory of a certain very sexy man.

Chris focused on me, and I knew what he was basically going to say before he opened his mouth. "We need to talk about everything that has happened."

I rubbed my fingers down the side of the glass then wiped the condensation off on my pants. "I figured as much."

"Drew filled me in on the case from what he knew, but he wanted me to ask you a few questions."

The mention of Drew brought back a flash of our bodies together in the shower. I was tempted to roll the cold wet glass over my forehead to cool it.

"What does he want to know?" My voice was clipped as I spoke, and Chris picked up on it and looked at me a little harder.

"Well, he never had a chance to ask you about your dinner with Rob. He wanted to know if Rob said anything to you about the case or the court orders."

"Oh, shit! I forgot about those!" I stood up and put my glass down on the coffee table so fast I almost spilled it before I took off into the bedroom to get the copy Rob had given me at dinner.

When I came back, I sat back down on the couch, and Chris moved over to sit beside me. I unfolded the papers and started reading down the list.

"Shit, there is no way that Gary is not involved." I pointed to a number that kept showing up. "This is his phone number."

"Wow, yeah, no wonder he didn't want you to see that. There must be at least thirty, thirty-five calls in those two days alone on that page."

I started counting, "Thirty-four to be exact." I stopped to think. "Do you have a calendar around here?"

Chris pulled out his cellphone, "There is one on here." He put in his passcode and opened the calendar application before handing it to me.

I counted back the days. "These calls started the day of the burglary at Timmons's house and into the next day."

"Maybe we need to get another court order to go back a little further and see how often he was contacting him before that," Chris suggested.

I glanced at him before turning the page, "It might be worth it." I studied the second page, "His number only appears twice on here and that is two days later, both calls are less than a minute and made to Gary from Timmons." I flipped to the third page. Gary's number wasn't there.

Chris was scanning over the pages with me. "Do any of these other numbers look familiar? This one here," he pointed at a number, "is called a lot. Do you know who that belongs to?"

I shook my head, "Unfortunately, no. Without my cellphone, I can't look to see if any of them match anyone else from the unit. You're going to have to ask Drew that."

"What happened to your cellphone?" He leaned away from me now that we weren't inspecting the pages.

"I lost it when Rob was shot." I set the papers down on the coffee table and reached for my glass again. The scene played over in my mind in slow motion, and I could still hear the tires squealing and the sound of the shot echoing through my head. "Drew was supposed to come over that night, but he had to go out on a homicide. I guess Rob found out about that and called me to ask me to dinner." I leaned my head back on the cushion and stared at a painting of a mountain landscape hung on the wood-paneled wall. "We met at a steakhouse and sat around talking and eating for a few hours." I glanced at the court order results lying on the table, "He gave me those just before we left." I felt tears welling up in my eyes. "He walked me out to my car, and I was giving him a hug goodbye when," I shut my eyelids and felt the tears spill over the side. I swallowed and tried to hold back a sob. Chris rested his hand on my thigh in comfort. "I heard tires squeal, and then I remember slamming against Rob. We fell. The shot echoed around us, but I didn't comprehend it at first."

"Do you remember anything else about what happened?" he asked softly.

I shook my head from side to side. "No, I was so focused on Rob that I didn't even think to look around." I hung my head. "If I had, I might have at least gotten a description of the car."

Chris squeezed my leg just the slightest bit, and I welcomed his compassion even if I didn't deserve it.

"Mack, don't beat yourself up about that. You know exactly what happens in situations like this; you get tunnel vision and yours was on Rob. There is nothing wrong with that."

I nodded, "I know. I know. All I could see at that moment was the blood on his lips, and the stain growing on his chest. I remember dialing nine-one-one and talking to the call taker, but then the pain in my shoulder became too much. Someone took my phone from me, and I never saw it again."

Chris released a sigh and sat back away from me again. "It's probably better that you don't have it. They can't trace you."

"True."

"I'll speak to Andy when he calls and ask him to check the numbers." He glanced at his watch. "What time does he normally go to lunch?"

"Anytime between eleven and one usually, depends on what we are working on." I bit my lip as I started to think about something else.

"Well, it's after eleven now, so he should be calling soon." He stood up and picked up my glass, "You want some more?"

I nodded and continued to chew on my lip.

He set it on the table when he returned and fell back into the chair across from me.

"There is something else I should probably tell you about." I studied my one of my fingernails as I picked at it.

"Something else that happened at the shooting scene?"

I gave my head a quick shake, "No, something that happened a while ago, something that I never reported." I tossed my head back to stare at the log ceiling. "Hell, I never told anyone other than my sister about it."

Chris remained quiet, patiently waiting for me to string my

words and thoughts together.

"It's something that Gary was involved with years ago. I don't know if he still is, but he was." I peered at him and met his questioning gaze.

"Something illegal?" He watched me carefully as I nodded slowly. "Okay, what is it?"

I closed my eyes. I had never told anyone other than Cindy, and that was hard enough. I knew that once I said this, heads were going to roll, but maybe I had been wrong to keep it a secret all those years ago. Shit, I knew I had been wrong, but keeping it secret had been the only way to keep it quiet for my own sake.

"I was married to Gary, did you know that?" I looked him straight in the face as I asked.

"Andy mentioned it." He shifted in his seat and rested his chin on his palm.

"When I was married to him, he was a sergeant and in charge of the narcotics division. I was pretty new to the job and working patrol." I stopped to remember when I had met him. His good looks and charm had bowled me over. What an idiot I had been. "He kind of swept me off my feet." I let out a nervous laugh although it wasn't funny. "Anyway, we got married, and I had this incident that involved a woman with quite a bit of heroin on her person. I made the arrest, did the charges, and then came to find out that the charges were withdrawn later at the court." I sat up straighter on the couch and uncurled my legs, stretching them out in front of me and resting my heels on the coffee table. "I did some digging and found that Gary was the one who had the charges pulled. When I questioned him about it, he gave me a great explanation. Told me that he flipped her and turned her into a confidential informant." I paused for a moment.

"Nothing wrong with having a new CI," Chris stated.

"No, you're right, there isn't. It was the way it was done that was the problem." I lifted my glass and took a drink, more to steady my nerves than for any other reason. "I walked into his office one night and found him in a compromising position." I met his eyes head on and watched them grow in size as he got my drift.

"He was having sex with the CI?" he asked.

"Not mine, but another one. I flipped out, of course, and took off out of the office." I picked at my fingernail again as I remembered the embarrassment and anger I'd felt seeing him with another woman on his desk. Chris was quiet for a few moments, either digesting what I'd said or giving me time.

"What happened after that?"

"My shift was over, and he wasn't supposed to be home for a while, so I packed up his shit and put it on the front porch."

"You're a better woman than some." He laughed to ease the tension. "Some women would have burned it or cut it into shreds."

I smiled, "The thought crossed my mind, but that's not the worst of it."

"There is something worse than him banging some dirty ass CI on his desk and you finding him in the act?"

I laughed, "Oh yeah. See, I went on the computer that night trying to calm down and decided to go through his files. He was stupid enough to put some things on there, some very seriously incriminating things."

He dropped his hand from his face and stared at me, "What things?"

"Gary had made videos of his encounters." Wow, I said it. I actually said it out loud.

His mouth opened, and he was about to speak but closed it again before he did. "You're kidding me?"

I shook my head sadly, "Wish I was. I found twelve total videos, and one of them was the woman I arrested." I contemplated if I should say the rest. I told him this much; I had to finish it. "Eleven of them were CIs and the twelfth one," I swallowed and kept my eyes trained on my hands, "was me." I was afraid to look at him. I was mortified about having been videotaped while we took a quickie in his office. That could have gotten me fired and was another reason I had never said anything.

His voice was soft as he asked, "Did you give consent for that,

Mack?"

"For the sex or the video?" I tore my fingernail off.

"Either, both."

"We were married. I didn't have a problem having sex with him. It was exciting to do that at work. I was caught up in the moment and his seduction." I lifted my head and met his gaze directly. "I did not, however, give my permission to be videotaped in the act."

He leaned forward in his chair and put his elbows on his knees. "Why didn't you report him?"

"Oh, I threatened to, I did, but he refused to give me a divorce and threatened to post my video online for others to see. My professional reputation would have been ruined. I swore I would never tell anyone as long as he gave me the divorce."

He flexed his hands as they hung between his knees. "So how did you come to work for him in investigations?"

"Since the day I joined the force, I have wanted to be a detective. I had filled out the paperwork to test for the position, just about the same time that he made lieutenant and was transferred. It was sheer coincidence; at least I think it was." I wondered now. "You know how hard it is to even get a police job, much less getting into investigations. The academy has almost two hundred cadets graduate each year, and only a handful of them ever get jobs around here. That's why I never looked anywhere else. It was awkward at first, but we found a way to work together, as long as we kept our distance from one another." I thought for a moment, "I don't know if this has anything to do with what is going on now, but I figured it was time to bring it up."

"Does Andy know about this?"

"Oh, hell no," I practically shouted, "and I would prefer it if he didn't."

"Mack, I gotta tell him about this. Wait, do you have any proof of this?"

"I made copies, but I assume mine was blown up in the explosion."

"Is there another copy?"

I nodded.

"Where?"

"My sister has it."

He had just started to speak when his cellphone began to ring, "I need that copy." We both looked at his cell, "It's Andy. Do you want to tell him or do you want me to?"

I didn't even have to consider that, "I don't want to talk to him." I stood up. "I'm going to go lie down for a little while."

I heard him say hello to Drew just as I reached my door. I closed it when I heard him say, "I have some very serious information for you."

Chapter 32 – Drew

The air in the unit was electrified; we were all walking on eggshells. Gordon and Chad seemed to be the only ones unaffected.

Gordon spent most of the morning typing away at his computer and making phone calls. Once in a while, he would ask me to help him with something or question me on something a witness had said at the latest homicide; otherwise he kept to himself and stayed busy.

Chad was writing his report of the explosion at Mack's house and was on and off the phone with an agent at the ATF. He seemed encouraged by some of the information he was given but wouldn't share anything with me. I did, however, find out the name of the agent he was working with and planned to put a call into him as Agent Cooper, not Detective Bradley.

The door to Gary's office stayed closed, even after Bria walked out. Right before lunch, Bria left to take care of an interview at the child safety center. Will bounced in and out of the office and kept his attention on his own things, although every once in a while, I would catch him watching me.

Jose and I didn't talk, but from time to time, we would have a silent conversation with our eyes about something that was happening in the unit at the time.

Mack's name wasn't mentioned again, and I was relieved. I didn't want to have to keep repeating that I wasn't going to tell anyone where she was.

At lunchtime, I slipped out of the office and used my FBI-issued phone to place a call to Chris. My heart beat faster with the hope that I would talk to Mack. All morning I had missed her and wondered if Chris was taking care of her. Did he clean her wounds and bandage them up? Did he make her take her medicine?

One question was more important than the rest though: Had he learned anything?

Chris answered on the third ring, "Hey, how are things going down there?"

"Interesting to say the least. Lots of stepping around each other. How are things there?" I really wanted to ask how Mack was, but I phrased it to be less intimate.

"I have some very serious information for you," he replied.

He gave me a list of the other phone numbers that were on the court order to check into and explained what had happened when Rob had gotten shot. I listened, but I didn't want to.

Hearing the details of the shooting reminded me that I needed to call Drake and Rose and check on them. I would do that tonight. Maybe I'd go visit them to keep myself busy. I'm sure they were trying to get all the funeral arrangements made, I could help. Not that I wanted to bury my best friend, but to help honor his memory, I would.

"There's more," Chris stated in a serious tone.

"More? About what?" I leaned my elbow on the console between my two seats.

"Mack told me about something Gary was involved in years ago. It's the reason they were divorced," he filled in.

"He cheated on her. I already know that. She told me before that was why they had been divorced."

Chris chuckled into the phone, "Andy, this was more than cheating. The guy was flipping women who were arrested to become CIs and having sex with them on the job."

"What?" How had Mack known about that, and why the hell

didn't she tell me?

"Not only that, but he videotaped the encounters." His voice was serious but also held a note of humor.

"You're kidding, right?" I scanned the parking lot while I tried to absorb what he said.

"No, she has a copy of the video. Well, she doesn't anymore, but her sister has a copy of it."

"I need to get ahold of her sister and get that." I was already trying to remember what Mack might have said about her sister and where she lived.

"One more thing," his voice lowered again, all humor gone now.

Dread filled me, and I was afraid to ask what "one more thing" was, but I did. "What?"

"Mack's in one of the videos, too."

Son of a bitch! "Did she know she was being taped?" My hand started to cramp, and I realized I was squeezing my cellphone.

"No, she didn't know," he replied, and I was about to ask another question when he continued, "They all took place in his office, even Mack's."

"Holy crap!" I bounced my head against the headrest a few times. "Why didn't she say something about this before?"

"It was how she obtained her divorce. She swore she would never tell in exchange for him signing the papers. Besides, she was embarrassed as hell about it. She knows her job is on the line for that."

"They can't hold her responsible for being videotaped without her knowledge," I spat back at him.

"No, they can't, but she had sex on the job, in the office."

I winced. "Is there anything else?" I asked, afraid he would give me more to ponder.

"No, that's it. She just went to lie down again, but when she gets up, I'll get her sister's information and text it over to you."

"Alright, thanks," I paused, "how's she doing?"

"Physically, she's fine. I cleaned her up, had to deal with a little infection, but it should be okay. The pills make her tired, but that's to be expected." I heard water running in the background.

"And mentally?" I asked.

"Mentally, she's messed up. She was emotional talking about Rob's shooting, which is understandable, but she couldn't remember anything else. She went into shock pretty fast when it happened." He paused, and I heard a door open and close. "She was pretty upset when she told me about Gary and didn't want me to tell you."

"Why the hell not?"

"Why do you think? She cares about you, or so you say. I didn't see any signs of it today, in fact she barely mentioned you." Ouch, that hurt. "She doesn't want you to know about the sordid details of her life, although I am sure she understands the need for it."

I didn't know how to answer him, so I thanked him again for the help and told him I would wait for the other information and check into the phone numbers. We said our goodbyes, and I hung up feeling a bit put out.

She hadn't talked about me? Was she angry that I left her there? I thought she understood that we were trying to keep her safe and allow her to heal—or was she embarrassed about what she had told Chris?

Either way, I would get her on the phone later. I couldn't afford to go there to see her, not now. I could only assume I was being watched.

After I hung up with Chris, I turned my iPhone off and slipped it into the hidden compartment in my dash. There was also a hidden compartment in the back hatch area where I stored my agency laptop and extra duffle bag. Everyone thought this was my car, but it was actually on loan from the FBI and registered to a person who had a fake identity.

After entering the passcode in my unit cellphone, I opened the contacts to check the phone numbers Chris had given me. I had no idea how many times each of these numbers appeared on the court order, or if they were a caller or receiver. Chris had only asked me to see if I could match the numbers to anyone in the unit.

I looked for Bria's number first and, Bingo! I looked for

Gordon's, and there it was. Damn, I was hoping he wasn't involved. Maybe he had just been in contact with him about his burglary and not this other investigation. I checked for Gary's number, but it didn't match my list.

I pulled up Jose's contact information and held my breath as I checked over the list. I expelled the air from my lungs in a burst when I saw it was not one of the numbers given to me. Thank God for small favors. Chad's name was next, and then Mike's. Neither of their numbers appeared. Will was the last one to be checked, and I wasn't surprised to find his there. Something this morning told me he was just too interested in me and Mack to not be. Now this was starting to make sense. Will was a gang man, and this could very possibly be gang related.

I started my car and drove to a fast food restaurant a few blocks away. While I stood in line, I heard someone walk up behind me and heard him bend down but paid no real attention to him as I contemplated my conversation with Chris.

A deep voice interrupted my thoughts, "Sir, you dropped something." I turned to the man and quickly took in his features— something all agents did out of habit formed by years of training. He had long brown hair pulled back in a ponytail and a bushy beard with gray strands mixed in with the brown. I glanced at the paper he held in front of him. He gave me just the slightest nod. I accepted it unobtrusively and slipped it into my front pocket.

"Thank you," I commented before I stepped up to the register to order my food. The employee gave me my tray and told me it would be a minute for my sandwich. I stepped aside so the helpful stranger could order.

From the corner of my eye, I took in the heavy black leather jacket and blue jeans. There was a chain hanging from his belt that attached to the wallet he held in his hand. I hadn't dropped anything, so what was this biker guy passing on to me: a warning?

My heart beat faster as I lifted my meal tray. The man glanced at me and I nodded as I turned to fill my drink.

I pushed my cup against the ice machine lever right as the man stepped beside me.

"I know who you are," he said softly, and I pulled my cup away from the lever. "Fill your drink up."

I did what he told me to do and started putting soda into my cup.

His voice was quiet, and I strained to hear him speak. "Mack's not involved in this." How did this man know who I was or about Mack?

"Who are you?" I asked.

He laughed, "Laugh."

I pretended to do as he said, but it sounded hollow. Obviously, we were being watched, and he was taking a chance talking to me, but who was he?

"Keep her safe," he said as I stepped away from the soda fountain. I scanned the room, taking note of what was outside the large plate-glass windows. Another biker stood outside by two Harleys. He was staring at me.

I snapped the lid on my cup, grabbed a straw, and was about to turn when it dawned on me, "Mike?"

He pushed his cup up to the ice lever, "Yeah."

I spun around and moved toward a table. I glanced at the other biker; he was following my movements. Neither of them wore their colors, but I had no doubt they were from one of the Outlaw Motorcycle Gangs in the area. I found a seat and forced myself to go about eating the food in front of me.

I had not realized that Mike was that deep into his undercover work. What information did he pass on to me? There was no way I was going to take a chance of reading it now. I pulled out my cellphone and pretended to read something on it. I was almost finished with my sandwich when I heard the guttural sounds of two Harleys being started outside. I forced myself not to look at them.

The deep vibrating sounds of the bikes echoed inside the restaurant and, as they drove away, I finally turned to watch them pull out onto the main road. The paper burned a hole in my pocket, but I refused to pull it out. Someone else might still be watching.

It wasn't until I walked into the back door of the station that I felt safe enough to remove the paper and unfold it.

I read over the short note and was glad to know I wasn't far off from my thoughts. He'd listed the people involved and an address. I wasn't sure what that address was for, but I would check later when I was off work and could use my own computer.

I slipped the paper back into my pocket and went back to the unit.

Chapter 33 – Mack

I tried to sleep, but with my eyes closed, crazy images rushed through my mind and kept me on the edge of consciousness. My shoulder started to throb again, and I wished that I had taken another pain pill before I'd hidden away in my room.

When my stomach growled, I sat up, frustrated. I climbed out of bed and went in search of Chris, food, and hopefully a pain pill.

I found Chris in the kitchen making some sandwiches. "I hope one of those is for me," I said as I slipped into a chair at the table.

He cast a glance over his shoulder. "I kind of figured you would be out soon looking for food. I was going to wrap it and put it in the fridge, so it was ready when you woke up."

"No need now. I'm starving!" He cut the sandwiches in half and turned to place a plate in front of me. "I love roast beef." Saliva filled my mouth, and my stomach rumbled again. "Do pain pills normally make you hungry? Because I'm freaking starving." I picked up the sandwich and tore into it. Chris laughed as he dropped a napkin on the table next to my plate. I swiped it up and wiped tomato juice running down my chin. "You like to cook?"

He pulled the chair back across from me. "I've been single my whole life. If I wanted to eat decent meals, I needed to learn. I actually took a few cooking classes; so yeah, I enjoy cooking. Would

259

be nice to have someone to cook for once in a while, though."

"Never been married, huh? Do you have a girlfriend?" I took another bite, savoring the taste on my tongue.

"It's hard to keep a girlfriend with my schedule. I do a lot of undercover work and travel. Cooper used to be my partner until—" he met my eyes and realized what he was about to say.

I smiled to let him off the hook, "Until he moved to Los Angeles. Is that what you were going to say?" His right eye twitched momentarily.

"Yeah," he laughed around a bite of food. I watched his Adam's apple bob as he swallowed, "I didn't know you knew he was from California."

I put my sandwich down, wiped my mouth, and balled up the napkin in my fist. "Let's just say I found out by accident. He didn't tell me."

"And that pisses you off, right?" He stood up and moved to a cabinet where he pulled out a bag of chips.

"I won't deny that it upset me to learn that he wasn't from around here. I should have been pissed off about him lying to me about being undercover, but I get that." I stopped to use the tip of my tongue to get a piece of food out from between my teeth and cheek. "What I don't get is how he could get involved with me when he has a life on the other side of the country," I paused, "unless he was using me this whole time." I contemplated my half-eaten sandwich. Why did that hurt more than knowing he had a family out west?

"It's not my place to get involved with this, but I will tell you, no, he wasn't using you. He does care about you, Mack. It's obvious to anyone who sees you two together. I could tell the moment he walked in the door behind you."

Knowing that he cared about me did not help. I knew he had still lied about his family. I was tempted to ask Chris about it, but he had already said it wasn't his place, and asking him didn't feel right. When I finally had the courage to face Drew again, if I ever did, I would ask him.

"I told him about the phone numbers. He is going to check into them." I nodded as I chewed and picked up a chip from the edge of the bag. "I also told him about the other information with Gary."

I stopped with the chip halfway into my mouth and peered at Chris. "What is he going to do about it?" I held the chip in front of my mouth.

"Not sure. He didn't say, but he does need your sister's information so he can get the evidence."

"Can I call her and warn her?" I popped the chip between my lips.

He shook his head as he replied, "No, her phone might be tapped. We can't take that chance right now."

"At least she knows about Drew, if he goes to her and says I'm in trouble, she'll give it to him."

"You told your sister about him?"

"Of course I told my sister, she's my best friend. Girls have to talk, you know." I tried not to laugh as I spoke.

"Oh, I know how much you girls talk." He pointed at my plate, "Finish your sandwich. Do you think you can stay awake long enough to watch a movie?"

"Yeah, I think I might be able to."

It turned out that we both fell asleep in the middle of the movie. I woke up to the sounds of heavy gunfire and sat straight up, swiveling my head around to find that the sound had come from the surround sound speakers. Chris was still passed out in the chair across from me. His neck bent at an odd angle that I was sure would cause him pain later.

I found the remote and turned the volume down and went in search of a drink.

I was pouring a soda into a glass when an ear-screeching beep went off twice. It scared me so bad I dropped the can onto the floor, coke bubbled out of the can over the wooden floor planks. I heard Chris jump up and run to his room.

Funny, he could sleep through gunfire, but the beeps woke him out of a dead sleep. I peered into the living room to see him disappearing into his bedroom on the other side of the living room.

I forgot about the soda can and followed him. I stopped at the threshold as I took in the closet full of electronics that faced me. Multiple television screens were inside along with other electronic boxes with flashing LED lights. I went to stand beside him.

On one of the screens, there was a car sitting at the end of the driveway. We both watched as a man climbed out of the car and walked to the back driver's side. He slammed his hand on the roof of the car and went back to the driver's door for a minute. Then he walked to the rear of the car and opened the trunk. I held my breath waiting to see what he was doing.

Chris and I both relaxed when we saw him pull out a jack. He had a flat tire.

"Pretty intricate system you have here." I studied the rest of the machines as Chris continued to watch the monitor and flipped through other views around the property to make sure this wasn't a diversion.

"Yeah, it's one of the best." He was all business as he continued to scan the other camera views.

"I better go clean up my mess. I dropped a soda on the floor when the alarm went off." He grunted, and I left him to watch the poor man change the tire.

About twenty minutes later, the alarm sounded again, and I tensed at the high pitch. I got up and went to his door. He was seated in a chair in front of the screens.

"He's leaving. He tripped the alarm when he turned his car around." He clicked on the mouse, and I watched the screens change. "I think we're good." He clicked a few more screens and finally stood.

"How many cameras and alarms are out there?" I asked as we went back to the living room.

"Twelve cameras and about two dozen alarm points. We're in the woods, so there are a lot of odd angles and trees to work around." He went into the kitchen while I sat down on the couch.

I heard the microwave turn on, and a minute later the sound of popping: Snack time!

When he came back in, he had two bowls of steaming popcorn and handed me one. "Let's finish watching the movie. What's the last thing you remember?" He picked up the remote and waited for me as I tried to remember.

"They were in the bedroom, hot sex scene, I think." I popped some popcorn in my mouth.

"You fell asleep during the smoking-hot sex scene? What is wrong with you, girl?" He hit the menu and started looking for the scene so we could start over from there.

I wasn't going to tell him that watching the scene had only reminded me of Drew and our time in the hotel.

"Before we watch this, I need to send Coop a message with your sister's info."

I relayed the name, address, and phone number and told him to add that he should call me Macky. My sister would know it was okay to give it to him. She was the only one that ever called me that. Chris smirked as he added that piece of information.

"Don't even start," I threatened him playfully as I threw a piece of popcorn at him.

We finished watching the movie without falling back asleep and decided to play a game of scrabble before we fixed dinner. Chris's phone beeped about an hour later, and he flicked a glance at me, "Cooper has the information. He is headed to your sister's now."

I glanced at the clock on the wall in the kitchen, "He won't get there until after nine. Is he going to drive back again right away?"

Chris typed on his cellphone screen and waited. "Yeah," he laughed. "Let me read his reply directly. 'Tell Macky I'll be fine.'" Chris let out a big belly laugh.

"That's not funny," I tried to contain the laugh, but it came out anyway.

Chris typed for a few more seconds, then set his phone down and went back to looking at his scrabble letters. His phone pinged one more time, and he picked it up after he put his word on the board. He sent me a quick glance and typed back a reply, pushing the button on the side to darken the screen before putting it down.

I had the distinct impression they were discussing me, but I didn't care. It didn't matter what Drew said. He was history, or would be as soon as this case was over. Then, I could go back to my life.

I stared at the board. Holy hell! What life did I even have left? My house was gone, my car, too! Oh no, my Mustang! I put my forehead to the table.

"You okay, Mack?"

I mumbled from where I was, "Those pricks blew up my Mustang!"

"They blew up your house, too, but you're worried about your car?" he sounded confused.

I lifted my head and gave him a direct stare. "Yes, they blew up my car! Who cares about my house? They blew up my car! You don't just go blowing up things like that!"

I sounded irrational even to myself, and as Chris's eyebrows arched high over his eyes, I knew he thought I had lost my mind.

"Damn it!" I swiveled in my chair and stood up, suddenly restless. "They blew up my house! Everything I own!" I stomped the window. "Those pricks took everything I had and destroyed it, and now...now my job is in jeopardy." I stared out the window at the darkening woods. "For what?" I yelled as I spun around and stabbed Chris with a heated glare. "What the hell was so important that they had to destroy everything I had? Those bastards tried to kill me and killed Rob? Why?"

I didn't expect an answer, and the anger bubbled inside me until it started to run over into my eyes. Tears began to slip down my cheeks. "They have taken everything from me." I hung my head and sobbed.

Chris pulled me into his arms and held me as I cried. I fisted the back of his shirt where my right arm wrapped around him. He stayed quiet until my crying started to subside.

"Not everything, Mack. You're still alive and you still have Andrew."

I sputtered and began to laugh, pulling out of Chris's consoling arms and wiping the dampness off my face. "Yeah, okay!"

"What's that supposed to mean?" He wore a perplexed expression.

I laughed again, "I had Drew! To be more specific, I had Drew twice—but did I really ever have him? No!" I spun around and stalked to the other side of the room. "He's no better than Gary! Why do men think they can go around cheating on people and not get caught? Huh? Why?" I raised my good arm and held it out to the side as I questioned him. He appeared more confused as I ranted, but I didn't care. My shoulder throbbed, and I was pissed. Everything had finally come down on me, and my emotions were in an uproar. "Where is my medicine? I need to take a pain pill, and then I am going to bed."

Chris started to move towards me, and I held my hand up, palm out, "Stop. Just tell me where they are. I want to be alone."

"They are on the kitchen counter." I knew he was staring at me as I went to retrieve the vial. I grabbed a can of ginger ale from the fridge and went straight to my room without another word.

He probably thought I was an overemotional female, but I really didn't give a shit. I wanted to take the pill and forget about everything for a little while longer.

Chapter 34 – Drew

The rest of the afternoon was quiet. Bria was gone for most of it, as was Will. Gary stayed in his office, and I only saw him once when he came out to get some coffee. He had paused at the side of my desk as if he wanted to say something but changed his mind and went back to his office.

I took a moment to let Jose know that Mack was doing well and asked him to help keep his eye out for anything between Bria, Gary, and Will. He said he would check into some things on Will and see if he could find out anything else.

I also slipped him the phone list and asked him if he could check the numbers to see if he could figure out to whom they belonged. He told me he'd work on that from home, so no one would know.

When I left at four, I pulled out of the parking lot and turned on my other phone. A few moments after it booted up, the text messages from Chris came down with the information about Mack's sister—or should I say Macky?

I could not imagine someone calling her by a nickname like that. It was too feminine to fit her. I punched in the address on my GPS and sighed—a five-hour drive. It was going to be a long night.

I acknowledged Chris's text messages and stared at the screen when I read his last message, *FYI, somehow she knows you are from L.A.*

Did you tell her? I typed back.

No, I did not. She made mention of it earlier.

Shit. *I never told her. How the hell did she find out?*

When he didn't respond back right away, I set up my Sync on my car and pulled back on the road. I had a long ride ahead of me.

How had Mack found out I lived in L.A.? I had never mentioned it, and if Chris didn't either, then how the hell did she know?

I checked my phone when I stopped for gas and to get a cup of coffee. There was a message from Chris to call him when I could.

"What's going on?" I said when he answered the phone.

"She went into meltdown status right after I last spoke to you."

"What do you mean meltdown status?" I stood outside of my car, leaning on the back tailgate.

"It all hit her. Losing her house, the fact that her job might be on the line now, she even freaked out about her car. Man, did she freak out about her car."

I cringed, "You have no idea how much she loved that car."

"Obviously," he replied slowly.

"Did she say anything else?" I scanned the parking lot, looking for any cars—or more exactly, tails—that might be following me.

"I don't know how she knows, Andy, but I think she knows about your kids and Annabelle."

My heart skipped a beat and I stood up straight, "What?"

"She made a comment in her tirade about all men being cheaters."

"Shit." I hung my head. She had no idea what the truth really was. No wonder she didn't want to talk to me. "I'll explain it all to her when this is over. She'll understand." She has to, I told myself.

"I hope so, for your sake."

I thanked him for the information and apologized to him for having to deal with the emotional woman stuff. I knew it wasn't the first time he'd had to do it, but no man wanted to deal with a hysterical female.

I climbed back in the car and got back on the road. I didn't see a tail behind me, but that didn't mean I wasn't being followed. I was leery about going to her sister's house, but I had no choice. I needed that evidence.

It was around eight-thirty when I pulled up in front of a large two-story house in an affluent neighborhood. Lights were on in one of the front rooms. At least they were home. That would have sucked if they weren't.

I made my way to the door, stepping over a roller skate that lay in the driveway. That's right, her sister had a couple of kids. Mack had mentioned that.

I knocked on the door and wondered what kind of reception I was going to get from her sister. A man almost my height answered the door. "Can I help you?"

"Hello, my name is Drew Bradley. I'm a friend of your sister-in-law. Would Cindy be home?"

"Sure, come on in. I'm Jeff, Cindy's husband. Is everything alright? I know Cindy was trying to contact her, but she can't seem to get ahold of her."

"She is safe." I left it at that for the moment. Jeff studied me for a minute then left me in the living room while he went to get Cindy.

When she entered, she eyed me from head to toe. "Hmm," she said when she finished, "so you're Drew?"

"Yes, ma'am." I held my hand out and she shook it.

"Have a seat. I understand my sister's dilemma now." She smirked as she took a seat opposite me on the couch. Her husband sat beside her.

I had no idea what she was talking about. What dilemma? "Excuse me?" I said as I sank down into the luxurious cushion of the wingback chair.

She laughed and waved it away with her hand, "Nothing, girl talk. What can I help you with, Drew? Where is my sister?"

I cleared my throat, "Mack is in a safe house right now."

She sat up straighter, "A safe house, why?" Jeff moved closer and took her hand.

"The night that Mack left here, she went home and was out to dinner with a friend. They were both shot that night." She sucked in a breath, and her hand flew to her chest.

"She's okay. It was only a shoulder injury," I was quick to let her know she was alive.

"Why? Does it have to do with this case you are working on?"

"Yes, it does." I sat up to the edge of the chair, "Cindy, I need your help."

She appeared confused, "What can I do?"

"You have some evidence that she gave you for safekeeping. I need that."

"What evidence?" her husband spoke up for the first time.

She turned to look at him, "Mack gave me a disc to hold on to. It has some evidence against Gary." She turned back to me, "How can I trust you? Are you really FBI?"

I smiled, smart girl just like her sister. I pulled my FBI credentials out of my back pocket and handed them to her. She studied them and then looked up at me.

"She also told me that you call her Macky." Tears sprang to her eyes, and she struggled to hold them back.

"Okay, I believe you. She would never admit that to anyone, unless it was important." She handed me back the leather wallet that held my badge and ID. "I can get you a copy of it, but I'm keeping the original, just in case."

"Good idea." I thought for a moment, "Actually, could you make two copies?"

"Sure, who is the second one for?" She stood up.

"I am going to have you mail the second copy to my supervisor at headquarters, just in case something happens to my copy."

"This case is that dangerous?" she whispered.

"Two people have been killed, and Mack was shot. Her house was also burned to the ground after an explosion there."

She sank back to the cushion, and her husband moved to put his arm around her. "You're kidding me, her house?" She stared at me with a vacant expression on her face. "Wait, what about her car?"

"It's gone, thanks to the explosion."

"Oh, man, she loved that car." She stood back up and dwelled on that for a moment.

"I know." I smiled sadly, and she turned to leave the room, walking towards the back of the house.

"Is Mack really alright?" Jeff asked when Cindy was out of earshot.

"Yes, she is. She is in a very safe place and with an agent trained for special protection." I leaned back in the chair. He continued to sit on the edge of the sofa and clenched his hands into a fist as his elbows rested on his knees.

"It was really only a shoulder injury?" His head snapped up just as he finished, "Wait, that was her, the one that was shot and injured and an agent was killed outside the restaurant."

I nodded, unable to voice who that agent was.

"Ironically, I figured she would have been there investigating it, not being the victim." He shook his head and stared at the coffee table with a vacant look in his eyes.

"The bullet went through her shoulder. It was a clean hit, and she was released a few hours after it happened. I've had her in hiding since."

He barked out a laugh, "I bet that is going over well." I thought back on the emotional outburst that Chris had told me about.

"You have no idea." I gave him a wry smile.

We chatted for a few minutes while we waited for Cindy. When she returned, she had a pad of paper with her that she handed to me.

"Here, write the address for your supervisor. I'll make sure it goes out first thing tomorrow morning." I wrote the address down and handed the paper back to her. She held the disc in hand but did not hold it out to me.

"You know what's on here, right?" She tapped the disc case on her pad. I nodded and flicked a glance at Jeff who was observing us.

"And you know she is there, too," she said softly.

"I will do everything I can do to keep her safe, Cindy. I promise you that. I care about your sister, more than even she knows."

She absorbed the words and finally handed me the disc. A few minutes later, I was out the door and on my way back to my apartment.

The thoughts whirled so fast in my mind that I didn't think I would need caffeine at all on my way home. I glanced at the disc beside me. If there was a way to remove the video of her, I'd do it in a heartbeat, but I knew I couldn't. That would be altering evidence.

The ride home was uneventful, and with little traffic on the road, I was home a little after one. I passed out in bed as soon as I lay down.

I wasn't sure if I was just tired when I woke up or if the feeling of impending doom was from something else. I dressed and headed into the station.

Jose was at his desk, but Gary wasn't in, and neither was Bria or Will. The bad feeling intensified.

"Any idea where they are?" I asked Jose as I set my coffee cup on my desk.

He shook his head, "No, I was wondering that myself." He rolled his chair back and pulled a file out of his briefcase. "Here, this is what I found on the phone numbers."

I took the file and sat down at my desk before I opened it. I started to close it when I heard footsteps, but didn't when I saw it was only Gordon.

"Morning, guys," he called out as he set his satchel down beside his desk.

Jose and I both called out our greetings, and then I dug into the information that Jose had found. Some of the phone numbers were business listings and seemed legitimate. I bypassed those and moved further down the list. I stopped when I saw the information about one certain number.

I turned to Jose; he glanced at me over his screen. I stood up and moved to the side of his desk. I glanced over my shoulder and saw Gordon on the phone.

"How did you find out that information?" I whispered to Jose.

"I hacked into Will's contacts."

I snorted. "You need to come work for us. I didn't get a chance to tell you, but I met Mike yesterday."

His surprise was evident, "You did?"

"Yeah, he slipped me some information when I went out to lunch."

"No shit?" Jose leaned back in his chair. "It must have been important information for him to reach out of the gang. He's pretty deep in there right now." He tapped his pen on the desk. "What information did he give you?"

"He confirmed who was involved. While Mike seems to be deep in his gang work, Will seems to have taken it a bit too seriously. He's gone rogue and is probably the one who pulled Bria and Gary in." I walked back to my desk, "Now, we just need to figure out how to take them down."

My phone rang, and I answered it without thinking.

"Bradley, it's Gary." I gripped the handset tighter. Why was he calling me? And was he whispering?

"Yes?"

"You need to get to Mack, and you need to get to her quick. I can't say any more, just get to her." I heard him disconnect, and I stared at the receiver. Why had he been whispering?

I set the phone down slowly and spun around to face Jose. My stomach twisted, and my hackles went up.

"Jose, can you trace Gary's cellphone? Or Bria's?"

He looked at me curiously, "Yeah, if they have it on, why?"

I peered over at Gordon. He stood up and walked out of the unit tapping a pen in his hand as he did.

"Gary just called me and told me to get to Mack. See if you can find out where they are."

"Shit," Jose responded and immediately started clicking his mouse and typing on the keyboard.

I walked around the back of his desk to watch him. When the screen came up showing the GPS location of Gary's cell, my heart skipped a beat.

"Bring up Bria's phone." I leaned closer and felt my hands get clammy.

"She's on the highway heading north, too." He looked up at me over his shoulder.

"Son of a bitch, they found her." I moved back to my desk and grabbed the file he gave me along with my bag.

Jose was already out of his seat and pulling something out of his drawer. A small caliber handgun lay in his palm, "My backup." He slipped it into his pocket.

"Good, I have a feeling we are going to need all the backup we can get." Jose grabbed a laptop bag from behind his desk, and we ran out of the building.

Chapter 35 – Mack

I didn't want to get out of bed. I was embarrassed at the way I had acted the previous night. How old was I the last time I threw a temper tantrum and freaked out emotionally? I had to have been a teenager. Even with the incident with Gary, I hadn't flipped my lid.

With a heavy sigh, I climbed out of bed and went to brush my teeth. I looked down at my lounge pants and t-shirt and shrugged. There was nobody here to impress.

The cabin was quiet, and I searched the cabinet for the coffee stuff. After finding it and getting it started, I opened the fridge to see if there was something simple I could make for breakfast. Cereal was about the easiest thing to accomplish, but I doubted Chris would be happy with that.

"Don't even think you are cooking." I jumped when I heard his sleepy voice behind me.

"Don't sneak up on me like that!" I adjusted the sling strap around my neck while he winked at me.

He set his phone down on the table and went to pull down two coffee mugs out of the cabinet. "How do pancakes and bacon sound?"

"Like heaven." I sank down into a chair while he moved around the kitchen getting things ready. He put a mug of coffee in front of me when it finished gurgling. "I need to apologize to you."

Chris was mixing the batter for the pancakes and paused to glance my way. "No, it's okay. I get it." He went back to stirring.

"No, it's not okay. I totally freaked out yesterday, and that is not me." I took a sip of my coffee. "I'm sorry about that."

He set the spoon down and turned around to give me his full attention. "Mack, most people would have fallen apart a lot sooner and still wouldn't have picked themselves up. It is completely normal to break down."

I shook my head, "But I'm not normal." As soon as I spoke, I realized what I'd said and burst out laughing.

"Good to know," Chris joined in and turned back to the pancakes.

"After breakfast, you want to finish that game of Scrabble? I was beating you. I need to make that official."

"Yeah, we'll see about that."

We chatted while he finished cooking breakfast and ate.

"Why don't we take showers, let me dress your shoulder again, and then we can finish our game," he offered.

I agreed, and while he cleaned up the kitchen, I took the first shower.

I was sitting in the kitchen waiting for him when his cellphone rang. I looked at the screen and saw "Cooper" on it. Drew was calling. The sight of that name on the screen brought up a sad feeling, and I lifted the phone and stared at the name. I pushed the button on the side and turned the volume to off. I laid the phone on the table facing down.

If Drew left him a message, the blinking light would taunt me. Turning it over, I'd never know.

I looked around in the cabinets until I found the little medical kit that Chris had used on me before. I opened it up and began removing paraphernalia that I had seen him use the last time.

When he finished with his shower, I was sitting on the table waiting for him.

"Well, aren't you a good little patient?" he teased.

"My way of apologizing for my psycho scene yesterday."

"If you really want to apologize, you can let me beat you in Scrabble," he said as he pulled gloves on.

"No way! I'll be nice and help, but I'm not throwing a game for your ego."

He shrugged, "It was worth a try." For the next few minutes, we joked around while he cleaned my shoulder and put more medicine on it. He told me to keep the sling off for a while and to try to use my shoulder a little bit. I was more than happy to free my arm of the sling.

We sat down to finish our game, and I purposely used my left hand at times to give some movement to my shoulder. We cleaned up the game, and I realized my shoulder was starting to throb again. I went to get the vial of pain pills from my room.

Chris gave me a snack bar to eat so it wouldn't upset my stomach and I lay down on the sofa, knowing full well I would be asleep in a few minutes.

The tree was screaming at me, and I couldn't figure out why. I only knew that the sound was so high pitched that it hurt my ears and wouldn't stop. I heard my name being called, and I stared at the mouth on the tree. It wasn't saying my name. I felt someone grab my arm, and I jumped.

Chris was in my face, "Mack, you gotta wake up. Come on. They found you."

"What?" I was disoriented. The screeching was the alarm in the house. It had invaded my dream. The trees had been telling me to run.

"Mack, there are people outside. Come look at the monitors and see if you recognize them." He pulled me up off the couch as another beep went off, and I cringed.

As we went to his room, I noticed all the curtains were pulled tightly closed. Were the doors locked?

I entered the room, and stood in front of the monitors. My heart was thudding loudly in my chest. I knew it wasn't exactly from fear but from being forced awake with such extreme measures.

I blinked, trying to focus on the screens in front of me. "Do you know who they are?" he asked quickly, and I nodded.

I pointed to a woman in the right screen, "That's Bria." She was holding a gun in her hand. No way in hell was she going to take me down.

"That's Gary." He was standing back away from the rest of them, looking around. Was he waiting for more people, or trying to escape?

"I don't know those four." I paused and squinted at another screen, "Wait, son of a bitch, that's Will!"

There were three coming from the back and three from the front. Did they think they were going to just bust in and kill us? They all had guns in their hands.

"How secure is this house?" I squeaked out. There were six of them and two of us, and I didn't have a gun. I assumed Chris did. How good of a shot was he?

"It's pretty secure." He turned and walked away, "Have you seen my cellphone?"

Immediately, I remembered his phone ringing a few hours ago. Guilt assaulted me as I realized Drew had most likely been calling to warn us. "It's on the kitchen table." I went to the door, "I forgot to tell you that Drew called earlier."

He picked up the phone and looked at the screen. "He called eighteen times!" He spun around to look at me.

"I turned down the volume the first time he called." I held my hands out, "How was I supposed to know it was an emergency?"

A second sensor went off, and Chris rushed into the room with his cell to his ear.

"Yeah, my volume was down, and I am well aware that they are coming. They are already here. Where are you?"

He stared at the screens relaying the information that I had told him about who was out there.

"Are there any other agents in the area?" he asked, and I heard Drew's voice but couldn't make out the words. "They are crossing the second perimeter, so about fifty yards out. No way I can get her out of the house now." Chris walked away from the monitors and to another closet. "Yeah, we are fine with that." He pulled the folding door back to reveal a large gun cabinet. Yes!

I watched him as he did the combination and pulled it open. There were at least ten different guns inside of all different sizes and calibers. He opted for an AR-15 rifle. I knew I would not be able to handle something that heavy with my shoulder, not if I wanted to be accurate. I searched the inside and found a .45 caliber Glock. I slid back the chamber, already loaded. Good.

I searched the side and found two magazines. I slipped them into the waistband of my lounge pants. How I wish I had jeans on so I could put another in my pockets. Wait, I had jeans. I pulled the magazines out of my waistband and tossed them on the bed running from the room.

"Mack, where the hell are you going?"

I entered my room and dropped my lounge pants to the floor. I yanked open a drawer just as Chris ran through the entrance and did an about face. "You pick now to worry about what you're wearing? Good God, woman!"

"No, I need a tight waistband and pockets to hold the magazines." I yanked up the pants and kicked my sneakers out from under the bed. "I need you to untie those for me."

"Seriously?" he asked but bent down to snatch one off the ground.

"If we have to run, do you think I would get far in flip flops?" I sneered at him, not meaning to.

"Okay, true." He dropped the one and picked up the other one. I slipped my foot into the shoe and bent to lace it up, but I jerked when I stretched my shoulder further than it wanted to go. He pushed my hands out of the way and dropped down on his knee to tie the shoe. I pushed my foot into the second one, and he tied it and stood up just as another alarm went off. "They're within twenty-five yards."

He took off out of the room, and I was right behind him, my left arm tucked tightly into my side. I ignored the stabbing pain that using my arm had caused. He stopped so fast before he reached the door that I almost slammed right into his back. He turned around to run to the coffee table. After hitting a few buttons, the room was filled with the noise of a car chase. Smart, they wouldn't be able to hear us.

I went into his room and straight to the monitor. "Chris!" I yelled. He ran into the room and stopped at my side. "Please tell me that's not what I think it is." The screens weren't color, but it wasn't hard to make out what two guys were carrying. "What the hell do we do now? They might not be able to break the doors down, but they can burn the building up." We both stared at the screen and watched the two men get closer to us carrying large gas containers.

Chris's phone began to ring, and he jerked it to his ear, "You better call the fire department."

I heard Drew yell on the phone.

"No, not yet, but they are about to set it on fire. They brought two large gas cans."

Chris paused, listening to Drew. "No, there is no way to safely get out, but we might have to take a chance and make a run for it if it gets too bad inside. How far out are you?"

He paused and listened for a moment. "You better hurry the hell up! And get some local police cars heading this way."

He hung up the phone and put his hand on my good shoulder. "I'm sorry about this, Mack. I don't know how they found us, but I will do everything I can to get us out of here alive."

"It's not your fault. I'm sorry you're in this mess." I looked into his face. Tension etched his features.

"Protecting you is my job." He gave me a tight-lipped smile.

"And it's mine too, to protect you. It's what we do. So you watch my back, and I watch yours."

He squeezed my good shoulder, and we turned back to the screens.

They were pouring the gasoline around the foundation of the house. Another alarm went off, and Chris pushed a button to silence it. We were well aware that they were right outside. As the liquid ran to the ground, I could imagine the smell.

I inhaled subconsciously, but the fumes did not reach inside, not yet at least.

"If we have to run for it, head east. There is a road that way. Flag down a car."

I nodded.

We watched as they dropped a match onto the gasoline and flames flickered up and spread rapidly around the cabin. I shuddered. How long would it take for the fire to make it inside? Or worse, the smoke?

Chapter 36 – Drew

"Why the hell aren't they answering the damned phone!" I wasn't asking a question. I was beyond questions. I was ready to freak the hell out! Okay, I was already freaking out.

"How the hell did they find her?" I had been dwelling on the question the whole trip.

"Did you have your unit cellphone with you?" Jose asked.

I wanted to slam my head into the steering wheel! I had been so glad that she didn't have her phone with her, but I had forgotten about mine. How easy I had made it for them. All they had to do was access my phone and pull my GPS records. I had given her to them on a silver platter!

I glanced at the speedometer, eighty-five. I pushed it above ninety.

"They're there," Jose said tensely beside me. "Should we call local units in?"

"How much further is it?" I didn't dare take my eyes off the road as I asked. I had the police lights activated and cars were moving out of my way, for the most part. From time to time, I came up on drivers that weren't paying attention, and I'd hit the siren. They moved quickly after that.

"About twenty miles," he answered from the passenger seat. The whole ride, he had been watching their progress on his laptop. Gary's car had been driving the speed limit, and that was the only way we had been able to gain on them.

"Shit!" My phone started to ring and I snatched it up, "Thank God!" I hit the answer button. "Where the hell have you been! They found her!"

"Yeah, my volume was down, and I am well aware of that; they are already here. Where are you?"

"We are about twenty miles out. Jose is with me. We've been tracking them. Who is there? Can you tell?"

"Yeah, there are four she doesn't know, but Bria, Gary, and Will are there. Are there any other agents in the area?" Chris asked me.

"I put a call into Todd. He was going to put a call out to anyone in the area. How close are they? Can you get her out of the house?"

When he told me they were crossing the fifty-yard perimeter, I knew it was too late. Damn it. Why had his phone volume been turned down? What the hell had they been doing?

"Do you have enough firepower in the house?"

He told me they were fine with that, and I told him I would call Todd back and find out what I could about other agents.

I hit Todd's number, "They just arrived on location. We are about—" I paused and glanced at Jose.

"Fifteen," he threw out.

"We are about fifteen miles out and traveling at about ninety." Todd told me there were three other agents in the area that were en route to the location. We would all arrive at about the same time.

I hung up and dialed Chris back for him to announce, "You better call the fire department."

"What the hell are you talking about?" I yelled into the phone. I wasn't in the mood for jokes. "Please tell me they did not set the cabin on fire."

Images of Mack's house burning crawled into my mind. I couldn't let that happen. "Isn't there a safe way out?"

Chris's words put a chill down my spine, "No, there is no way to safely get out, but we might have to take a chance and make a run for it if it gets too bad inside. How far out are you?"

"About ten miles. Another few agents are coming."

"You better hurry the hell up! And get some local police cars heading this way." I heard the tension in his voice, something that was never in his voice unless it was life threatening.

"I will." I hung up the phone and told Jose to call nine-one-one and to get cars en route.

We were five miles out when I saw the smoke. "Oh, shit."

Jose looked up and repeated my comment. I heard him speaking to the operator and explaining there was smoke rising from the tree line. I pushed the gas harder and hit my siren to get around another car.

My phone rang when we exited the highway, four miles out from the cabin. I tossed it to Jose so I could focus on the roads and traffic.

"There are two agents on scene; they are waiting for you."

I nodded and drove around two cars on the opposite side of the road. I didn't dare use my siren now. We were getting too close.

The smoke was billowing into the sky, and I wondered how Mack was holding up. I said a silent prayer that they would be alright.

We found the other agents, and they advised that local police were just a few minutes out. I didn't care where the hell they were. I jumped out of the car and took off on foot. I heard thudding behind me and glanced to see Jose right behind me. One of the other agents was following close behind and arching to the left to take a different approach.

I heard sirens off in the distance, just about the time I had my first view of the cabin. Flames were licking over the entire outside and focusing on the roof. I watched as a piece of the roof collapsed into the house, and my heart skidded to a stop.

I forced myself to stop and scan the area. I saw someone running around the back of the house. Jose saw him at the same time and took off after him.

There was another person out front. I could see a leg from behind a tree. I moved closer and ducked behind a bush. It wasn't the smartest cover because it wouldn't stop a bullet, but it did conceal me for the moment until I could figure out my next move.

I heard talking and peered around the tree. "We have to get out of here; this isn't going to work." Gary spoke to Bria as he stood in front her.

She squared off her shoulders, "We are not going anywhere until I know she is dead."

"Jesus, Bria! She is going to be lucky to survive this," he gestured towards the burning cabin, "we have to get out of here before we get caught."

She laughed, and I clenched my jaw. "What are you afraid of, Gary? We can say we were rescuing her from a kidnapping and arrived here after the place was on fire. Those other guys already took off. At least we can come up with a plausible excuse for us being here. I'm not leaving until I know she is dead. The only thing that would be better was if her boyfriend was in there with her."

I slid sideways and inched towards another tree. Bria was facing away, but Gary was facing me. If he saw me, would he do something to alert her? Even though he had called me to warn me, I couldn't trust him.

I stared at the cabin. I had to move fast, or I would never get inside.

I saw Will walk back from the house down the driveway towards the cars. If he reached the car, he would see the other cars and know we were here. I turned to the other agent and pointed at Will. He acknowledged me with a nod and moved that way.

I held my gun in front of me but pointed low. I was going to have to take the chance that Gary knew I was there. I had no other way to approach.

I stepped out, and his eyes instantly flicked my way. A large crack came from the house, and I heard a chunk of the ceiling fall in. I forced myself not to falter and to keep moving. I would never be able to help her if I stopped to stare.

Sirens were closing in around us. I wasn't sure if it was from police or fire, but I didn't care.

Gary put his eyes to the ground. Was he waging an internal

battle? Bria shifted, and I thought she was going to turn in my direction.

Just before she did, Gary pulled his arm back and slugged her so hard her head snapped back, and she went straight to the ground. Her weapon bounced on the dusty dirt driveway.

Gary met my eyes and shrugged, "I've wanted to do that for a while."

I almost laughed.

I tossed my cuffs at him and said, "Lock her up."

He didn't say anything else, and I heard gunshots coming from the driveway. I spun around with my gun pointed out in front of me. Someone yelled, "FBI, put your weapon down."

Another round of shots echoed in the trees, and all was quiet. I didn't know who was shot, but someone must have been for it to have become so deathly silent. Another large cracking noise came from the house, and I spun around.

Gary stood next to me, "Is there a way in?"

I pulled my phone out and hit Chris's number. "Unlock the door! Where are you?"

He was coughing, and I heard Mack coughing next to him. "Master bathroom," he managed to rattle out between coughs, "unlocked."

I ran towards the house, Gary was close on my heels. "What the hell do you think you are doing?" I yelled at him.

"I let her get into this mess; the least I can do is make sure she lives to get out!"

I turned back to the house just as a loud air horn came from the road: fire trucks. No time to wait. I spun the knob on the door handle and pushed my way inside.

Flames licked along the interior, but there was an area that we could enter, for now. I glanced at the roof; it looked ready to collapse the rest of the way very soon.

We went into the cabin bending over, trying to keep our heads down and out of the worst smoke. I held my arm over my mouth and nose, but the smoke burned my eyes, and they watered.

I felt my way to the master bedroom along the side wall where the fire had not yet reached. The door was closed, and Gary and I had to push to get it open. Timber had fallen on the backside, but the flame had gone out and it only smoldered. This room had the least amount of damage. We reached the bathroom just about the time that the smoke started getting to us.

I heard Gary coughing from behind me. The smoke was thick, and I used my hands to feel my way to the bathroom from the memory of the one and only time I had been here. Gary was holding onto my shirt so he wouldn't get lost in the black smoke.

We reached the bathroom door and pushed it open. "Mack! Chris!" I yelled and began to cough from sucking in the smoke.

I heard hacking before I heard Chris's voice, "Over here."

When I reached his side, Mack was unconscious, leaning against him in the bathtub. He held a wet cloth over her face. "She still has a pulse, but it's thready. Get her out of here."

I didn't need any further prompting. I swung her limp body over my shoulder and turned. Gary helped Chris stand and put his arm around him to help him out of the house. His oxygen levels would be low enough for him to pass out from the slightest exertion.

The front door was in sight, and I was imagining the fresh air that would fill my burning lungs as the first fireman stepped into view.

We burst through the door, and another fireman ripped Mack from my arms. I fell to my knees as the coughing wracked my body. Tears blurred my vision; I wiped at my eyes, but that only made them burn more.

From my hands and knees, I saw Gary put Chris to the ground and sink beside him. They both fought for fresh air and tried to purge the bad. Mack was lying in the dirt ten feet from me, and I could see several people on their knees working on her.

"Mack," I tried to say, but it came out as a choking cough. I began to crawl towards her.

A stretcher came between me and her before I could get to my feet. They swung her body onto the stretcher and started pushing her away even as someone else secured the safety belts.

Someone pushed me back to the ground and fit an oxygen mask over my face. I needed to go to Mack, but the pure oxygen felt incredible to my burning lungs.

I closed my eyes and prayed that Mack would make it. She couldn't go through all this and die from smoke inhalation!

I heard a siren spark up and race away from the scene. Another stretcher appeared, and I was helped on to it. Someone squeezed my shoulder, and I opened my eyes to see Jose.

"I got the one that took off that way. One of the agents was shot, but he will be okay. Will was killed."

I nodded my understanding, knowing I wouldn't be able to talk without coughing.

"You got Mack out?" he watched me carefully, I nodded.

"Gary helped you?" He looked over to the side and I nodded again, but he was looking away from me.

Jose walked away, and I lifted myself up on my elbow to see where he was going. When he reached the stretcher that Gary was on, he snatched his cuffs off his belt and picked up Gary's wrist.

Gary wore an oxygen mask and met Jose's hard gaze head on. Jose clamped the cuff around his right wrist and then around the side bar of the stretcher. Gary dropped his head back to the stretcher, and I lay back down.

Bria and Gary were in custody, and Will was dead. I knew there were others that were involved, and we would find them, but for now, my job was done.

An EMT came to push my stretcher into an ambulance. As the door closed on the back, it felt like this chapter of my life was over. With my job finished, it was time to go home.

Chapter 37 – Mack

"The roof is going to collapse; we have to get to a smaller room." Chris tugged me away from the monitors.

The smoke was thickening inside, and we were both starting to wheeze. "But Drew's here!" I yelled and tried to pull away to go back.

Chris grabbed both my arms and faced me, "Mack, if we don't get into the bathroom, we are going to die before he gets in!"

I saw the fear in his eyes. I nodded, and he pulled me along beside him.

We went into the master bedroom just as a patch of the ceiling collapsed into the living room.

Chris yelled, "Get in the bathroom."

He pushed me, and I tripped over my own feet. My heart thudded, and the smoke burned my eyes and lungs. He slammed the door shut and grabbed a towel. He turned to the tub and spun the tap handle.

"What are you doing?" I asked him as I rubbed my left shoulder, the pain streaked through it.

"Putting a seal on the door." He wet the towel and twisted it before pushing it up against the bottom of the door. He looked at the top, "Not much I can do for that." He turned back to me, "Get those other towels wet, and your clothes, too." I didn't move, "Now,

Mack!"

The sound of another section of the roof falling in snapped me out of my zone, and I stepped into the bathtub and turned on the shower nozzle. I stood under the water and allowed my entire body to get soaked, gun and all.

Chris tossed towels in at my feet and then climbed in behind me. I moved out of the way so he could get wet.

"Sit down in the bathtub. I'm going to cover you with the wet towels."

"What about you?" I asked him before I sat, "You have to get in here, too." He nodded and climbed in behind me. I leaned back against his chest, and we started pulling towels over our bodies.

Even with the towel against the door, the smoke encroached on us. Most of it seeped in from the roof. We sat in the tub and listened to the flames crackling around us. The sound of my heart beating almost drowned out the sound of the fire, but not quite.

Chris held me close. I think he needed the reassurance as much as I did. I coughed harder, and he put a towel over my face. "Here, hold this over your mouth. It will help filter the air." I watched as he did the same.

I began to feel nauseous and sleepy. I knew I was losing consciousness. How much longer until they reached to us? Where the hell was the fire department? Would I ever see Drew or my sister again? Was I going to survive being shot, just to die in a fire?

The questions flew around in my mind as I grew more tired and coughed more often. I heard Chris's phone ring, but I was already fighting to keep conscious. I couldn't understand what he was saying.

The last thing I remembered was Chris holding me tight and kissing my head, "Hold on, Mack, he's coming." I heard his voice trickle into my mind and then everything went black like the smoke that swirled around us.

No! No more alarms! Turn them off! I twitched and tried to find the source of the alarm going off.

"Hey, hold still, you're okay." I felt arms holding me down, and I struggled to fight. A sharp pain went from my shoulder straight into my neck, and I think I let out a scream before everything went dark again.

There was cold air rushing into my nose. I didn't like it, but it was better than the dark stuff that had burned my nasal passages and throat. I coughed. I felt like I had been sucking on charcoal.

Darkness claimed me again just as Drew's face came to mind.

I awoke in a hospital room. I was well aware of where I was: light pea green walls, an uncomfortable bed, a beige curtain hanging by my side, and a tube under my nose pushing cold air into it. I just didn't remember why, not at first. I blinked to clear my eyes, and as they cleared, so did the haze surrounding the events.

Something moved in the room, and I turned to the noise. Drew sat in the corner with a computer sitting on his lap; he was typing. He must have felt my eyes on him. He did have an uncanny way of knowing when I was watching him.

He raised an eyebrow and gave me one of his heart-stopping smiles. Good thing I was in the hospital, because when my heart gave out from staring at him, they could bring me back to life to do it again and again—or maybe not.

"Hey, sleepy head." He closed his laptop and set it aside. I watched his every move. The case was close to being over, and I knew that his time here was limited. He needed to go back to his life, the one with his family that he hadn't told me about.

He sat on the edge of the bed, "What's wrong? Are you in pain? I can have the nurse come in and give you some medicine."

"No, I'm not in pain." I shifted in the bed to get more comfortable and to move away from him just a tiny bit. He noticed.

"We need to talk, Mack."

"Yes, we do, so tell me what happened when you came to get us. Who was behind it all, and what the hell were they doing?"

"That's not what we need to talk about."

"That is all there is to talk about, Agent Cooper."

A hurt look passed over his features, and his forehead wrinkled. "Wow, Agent Cooper, really?"

I stared at him, unable to find a witty comment to make back.

"Mack, we need to talk about us."

I shifted, not uncomfortable with my position, but with the look in his eye.

"There is no us. There is a me, and there is a you, and then, of course, there is your family."

He watched me for a minute and then broke out in a grin. "You think I'm married and have been cheating on my wife, is that it?"

"Aren't you?" I threw back at him. I was angry that he wanted to have this talk while I was stuck in a hospital bed and not able to put distance between us.

He shook his head, "No, Mack. I'm not married. I never lied to you about that. I have never been married."

I eyed him carefully. "But you have kids. Are you going to deny them, too?" I spat out.

"Nope, Alexandra and Andy are mine. They are twins, and Annabelle is their mother, but I am not and never have been married to her." He reached for my hand. I allowed him to lift it because I was intrigued by what he was saying.

"I met Annabelle in college, we had a relationship, and she got pregnant. I asked her to marry me, but she knew I was just doing it because I felt I needed to." He paused and had a faraway look in his eye. "Don't get me wrong, I love Anna, but not like I should love someone I want to spend my life with." He paused, and I wondered if he was going to tack something on there about me. He didn't and after a few seconds, continued, "I stayed in the area so I could be close to the kids. We didn't ever live together, but we shared custody. We are good friends, that's all, just good friends."

My heart thawed a little bit, but I remembered that he still had kids, children that needed him on the other side of the country.

He took a deep breath and sighed, "Annabelle has brain cancer."

My jaw dropped open, and I found myself squeezing his hand. "How bad is it?"

He looked down at our hands and ran a thumb over my knuckles. "I spoke with her oncologist the other day; it's not good. They have been doing treatment, but the tumor is still growing, and they can't do surgery on it now."

"So she's dying?" I asked him quietly and he closed his eyes.

"Yes, she is." He opened them again and focused on me. "That's why I have to get back. Since she was diagnosed, I have been living in the guest room helping her out with the kids. The doctor thinks she only has a few months. The kids don't know that yet."

"Then you have to go." My heart was breaking for the two beautiful children whose picture I had seen on his phone. Their father should be by their side.

"I will, but I want you out of the hospital first."

I shook my head, "Drew, you don't need to stay here. You need to get home to your family. I will be fine, I promise."

"I know you will be, Mack, but I want us to be able to spend one more night together. I want to hold you and love you, one more time." He leaned down and kissed my forehead. "I don't know when I'll be able to get back this way, or what is going to happen when I return, but I do know that I want one more night with you."

I smiled at him, "I want that, too, more than anything." I stared into his eyes, and realized the depth of my feelings for him. He'd gone from being this sexy kid to a damned good investigator to an amazing man, and my heart grew just a little bit larger knowing the feelings I had for him lived within its beating walls.

He gave me one of his heart-thumping grins that made me giggle and leaned down to place his lips on mine as if to seal the deal.

"When do I get out of this joint?"

Drew laughed, "Tomorrow, you can go home tomorrow." He squeezed my hand.

"Okay, I think I can wait till tomorrow, so, since I can't have my way with you here and now, why don't you tell me what I missed while I was vacationing at the cabin?"

"Vacationing, is that what you call it?" He moved to sit further on the bed.

"Yeah, you're right, so not a vacation."

"Well, you know Will was involved right?" I nodded. "He is the one that pulled Bria into it and, in turn, Gary. They were stealing the cars, putting hidden compartments in them, and filling them with drugs to smuggle out of the country."

"Why would they use stolen cars? Why not just buy older cars."

"Because Timmons was in on it. He was able to give them documents that changed the identity of the cars, making them easier to ship. He also had new VIN plates issued for the cars; that's what was in the file you knew was missing. It was a list of the bogus VIN numbers."

"Aha! Okay, I get it." I thought for a moment. "How deeply was Gary in on it?"

He squeezed my hand, "Pretty deep, but he is cooperating. I actually ran into Mike, and he gave me some information about where the cars were being stored. We hit the warehouse early this morning, recovered four cars, and rounded up a few guys. Gary has given up a few more names and is filling in the details in return for a shorter sentence and a prison far away."

"So he's going to get a lighter sentence for this?" I wasn't sure I was happy about that.

"That's just for being involved in the stolen cars. He is still going to have to answer to charges for the sex tapes he took."

"Oh." I looked away. "Did you see them?" I could feel my cheeks heating up.

"No, I told them that wasn't my business. I think Jose is helping with the internal investigation for that, so you can save your embarrassment for him." He squeezed my hand, "And, by the way, the fingerprints from your house matched the same guy whose footprints were found at the one burglary and the homicide. We picked him up in the warehouse raid, and he made full admissions."

The door cracked opened, and Jose stuck his head in. "She's awake!" He walked over, patting Drew on the back. "You know he saved your life, right?"

Drew looked away sheepishly.

"No, what happened? We didn't get that far into the story."

"Well, Gary called him at the station and kind of gave away the fact that they were on their way to kill you. Drew turned into a mad man when he kept calling Chris's phone, and there was no answer. I swear my life flashed in front of my eyes so many times while he was driving." Drew rolled his eyes. "When we arrived there, the roof started falling in. Drew ended up getting Bria in custody."

"No, wait, Gary is the one who knocked her out and cuffed her," Drew added quickly.

"Gary knocked her out?" I laughed, "I would have loved to see that."

"It was priceless, but Gary ended up helping me get you and Chris out of the cabin."

"How is Chris doing?" Suddenly, I realized that no one had said anything about him, and I wondered if anything had happened to him.

"Relax, Mack, he's in the room right next door, and he's fine."

I released the air from my pained lungs, thankful that he was alright.

There was a knock on the door, and we all looked to see who was pushing it open. Tears filled my eyes as I saw my sister's face.

"Oh, Macky!" she ran into the room and bent over to hug me. I felt Drew climb off the bed to give her room to get to me.

"Macky?" I heard Jose say out loud. "That's your nickname? Macky?"

Drew grinned, "Yeah, be careful with that, though, only her sister is allowed to use it."

Cindy pulled back and looked at me, "I'm so glad you are alright."

"I am, thanks to Drew." He came around to the other side of the bed and held my hand.

Cindy leaned down to whisper in my ear, "You're right. I melted right down onto the couch the first time I saw him."

We both laughed and looked at Drew who raised his eyebrows in question.

Chapter 38 – Drew

I hung out at the hospital for a while but had to leave to run some errands. Cindy would be at the hospital to watch over Mack in the morning.

That morning, Jose and I had someplace else we needed to be. He stood beside me in full Class A Uniform and helped carry Rob to his final resting place. It was a difficult ceremony, and one that I hoped to never have to attend again.

I finally arrived at the hospital around three. When I entered her room, she was sitting on the edge of the bed dressed in lounge pants and a t-shirt. She looked apprehensive.

"What's wrong? You feeling alright?" I asked as I sat beside her and took her hand.

She nodded and then changed in mid-nod to shake her head. "I'm supposed to leave today, but I have no place to go."

I put my arm around her back, "All taken care of."

She looked up at me. "What do you mean?"

"You are going to be staying at my apartment. The FBI is going to allow you to stay there until you find something else and get settled. It's fully furnished. You even get to use the Explorer. I know it's not as nice as the Mustang, but it will get you from point A to point B."

The tension seemed to melt away from her face with each word I spoke. "Really?"

"Yes, really." I pulled her to me and held her close. "You almost ready to go?"

"Just waiting for my final papers." Just as she finished speaking, the door swung open and a nurse walked in with a clipboard. She went over the documents, and then Mack signed them and received her copies.

"Is my sister here?" she asked as she climbed into the wheelchair.

"No, she and Jeff are going to come over later tonight for dinner. They wanted you to get some rest." I winked at her, and I saw her cheeks start to color.

Mack was unusually quiet on the ride to my apartment. Well, I guess it was hers now, since I was leaving in the morning. I hadn't told her that part yet. I didn't want to ruin our evening.

When we arrived, I kept my arm around her as we climbed the stairs and I unlocked the door. She stepped inside and looked around while I closed and locked the door behind us, "Strange to think I will be living here, and you won't."

I rubbed her forearms gently. "I know, but the funny thing is I find it comforting that I will know exactly where you are."

She leaned her head back onto my shoulder, "I guess."

I let go of one of her arms and turned her to face me. "There is no guessing about it. I'm going to miss you like crazy MacKenzie. Knowing that at night you are laying your head on the same pillow that I did will make it easier for me."

She stared into my eyes. "I'm going to miss you, too," she said softly.

I lowered my head and took her lips. They opened immediately for me, and she put one arm around my shoulders and the other around my waist. Her body fit so perfectly against mine.

The kiss grew in urgency faster than I could have expected, and before I knew it, she was tugging at the end of my t-shirt to get it out of my waistband.

I grabbed her hands and pulled them around front while I dragged my lips from hers. She was about to say something when I let go of her hands and scooped her up into my arms.

Her lips found my neck as soon as she was level in my arms, and I carried her to the bedroom. I let her body slide down mine as she continued her assault on the sensitive skin of my neck. I shuddered as the feelings ripped through me.

She kissed her way up to my chin and nipped at it. I absorbed the feel of her against my body as I ran my hands down her back and under the edge of her shirt. She shivered as I trailed a finger up her spine.

We tumbled to the bed, and I forced myself to be careful with her shoulder. It had only been a few days since she had been shot. So much had happened since we had met two weeks ago.

Her hands caressed every part of my body that they could find, and I helped her find a few more by taking my clothes off and removing hers.

The feel of her breasts against my chest caused my groin to kick. What was it about this woman that had me in overdrive the moment our bodies came together?

Neither of us said a word, but we didn't have to. Our touches, our looks, and our kisses said it all. I grabbed a condom before we became too engrossed in our lovemaking, and as I entered her, I leaned up on my elbows and gazed into her eyes. I saw my own feelings shining back: I loved her, and she loved me.

Our lovemaking was slow and consuming. It brought us both to heights we could have only imagined, and when we came down, we held onto each other like there was no tomorrow.

I guess there really wasn't, since I would be flying across the country in the morning. That thought weighed heavily on my heart, and I knew Mack could feel the change come over me.

"What's wrong?" she asked as she snuggled deeper into my chest.

"My flight is tomorrow at nine."

She stiffened ever so slightly and didn't say anything for a long time. "What time do we have to leave?" she finally asked.

I leaned so I could peer into her face. "You don't have to take me to the airport."

"I know I don't, but I want to." The smile that graced her lips was sad, but it was a smile.

I pulled her back into my chest, "I'd like that." I ran my hand down her back, "We need to leave at seven."

"Okay," she whispered.

The afternoon went too quickly. We made love again and then dressed so I could cook dinner for her sister and brother-in-law. The meal was nothing special, but the company was awesome. It reinforced the thoughts I had, that Mack and I should be together.

When we fell in bed that night, we made love in a way that connected our souls not just our hearts. She lay on my chest, softly breathing, and I wasn't sure how I was going to get through tomorrow and saying goodbye to her. My chest ached just imagining it.

The sun broke the horizon, and I woke as the first beams of light hit the ceiling. I turned to find her studying me. "Morning."

"Good morning," she whispered as she curled her body into mine.

I wrapped my arms around her and felt my groin awaken when she ran her fingers over my stomach muscles. She teased them and slowly moved lower. I groaned as she teased one finger down the length of me.

She lifted her head and stared into my eyes, "Make love to me one last time."

I wrapped my hand around her neck and held her still. "This will not be the last time, Mack."

She gave me a half smile and leaned in to kiss me. Her naked body came in close contact with mine and stoked the fire deep within me. A hunger and need to prove her wrong roared through me, and I flipped her over and devoured her lips.

I took her harder this time than I had ever taken her, and she gave as good as she got. We both knew that our time was running out, and we fought to use every moment to the best of our ability, and did we ever.

The ride to the airport was quiet. We held hands and snuck peeks at one another. The closer we were to the airport, the tighter our hands became clasped. When we pulled up to the terminal I wondered whose hand was going to crush the other's first.

I turned in the seat and looked at her. I pushed some hair behind her ear. What did you say when you were leaving someone you knew you loved? What could be said to make it easier on either one of us?

"Mack," I started to speak, and she twisted in her seat and opened the door. I stared at the back of her head as she climbed out.

I made sure the key was in the ignition and walked to the back of the SUV. Mack crashed into me and threw her arms around my neck to embrace me, placing a punishing kiss on my lips.

I am sure the kiss was a little too much for a public arena, but I didn't care. I had no idea when I would be able to hold her and kiss her again. I felt my emotions whirling, and I wanted so bad to get back in the car and head back to the apartment, but I knew I couldn't.

She slowly ended the kiss, and we rested our foreheads together. I pulled back to see tears trickling down her cheeks. I swiped at one of them and fought to hold my own back.

"Mack," I tried to speak again, but she put a finger to my lips.

"No, don't say anything, no goodbyes, no promises. I know. Kiss me and walk away, please, just kiss me and walk away."

I shut my eyes in an attempt to control my emotions. If that would make it easier for her, then I would do it. I stepped out of her arms and opened the hatch, lifting my two suitcases and briefcase out and setting them on the sidewalk. I closed the hatchback and faced her.

The tears were still present in her emerald eyes but no longer running down her cheeks. I opened my arms, and she stepped into them. The kiss was bittersweet and didn't last anywhere long enough. Eternity wouldn't have been long enough.

She let me end the kiss, and without looking at her, without saying a word, I turned to the sidewalk, put my briefcase strap over my shoulder and picked up my two bags. I took a few steps when I heard the car door close and was just about to enter the building when the car started. I paused, unsure if I could take the next step.

In the reflection of the glass, I saw her glance my way, wipe her tear-stained face, then put the car in gear and pull away. I stepped into the terminal.

Chapter 39 - Mack

I heard my cellphone ping, but I ignored it. I was trying not to fall apart. It was hard enough to drive while swiping the tears off my cheeks every two seconds. I wouldn't have been able to hold it together if I had seen a message from him.

I had told him to walk away without a word. It was easier than the two of us standing there trying to declare a love that might never get fulfilled.

After a few miles, I was able to pull myself together and get back to his apartment. It would always be his apartment, and I wasn't sure if I would ever change the sheets. I know, gross, but I wanted to keep his scent with me.

I remembered one time saying I wouldn't be able to sleep with his unique smell filling my nose, but now I think it would be what helped me drift into a dreamland filled with loving families and hope.

I unlocked the door and stepped inside. The tears assaulted me without warning, and I sank to the floor. I felt like a blubbering idiot and blamed it on all the bad shit that had happened, not the fact that Drew was gone.

I lifted my sorry butt off the floor and went to make coffee. We had stayed in bed until the last moment, and neither one of us had complained.

As the coffee brewed, I sat down at the small table and picked up my cell. Should I look at it now, or would I fall apart again? Suck it up, girl! He's gone! Read his message already.

I woke up the screen and clicked on my text messages, I had one from my sister and two from Drew. I figured my sister would be picking up my pieces later, so I read the ones from Drew.

Mack – I know you didn't want me to say anything, but I had to tell you that I left a promise for you back at the apartment. Look under the pillow.

The second one said, *What do you think?*

What did I think? I was intrigued by his text, and I went in search of his promise. I stood staring at the pillow. I moved slowly towards it and lifted the pillow by the edge.

On the bed lay two silver boxes numbered with a #1 and #2 on them, both jewelry style, and a note. I lifted the note and unfolded it.

I miss you already, and I just left.

I laughed and cried at the same time.

I went back to reading, *I wanted you to know that you are the most incredible woman to ever grace my life. I don't know how I will function without you, but I wanted you to know that I PROMISE that I will be back. Someday, I will be back. I know I can't ask you to wait for me, but I can give you something that might help remind you that I will come back. Look at box #1.*

I set the note down and reached for box one. When I lifted the cover I sucked in a breath. A ring sat inside, but not a large gaudy engagement ring. This one was a simple platinum band with a small design and a few delicate diamonds. I lifted the ring and picked up the note. Was he proposing?

This is not an engagement ring, this is a promise ring. Someday I will be back, and I will take that ring off your right hand and place it on your left hand next to your engagement ring. Until then, consider it a promise ring. Now put it on.

I shook my head but did what he said and slipped it onto my right ring finger. It fit perfectly, surprise, surprise.

I lifted the paper and resumed reading, *Now open box #2.* I set the paper back down and lifted the box; it was heavier than I had expected. I shimmied off the lid, and my mouth dropped open.

Inside was his second shield. The one he had carried when he worked for the unit. I placed the gold plated badge into my hand, and my tears fell on it.

The note lay on the bed, and I leaned over to finish reading it, holding his badge close to my heart. *Hold this for me because, someday, I'm coming back to be your partner. Whether it is as a partner in crime or a partner in life, I'm coming back.*

I laughed and picked up my phone that I had set down on the bed beside me. I pulled up his last text message and typed back, *You're bossy!*

I know. Well?

I lay the badge down on the bedspread and turned around to grab mine off the dresser. I turned my camera on and put my hand between the two badges and snapped a picture of it. I grinned as I loaded the picture into the text message and typed out the words, *Okay, partner.*

I could imagine him laughing as he read it. When he answered me back, emotions lodged in my throat.

I have to go, we are boarding.

Have a safe trip. I typed quickly.

I will. MacKenzie...

Yes, Andrew? It was the first time I had used his real full name.

I love you. His words shimmered on my screen as the tears crowded my eyes.

I know.

Epilogue - MacKenzie

Drew had been gone for six weeks, and I felt the weight of his departure constantly. We spoke daily on the phone and sent emails once in a while, and late at night, as I snuggled down into the bed he had once slept in, we would chat via text. Sometimes it would make me feel like a teenager, all giddy and stuff.

Those moments when it was dark outside, I was able to pretend that everything else in the world didn't matter and that one day we would have a chance to move forward with our own relationship.

The light of day brought back the reality of our lives.

Drew had kept me updated on Annabelle, and she was in a new form of treatment that seemed to stall the growth of the tumor. No one knew if it would stop completely or if it would get worse. For now, even I had to hope for the best for her, even if she was keeping Drew from being with me. For the kids, I prayed she would live.

I went back to work a week after the fire and took physical therapy twice a week for my shoulder. I was healing nicely, but it was still an occasional painful reminder of what had occurred.

With great sadness, I went weekly and placed fresh flowers on Rob's grave. I even ran into his parents one time, and they welcomed me with open arms, a forgiving but bittersweet embrace.

Jose and I had talked at length about the videos, and while I was reprimanded by my superiors for my behavior, they knew the circumstances and did not hold my actions against me. I was thankful that nothing would be put into my file about that incident, and the suspension that Gary had forced on me was removed. My jacket was once again, spotless. In fact, I had even received a commendation added to it for my work on this case.

Gary had continued to cooperate with the authorities and helped to tie the case up nicely. He'd had an affair with Bria and had been stupid enough to trust her with his dark little secret. She ended up holding it over his head and used his clout and her knowledge of his behavior to pull him into her criminal activities. Her husband had absolutely no clue and was now on a leave of absence more because of embarrassment than anything else.

I even went to visit Gary once in jail and allowed him to apologize for everything. I believed he was sincere and accepted it. I felt sorry for him, in a way. Well, not really, but it sounds good, doesn't it?

That part of my life was behind me now. I was up for promotion soon and was made acting supervisor of the investigations unit. There were a few new faces in our group, and they knew they had to dot their Is and cross their Ts. There was no way we would allow rogue cops to work amongst us again.

My fortieth birthday came and went just after Drew returned to California. Drew sent me a present, or rather, had Jose deliver it. It was a brand new shiny Mustang GT in bright red. It even had a big bow on top and a custom license plate that read "Macky". I laughed till I cried, and then laughed some more.

I sat in the doctor's office waiting for my final checkup from the fire. Worker's compensation required I be checked one more time before closing my file on that incident.

"MacKenzie, it's good to see you again." I smiled as Doctor Bruno entered and shook my hand. She was about my age and had been my doctor for years.

"Nice to see you, too. Take no offense, but I hope this is the last time I do see you for a while."

"No offense taken." She sat down on a stool and flipped open my file. "How are you feeling? Any breathing problems or dizziness?"

"No, not at all. I feel pretty good, tired but other than that, I'm great." We shared a smile.

She scanned over my paperwork, flipped through a few pages and stopped at one, running her blunt fingernail down over a list of numbers.

"Well, we have all your blood work back, and it looks like everything is fine, actually more than fine." She spun on her stool and turned to face me.

I noticed a Cheshire smile on her face. "How is it more than fine?"

"MacKenzie, do you know you're pregnant?"

Did the world just spin off its axis? Because I swear the room tilted. "What?"

"Looks like your hormone levels are higher than they should normally be. When was your last period?"

I stared at her like she had two heads. She had just dropped a bomb on me and wanted me to remember a date? Was she kidding?

"I don't know," I forced myself to say.

She turned away and pulled a calendar off the desk, pushing it towards me. She actually wanted me to figure this out. Shit, she was serious.

I stared at the piece of paper covered with square boxes and little numbers in the corners of the boxes. It could have been a chemistry chart.

I brought my face back up to hers, "Are you serious?"

She moved closer and rubbed my arm, "Obviously, this is a surprise."

"Ya think?" Gee, I wonder what gave me away. I turned back to the calendar and tried to process my thoughts. Okay, when did Drew leave? I flipped the calendar back a page, he left here. He showed up in our unit on this day, and lo and behold, I had started my period the week before and hadn't had one since.

Why didn't it even cross my mind before now? Why? Because I

had figured it was the stress causing it or the fact that I got shot or something stupid like that. Like getting shot in the shoulder was going to affect my uterus. Get real, Mack!

It was all crystal clear now. That first time we had sex in the shower, he had entered me and then remembered he wasn't wearing a condom. They weren't kidding; the little drop of pre-cum could be potent. What did they say? He had strong swimmers?

I tapped on a date, "That was the first day of my last period." I pushed the paper towards her.

"That far back? And you had no idea?"

I shrugged, "I guess I didn't pay much attention to it."

"Any idea what day you might have conceived?" she asked as she began to write the date down in my file.

I tried to laugh, but it sounded strangled even to me, "Oh yeah, I know exactly what date."

Before I left the office, she handed me a bunch of papers and told me to get in touch with my OB/GYN. This would be the first time in my life I would use the OB part of that title, and it scared the hell out of me.

I sat in my bright red birthday present and rubbed the steering wheel while I glanced in the rearview mirror. Would a child's car seat fit back there?

"Holy hell, I'm going to be a mother!" My thoughts then shifted to, "Oh, shit, what the hell is Drew going to say?"

About the Author

Stacy Eaton is a police officer by profession. Currently, she is working as the department investigator and enjoys digging into cases and putting the pieces of the puzzles together.

Stacy resides in southeastern Pennsylvania and is the wife to a police officer and the mother of two. She is very proud of her son who is currently serving in the United States Navy and equally proud of her nine year old daughter who works hard in her Tae Kwon Do studies.

When Stacy is not working her demanding job, or spending time with her family, she works on her business and volunteers with the World Literary Café. She is also on the Board of Directors of her local Domestic Violence Center. When there is time, she writes.

Be sure to visit www.stacyeaton.com for updates and more information on her books.

Check out Chapter 1 of "Liveon ~ No Evil"
Released November 2013

Chapter 1

October - Jacquelyn

There are two things that inevitably happen whenever you are picking someone up at the airport. First, you could be running late, and when you finally arrive, you find the person you're meeting standing by the curb tapping their foot with impatience because their plane got in ten minutes early. Or, you might be extremely early just to find out that the plane is running way behind schedule. The latter would be today.

So here I find myself standing in the United Airways terminal at the Philadelphia International Airport looking up at the arrival screen and re-reading that my friend's flight is still thirty minutes out. Freaking wonderful. Like I've got nothing better to do than to sit around and wait for Rebecca to get in.

Oh wait, I don't have anything better to do. That's right. I have no life other than my extremely busy career and hanging out with a few friends once in a while. I don't have a family waiting at home for me or any pets that need attention. It's just little ole me, Jacquelyn Liveon.

I glanced around and found a nice, solid white pillar to lean against where people couldn't walk up behind me. I don't like people where I can't see them, especially ones I don't know. As a police officer, it's been ingrained in my brain that you always know what's at your back. No matter where I am, I always prefer to be against a wall or facing the doorway so that I can see what's coming my way. I don't like surprises, ever.

I stood against the cold stone and scanned the area for a few minutes. If I have to be in a crowd, which I'm never really comfortable with, I like to people watch. People watching is another thing that police officers like to do, more out of habit than anything else. By watching closely, we can read what's going on. We rely heavily on body actions to tell us when a person is being honest or about to become aggressive.

As I glanced around, I saw a guy trying to pick his right nostril without being seen; he wasn't doing a very good job at it and I wrinkled up my nose and continued to observe the crowd. A woman in a tight white pencil skirt—totally inappropriate for flying, in my opinion, was trying to work a wedgie out of her butt crack by walking funny. She was getting quite a bit of attention and not just from me. Several tired looking male businesspersons rolled their briefcases or overnight bags watched her walking wiggle. At this time of night, they were probably just making it home after a long day of work. Sad to think, she was their entertainment.

It wasn't all that busy here since it was nine o'clock at night. The rush over for the day, but there were still a good number of people wandering and waiting. I looked at my watch, another twenty minutes until Becca's plane landed. I wish I'd grabbed a cup of coffee before I got here; I passed a popular coffee shop about ten minutes away from the airport, but I was worried I'd be late if I stopped. Being the good friend that I am, I had passed up on my need for caffeine. There weren't any coffee stands on this side of the security gate either, so I had to wait until we left to get my much needed fix.

I pulled out the cell phone that I'd slipped into the side pocket of my cargo pants and browsed through some work emails that I hadn't had a chance to answer. Occasionally, I lifted my head and glanced around, keeping my eye out for any trouble. It was a hazard of the job, never fully being able to relax, always waiting for something bad to happen, or for someone to yell for help.

I went back to my emails after watching a family drag four suitcases and two tired children past me. Maybe it was the energy that caught my attention next, or just the fact that there was a lot of movement to my right, but I turned to see an entourage of people coming in from the parking garage. They climbed onto the walking escalator; you know, that moving sidewalk that makes you feel like you're walking three steps for every one you actually take.

I personally loved those things, but I hated when I got on and lazy people were blocking both lanes. There were signs above that explained how to use it in both words and pictures, but obviously, the entourage wasn't paying any attention. They were the type who'd get under my skin because they stood in a large group and blocked the passing lane.

Everyone appeared happy and they were talking over one another. There were six people in the group, two men and four women, all dressed casually but expensively, and they appeared to be traveling light with only one small bag for each of them. I watched as they climbed off the walking platform and looked around, unsure of exactly where they were going.

I figured they were either going to step into the security line or step up to the ticket counter. They did neither. They continued to mill around and talk, blocking the exit off the moving platform.

I heard giggling to my left and turned my head to see two young girls, probably about eighteen, chortling to themselves and staring at the group. They took out their cell phones and started snapping pictures. When I looked back at the group again, I noticed that one of the men was smiling down into a woman's face. She beamed brightly back up at him.

"Wait till everyone sees these pictures of Ryan Palmer!" I heard one of the girls giggle.

"Oh my God, he is so freaking hot," the other one replied.

Ryan Palmer was a film star, I knew that much, but not much else. He's probably in his late twenties, maybe early thirties, and from the few movies I'd seen of his, he was a pretty good actor. As I watched the group, I saw the man glare at the young girls and quickly look away, turning his back on them to shield his face. Huh, it really was him.

"Did you see that? He just looked at us!" I heard the giddy voices of the girls giggling as they spoke back and forth to each other. Man, to be young and silly again. *Yeah, or not.* I rolled my eyes.

Just then, an airport police officer walked up and told the girls if they didn't get outside and move their car right this second, it would be towed. It was my turn to chuckle. I could only imagine how much that towing bill would cost. I watched as the girls followed the police officer, turning to look over their shoulders at Ryan one more time before he was out of their sight.

I glanced back at the group and saw that Ryan was now eyeballing me. I held his stare for a moment and then looked away. He was most likely wondering if I was trying to snap his picture, too. I shook my head. Not likely. I was not a groupie of any sort, and the thought of falling into the hoopla of some mega movie star was not my deal.

I put my cell phone away and crossed my arms over my chest. I looked over the crowd that had gathered in the area, many of them rubber necking to get a peek at the six people congregating as more and more people began to recognize him. I surveyed them as I waited. One man, about thirty, seemed a bit out of place. It was about seventy-five degrees outside—warm for a fall night—but he was wearing a heavy jacket. Immediately, my instincts were on alert.

I observed him as he peered nervously around; he shoved his hands deep into the pockets of his jacket. I could see a slight sheen of sweat on his face. The fine hair on the back of my neck rose rather quickly. I followed his train of sight and found that it led right to Ryan's group. Ryan was inspecting me again, and I considered him for a moment. I could tell his eyes were a bright blue even from the distance between us. I wondered how much brighter they would look up close. I blinked and looked at the floor. *Where did that even come from?*

I turned my attention back to the suspicious guy, taking in every detail about him. From his thinning brown hair to his metal-framed eyeglasses, all the way down to his ratty Nike sneakers. Something was up, and it wasn't going to be good. *Figures.* I left my off-duty weapon at home. I shook my head at my own stupidity; I never leave it at home. It's always the one thing that you need when you don't have it—right now being the perfect example.

The man continued to peer around nervously and always returned his sight to the group who had now moved over near a window. I continued to keep my eye on him, and I found myself standing up straight, no longer leaning against the pole. My arms came down to my sides and I scanned the large area quickly to see if there were any police officers in the area. Nope, none. Great…just great.

As the movie star entourage started to move toward the security line, the strange guy tensed, and I noticed that there was a bulge in his pocket that caused the material to droop. Based on its outline, he appeared to be concealing something heavy. If I took wild guess, I'd say that it was probably a gun. Little jolts of adrenaline started to spike through me. This could get really ugly, fast.

The man followed the group toward the security checkpoint. He had to walk quickly to catch up, his strides longer than what was reasonable for a man of his size. I kept pace right behind him, ready to move when I saw a chance. The group was so involved in itself; they didn't notice anything happening around them. Normal behavior for most people.

One of the ladies in Ryan's group dropped something on the ground, and two of the other women stopped to wait for her to pick it up. Ryan and the other two people in his traveling group continued on, oblivious to what was going on behind them. They were separated now, easier to pick them off. This was not good, I moved closer to the suspicious man.

When they were about forty feet from the security checkpoint line, the man began to pull out his hand, and in his palm was a semi-automatic pistol. My instincts had been dead on. I stepped into action without a second thought. Why I did what I did, I will never know; but it was just the start of things to come.

Instead of grabbing the guy or going for his gun, I stepped in front of him, blocking his view of Ryan, who apparently was his target. At the same time, I put my hand on Ryan's arm to gain his attention and push him back. He turned to me but my focus was already on the man holding the gun, my back to Ryan. I felt him stiffen beneath my touch, or maybe that was the wave of fear that flew out of him and slammed against my back.

I looked the guy in the eye, but he didn't see me; his gaze was trained over my head at Ryan. Although his attention was on the man behind me, he pointed the gun directly at my chest. A fierce stab of adrenaline surged through my veins at the sight of the muzzle. I heard a woman scream, but I didn't look to see where it came from. It sounded like it came from a distance, but my tunnel vision had kicked in and the outside world faded as I concentrated on the subject in front of me.

"Whoa! What's going on?" I asked him quietly.

The man's gaze flicked to me quickly and then moved back to Ryan. "Move!" he yelled.

"Sorry, but I can't. Why are you pointing a gun at me?" I asked him, purposely keeping my voice low. Rule number one for any hostage negotiator was to always remain calm and talk softly, to try to get the person to stop and listen.

He regarded me again, glanced at his gun, and then looked back up at Ryan. "I'm pointing it at him, not you. Move!" he said loudly, although not quite shouting this time.

"Wait a minute, why do you want to point a gun at this guy?" I pointed to Ryan over my shoulder. I still stood directly in front of him and his fear continued to roll over me like a stormy night on the beach. Thank God, I didn't normally get sea sick.

The gunman directed his attention back to me, this time keeping eye contact as he spoke. "Because I'm going to kill him. Now move, or I'll shoot you, too!" His voice rose with each word.

"Why would you want to kill this guy?" I turned to glance quickly behind me and saw Ryan staring over my head at the man with the gun.

"Because my wife is in love with him!" he shouted. I almost found this funny. *Almost.* Half of the world's population of women was probably in love with the Ryan. He *was* smoking hot, but you wouldn't hear me say that out loud to anyone.

I heard a small grunt behind me, and I wanted to turn around and slug Ryan; instead, I turned myself sideways, and inspected him closely, taking him all the way in. Yeah, he was drop dead gorgeous, but I was able to control my drooling. I learned a long time ago that if someone thought they were good looking, they wouldn't get a bit of attention from me. It only made them more conceited, and I didn't feel the need to contribute to that.

Ryan was peering down at me as I looked him over. Our eyes met for a moment, and when I saw the light blue flecks in his dark blue irises, my heart skipped a beat. I forced myself to turn and face my opponent before I could notice anything else about Ryan.

"Your wife is having an affair with *that?*" I made it sound like Ryan was a total loser, but I was purposefully playing on the guy's feelings.

I felt Ryan's body heat against my back as he stepped closer to me—why I didn't know—but I was torn between wanting to lean back into him and turning around to push him away. I did neither as I observed the profusely sweating man holding the gun in his shaky hand.

As the guy gawked at me in surprise, he glanced at Ryan. I broke my tunnel vision enough to glance around and saw that there were quite a few armed officers in the area now, but unfortunately, they were not well placed. If one of them tried to fire a shot and missed, it would sail past us and strike someone on the other side. We were at a T intersection of the terminal and there was a growing crowd of onlookers. I had to get this guy to calm down quickly before it escalated.

"No! She's not having an affair with him; she's just in love with him. Everything is about him!" The gun in his hand wobbled up and down with his words. "She has pictures of him everywhere in our house and she is constantly watching his damn movies and telling me I need to look more like him." He said the last part bitterly; and, if it was because he was being honest with himself, there was no chance in hell he'd ever come anywhere close to looking like Ryan.

"So you want to kill him, *why?*" I asked quietly, as I drug out the last word, trying to keep him calm so that I could continue to talk to him.

He furrowed his forehead, and anger passed over his features. He pointed the shaky gun out further toward us. "If he's dead, then she can't love him anymore," he said sternly. I didn't think his reasoning was very sound, but, hey, whatever; they were his thoughts, not mine.

"I don't think killing him is the answer." I took a slow deep breath and hoped that what I was about to say would get his attention long enough so that I could get the gun away from him. "If you kill him, you will go to jail, and then you won't have your wife at all." I took a very small step toward the man, more of a foot shuffle then a step. "Is that what you want?"

The man scrutinized me, tilting his head to the side, and then glanced over my head at Ryan. He was thinking about what I said. I could almost see the hamster wheel turning in his mind. I took another small shuffle in his direction.

He glanced down at the floor, and for a second, I thought maybe he noticed my foot shuffle. I took the opportunity to make eye contact with one of the armed officers. I put my hand out to the side as if I was pushing something away. He seemed to understand and he murmured into his lapel mic. I watched as he and two others started to move slowly backward, just a few feet.

I nodded as I saw the movement in the corner of my eye stop. These guys were good, I had to give them that.

"No. Of course I don't want to go to jail. I would rather be dead!" He glared at me, squinting his hazel eyes behind his wire-framed glasses.

He surveyed the onlookers who gathered, and I took the opportunity to take another small step toward him. I was only a couple of feet from him now.

"You don't really want to die. Imagine the pain that would cause your wife." My voice was soft to keep the conversation between us and away from all of the noisy people who were gathering.

"Yeah, I do." He glared hard at me now and a bead of sweat ran down the side of his face.

I maintained eye contact with him, keeping my hands low and in front of me with my palms out to show him I was not a threat. I heard some commotion off to my right, and when I heard the voice, I almost laughed.

"Really, Jack!" a female's voice called out just loudly enough for me to hear. I fought back the laughter when I realized that Becca's plane must have landed, and she was now standing there being held back behind security until we got this issue resolved. If she was able to, she would've walked right into the scene with me.

"I don't think you really do." I cocked my head to the side as I continued to study the man. "Why don't you give me the gun before someone gets hurt?"

He tensed as I spoke, glancing over his shoulders again at the police officers who were surrounding all of us. Two had rifles trained on him, they could easily take him out at their distance, but there was a chance that the bullet would pierce his body and travel through to strike someone on the opposite side.

"No," he said and stepped back, pointing the gun at my head as he raised it. Okay…not a good feeling. My heart sped in my chest as the adrenaline pumped harder. I heard Ryan shift behind me, but I didn't move. I saw the officers on both sides of us tense. I pushed my hands down toward the ground, hoping that the officers might catch it and calm down a moment before they tried to neutralize the threat.

"I know you don't really want to hurt him. If you do that, it will only hurt your wife and your family, and then you'll spend the rest of your life in jail." My voice belied my racing heart and remained calm. I should get an Oscar for my performance here; maybe Ryan could nominate me. That is, if we lived through it.

"But what am I supposed to do?" he asked, and I realized that I had just hit a crucial point. He was responding to me.

"Hand me the gun, and we can figure it out." I took a step closer to him and started to raise my left hand toward the gun, keeping my palm open and low.

I heard gasps and murmurs all around us. I could see flashes going off, bouncing off the glass of the terminal walls, and I knew people had cell phones and cameras out and were snapping away at the dramatic scene in front of them.

I locked my eyes on his. He glanced around nervously and then back at me. He now had the gun pointed at my chest again.

"Please," I said, and took one very slow step toward him.

He stared at me for a long moment, and then contemplated his gun. He nodded once, and everything around us got quiet. Like really quiet, like dead silent. Maybe it was just my tunnel vision kicking back in that blocked everything else out, but I think every person watching stopped breathing at the very moment that I took my next step. I was so focused on what I was about to do, that I neither paid attention, nor cared, what anyone else did. It only mattered what happened in the next few seconds.

I slowly reached out with my left hand to take the gun from him. It was still pointed at my chest, but he was lowering it. I searched his face for any adjustments that might mean he was changing his mind. Just as my hand came in contact with the barrel of the gun, everything moved in slow motion.

I stepped forward with my left foot and planted it solidly on the ground. As my hand wrapped over the top of the gun covering the slide, I pulled up on the gun, and his hand released its grip. I twisted slightly to the left, bringing my right leg up to hip level and extending it directly into his midsection. It must have been the extra adrenaline that rushed through me, because he flew about eight feet back and slammed into the thick glass observation wall.

I immediately grabbed the gun with my other hand, pushed the button on the grip to release the magazine and slid back the top slide. I heard the magazine clank to the ground and watched as the chambered bullet flew out and rolled away. I locked the slide back and flipped the gun upside down to hang on my finger with my arms above my head. I was not a threat, and I wanted everyone to know that.

Four officers jumped on the guy as soon as he landed on the ground. The gunman was too surprised to fight and laid there considering me with hurt in his eyes. I turned away to look at an officer who was coming toward me. He reached to grab the gun from me, and I pulled it back.

"Either put gloves on or give me an evidence bag. You don't want your prints on this." He looked surprised, but nodded and pulled out some nitrile gloves from his belt pouch.

Another officer approached, and I glanced over my shoulder to where Ryan and his group were all huddled around each other. The woman he had been talking to earlier had her arms wrapped tightly around him. His back was to me, which I told myself I was grateful for.

"You might want to get them someplace secure." I smiled at the new officer and tipped my head toward the group.

He spun around to talk to someone and then looked back at me just as Becca walked up. "Jack, I can't take you anywhere can I?" She laughed.

"It's your fault. Your plane was late." I joined in with her laughter. My adrenaline still ran high and laughing was the easiest way to deal with it. I would crash later and wonder what the hell had possessed me to do what I'd done.

"I assume you're a badge?" A new officer with the Sergeant stripes on his arm asked as he watched the banter between Rebecca and me.

I nodded. "Where do you want me to write my statement?" I raised my eyebrows in question as I slipped my shaking hands into the pockets of my cargo pants.

He laughed and started to walk away as he led us to an unmarked doorway. He put a piece of plastic up to the panel, and the lock released. As I went to step through the frame, I turned one last time and found Ryan watching me with an intense look on his face. It was a look I didn't want to acknowledge, so I stepped through the doorway instead.

"Can you make sure I'm kept separate from that group back there?" I asked the Sergeant who was leading us.

He glanced at me, and I smiled shyly and shrugged. "Sure," he said while he led us into a group of offices. Several officers were milling around, and I saw a television hanging in the corner above everyone's heads. Seeing the TV reminded me that during the incident, there were numerous flashes. I wondered how bad the fallout was going to be and where my photos would show up. I physically cringed at that thought. I hated attention.

The Sergeant walked me back to a sparse interview room and I sat down to fill out the paperwork that the prosecutor would need from me as a witness. I waited while the Sergeant read it over and we both signed the form. He asked me a couple more questions and then told me I was free to go.

As we got up to move out of the room, I heard Becca laughing in the hallway. I rounded the corner and saw her staring up at the television. "It's all over the news!" She laughed.

Great! I turned back to the Sergeant. "Do you think you could get me out a back way? I really don't want to deal with that circus," I said as I pointed at the television. They were already interviewing witnesses.

"What? You don't want your moment in the spotlight? You just saved that guy's life!" I wasn't sure if he meant Ryan or the man who held the gun, but either way, a life had been saved—maybe two or three if you counted mine.

"Not my idea of a spotlight." I laughed softly. "I would appreciate a bit of professional courtesy. Could you possibly not tell them who I am? The Palmer group that is?"

He considered my words for a moment. "Wow, you really don't like the spotlight, do you?" He grinned. "Sure, if that's what you want."

Becca and I followed him down another hallway. A few minutes later, we were out of the maze of halls and in the parking lot. With no press around, we quickly made it to my truck without seeing anyone.

It wasn't until we climbed into my Jeep that Becca spoke. "You do realize that you just saved the hottest man on the planet, don't you?"

"Whatever, Rebecca."

"If I were you, I would have been all over that! How come you didn't want him to know who you were?" I turned to her as I backed out of the parking space.

"Why would I? The last thing I need, or want, is some crazy thank you. They would turn this into a huge publicity stunt." She laughed as I put the vehicle into drive.

"I can't figure you out. You just saved a man's life—not to mention the hottest freaking actor alive—and you don't even want him to know your name. You never know, maybe he might want to give you a personal thank you gift." She nudged my arm with her hand, and when I peered at her, she winked.

"Oh, give me a break, Rebecca. He's not my type," I muttered as I pulled up to the window and paid for my parking.

"Jacquelyn Liveon, you are the strangest person I know. Anyone else would be begging for that guy's attention. You could have it and yet you turn and run away." She was shaking her head at me.

"I'm not running away. I just don't need the attention, Rebecca. Can we just drop this? How was your training?" I pulled away from the tollbooth and we headed for the highway.